THE
DARKNESS
OF EVIL

The Works of Alan Jacobson

Novels
False Accusations

For up-to-date information on Alan Jacobson's current and forthcoming novels, please visit his website, www.AlanJacobson.com.

THE
DARKNESS
OF EVIL

A KAREN VAIL NOVEL

ALAN JACOBSON

OPEN ROAD

INTEGRATED MEDIA

NEW YORK

Select book cover text are set in Caudex. The Caudex font is Copyright © 2011 Hjort Nidudsson.

Author photograph: Corey Jacobson

ISBN-13: 978-1-5040-4171-3

Published in 2017 by Open Road Integrated Media, Inc.
180 Maiden Lane
New York, NY 10038
www.openroadmedia.com

For Kevin Smith

During Kevin's decades-long career in publishing, he has edited and sharpened prose, uncovered weaknesses and writing tics, and guided authors on the path to refining their craft.

While working closely with me on nine books over a span of nine years, Kevin has become as much a steward of my characters as I am. We've come to talk bluntly, but good-naturedly, to each other as only fellow New Yorkers can—resulting in a level of honesty that gives me complete trust in his opinion. His ability to home in on a scene, or paragraph, or sentence, or word, that isn't quite right—and then brainstorm with me until we find a solution—is something I've relied on to bring an extra shine to my novels.

The Darkness of Evil is the first work I did not title myself—and it's only fitting that the novel that's dedicated to Kevin is the one that he named.

THE

DARKNESS
OF EVIL

"It's hard to distance yourself from so much evil and darkness when that person is your dad. You just think, How can I be a part of something that ends up so terrible?"

—CINDY DYKES,
daughter of murderer
Jimmy Lee Dykes

"Forgiveness is there between the lines . . . she recalls all that we did as a family—many good memories . . . That is true love from a daughter's heart. What else can a father ask for?"

—SERIAL KILLER DENNIS RADER,
December 2013 letter to *The Wichita Eagle*
from the El Dorado maximum-security
correctional facility

"To take one human life is an outrage; to take five is carnage."

—JUSTICE ALBERT SACHS,
when sentencing serial killer
Colin Ireland

1

Did he ever sodomize you?"

The bright lights in the television studio bore down on Jasmine Marcks and caught a glistening tear as it coursed down her cheek.

FBI profiler Karen Vail clenched her jaw. *How could this woman be so callous?*

"No," Jasmine said. "He saved that for his victims, the ones he killed."

Talk show host Stephanie Sabotini waved her hand in the air, as if dismissing Jasmine's answer. "You never really say in your book that you feel guilty. Don't you feel remorse? An ounce of guilt?"

Jesus Christ. What's she supposed to feel guilty about?

Jasmine wiped at her moist cheek with a couple of fingers and tilted her head. "What?"

Vail tried to remember the cute floor director's name she was introduced to shortly after arriving. *Theo.* Vail stepped quickly to her right and elbowed him.

Theo was focused on his cameraman and startled a bit as he turned to Vail.

"That's enough. Tell Ms. Sabotini she's gone too far."

"Nothing I can do, Agent Vail. Miss Marcks agreed to the interview."

Vail wondered if Jasmine's publicist, munching on catered food in the green room, was watching the show. "Jasmine's been through enough. She's here to promote her book, not be interrogated and chastised."

Sabotini leaned forward in her seat. "I find it hard to believe that you and your mother were oblivious to what was going on. I mean, your father was a *serial killer*. You were his daughter and you say you loved him, that he was a good father."

Vail grabbed Theo's arm. "Now. Tell her to back off. Or I'll go over there and tell her myself. While the camera's rolling."

Theo repositioned the headset mic in front of his lips. "Stephanie, the FBI agent's having problems with your questions. She wants you to back off."

Sabotini's eyes narrowed slightly and her head jerked slightly right, as if she took umbrage at Theo's remark. She refocused on Jasmine, who was answering the host's question.

"I was a kid. He treated me like I was a queen. I was like any other girl who loved her daddy. How could I know he was a serial killer?"

Sabotini glanced into the darkness and found Vail, whose angry gaze was fixed on her face. She cleared her throat and said, "How about we get back to your book, Jasmine?"

What a terrific idea. Vail nodded a thank you to Theo, who winked at her and arched his brow flirtatiously. Vail scratched a phantom itch on her cheek with her left hand, showing him her engagement ring. *Taken. Sorry, buddy.* She turned back to Jasmine, who was already answering Sabotini's follow-on question.

"It's not like my father turned to me one day and said, 'Honey bear, I killed fourteen people.' But he did say some weird things that, when I was older, started to make me think, reevaluate some of the things he'd said to me over the years."

"When you were a teenager," Sabotini said, "you found some duct tape with blood on it. And you went to the police."

"Well, when combined with the other things, yeah, the tape made me think something wasn't right. I saw articles in the paper, reports on the news about the Blood Lines serial killer in Virginia. They said he used a knife to carve parallel lines on his victims' stomachs—and they also said he used duct tape to tie up his victims. I saw my dad come home once with blood on his shirt. Wasn't much, but my mom saw it. He told her he cut himself on his truck and she didn't need to worry about it. But I started thinking, duct tape, blood . . . what if my daddy was the killer? I got scared. I thought the police could tell me if he was the one."

"You were only fourteen. Did they believe you?"

"Not really. They brought him in and questioned him along with a bunch of other men from the area, to make it look like they weren't targeting him. And they didn't let on that I was the one who told on him. But . . ."

"But they didn't arrest him."

"They said they had no evidence."

"Right," Sabotini said, "but four years later, you found some more duct tape."

Jasmine nodded, her gaze off somewhere behind Sabotini, into nothingness, like she was reliving the memory. "I found it in the trunk of his car. There was blood on the roll, on the inside, on the cardboard. I went back to the police and told them, again, that I was worried my father was the killer."

"And they believed you this time?"

"No. But I told them I was not leaving until I talked with the detective. So I sat there for an hour and the detective finally came with a social worker because I wasn't eighteen yet. I started telling him things my dad did over the years, times when he'd disappear for hours at a time, late at night. I'd wake up when he came home, three or four in the morning. I once came out of my room and asked him where he'd been. He didn't smell like booze, so he hadn't been out drinking."

"What'd he say?"

"His favorite answer. 'Don't worry about it, darlin'.'"

"Maybe he was having an affair."

"Maybe. But it always happened the night before another body was found. I started writing all these things in a journal, just in case I was right, in case he was the killer."

"What other things were there?"

"Those are in my book, Stephanie," Jasmine said with a wry smile.

"They are indeed. Let's get back to that roll of duct tape you found. The second one. It later became key evidence."

"Right. The DNA was contaminated, so that was a problem. But there was something else. An issue with forensic procedure. Chain of custody."

"Even if it was considered 'tainted' evidence, why didn't they question him?"

"They told me they didn't want to tip him off. So they looked into his background and investigated without him knowing."

Sabotini leaned back slightly in her seat. "But that still got them nowhere. Isn't that when they called the FBI?"

"Their profiling unit. The police never could find much in the way of forensics at the crime scenes, so they needed someone to find another way to identify the killer. The agent gave them a profile that turned out to be very important."

"Thomas Underwood," Sabotini said. "We invited him to appear with you, but we were told he was unavailable. Instead, we've got his stand-in, Karen Vail, who's going to join us in a few moments to talk about ways of keeping ourselves safe from people like your father."

I'm a stand-in?

"Another three years passed before he was arrested," Sabotini said. "How did you handle that, living with your father, someone you suspected of murdering eleven women and three men?"

"The police told me they couldn't find anything linking him to the murders. The duct tape had only his blood and DNA on it. Bottom line, they said they had nothing proving, or even suggesting, he was the killer they were looking for. I believed them and started to relax. I started questioning everything. I was young, I told myself. Maybe I misinterpreted the things my dad told me. I realized, being older now, that there were different ways of taking what he'd said." She took a deep breath. "It was only me and my dad. My mom had passed by this time, and you know, like I said, he always treated me like a queen. Even when I thought he might be the killer, it made me apprehensive—I really just wanted to *know*, one way or another. But I never felt like I was in danger."

"What about after the police told you they had nothing connecting him to the murders? Did that ease your mind?"

"Well yeah, I felt relief, of course. But I also felt stupid." She looked up at the ceiling, took a breath. "I felt like I betrayed my own father. Going to the police . . ." She shook her head. "I felt really, really guilty over that for a long time."

"When the police came to your door to arrest him, what was that like?"

Jasmine hesitated a moment, looked up again, searching for an answer, the bright white lights reflecting off tears pooling in her lower lids. She came off as articulate, honest, and photogenic: an athletic blonde with Nordic features. Easy to promote, easier to book on TV, with a compelling story.

"I went through a range of emotions. Shock. Anger at the police for getting it wrong—I mean, he'd killed a lot more people since I first went to them. Then there was betrayal—I mean, Roscoe Lee Marcks, my father, my *dad*, the man who tucked me in at night and gave me hugs and kisses, really *was* a serial killer. He murdered people. Lots of people. And he wasn't just any serial killer. He was the Blood Lines killer, a man who kidnapped women and men, tossed them into a panel van, tortured them, reviving them repeatedly, before slicing their bodies and cutting off their genitalia." Her voice caught and she looked down.

Sabotini tilted her head in mock empathy, bit her bottom lip, and waited for Jasmine to compose herself.

Jasmine looked up and dabbed at her teary eyes. She cleared her throat. "It's hard to explain what it feels like knowing that this coldhearted, brutal killer was my loving father. You start thinking, Why didn't he kill *me*? Was I ever in danger? When he got mad at me when I broke his favorite watch, was I—was he thinking of *killing me*?"

Vail glanced at the clock. They were due for a commercial break and then the focus of the show would pivot to her. She could not wait; Jasmine looked stressed and needed the interview to end.

"At first I had a tough time accepting it," Jasmine said. "But when Detective Curtis came to my house with Agent Underwood and they started going through things, what they knew, the type of person they were looking for, it sounded like a match for my father. That's when I realized it was not going to end well."

Vail snorted. *Depends on your perspective. It certainly did not end well for Roscoe Lee Marcks.*

2

Ninety minutes later Vail walked into her office in Aquia, Virginia. Her boss, Assistant Special Agent in Charge Thomas Gifford, was chatting in the hallway with her new unit chief, Stacey DiCarlo.

"How'd she do?" Gifford asked.

"The host really laid into her, asked some tough, very direct questions. Not exactly what she needed. I took care of it. She backed off but it was still emotionally trying."

"And I *still* think this hand-holding is a waste of Bureau resources," DiCarlo said.

Vail had been through this with her multiple times during the days leading up to the interview and did not feel like getting into it again.

"The reason for having Agent Vail there," Gifford said, "was to support our mandate to educate the public on staying safe. Not to hand-hold a witness."

Hmm, an assist from an unlikely source.

"I still don't think it's a good use of our time," DiCarlo said. "Or taxpayer money."

Gifford shoved both hands into the pockets of his slacks and rocked back on his heels. "Your concerns are noted. Thanks for your input."

DiCarlo frowned, then turned and huffed off down the hall. Gifford gestured with his chin for Vail to follow him into his office. On the way in, Vail nodded at Lenka, Gifford's assistant, and took a seat.

"How do you like your new unit chief?"

Vail glanced around. "Is this a trick question, sir?"

He threw out his hands. "Just trying to take the pulse of the unit."

"We think she's an asshole. She knows nothing about criminal investigative analysis and wouldn't know a valid profile if it struck her in the face. And I've been tempted, let me tell you."

"Tempted?"

"To strike her in the face."

Gifford struggled to subdue his smile. "Off the record, she wouldn't have been my first choice to lead the unit. But . . . well, you know."

Vail tilted her head. "Know what?"

"We're supposed to increase the female head count. And with the success they've had with you, they're not only less reluctant to do so but they feel confident it'll work out well."

Smile and nod, Karen. That was a compliment.

"It's about the person, not the gender," she said. "Best person for the job, that's what matters. Sometimes that's a woman. Sometimes it's a man. But yeah, I think we do need more women in the BAU. We bring things to the table you men don't."

"I agree—but don't give Agent DiCarlo a hard time, okay? Let's give her a chance to find her legs."

Vail looked at him.

"Is that too much to ask?"

Maybe.

"That was not a rhetorical question, Agent Vail."

"Are you going to call me 'Agent Vail' when I'm your daughter-in-law? Just curious."

"In the office? Absolutely. Well, to your face, that is. You don't want to know what I call you when you're not around."

Funny.

"So let's get back to Jasmine Marcks. You think she's going to be able to handle herself on book tour when you're not there to run interference?"

Vail thought about that a moment. "She made it through a childhood with a father who was a serial killer, and she dealt with the emotional stress of the trial and the intense media scrutiny. She'll be fine. She's tough."

Vail's Samsung vibrated. She glanced at the screen and saw Jasmine Marcks's number. "Guess who."

"Go on," Gifford said with a wave of his right hand. "Take it."

She swiped to answer and brought the handset to her ear. "Jasmine. Everything okay? I'm in a—"

"I got a message from him. When I got home, it was in the mail."

"Message from who?"

"My father."

Vail glanced at Gifford. "What'd he say?"

"It's not what he said, it's what he didn't say."

Vail got up from her chair and began pacing. "Let's start with what he wrote. Then we'll worry about interpreting what he *didn't* write."

"That's just it. He didn't write anything."

Vail stopped and looked up. "Your father sent you a blank letter?"

"Right."

"Jasmine. Are you overreacting? I mean, if there's nothing in—"

"He's playing with my head. Trying to get even because of what I wrote."

"You got all that from a blank piece of paper?"

"Do you think I'm wrong?"

"Other than mentally screwing with you, is there anything else behind this? Are you in danger?"

After a second's hesitation, she said, "He's in a max-security prison a hundred miles away. No. I don't think I'm in danger. It just—it unnerved me."

"I get it." Vail pinched the bridge of her nose. "How 'bout I stop by, you can show me the letter. And we can talk."

"I'd like that."

"Give me a few minutes to get some things squared away. I'll see you soon."

Vail hung up and turned to face Gifford, whose face was scrunched into a squint. "I assume you figured out what we were talking about."

"I did. You're going over there because her father sent her a blank letter."

Vail sighed. "It spooked her."

"So much for being tough."

"We all have things that get under our skin. She's been through a lot. Hard to know what's gonna be a trigger."

Gifford muttered something unintelligible, then rose from his seat and turned to face his window. He rotated a thin rod and the green miniblinds opened wider, revealing the fresh snow that had fallen that morning. "You're not her therapist, you know."

"Don't say it, sir."

"Say what?"

"That I've been reduced to hand-holding."

Gifford let that hang in the air a moment—he was not verbalizing it because he did not need to. "Go. I'll tell DiCarlo I asked you to take something to headquarters for me. But this is a onetime thing. Your involvement with Jasmine Marcks is in the eleventh hour. We have pending cases that need your attention."

"I know."

Gifford turned to her. "Besides, we don't want to give your unit chief any reason to gloat."

3

Vail arrived at the Bethesda, Maryland, home of Jasmine Marcks an hour after she called. The house was a modest two-story colonial among larger and more robust residences, some a hundred years old and others recently constructed or remodeled.

Jasmine came to the door wearing the same stylish black below-the-knee dress she had selected for the morning's television interview.

"Karen. I feel so silly to make you come down here. For a blank piece of paper, no less."

"You didn't force me. You didn't even ask me. I came because I thought it was important."

"Come in," Jasmine said, standing aside and allowing Vail to pass.

Vail had been here a couple of times seven years ago when Jasmine's father was about to stand trial. Jasmine testified and Vail accompanied the prosecutor when she questioned Jasmine about what she observed as a teenager.

"You've still not met with my father," she said.

"I've asked. Every couple of years I make another request. Each time I get the same answer: 'We'll see.' He's purposely leading me along, yanking my chain. He leaves it open-ended so I have to keep coming back and asking. It's about the only power he's got left in a situation where he's told when he can wake up, when he can go to sleep, when and what he can eat."

"That sounds like something he'd do."

Roscoe Lee Marcks was the last case that profiling legend Thomas Underwood handled before he retired from the Bureau, just prior to Vail joining the unit. Gifford gave her the file to help get her feet wet, to ease her into the flow of things—and, Vail was sure, to see if she had the stomach to handle the brutality the agents in the BAU lived and breathed regularly.

Since the profile had already been finalized and reviewed with the Fairfax County Police Department, Vail was able to study, and learn from, Underwood's notes, analyses, and case management.

When Marcks was arrested, Vail began developing a rapport with Jasmine. After he was convicted, she and Jasmine stayed in touch periodically, mostly through email. But their contact grew less frequent.

"Coffee?" Jasmine asked as they sat down in the kitchen.

"I'd love some."

"How's Jonathan? How old is he now?"

"Almost nineteen. He's a freshman at George Washington University."

"No way. How did that happen? College? And a hell of a good one, at that. Smart boy. Like his mom."

"I'd say he certainly didn't get his smarts from his dad, but that'd be disingenuous. Deacon was many things, but before he started having problems, he was a bright man." *Not that it got him anywhere.*

"What's he studying?"

"Criminal justice." Vail chuckled. "Go figure."

"Uh-oh. Another cop in the family?"

Vail laughed again—but she clearly did not find it humorous. "Not if I can help it. Too dangerous."

Jasmine opened the cabinet and removed a filter, then placed it in the basket of the coffee maker.

"He's looking at law. Which would suit me just fine. A whole lot safer. And generally speaking, a whole lot more lucrative."

"Well, you know how that goes, right? You can try to influence your kids but in the end they do what they want. And let's not forget that whatever they choose to do in their careers, they've gotta be happy."

"Can't argue with that." *But I still don't want him carrying a badge and gun.* She glanced around. "So where's that letter?"

"Go on, take a look. That's it right there on the table."

Vail picked it up. It wasn't evidence—there was no crime— but she almost felt like she should be wearing gloves while handling it. She pulled out the paper and unfolded it. *What the hell did I expect? She said it was blank. But that did not fit a man like Roscoe Lee Marcks.* There was also a photo of a stuffed animal— torn from a magazine of some kind. "What's this?"

"What's what?" Jasmine stepped closer and brought a hand to her mouth.

"It was still inside the envelope. You didn't see it?"

She shook her head, still staring at the image.

"Why would he send you a picture of a stuffed animal?"

Jasmine turned away and went back to the coffee. "I had one just like that growing up. I used to go to bed with it every night."

"And your father sent this to you. With no note."

Jasmine set a mug of steaming java in front of Vail, purposely averting her eyes from the clipping.

"Did this stuffed animal have any special meaning?"

Jasmine stopped what she was doing and stood there. "Yes." She hesitated, then said, "I found it cut to pieces one day, in my bed."

"You're joking. You never told me about this."

Jasmine pulled a bowl of sugar from the cupboard. "It upset me. A lot. I remember crying, not understanding who would do it. Or why."

"Did you ever find out?"

"Never. My mom wasn't very nice about it. She said she'd buy me a new one, which she did. And she thought that made it all better. I loved Sparky. The new one wasn't Sparky. I had nightmares about seeing him all cut up for weeks. That's why I could never have a dog. Or a cat, or an animal of any kind. I just can't—" She shivered. "It'd just make me think of Sparky."

"You think your dad did it?"

Jasmine snorted. "What do you think?"

"Who else knew about what happened to Sparky?"

"I didn't tell anyone. It really freaked me out. I was afraid to talk about it. Besides, my dad told me to keep it to myself." She chuckled. "He said people may think I'm weird. They wouldn't understand. Hell, *I* didn't understand."

Vail set the magazine clipping aside and examined the blank piece of paper again. "You got a pencil?"

Jasmine drew her chin back. "Maybe. I mean, if you're not a draftsman or a sketch artist, who still uses pencils?" She rummaged through her drawer and handed Vail an old, yellow, chewed-up Eberhard Faber number two.

While Jasmine busied herself with pouring the coffee, Vail held the writing utensil at an angle, covering the white paper with soft, parallel strokes until she had shaded a good percentage of the surface a charcoal gray. "It's not exactly blank."

"What do you mean?" Jasmine came over and sat down next to Vail.

Oh shit. Shouldn't have said anything. "Mind if I take this with me?" Vail said as she folded it and placed it back into the envelope.

"What'd you find? What does it say?"

"Not sure. I think there are impressions. Like when you write, it leaves latent or visible marks on the pages below it. It's called indented writing. I'm going to take it over to the lab, have our techs take a look. Okay?"

"Yeah, of course."

Vail swallowed a mouthful of coffee. "Are you going to be okay on this book tour? The questions may not get any easier."

Jasmine cupped the warm mug between two hands. "I brought it on myself. Writing *The Serial Killer's Daughter* was cathartic in a lot of ways. I can't explain it, but it was something I just had to do. I had to write it. Obviously there are some unforeseen consequences."

"Stay away from the reviews. You don't need to subject yourself to that kind of abuse. There are some nasty people out there who think they know it all, who have nothing better to do but comment on things they have no clue about. Do yourself a favor and don't read that garbage. It'll just upset you."

"Okay."

"And I don't care if it's TV or radio, a local or national show, if there's anything you don't want to answer, if it's too sensitive or painful, turn it back on them. Tell them they're being cruel and you've been through enough. People will understand."

Jasmine took a drink.

"Did you get time off work for the tour?"

"I took my accumulated sick time. Almost three weeks."

"Still working for the state, right?"

"I've changed jobs a few times since you—well, since my father was convicted."

"Something in computers?"

Jasmine managed a slight smile. "You remember."

Now it was Vail's turn to laugh. "It doesn't happen often these days."

"I was a computer science major my first two years of college. Then I realized I wasn't very good at it, so I sat down with my adviser and, well, I cried in her office. She asked me some questions, gave me some forms to fill out, and told me I should become an accountant." Her eyes glazed over as she got lost in thought. "I looked at her like she was speaking a foreign language. But she said, trust me on this. So I did. And she was right. I have a thing for numbers."

Vail snapped her fingers. "Now I remember. Tax department?"

"My first job out of school. I'd interned for the state and showed a knack for finding things others missed. When I graduated they hired me. My supervisor liked me so much that he promoted me in, like, nine or ten months. Two years later I got a call from the state correctional system. It really wasn't any different from what I'd done at the tax department, but they were looking for someone with my skill set. Pay was better, hours were better, and the opportunity for advancement was pretty high."

"When was that?"

"Seven years ago. But two years after that a friend at work told me about this position at the Bureau of Prisons. Doing basically the same thing, only they paid a lot more. That was right around the time I started writing my book. Every night after dinner, 8:00 till 10:00."

"So instead of dating, you were writing a book."

"Instead of just about *everything*." She sat down, took a drink of coffee. "Once I got started, it was like freeing my soul from a self-imposed prison." Jasmine set her coffee down and laughed at her own comment. "I know that sounds silly. But when I shut my laptop every night, I slept better than I've slept since—well, since I was a teen."

"It didn't bother you being around a prison, being that your father was in a correctional facility?"

"Just the opposite, actually. I had a lot of pent-up anger. I really should've gotten help. But the book took the edge off. And going to work every day, seeing the prison, gave me a sense of comfort, knowing that my father was locked safely away just like the criminals where I worked."

"I can understand that."

Jasmine took another drink. "Besides, I was in the admin offices. I didn't have any direct contact with the inmates. Minimum-security facility—completely different animal. And it's not like my father was anywhere close. He was in North Carolina at the time, hours away, in a max facility."

"And now he's doing his best to reach out and touch you, making the seventy-five miles seem like a few blocks."

Jasmine closed her eyes. Her hand shook slightly and she quickly set the mug down. "It caught me off guard. I didn't expect to get that letter from him. And those questions this morning were . . . well, now I know what I'm up against." She laughed nervously. "I'll be fine."

Can you please be a little more convincing? Stop it, Karen. Shit, maybe DiCarlo was right.

"You *will* be fine," Vail said as she hugged her.

4

Vail drove to the FBI lab at Quantico to consult with Tim Meadows, the senior forensic scientist who had provided her with key assistance on many cases over the years.

The lab was a modern, freestanding facility down the road from the Academy constructed a dozen years ago. By the time the FBI was ready to move in, it had outgrown the building.

She found Meadows sitting on a stool peering into a microscope. Music was blasting from an iPod paired wirelessly with a speaker. She approached from behind and tickled his back with a finger. He startled and nearly fell off the seat.

She pressed "stop" and laughed. "Sorry, you had that thing turned up so loud I didn't think you'd hear me."

"Thank your buddies Uzi and DeSantos for that. I still haven't regained my hearing completely after that explosion."

"That was, what, three years ago? Hate to tell you, Tim, but it's not coming back."

Meadows frowned. "When did you get your medical degree, *Dr.* Vail?"

She raised a hand in contrition. "You're right. I apologize

again. I just figured, three years, you know? It's done healing. What'd your doctor say?"

"He told me my hearing loss is just that: a loss. It ain't coming back."

Vail looked at him.

"I'm not ready to accept it. I'm taking some kind of herbal tincture my friend stirred up." He leaned in close. "It's got cannabis in it. Some specially grown strain to help the auditory nerve. Said it'll help."

"I thought you were a man of science."

"I'm willing to try anything." He pressed "play" on the iPod and glanced back at her. "No, I don't mean that literally."

Vail pressed "stop" again. "I'm not here to visit."

"Of course not, because that's what a friend would do."

"Tim, I'm hurt."

"No you're not."

Vail could not help but smile. "No, I'm not. But I do miss mixing it up with you."

"Well, get to it, Karen. I was in the middle of one of my favorite songs. Not to mention one tough case. What do you got for me?"

"Something easy." She unfurled the letter from the envelope.

"What the hell is that, some preschooler's scribble?"

"Try again."

He took the paper and glanced at it. "Oh, don't tell me you were playing forensic scientist again. You've gotta stop watching that *CSI* bullshit. You know it's bullshit, right?"

"Why, because you can't solve every case in fifty-nine minutes?"

"Don't get me started."

Vail gestured at the paper. "This was sent by Roscoe Lee Marcks. To his daughter."

"And why are we handling this without gloves?"

"There's no case."

"You sure of that?" He lifted an eyebrow.

Vail felt perspiration beading on her forehead. "No. But I can track the letter in other ways. Through the prison. They scan incoming and outgoing mail unless it's from, or going to, an inmate's attorney."

"Let's first see if we've got something to be concerned about. What do you want to know?"

"It appeared to be a blank piece of paper. But now it looks like there's something written there."

"Hmm. You can see that through the mess you made scribbling with that crayon?"

"Pencil."

"Whatever." He shooed her away and hit "play" on his iPod. "Now go and leave me for an hour. I'll do my thing and text you when I've got something."

Vail was gone only twenty minutes—she had run into a friend on her way down the stairs and never made it out of the building—when Meadows's message came through:

you shoulda worn gloves

5

Vail ran up the steps and jogged into the lab. The music was off. Meadows had a stern face.

"You were able to get something?" she asked, pushing her shoulders back to force air into her lungs.

"No thanks to you. Not only did I use ALS," he said, referring to Alternative Light Source, "I used oblique lighting. But the pièce de résistance was ESDA."

"ESDA?"

Meadows grinned. "Another thing up my sleeve. Electrostatic Detection Apparatus. It creates an invisible electrostatic image that becomes visible when I apply charge-sensitive toners."

"Impressive."

"Except now you're gonna have to explain to your ASAC how you screwed this one up," he said, referring to her Assistant Special Agent in Charge. "Not to mention your unit chief. You've got a new one, I hear. Some . . . goddess named Di—"

"Yeah, just my luck." Vail drew in another deep breath and gestured to the LCD screen in front of them. "What'd you find?"

"A message. If it really came from Roscoe Lee Marcks, you're going to have to get some answers to figure out what it means. And verify that he actually sent this. Because there aren't any latents worth talking about other than yours and Jasmine Marcks's. We've got hers on file from when we had to rule hers out in the house when Fairfax County PD was drafting the arrest warrant for her father."

"What'd the message say? How long are you planning to keep me in suspense?"

Meadows made a point of checking his watch. "I guess this is long enough." He turned an LCD screen toward her and she saw the words:

Remember what happened to Sparky?

"Do we know what happened to Sparky?"

Vail swallowed. "Yeah. And it wasn't good."

"Do we have known handwriting samples on file for Marcks?"

"I—I don't know." She turned to Meadows. "I'm sure we do. But I came into the case after all the work had been done. I studied Underwood's behavioral assessment, read through the file to see if I could reconstruct his thought process, follow how he arrived at his conclusions. I didn't worry about the physical evidence too much because Curtis, the Fairfax detective, was dealing with that. Of course, in retrospect that seems ridiculous. But back then I was a rookie. What the hell did I know?"

"I suggest you find out. And you may want to pay Roscoe Lee Marcks a visit."

He may be in more of a mood to meet with me now. She smiled inwardly. *Thing is, even if he's not, he may have no choice.*

6

Potter Correctional Facility was a prison that exemplified punishment not merely by its strict rules and regulations but by its rustic building: over a hundred years old, its walls were roughhewn from stone, the mortar cracking and crumbling, moss coating its northern surfaces and weeds taking root just about everywhere.

It was cold in winter and, because of its West Virginia location and poor air circulation, hot and humid in the summer. For thirteen years there had been talk of closing it and relocating the inmates, but for various reasons the plans never moved beyond discussion and debate, cost projections and the politics of every special interest that had a hand in the pie. Litigation was tied up in the courts. The status quo continued—as did the complaints.

Potter was filled with murderers, rapists, arsonists, and child molesters. Truth be told, the prisoner rights groups and their paid legal counsel were the only ones who cared about the subpar conditions. Everyone else seemed to adhere to the sense that maximum crimes brought maximum security, which in this case begat maximum suffering. Or close to it.

After leaving the lab, Vail phoned Frank Del Monaco, another profiler in her unit, and asked him to locate handwriting samples for Roscoe Lee Marcks that they had on file and to scan and email them to Meadows.

Del Monaco was less than pleased to be given the unscheduled task, but Vail had done her share of favors for him over the years.

Vail followed the correctional officers to the interview room. Although the assistant warden had wanted her to meet Marcks with a slab of super-strength Lexan Plexiglas separating them and a phone line connecting them, Vail wanted a more informal environment given the strategy she had devised for their discussion. She listened to each of the man's objections then politely explained why she needed to do it her way.

Problem was, she had little control over how the interview was conducted: this was Bureau of Prisons' domain and her only recourse would be to go above his head to the warden, and she did not want to burn the bridge unless absolutely necessary.

He ultimately agreed and she now sat in a small room with two officers behind her. Marcks was led in, all six foot two and two hundred fifty pounds of him, and shackled to the table.

"Leave him handcuffed," Vail said. "But not to the table. I want him to be comfortable."

"Sorry, ma'am. I can't—"

"Agent. Or Special Agent. Or Special Agent Vail. But not ma'am." She faced Marcks but spoke to the guards. "Now please go check with Assistant Warden Thibeaux and you'll see that Mr. Marcks is to be handcuffed but not shackled."

The guard gestured to one of the other men, who left the room.

"He'll be right back to remove those," Vail said with a wink.

Marcks squinted. "Why are you going out of your way to make me comfortable?"

Vail shrugged. "I want to have an honest conversation with you. Hard to do that when you're chained to a table and your back and shoulder muscles start to burn."

Marcks canted his head slightly as if doing so would help him get a better angle on assessing her motives.

Vail needed to build a rapport with the man, to gauge the threat to Jasmine, to feel him out. In a best-case scenario, it would take multiple sessions. But she had to do it the right way if she had any hope of getting anything from him.

Seconds later, the door opened and the officer removed the shackles, then cuffed Marcks in front without a word. But on his way out, he turned to Vail and said, "If he bashes your head in, it ain't my fault."

She nodded at the two guards behind her. "You guys can go, too."

They gave her a look—probably similar to the one Robby, her fiancé, would give her if he knew what she was doing.

When the men left, and it was only Vail and Marcks sitting a few feet from each other, he laughed. "You carry a lot of weight around here."

"The assistant warden thinks I have a nice ass."

"I agree." Marcks laughed heartily—exactly the reaction she was hoping for. Break down the barriers that—had she sat down in a room with only a phone connecting them—would have prevented her from getting anything useful.

As he shifted his hands on the table, Vail noticed a three-letter scar on the inside of his left forearm spelling out "D.I.E." It reminded her of a similar mark she had seen years ago when a woman had used an eraser to obliterate her skin, the resulting wound healing with a thick keloid, as Marcks's had. More significantly, self-mutilation was one sign of childhood sexual abuse.

"And that may be the only time I'll ever agree with *anything* the assistant warden says, darlin'. Mind if I call you darlin'?"

Vail grinned. "What do you think?"

He pursed his lips and pretended to study her, then said, "Nah. I think you want to be respected."

She nodded slowly. "You're right, Roscoe. Would you mind if I call you Roscoe?"

"It's my name."

"I would appreciate the same respect I'm giving you. Is that a deal?"

"I can live with that."

"Do you know why I'm here?"

Marcks shrugged his large shoulders. "The Behavioral Analysis Unit's ongoing research project to study and assess serial offenders, continuing the work of Ressler, Hazelwood, Douglas, and Underwood."

Vail hiked her brow. "I'm impressed. Word for word from my letter."

"Letters," Marcks said. "I think we're up to six now, if I'm not mistaken."

"You're not."

"You've been very persistent, Agent Vail."

"It's my job. I think you could help us."

Marcks leaned back in his chair. "Now why would I want to do that? I mean, respect for you aside."

Vail tilted her head left, letting her red hair fall partially across her eye. She brushed it aside gently, an alluring enough move to be seductive yet ambiguously innocuous. She was sure it got his attention. "I was hoping that respect for me would be enough."

Vail knew he had not been in a room alone with a woman in about seven years. She had put on Robby's favorite perfume and was wearing a form-fitting blouse and well-cut pants. She wanted him distracted. And she wanted him to enjoy talking with her—because she needed this to become a regular occurrence while she built a relationship. Of course, that was her objective before Jasmine received the letter.

While that did change things, it did not alter her approach appreciably—because threats from inside a max-security prison like Potter generally did not present a clear and present danger. Generally. But there were exceptions. Still, Roscoe Lee Marcks was locked away for life without chance for parole. Unless he had someone on the outside to carry out a threatening act against Jasmine, she was safe.

If not unnerved. Or at least she would be when Vail shared with her the contents of the "blank" letter.

Marcks shrugged his shoulders again. "So what do you want to know?"

Wow. Can it be this easy?

"I've got a lot of questions."

"I'll give you three. How 'bout that? We'll start with those and go from there."

All about control. He'll dole out the answers, leave me asking permission for more.

"Fine," Vail said. "We'll start with three. You slice thin lines on the abdomens of your victims using an odd-shaped knife. A karambit. Why do you do that? What does it mean to you?"

"I count two questions there, Agent Vail. You sure you want to burn two at once, so quickly? And can I call you Karen?"

"Karen's fine. And the two questions are basically the same thing, just worded differently. So how about, "What's the meaning behind the thin lines you carve in your victims' abdomens?""

Marcks sucked his top teeth a moment, rolled his eyes toward the ceiling. "I don't like that question. Ask another. Not about the lines. And not about the murders."

Guess that's my answer. Not gonna be so easy.

"How about we talk about your daughter. Jasmine."

Marcks frowned. "Was there a question there?"

"You two had a unique relationship and I'd like to explore—"

"She had a normal childhood. She was loved. End of story."

"Except that she grew up—in her formative teen years—without a mother. It happens, but it's not entirely normal."

"I did the best I could. She had no female influence, you know? That was hard."

"You developed a strong bond with her."

He hesitated. "Yes."

"Why did you have to think about that?"

"We had a special relationship. A unique relationship."

"How so?"

Marcks laughed, then he raised his handcuffed wrists and pointed an index finger at her. "You're a sneaky little devil, you know that, Karen? Get me talkin' and not noticin' you've asked about a dozen questions when I only agreed to three. That's not really building trust, is it?"

How does he know about building trust? Has he read Douglas's or Underwood's books? He couldn't have—unless he read them before he was caught. Maybe it was just a good guess. "I thought we were having a conversation."

He yawned, making a show of it. "You know what? I didn't sleep too good last night. There's some shit going on in here and I have to watch my back. I'm really fuckin' exhausted. Can we do this next time? Promise we'll talk about my daughter." He looked past her, as if about to call for the guard.

But Vail was not ready for the interview to end. "How do you feel about Jasmine?"

Roscoe slowly settled his gaze on Vail. It was a threatening move, eerie in its deliberateness. "How do I feel about her?"

"She turned you in. You were caught because of her. You're behind bars. No chance of ever getting out. Because of her."

Marcks held her eyes a moment, then shrugged. "Wasn't a highlight of our relationship. How am I supposed to feel?"

"Did you read her book?"

"A news station sent me a copy hoping I'd give them an interview. Yeah, I read it."

"Did it make you angry?"

His right fist curled into a white-knuckled mace. "You have no idea."

"You want to get even?"

"How do you mean?"

Vail let the left side of her mouth drop sardonically. "You know." She leaned forward, as if sharing a secret. "Revenge."

"Against my own daughter? Because of some bullshit book?"

"Yeah. Like hurt her. Kill her. Cut off her limbs."

Marcks leaned back, narrowed his gaze, measured his response. "Now let's say I could do harm to my own daughter. My own flesh and blood. How would I do that?"

"You tell me."

He looked at her, long and hard. "Do something for me, Karen. Tell my little darlin' to be careful." He looked past her and banged his large fists on the table. "Guard!"

7

As Vail drove back toward Jasmine's house, she phoned Tim Meadows. After the disturbing end to her visit with Marcks, she wanted to know if they had supporting evidence that he had sent his daughter the letter.

"You get the handwriting sample Del Monaco sent over?"

"I did," Meadows said, "and I've got some good news. There's one characteristic in particular that's a bit unusual. A hitch in the uppercase S."

"But."

"How'd you know I was gonna say 'but'?"

"There's always a but with you."

"Well, here's the thing: both the known exemplar and the indented writing are small samples. It's a little tough to say conclusively based on only a few words."

"So . . . it's a probable match."

"Well, that's part of the but. In Questioned Documents examinations, the identification is either conclusive or inconclusive. There's some individuality and similarities in these writing samples, but . . ."

"There's not enough to go on."

"Right. If I was a betting man, however, I'd say he wrote it."

"Are you a betting man?"

"Nope. But that's irrelevant."

"I think I'm more confused than before I called you."

"Let me translate for the lower IQ agents I'm forced to work with: I believe it to be a match, but my report's gonna say inconclusive because to say otherwise would be asking for a sharp defense attorney to tear me a new asshole in court. Does that clear it up?"

"Now let *me* translate: you think it was written by Marcks but you're not gonna stick your neck out because you're covering your large buttocks."

"Now *there's* a language we can both understand." He paused a second, then said, "You think I've got a big rear end?"

Vail hung up and called Potter Correctional. Ten minutes later she had confirmation that a letter had been sent three days ago from Roscoe Lee Marcks. It contained a torn-out magazine advertisement and a blank piece of paper. They knew Marcks had a daughter, so they figured he was sending her a picture of a stuffed animal. Since it contained nothing overtly dangerous, they let the parcel pass.

Indented writing was *covert*, not overt, so she could not fault them for letting it through.

As Vail approached Jasmine's house, she received a text message from Stacey DiCarlo. She glanced at her Samsung Galaxy while driving and decided not to reply, mimicking those annoying announcements she saw in the movie theater: "It can wait." And when it came to her unit chief, she was more than happy to do just that.

Jasmine looked surprised to see Vail so soon. She had changed into workout attire—but she appeared to be nervous, as if she had spent the day stressing over the letter she received from her father.

"So there *was* something written on that paper," Vail said.

Jasmine studied her face a moment. "Come in."

Vail followed her into the kitchen again and they sat down. "Can I get you something?"

"I'm fine." Truth was, she was starving—but she did not plan on staying long.

"And what did it say?"

"It went with the picture of the stuffed animal. It read, 'Remember what happened to Sparky?'"

Jasmine banded her arms across her chest and shivered slightly.

"Obviously, it was a threat. But we have to keep it in perspective. He's in a maximum-security facility. He's never getting out."

"So you don't think I'm in any danger."

Vail hesitated. "I think we have to be smart about this. You should file a police report so that we can get the Fairfax County PD involved."

"Why?" Jasmine said. "It'll just mean endless questioning and a whole to-do over nothing. It is nothing, right?"

Vail averted her eyes. "I honestly don't know. But it's better to be safe than sorry. If your father has friends or if someone on the outside owes him for something, you could be in danger."

"Did you meet with him?"

"I did."

"And?"

"And . . ." *Shit, do I tell her what he said?* "For the most part he had normal reactions to my questions. He gave the impression he would never hurt you because you're his flesh and blood."

"But you didn't believe him."

"He's a violent criminal skilled in manipulation. No, I didn't believe him. He's telling me what he's supposed to say. And he did say I should tell you to be careful."

Jasmine clenched her jaw and nodded slowly. "I still don't want to report it. Just do whatever needs to be done."

"Jasmine, I'm . . . getting way outside the scope of my job. My unit chief's on my case. No pun intended. She—" Before Vail could finish the sentence her Samsung buzzed again. She held it up and said, "That's her. She wants me back at the office. She's concerned that I'm hand-holding you."

Jasmine stood up from the chair. "Okay. I'm sorry. I know, you're not a detective."

Not anymore. But sometimes I can't resist playing *one.* "Know anyone who was friends with your dad the police can look at, anyone who might be willing to do things, favors, for him while he's inside?"

Jasmine glanced around the kitchen, her eyes moving from one wall to the next but seeing nothing. "He didn't have many friends from what I can remember. A few, I guess, that he went drinking with. But there could be others I never met. One guy who's really scummy has probably had contact with my father. I saw him a few months ago at the market."

"You talked to him?"

"I caught him staring at me from the back of the store. Creeped me out. I turned and went back the other way and got the hell out of the place."

"Remember their names?"

"Vincent Stuckey and Scott MacFarlane. Those were his friends. At least the ones I knew. Booker Gaines, he's the creep I saw in the store."

"Gaines could be the guy to watch out for. He may've been keeping tabs on you when you saw him. It might not have been a chance meeting."

"You mean he may've been following me? For my father?"

"When did that article on you come out in *Time*?"

Jasmine's mouth dropped open. "About a week earlier."

Vail looked at her with a raised brow. No words were necessary.

"Fine." Jasmine massaged her forehead. "I'll file that police report so the detective can follow up."

Vail rose and gave Jasmine's right shoulder a squeeze. "Good."

"Should I just call the same detective who handled my father's case? Erik Curtis?"

"That'd be a good place to start. Give him those names. And if any of them contact you in any way, even if you happen to see them anywhere near you or your house, call Detective Curtis immediately." Vail's phone buzzed again and she glanced at the display. "Let me know if you have any problems. Or if you get more letters from your father. I'll be going back to see him again. If I find out anything else, I'll let you know."

She gave Jasmine another hug, then headed out the door, dialing DiCarlo on the way back to her car.

8

Erik Curtis sat down in front of Vail's desk. "Never been here before. Interesting place."

Curtis's New Orleans roots could still be detected in his speech. Someday she was going to invite him to a barbeque just to see if he showed up with a slab of alligator meat to throw on the grill.

"It's not as interesting as the subbasement at the Academy where the unit was started. Dark, quiet, deep below ground. This is just office space."

"I was picturing something more like the TV show. You know, *Criminal Minds.*"

"Seriously. Hollywood? That was what you thought my reality was like?" *Let me go summon our private jet. Wheels up in fifteen.*

Curtis shrugged. "Guilty as charged."

"Speaking of guilty," Vail said, taking a file and setting it in front of her. "Roscoe Lee Marcks."

"Bastard's still a thorn in my side, all these years later."

"Hey, at least he's a thorn who's residing in a federal penitentiary, locked away forever."

He worked his jaw slightly, as if conceding Vail's point. "So let me see this letter."

Vail pulled out a copy of the document and handed it to Curtis. "Not really a whole lot to 'see.'" She described the envelope Jasmine received and how she determined—or concluded—that Marcks had sent it. "No one else knew about what was done to Sparky. At least, no one who's still alive."

Curtis shifted his right leg, crossed it over his left knee. "So we basically know this douche bag is the one who sent the letter and he's . . . what? Toying with Jasmine? Or really threatening her?"

"Could be both. Don't know enough to say. Yet. But we have to take it seriously."

Curtis mulled that for a bit. "So what are you thinking?"

"Protective custody."

"Don't think I could sell that to my lieutenant. Not based on this." He glanced again at the paper Vail had handed him.

"Maybe start with regular well-checks, investigate Marcks, see if you can get a line on anyone he could be using for a job—guys who visited him, known associates. Maybe we can get a handle on whether or not he's actually going to act on this threat."

Curtis gave a tight nod. "I can do that."

"Jasmine's going to be contacting you to file a report. She's also got the names of three known associates of Marcks worth looking into. One may've been following her. Name's Gaines. Coincided with a front page *Time* magazine article—"

"I saw it. I'll follow up with her, look into it."

"Good. Now get outta here so I can get some real work done. I've got a unit meeting and my boss is on my ass."

"Speaking of asses, how's your husband?"

Vail looked up and locked her gaze on Curtis. "He's dead, Erik. Long story. I'm engaged to a DEA agent."

"Good for you. I think." He got up from his chair. "I had the hots for you. You know that, right?"

I do now.

"I—" she swallowed. "Nope, did not know that. But I'm . . . flattered."

"Yeah, well, you were married, had a kid. Jonathan?"

Vail rose and gathered up a case file. "Jonathan, yeah. Freshman at GW."

"Good. That's good." Curtis rocked back on his heels. "You're lookin' good, Vail. Guess you're the one that got away."

"Sorry." She glanced up at him, trying not to laugh. "You'll find someone." *It'd help if you cut your hair and joined a gym. But hey, there's someone for everyone.* "Keep me posted on what you find, okay?"

Curtis shrugged. "Of course."

VAIL WALKED INTO THE CONFERENCE ROOM a couple of minutes late. Gifford frowned, but it was DiCarlo's head shake that irked her. *Yeah, I'm late and I'm sorry, but get over it, lady. I was working. On that hand-holding babysitting case.*

Standing at the front, remote in hand, was profiler extraordinaire Art Rooney, one of two ATF agents—Bureau of Alcohol, Tobacco, Firearms, and Explosives—in the Behavioral Analysis Unit. He winked at Vail and turned back to the room, where nearly every one of the seats were taken.

"So as I was saying." Rooney hit the button and the first image splashed across the screen. "This was a month ago. Out

in the sticks, this house had three acres around it. Fire marshal believes the blaze was set in the living room and spread
rapidly—a key indicator of an arson."

"Accelerant?" Frank Del Monaco asked.

Rooney twisted his lips, hesitated, and said, "Denatured and
jellied alcohol. Sterno."

"From those catering canisters?" Vail asked. "Not a very
effective way of starting a hot fire. Or sustaining it. Right?"

"Right." Rooney forwarded to another photo, and then others: wide angle shots showing the crime scene and surrounding
land and close-ups of the fine ash and burned rubble—remnants
of kitchen appliances. "They're still analyzing samples from the
house. My guess is there was something else used other than
Sterno because that fire was damn hot. With intense fires we
typically see color changes or spalling in concrete, melted alu-
minum, deformation of steel, that type of thing—and we see
some of that here.

"There wasn't much left of the structure—cinderblocks for
the fireplace, the back and front steps outside, some metal from
a dishwasher and refrigerator. And that's about it. While those
are generally unreliable indicators of the presence of an accelerant, I'm convinced that the intensity of the fire is significant.
I'm sure we'll find something more potent than Sterno. Oh, we
also found traces of bone. There was apparently a body, which
is why homicide was called."

"Identification?" Tom van Owen asked.

"Not a whole lot left. No teeth, no long bones. They're running DNA. Homicide dick is Kevin McBride."

"And that's why we caught this case?" Vail said. "Almost no
forensics?"

"Yeah, that. Plus this isn't the first fire matching the MO. McBride said there were four more before this one, spread across a wide area. All in Virginia. And another they're now looking at from five years ago."

"I'm confused," Del Monaco said. "What in this crime scene says homicide? Sterno? Could've been left over from a party they had. The body could've been the homeowner. Smoking, watching TV, falls asleep, place goes up. Not like that doesn't happen. A lot."

Rooney's military demeanor helped him maintain his composure at times like these when others—Vail being the definition of "others"—would lose it with Del Monaco. "Too hot," Rooney said evenly. "I'm telling you, Frank, we're going to find a bonafide accelerant. And if not, we'll be going over those other cases to see if there's something that can clue us in on what to look for. We just need to dig deeper. The more info we have on the behaviors he left behind, the better we can establish linkage. And if we can establish linkage—well, you know the deal. If it is the same offender, we've gotta find him. He's not going to stop. These guys love their fires too much."

"And," Vail said, "if he's setting fires with people inside the houses, that's a whole other ballgame."

"Were there any distinguishable vapors at the scene?" van Owen asked. "Weather's been cold."

Rooney nodded. "Good point. Accelerant odors are sometimes detectable when the investigators make their initial inspection of the fire scene—and those smells are usually sharper on cold mornings. I'm told that they smelled something but couldn't identify it."

"Thank you, Art," DiCarlo said. "Agent Vail, you want to give us an update on Jasmine Marcks?"

He's "Art" but I'm "Agent Vail." What's up with that? Vail did not bother walking to the front of the room. She had no Power-Point to present. Just a verbal update, if that. "Some of you remember the Roscoe Lee Marcks case that Thomas Underwood handled before I joined the unit. I inherited the case and Marcks has been sitting behind bars at Potter Correctional doing LWOP," she said, using cop speak for life without parole. "Everything's been quiet until his daughter wrote a book about him. That seems to have stirred her father's pot."

"Why would he care?" Dietrich Hutchings asked.

"Because Jasmine was the one who turned him in."

"Oh, right. Duct tape or something?"

"Among other things," Vail said. "The profile was pretty much spot-on, but the nail in the coffin was the evidence she gave the cops. Her testimony blew away the thin alibis he had on the more recent murders. Not to mention the forensics they found at two of the later scenes. Anyway, Jasmine got a threatening note from him and—"

"And," DiCarlo said, "Agent Vail appears to have allowed herself to be drawn in to act as a babysitter."

Vail kept her death-ray gaze away from DiCarlo. And she held her tongue—both improvements in her demeanor that she had been working on the past few years, at Gifford's urging. She glanced at Hutchings instead, but he was wearing a politically correct poker face. "Fairfax County PD is taking it seriously, which I agree with. Detective Erik Curtis.

"I met with the offender at Potter Correctional, which I've been trying to do for years. After threatening his daughter, I felt he may have something to say and be more open to a sit down."

"And? What'd he say about his daughter?" Del Monaco asked.

"Nothing useful."

Hutchings spread his hands. "What was the threat? We can't be of much help if we don't have some details."

Vail told them.

Rooney, now seated across from Vail, lifted his brow. "Three issues here. One, is it credible, and two, if so, is he going to act on it, and three, what can he do about it? My sense is that you have to treat it as credible."

"Curtis and I agree. He's looking into known associates, tracking down visitors he's had the past year, the usual stuff."

"Is this surprising for Marcks?" Rooney asked.

Vail had to think about that. "I think so. He's a bad dude, no doubt about that. Underwood felt he exhibited some traits of psychopathy, but not the whole cluster. So he may have the ability to exhibit certain emotional responses. And if that's the case, it could simply be a case of building anger over the years. Disappointment, betrayal. And then the book comes out and it sets him off. He's pissed, he sends a letter that's designed to freak her out."

"I'm confused," DiCarlo said. "So you don't think there's a threat here?"

"It could be a case of frustration and anger. Or it could be something a lot more serious. We can't take that chance, especially when dealing with an offender like this, whether Jasmine is his own flesh and blood or not."

"Best guess?" Gifford asked.

"Best guess is this is a legitimate threat."

Vail's Samsung vibrated and she glanced at the display. It was someone calling from Potter Correctional Facility.

"I've gotta take this." She held up the handset as she rose from her seat, hoping neither of her bosses would object. They did not and she made it into the hallway. "Vail."

"I've got assistant warden Thibeaux on the line. Please hold." A couple of seconds later, Thibeaux picked up. "I had a message to call you."

"Actually, I think it'd be better if we do this in person."

Thibeaux paused. "Works for me. Don't you have a bit of a drive?"

"I'll need a couple hours."

"Call when you're fifteen out."

Vail started walking toward her car, dialing Curtis as she went. He answered almost immediately.

"Second thoughts about your engagement? Thinking that maybe you'd give me a shot?"

"Yeah. No. I got us a meeting with the assistant warden at Potter. Wanna take a ride?"

"YOU KNOW WE'RE PROBABLY GONNA HIT horrendous traffic on the way back."

"Worry about that later," Vail said as she glanced around at the rolling hills, forestland, and scattered farms. "I just figured, we want him to take this seriously, we need to sit across from him and look him in the eye."

They pulled into the Potter parking lot, the remaining daylight draining from the sky and the dense chiaroscuro clouds thick with the threat of precipitation.

They secured their guns in the trunk of the car and headed into the main entrance of the administration building. They signed in and were handed red laminated placards to clip to their clothing, a bold black *V* on the front. They were escorted from the visitors center to the main maximum-security cell block down a decrepit hallway, up two flights of stairs, and through another corridor that needed a paint job and some modern technology—on the order of fluorescent bulbs.

"You know they're doing away with incandescent lights," Vail said.

Their chaperone turned and glanced at her over his shoulder. "And this interests me, why?"

They arrived at Sean Thibeaux's office a moment later. The paunchy middle-aged man appeared through an adjacent doorway and waved them in. "I didn't know someone was joining us," he said to Vail's companion. "You are?"

"Erik Curtis, Fairfax County Police Department. Homicide."

"Curtis handled the Roscoe Lee Marcks case," Vail said. "I brought him up to speed on—well, what I'm here to discuss with you. Called him en route, thought he should come along."

"Uh-huh. Great," he said with the enthusiasm of a banana slug. He gestured to two guest chairs opposite his metal desk: standard 1940s-era seats that had never been reupholstered.

The hard, worn-out foam surface hurt Vail's bottom.

"So Marcks actually talked with you," Thibeaux said, settling his thick body into an office chair that looked considerably more comfortable. "You had a conversation that lasted more than three sentences. And he didn't bash your face in. I was surprised."

"We had a very nice chat," Vail said.

"Really?"

"No. He's a narcissist who tried to control the conversation. I let him run things because I was trying to establish a rapport. But it took a lot of effort to play along."

"And? Learn anything?"

"Just that he's a scary dude. Scratch that. Already knew that. But I'd be lying if I didn't admit it creeped me out. Not to leave this room."

"He won't hear it from me," Thibeaux said.

"I've got another meeting with him next week. Assuming he doesn't cancel."

"So we're here because of the threat," Curtis said, clearly not wanting anyone to forget he was in the room.

"Heard about that." Thibeaux brushed a lock of hair off his forehead and looked to Vail for an explanation.

"He sent a letter to his daughter."

"Okay. What'd it say?"

"It was a veiled threat."

The creases on Thibeaux's face deepened as he leaned forward in his chair. "And my guys let that through? What'd it say? I wanna see it."

"It was a blank piece of paper. Along with a magazine clipping—"

"Of what?"

Damn, I knew he'd ask. Hell, I'd ask. "Of a stuffed animal."

Thibeaux looked at her, a blank sarcastic look that said, "You gotta be kidding me." She knew it well because she had used it herself, many times. "A blank piece of paper and a photo of a stuffed animal. And you're calling that a threat?"

"There was indented writing. It asked if she remembered her stuffed animal from her childhood—her favorite stuffed animal, which had been dismembered and left in her bed."

Thibeaux sat back, his eyes narrowing in apparent thought. Then: "I'll loop in the warden, get his take, see what he wants to do. But he's a low-key guy, he doesn't overreact to things. And I have a feeling he's going to say this is nothing with nothing."

"That's a possibility. But I don't think that's what we're dealing with here."

"You agree?" Thibeaux asked.

Curtis nodded. "Yeah. I don't have to tell you Marcks did some pretty sadistic shit to his vics. You really wanna be the one responsible for his daughter's murder? Right after her book hits stores and *she's* hitting the talk show circuit?"

"Bring the warden in," Vail said. "I'd like to explain this to him myself."

Thibeaux contorted the left side of his mouth. "Wouldn't recommend that. The warden wouldn't take kindly to—"

"A woman telling him how to do his job?"

Thibeaux chuckled. "To the FBI telling him how to do his job."

"I'll take my chances."

"Suit yourself. Don't say I didn't warn you."

"I've been peripherally involved with this case for years. I'm concerned about Jasmine Marcks."

Thibeaux leaned back. "So it's personal."

"No." *Wait, is it?*

"All good cops personalize their cases," Curtis said. "It's what makes us human. If we turn off that spigot we wouldn't give a shit about the victims. And we wouldn't be very good at our jobs now, would we?"

Vail drew her gaze from Curtis back to Thibeaux. "Honestly, I couldn't have said it better."

Thibeaux worked his jaw, then got up from his desk and left the room.

"You know this ain't gonna go well," Curtis said quietly.

"Why?"

"Wardens are political appointees. A lot of these guys are clueless in terms of what really goes on in a prison. Most of what they do is manage bed space. Not very highly regarded. The black sheep of the Department of Justice."

"Well, let's hope this guy has some idea as to what's going on in his house. And what to do about it."

A couple minutes later, the door opened and Thibeaux motioned Vail and Curtis into the sparse hallway, then led them to a larger office. Larger, but not a whole lot nicer. In this borderline dilapidated building, there was just so much that could be done with aging, cracked cinderblock. Not to mention the lack of money to fund it.

Warden James Barfield's desk was immaculate, with neatly stacked folders on the left and a battered HP laptop on the right. It was an obsessive-compulsive's oasis in the bureaucratic mess of a correctional facility that was five decades past its prime.

"Sit, Vail." There was only one chair. "Curtis, you can stand."

Curtis frowned but did as instructed, taking up a position behind and to the right of Vail's seat.

"I'm told you wanted a few minutes to convince me that Roscoe Lee Marcks poses a danger to his daughter."

Vail folded her hands in her lap—less likelihood she would do damage with them tucked away there. "Not how I'd characterize it, warden, but I guess it's accurate enough."

"Well then, how would you *characterize* it?"

"It's our responsibility to keep Jasmine Marcks safe. And it's your responsibility to make sure Roscoe Lee Marcks doesn't do anything that endangers her. Our interests overlap so I don't see where we have to convince you of anything."

According to Curtis, that's not his responsibility at all. But it made so much sense. How could he argue?

Barfield chuckled. "Just like the FBI to tell me how to do my job." He had a southern drawl and said FBI slowly, emphasizing each letter distinctly, the "I" sounding like "ah." "My responsibility, as you put it, is to make sure these inmates do their time as instructed by a court of law, without causing harm to themselves or each other. That about sums it up, Agent Vail. Now, I don't know 'bout you, but I don't consider watching over an inmate's grown child as bein' part of that job description."

"Maybe it's just a matter of common sense." Vail forced a smile.

"We'd really appreciate your support," Curtis said, clearly aware of Vail's failed attempt at diplomacy.

"I'm sure you would." Barfield frowned and glanced at Vail. "We're already getting the materials together that Detective Curtis requested on Marcks's visitors. What more do you want?"

"Special attention," Curtis said before Vail had a chance to reply. "To make sure he doesn't have any contact with anyone, inside or outside, while we investigate."

"Can't prevent him from talking to his attorney," Barfield said as he busied himself with items on his desk. "And honestly, until and unless you charge him with something, there are rules I have to follow regarding prisoner rights."

"Just keep your eyes open," Curtis said, trying to sound reasonable. "That's all we can ask."

Barfield looked up. "Seems to me you were asking for quite a bit more than that."

"Actually," Vail said, "I was. We're talking about someone who was victimized as a young teen. And continues to be victimized as a young woman. Her father's an asshole. And he's a serial killer. The least we can do is try our best to make sure that Roscoe Lee Marcks doesn't conspire with anyone to kill her. Or rape her. Or mail her any more emotionally upsetting letters. Now maybe that doesn't fall under your job description as warden, but it falls under your job description as a decent human being."

Barfield grinned a broad, toothy smile. "Well, thank you, kindly, Agent Vail, for that inspirational kick in the rear. I'll take it under advisement. Now y'all have a safe trip back home. Be sure and come back again real soon."

"THAT WENT EXCEEDINGLY WELL," Curtis said as they walked back to their car. "Don't you agree?"

Yeah. Exceedingly well.

"You've lived in Virginia how many years?"

Vail squinted at the overcast sky. "Uh, I don't know, about ten."

"And you still don't understand southerners? Aren't you ever going to lose that New York aggressiveness?"

Vail fished out her car keys. "You know what they say."

Curtis grunted. "I know what *I* say. Shove it up your ass if you can't adapt. And take your Yankee ass back to New York."

Vail popped open her door and fell into the seat. "I was thinking more like, 'You can take the woman out of New York but you can't take New York out of the woman.'"

Curtis reached for his seatbelt. "I think that's what exorcisms are for."

9

Vail walked into her house and her chocolate brown standard poodle, Hershey, ran to the door, wagging his tail and holding a pair of her underwear and one of Robby's socks in his mouth. He jumped up to greet her, spit out the garments, and plastered her face with kisses.

"I missed you too, boy," she said, twisting her head to the side as she tried to talk without getting a wet tongue across her lips. "C'mon, let's go out."

Vail headed toward the side door, which led to the dog run. As she pulled it open, Hershey forced his way through and ran to his favorite spot to pee.

She grabbed a scoop of dog food and started back into the kitchen when her phone vibrated. She brought it to her face as she dumped the lamb kibble in the stainless steel bowl. "Hey Jasmine, how's—"

"Someone was here, in the house."

"How—are you there now?"

"I just got home and the side garage door was open. And then I heard a car door slam and I ran to the window and saw a beat-up old Toyota or Honda driving away."

Awesome. That narrows it down to only a few million vehicles.

"Did you get a license plate?"

"No, I—I ran inside and called you."

"Okay, get back in your car and go somewhere safe—get a coffee at Starbucks. It'll be busy. I want you around people. I'll call Detective Curtis, have him check your place out, make sure it's clear, okay?"

"Yeah. I'm—I'm just . . . this isn't like me but I'm . . ." She took a breath. "You know what? Forget it, I'm fine."

"It's okay to be scared. Do what I said. We'll get this sorted out. I'll call you back soon."

Vail let Hershey in as she dialed Curtis. It went to voice mail and she left him a message to meet her at Jasmine's, then headed out to Bethesda.

It was the tail end of rush hour and the last thing she wanted to do was get slowed by traffic. Her stomach was rumbling and her back was sore, having spent the better part of the day on the road. Though not standard issue, Vail had picked up a portable magnetic auxiliary light a few years ago for situations such as this. After affixing it to her roof, she was able to work her way through the congestion.

While en route, Vail called the Fairfax Police Department's PSTOC—Public Safety and Transportation Operations Center— and had Curtis pulled out of an interview room. He was not sure how soon he could make it to Jasmine's house, but he requested that a patrol car and a crime scene unit be dispatched.

Vail texted Jasmine and told her that both she and the police were en route. When she arrived on scene thirty-five minutes later, an officer had cleared the house and was waiting outside with Jasmine.

"I told you to go to Starbucks."

"I did. But when I got your text I turned around and came home. The police were already at my front door."

The crime scene technician opened his toolbox and pulled out gloves and booties. He tossed a handful to Vail, who gave a pair of the blue shoe covers to Jasmine. "Slip these on."

"What for?" she asked as she knelt to pull them over her tennis shoes.

"To preserve the crime scene."

Jasmine looked up from her crouch. "Crime scene? My *house*?"

"Anything missing?"

"I don't know. I did what you said, left right away."

"Take a look around. But don't touch anything."

Ten minutes later, Erik Curtis walked in, a scowl stretched across his face. "When I got home I found my brother in my kitchen, eating *my* New York strip steak. Before I could rip him a new one, I got a call that they've grabbed up a suspect in one of my cases so I went back in. And now this."

"Strip steak, eh? You don't hate *everything* that's from New York."

"As long as I can put it over a hot flame, I'm good." He gestured at Jasmine. "So what's the deal?"

Vail related what happened, then motioned him to the front porch. They stepped outside into the darkness and walked ten or so feet down the brick path. The street was not well lit, the nearest house a quarter of a block away. Curtis whistled to an officer and told him and his partner to begin a canvass of the neighborhood in case anyone saw the car or the person who had been inside Jasmine's house.

"Find anything on those three known associates?"

Curtis snorted. "And when was I gonna do that? I was stuck in the car with you all day."

"Stuck? With me?"

"You know what I mean." He shrugged. "I'll get on it tomorrow."

"Could be one of them who did this."

Curtis nodded absentmindedly. "Hopefully someone got a license plate or make and color of the vehicle. Maybe forensics will help us out."

"So what are we going to do with Jasmine?"

"I'll make a call, see if I can get a car stationed here tonight. And then . . ."

"Yeah, and then what?"

The voice came from behind them. Vail turned. It was Jasmine.

"We'll figure something out. We won't leave you unprotected."

Jasmine bit her lip and nodded, searching Vail's face as if evaluating the veracity of her statement. "You really think it's safe here?"

"The moment it's not, I'll get you out. Promise."

Jasmine nodded acceptance, then turned and walked back into the house.

"What do you think?"

"I think someone's screwing with her," Curtis said. "And I think she'll be fine here. Because if that someone wanted to hurt her, he could have."

Vail backed away from Curtis, heading toward the house. "'Someone' doesn't cut it. We need to find out who it is, if he's working with Marcks, and if he's serious about hurting her or just trying to send a message."

"Got it on my list, Karen. Tomorrow we'll have some answers."

Vail shoved her hands into her pockets. "Let's hope so."

10

Roscoe Lee Marcks walked into the inmate showers, a large white tile room with industrial steel shower heads hanging from the low ceiling. It was a communal area without privacy, a place where larger men derided smaller men based on the size of their genitals, their sagging asses, or anything else they could insult—or use to their advantage. The pecking order of a federal penitentiary was clearly defined and did not offer much opportunity to better your lot in life . . . particularly among those who were *doing* life.

Marcks did not have to worry about being ridiculed or intimidated because he was often the perpetrator and never the recipient.

"Fuck you looking at?" Marcks yelled across the room.

The target of his challenge was not, in fact, looking at Marcks; his back was turned and he had to be told that Marcks was talking to him.

The man, Patrick O'Shea, rotated slowly. He was larger than Marcks, both in bone structure and muscle mass. No one had challenged him since he arrived at Potter. As a result, when O'Shea tossed his bar of soap to the floor and advanced on Marcks, all the inmates in the vicinity scattered to the periphery, wanting no part of what was about to transpire.

Marcks stood his ground, nonchalantly tilting his head to the left as O'Shea closed on him. There was nothing that could happen here other than a physical confrontation. Regardless of the reputation of these men, the instigator could not back down and neither could the one who was called out.

"You outta your fuckin' mind? Or you juss lookin' for a beatin'?"

Marcks did not hesitate. A quick, hard jab to the jaw landed firmly and O'Shea staggered noticeably. But the larger man recovered his balance immediately and took a long step forward, blocked a hook, and grabbed Marcks by the back of his neck. And then he pounded his right fist into Marcks's cheek, followed by a crushing blow to his temple.

Marcks's legs buckled and his eyes rolled back.

O'Shea grabbed Marcks by his thick charcoal gray hair and flung him like a discarded sack of potatoes across the room and into the wall. Marcks stuck his left arm out and, with a resounding thud, broke the impact.

It was nothing, however, compared to the sound his skull made when it hit the tile.

An alarm sounded. Shouts from the approaching guards:

"Break it up!"

"Everyone against the wall!"

Three officers entered, two with their backs to Marcks, facing the prisoners, while the other attended to him as he writhed feebly on the wet floor, moaning as he attempted to get to his knees.

Alarms sounded in the distance, fading off as he dropped in a heap to the cold, blood-slimy tile.

◆   ◆   ◆

"HE NEEDS AN MRI. I can set his broken ulna, but there's no point. They can do that at the hospital. He needs to get there STAT. I'll ride with him."

Marcks kept his eyes shut. But he knew that voice well: Sue Olifante, Potter's nurse practitioner. The doctor, Lester McQuade, or More-or-Less McQuack, as the inmates called him, was off on Saturdays. Rumor had it that he worked for the Bureau of Prisons because he was not good enough to have his own practice and could not secure a position at a clinic anywhere in the country. Once word of that broke, the prisoners did not hesitate to mock him at every opportunity. McQuade took the abuse—because he had to. And because it was true.

Why any sane person would want to spend his days around dangerous, hardened, violent criminals—the scum of the earth, as he once put it—was clear: because he did not have a choice. Student loans, years in school, mouths to feed at home . . . Olifante and McQuade were cut from the same grease rag: hacks who could earn a decent salary at Potter, even if it meant spending their days knee deep in the filth.

But Olifante had found a confidante in Roscoe Lee Marcks. Marcks was a good-looking man who knew how to talk to a woman, how to charm her, how to make her do what he wanted. He put such skills to work on Sue Olifante, and to a good end.

"I'll have the transport van brought around back," the correctional officer said.

Olifante glanced at the man. "Double time it. He's hurt real bad and every minute counts. Head trauma's very serious."

He ran off. Olifante gathered up a cast-like brace and slipped it over Marcks's left forearm, then inflated it.

Moments later, three guards appeared with ankle and wrist restraints.

"What do you think you're doing with that?" Olifante asked, hands on her hips.

"Prisoner's gotta be secured for transport," one of the officers said.

"And just how are you going to do that with his fractured ulna? Best I can tell, it's broken in at least three places."

The guard moved closer to evaluate the situation.

"I've got a compression splint on him," Olifante said. "The cuffs won't fit—and even if they did, they'd do permanent damage if they tore the median or ulnar nerves. Just secure his ankles. With this head wound, he probably won't even regain consciousness."

"If he escapes," the young guard said with a shake of his head, "this is gonna come back on me. I got a wife and—"

"You are?"

"Sanders. I'm accompanying the prisoner to the hospital."

"I'll be in the van with him, too," Olifante said. "If he escapes, I'm the first one he's going to kill. You think I'm suicidal? I'll be fine. And you'll be fine, too." She secured the IV line with tape and checked the drip chamber. "Besides, he's not going anywhere with this needle in his arm. I've got him sedated."

The door opened and two correctional officers stepped into the medical suite, fastened the ankle restraints, and pushed the gurney out to the sally port.

A moment later, Marcks was loaded into the back of the twenty-foot-long cabover transport vehicle. It doubled as an ambulance during times like these—which had become more frequent in recent years. Potter's decrepit condition was not limited to the prison blocks and administrative wing, but the medical facilities as well. The surgical suite was rudimentary and borderline functional for simple procedures. The x-ray machine, however, dated back to the 1920s, the early days of its use as a valuable diagnostic tool, and the CT scanner was a first-generation unit purchased secondhand twenty years ago when the local hospital closed its doors.

Olifante watched as the dour-faced Sanders and another guard secured the gurney to a locking mechanism on the interior wall. After the other officer left, Sanders checked that his sidearm was firmly seated in its holster. "You sure you wanna make this trip? It's twenty-five minutes each way."

"I'm fine," Olifante said. "Let's go. Every minute counts."

"All right, let's move it out!"

The doors clanked closed and the truck lurched, pulling out of the sally port and eventually onto I-95.

"He's a fucking serial killer," Sanders said. "If he goes, he goes. Know what I mean? Why do you care so much?"

Olifante snorted. "I'm a medical professional. Every life has equal value. That's all that matters. Right now he's my patient. What he's accused of doing doesn't matter to me. And unless we get him to the hospital quickly, he may not live much longer."

Ten minutes later, Marcks stirred on the gurney. Then he moaned.

"He's regaining consciousness," Olifante said.

Sanders shifted in the stool he was sitting on in the corner of the cargo area, no more than eight feet from the gurney. "I thought you had him sedated."

"Have to be careful with brain trauma. Too much sedation and I could kill him."

Olifante moved closer and pulled a stethoscope from her scrubs pocket. She took something else out and palmed it.

"That's close enough," Sanders said.

"And how am I going to listen to his heart without touching his chest with the stethoscope?"

Sanders gritted his teeth. "Be quick about it, then back away."

Olifante threw him a look of disgust, then leaned over Marcks's torso, placing an object in his left hand out of view of the guard.

With leopard-like quickness, Marcks grabbed the back of Olifante's neck with his right hand and yanked her close. She screamed: nothing fake about it. Pure, unfiltered surprise. And horror.

"Fuck!" Sanders drew his sidearm.

Marcks dug his thumb into her windpipe. "Drop that gun or I'll choke her to death."

"I'm *not* dropping my gun," Sanders said firmly. "But you're gonna let her go."

"You know who you're talking to, boy?"

Olifante struggled, her face shading deep blue.

"I'm gonna give ya to three," Sanders said, raising his SIG to eye level.

That was when Marcks produced the scalpel that Olifante had slipped him and brought it against her carotid. He had an awkward grip with the splint in the way, but what mattered was the exquisite sharpness of the blade against the woman's skin. One movement, a sudden lurch of the truck, and she would bleed to death.

Olifante cried a muffled plea, as best she could with what little breath she had left in her lungs.

Sanders rushed forward and shoved his gun against Marcks's groin. "Drop the fucking scalpel!"

But Marcks was too skilled a criminal. And Sanders was too hapless an officer to stop him. In an instant, Marcks drew the blade across Olifante's neck, spurting blood into Sanders's face—and then stabbed the guard in the eye.

Sanders screamed—a shrill cry. He dropped his SIG and Marcks sat up in one motion and grabbed Sanders by the hair. He yanked the man's face toward his and shoved the protruding scalpel deep into his brain.

Sanders's knees buckled and he sagged against Olifante's fallen body.

Marcks gathered up the SIG, located the guard's key, and unlocked the ankle restraints.

He pushed Olifante's dead body aside and slid off the gurney. He was surprised the driver had not heard Sanders's shriek of alarm. Then again, with the road noise and what sounded like the radio playing in the cab, the man appeared to be unaware of what was happening. The truck continued on its course, not slowing or changing direction.

Marcks pulled the slide back and chambered a round, laughing at the guard's poor training. The weapon was not even ready to be fired. *Jesus Christ,* he thought. *Don't they teach these guys anything?*

There was no window into the cab, so there was some guesswork involved. But Marcks did his best, lined up his shot, and pulled the trigger repeatedly until he had emptied the magazine.

The noise was deafening in the closed cargo space. But the truck veered onto the shoulder of the road, then struck something and rolled onto its side.

Once it came to a rest, Marcks righted himself and searched Sanders's pockets. He found fifty bucks but no ammunition. The handgun was now of little value, so he tossed it aside. Until he could find a knife, which would be a great deal easier to obtain than a firearm, the scalpel would have to suffice.

He pulled another thirty dollars from Olifante's pockets. Although there was some risk involved, he would at least be able to feed himself for a while. But the true prize was a cheap cell phone Olifante had purchased for him, programmed with the numbers he had requested. Without question, Sue Olifante was a godsend. He owed her his freedom.

He gave her a kiss on her bloody forehead, then exited the vehicle.

11

Vail stood at the front of the modest lecture hall, Jonathan seated in the third row at the far right. He had declined to introduce his mother, instead letting the professor do the honors, not because he was embarrassed by her or was afraid of public speaking, but because he felt it would seem self-serving.

The professor, however, did not share the same concern, as he made it a point to note that the FBI profiler guest speaker was the mother of one of their fellow students. Vail could not tell, but she was fairly certain that her son's face shaded red.

She turned away and focused her gaze on the outsized circular white column that was situated directly ahead of her, in the middle of the room.

The professor finished his remarks by noting that her talk was being recorded by "lecture capture" so they did not need to worry about taking notes.

Wonderful. Better watch what I say.

Vail stepped in front of the substantial oak lectern, which was wired with audiovisual equipment, a computer monitor, keyboard, and mouse.

"Thank you, Professor Winfield. It's an honor to be addressing you guys this afternoon." She inserted a flash drive, double-clicked her PowerPoint file, and swiveled to face the expansive motorized projection screen behind her to make sure it was displaying her first slide.

"I remember sitting in one of my criminal justice classes when a detective came to speak to us. I found his talk inspiring and I hope to do the same for some of you today. I also think back very fondly on the time an FBI profiler came to speak to my class, and, well, that ended up changing my life.

"I'm going to leave the last twenty minutes for questions because hopefully what I'm about to discuss will get you thinking. Listen to what I'm saying. Challenge it. Ask questions—because thinking critically is a key to just about anything you do in law enforcement, whether it be forensics, prosecuting offenders or—God forbid—defending them." She smiled, but they all wore serious expressions.

Get on with it, Karen. You haven't won them over yet. Jonathan's probably rolling his eyes. Don't look at him.

Vail swiped her finger across the screen and the next PowerPoint slide appeared: a red and black header reading "Violent Crime" appeared above a photo depicting a puddle of blood beside a victim's chalk outline.

But as she opened her mouth to speak, her phone vibrated. She pressed a hand against her pocket, hesitated a second, then pushed forward.

"Many of you have heard of the Behavioral Science Unit from the movies or TV shows. Although it's been renamed the Behavioral Research and Instruction Unit, its focus has remained the same since it was started in the early seventies."

Her phone vibrated again, and again she let the call go to voice mail. "Simply put, the goal behind behavioral science is to study, and understand, human behavior. More specifically, BRIU, as it's called—because the government loves its acronyms—focuses on criminal behavior so we can gain insight into who these offenders are, how they think, and why they do what they do. If we can understand that, it'll help us solve crimes and potentially head off future criminal activity. Now if we drill down a bit deeper, the criminal behavior we're most concerned with in the BRIU, and my unit, the Behavioral Analysis Unit, is violent crime."

Her Samsung vibrated a third time.

Someone's determined to reach me. Vail glanced at Jonathan, then the professor. "Excuse me for a second." She fished out the phone and checked the display: Erik Curtis. *Answer it?*

Vail did just that—and got an earful.

"Jesus, Karen, were you on the shitter or something? I've been trying to reach—"

"I'm teaching a class at GW—"

"Oh—sorry. Sorry. But I thought you should know that the officer we put on Jasmine's house is, well, he's missing."

"Missing? What the hell does that mean? He's a goddamn police officer." She caught herself, glanced up at the class. *Jonathan's gonna hate me. If not for the interruption, for—*

"He's not reporting in or responding to his radio. Karen, you there?"

"I'm here. I assume you're searching for him? Is Jasmine okay?"

"She's fine. I'm on my way but I'm told she's not there. Trying to verify. Can you get over there? She's got some kind of bond with you, a women's th—"

"I'll be there as soon as I can. Give me an hour."

She hung up before Curtis could object. *I'm not supposed to be babysitting her. Curtis can handle this.*

"I apologize for the interruption. One of my cases." She rubbed the creases in her forehead, looked at the PowerPoint, and gathered her thoughts. "Okay, so let's pick up where we left off. The BAU, where I work. Anyone interested in understanding why offenders do what they do? How about walking into a crime scene and picking up on hidden clues about the killer that no one else sees? But *you* see them because you're trained to see them, to put it all together, to understand who committed the crime—and why.

"It's very powerful. Think of it like a foreign language that you don't know how to speak. It sounds like gibberish. But once you learn it, you start to see things differently, you understand what's being said. You understand the nuances of a language very few others can comprehend. Let me give you an example."

Her phone buzzed again. She closed her eyes as she fished out the cell. A text message from Curtis.

found missing officer
hes dead
killed like the others
like the other blood lines vics
wtf

Vail swallowed. She was staring at her screen, her thoughts zipping by so fast she could not process them. None of this made sense. The Blood Lines killer was behind bars ninety minutes from here. For life.

"Agent Vail," the professor said. "Are we interrupting?"

"I, uh—I'm sorry, a case. It's—"

Her phone vibrated again—in her hand. It was Gifford.

She slowly brought the handset to her face, almost afraid to answer it.

"Yes sir."

"Karen, I know you're offsite at GW, but you need to take a rain check."

She brought two fingers to the bridge of her nose. "I heard about the officer."

"What officer? I'm calling you about Roscoe Lee Marcks. He escaped two hours ago."

Vail felt dizzy. *This can't be happening. Fuck.*

She glanced up, hoping she had not verbalized that thought. All eyes were on her but no one appeared shocked. Then again, these were college students.

"US Marshals have mobilized," Gifford said. "Call Deputy Lewis Hurdle. DiCarlo's texting you his contact info."

Vail swallowed and looked across the lecture hall at Jonathan. "Yes sir."

"Leave now. I'll have Lenka call the professor and reschedule you."

"Okay sir. Yes sir. On my way." She slipped the phone back in her pocket, adrenaline hitting her bloodstream with the abandon of a broken dam. "I'm uhh . . . I'm very sorry. I must sound like an idiot, but I've been ordered to—I've got a—there's a situation I have to deal with and—we'll have to reschedule." She grabbed her flash drive and the screen behind her went blank.

"My office will be in touch," she said to Winfield, avoiding Jonathan's gaze, as she bolted for the door.

◆   ◆   ◆

VAIL DID NOT HAVE TO CALL DEPUTY HURDLE. He
phoned her by the time she reached her car.

"On my way," Vail said as she chirped her car remote.

"No need," Hurdle said. "We got this."

"What do you mean, 'We got this.' I was ordered to get with
you, help the task force find Roscoe Lee Marcks."

"I know what our job is. All I'm saying is you don't need to
do it. We got this. We're good."

Vail turned over the engine and pulled out of the parking
spot, trying to restrain her building anger. "Who's we?"

"Capital Area Regional Fugitive Task Force. This is all we
do, Vail. We catch assholes like Marcks. And we do it better
without anyone meddling in our business."

"Good to know. What address am I driving to?"

Hurdle slowed his speech and lowered his voice. "Am I not
making myself clear?"

"Crystal. I'm ignoring you. Now, you can give me the address
of the command center, or I can have the FBI director talk with
the attorney general and have him get the address for me. I've
got the director on speed dial."

I love saying that.

There was a pause.

So predictable.

"Check your phone." The line went dead.

And the info hit her cell seconds later.

VAIL PULLED INTO THE PARKING LOT of the Mason District Station of the Fairfax County Police Department, where a

black RV sat, gold lettering proclaiming "U.S. Marshals Service Mobile Command Center," along with the five-pointed silver star that dated back to the agency's origin in 1789.

A conspicuous satellite dish and corkscrew communications array projected from the top of the vehicle.

As she started to get out of her car, Curtis's Ford glided into the spot next to her.

She had called Curtis and told him to divert there, if possible. He said he could, as his partner was already on scene at Jasmine's house.

"Thanks for the heads-up."

"Figured you'd want to be looped in from the start."

"You figured right. Gotta watch these marshals. They think they know everything there is to know about catching bad guys."

"They do." She noticed Curtis's look, so she added, "Hey, I give credit where it's due. The marshals on the fugitive squads know their shit. They've got fugitive tracking in their blood."

"You admit that?"

"Before we walk in that trailer?" she said, gesturing at the RV. "Hell yes. But they'll also piss you off because they don't pass up any opportunity to let you know that they're the best."

"This isn't your first rodeo with them."

"I've heard stories."

Curtis gave her a dubious look. "I could *tell* those stories. Did a couple years on the task force a while back."

"We'll just make this a meet 'n greet so we can get over to Jasmine's place. I know you've got a guy there now, but—hey, who'd they give you?" Vail knew that Curtis's former partner died of leukemia. "Anyone I know?"

"She's new. Out-of-state hire. Checkered history, what I'm told. Lucky me."

Vail locked her car door and started toward the marshals' command post. "You ask her about it? You've gotta know who's covering your back."

"I will. We only met yesterday. They had me with some burned-out train wreck after Lonny died. He finally retired—actually, he'd checked out a year ago, but I convinced him to make it official before he got us both killed."

They ascended the wooden steps and pulled the trailer door open. It was well outfitted, with built-in workstations and LCD screens lining the periphery. She had seen one of these mobile command centers before, on a larger scale, in New York City.

Several people were there, including a man in his early forties dressed in tactical pants—her favorite 5.11s, by the look of them—with a two-day beard and a rumpled button-down concealed carry shirt . . . the professional's way to pack a weapon without anyone noticing while keeping it instantly accessible. "Lemme guess. Vail. Right?"

"What was your first clue? The red hair? Or the breasts?"

His eyes gave her the once over. "FBI badge on your belt."

Good save, buddy. "The badge does attract attention."

"Just like you people."

"How's that?"

Hurdle nodded at Curtis. "Who's your friend?"

"Erik Curtis. Fairfax County Police."

"Uh-huh. Figured you'd show up."

"Well," Curtis said with a half-smile, "you *are* in my parking lot. Good to know we're not gonna have any problems working together."

"Before we talk about working together, I was told you were on the task force several years ago."

"Whoever told you that seems to be a reliable source." Curtis grinned again.

"Yeah, he is. We'll have OPR do a backgrounder on you PDQ," he said, referring to the Service's Office of Professional Responsibility. "Make sure there've been no warrants issued and no bad shit smeared on you since you left the task force. Everything checks out, you're back in the saddle. That's the official line. Unofficially, look in my eyes."

Curtis did as instructed.

"Anything I need to know about? Anything that would come up in the background check that'd make it impossible for you to serve on CARFTF?" he asked, ignoring the silent "F" and pronouncing it "cartif," for Capital Area Regional Fugitive Task Force.

"Nothing."

Hurdle studied his face a moment. "You're onboard as of now, on my authority. You'll be deputized as soon as the paperwork comes through. If we do our jobs efficiently, and the FBI doesn't get in the way, we'll have this Marcks dude wearing handcuffs before the ink's dry on your application."

Vail lifted her brow. "You sound very confident." *And more than a little condescending.*

Hurdle walked toward them and leaned against the adjacent work table. "Damn straight. I've been tracking down these assholes for eighteen years. I know what I'm doin'. You people are here because it's the right thing to do. Cooperation with state and local. And FBI, in cases like this, because—well, because some clueless idiot bureaucrat, who knows shit about what we do, decided we have to work with you people. I get it—but that don't mean I gotta like it. Or that it makes sense."

"You didn't really think the intimidation act would work with me, did you?"

"'Course not. I try it all the time with the Fibbies, never works. Can't blame me for trying." He cracked a smile—which looked genuine.

"Bottom line," Vail said, "is—"

"Bottom line is that we're gonna catch Roscoe Lee Marcks. And you guys will claim all the credit for a job well done. Ask any marshal on any task force in the country, he or she will tell you the same thing. That's it in a nutshell."

Perhaps that nutshell is more than a little cracked.

"I can do this shit in my sleep, Vail."

"I can't speak for anyone else, but I'd rather you keep your eyes open on this one."

"The question is not *if* we'll get him," Hurdle said, ignoring her. "It's when. How long's it gonna take us? Don't know. But we will get our man. Assuming *you* don't fuck up."

"Me?"

"You. I work dozens of these cases a year. In eighteen years, that's a lotta violent fugitives. And I gotta say, the FBI always does its *best*." He paused and looked into Vail's eyes. "To grab the limelight. And yeah, screw things up. You guys don't play well in the sandbox. You don't share your leads. But you sure do look good on camera."

A number of responses populated Vail's thoughts—and none of them were polite or politically correct. Instead, she said, "Guess I'll have to do *my* best. To prove you wrong."

"Don't get my hopes up."

"You got any problem with the county police?" Curtis asked.

"Not generally, no. You guys are serviceable. Know your place."

Vail and Curtis shared a look of disbelief.

"Okay," Hurdle said, turning his back on them and walking toward the front of the room. "Let's get started. Rest of the task force will be rolling in within the hour. You know how this works?"

"I've got an idea," Vail said.

"There are regional task forces—Pacific Southwest Regional Fugitive Task Force, Southeast Regional Fugitive Task Force, this one, the Capital Area Regional Fugitive Force, and so on. We apprehend the most violent and dangerous fugitives in DC, Maryland, and Virginia. Like I said, we work with federal, state, and local law enforcement."

"Even though you prefer not to," she said.

"Even though. Yeah." He gestured to a map mounted on the wall. "Districts can have their own local task forces, too. So the Marshals Service in the District of Arizona has warrant squads in Phoenix, Tucson, and Yuma that track fugitives in their area." He turned back to them. "Overall, there are about sixty local fugitive task forces. Most are full-time. Why? Because we've got a lot of bandits out there tryin' to avoid doing their time."

"You know about the officer's murder, I take it?" Vail asked.

"What officer?"

"The one who was watching Jasmine Marcks's house."

Hurdle ground his jaw. "No." He checked his watch. "When did this happen? And what—"

"Curtis and I are headed over there now. Want to tag along?"

Hurdle cursed under his breath, turned to a man behind him and issued some orders, then grabbed his coat and followed Vail out the door.

THEY ARRIVED TO FIND CRIME SCENE TAPE encircling the entire block where Jasmine lived. Police cruisers blocked the entrance to the street and personnel milled about, mouth vapor offering proof of the chilly temperature. A police helicopter buzzed by overhead.

Vail and Curtis pulled up seconds before a car driven by Hurdle. They got out and walked along the asphalt to the vacant police department sedan. Its door was open and a crime scene technician was kneeling, dusting for prints.

"I don't see no blood," Curtis said.

"That's 'cause he wasn't killed here," the man said. "In a planter, up the block."

"Karen!"

Vail turned and saw Leslie Johnson—her former partner from when they were rookies with the NYPD. *What the—*

"You lookin' good. Robby been treating you well, looks like." She advanced on Vail and threw her arms around her, dreadlocks swinging into Vail's face.

"What are you doing here? How come you didn't call me? We would've had you over for dinner."

Johnson pulled back. "Lots has happened. Shit with the department went down. So I moved here, got a gig with the PD. Yesterday was my first day on the job. Took a big pay cut, busted down to a detective again, but all—"

"Wait," Vail said. She glanced at Curtis, who was observing this with a modestly open mouth. "You're Curtis's new partner?"

"You two know each other?" Curtis asked.

"I knew they gave you that detective's shield for a reason," Vail said with a shake of her head. "Must've been the hug. Or when I asked why she didn't call me." She turned back to Johnson. "Why *didn't* you call me?"

Johnson shrugged. "Things didn't end good in New York. My mom's out here in Silver Spring, so I put in some applications. Fairfax County had an opening. Only been here a few days. Wasn't kidding, yesterday was my first day."

"I wanna hear all about New York," Vail said.

"Makes two of us. Including what went wrong." Curtis lifted his brow. When Vail glowered at him, he added, "Hey, that was your idea half an hour ago."

"Later," Vail said. "We've got a murder that needs our attention. We'll catch up. Dinner or lunch or something."

Curtis gazed skyward at a police helicopter that was circling overhead. "So what's the deal here?"

"What happened to Hurdle?" Vail rotated her neck, scanning the area for the marshal. She did not see him, so she faced Johnson.

Johnson pointed toward the house. "Woman who lives here, Jasmine Marcks, woke up this morning and looked out her window at 7:55 AM and saw the officer out there in his car."

"Where *is* Jasmine?" Vail asked.

"Don't know. Not here. I was able to reach her by phone. She refused to disclose her location. But she gave me an accounting of what happened. Got her number if you want it."

"We have it."

"We're gonna need to meet with her," Johnson said. "I told her—"

"Got it covered," Curtis said. "I'm sure it won't be a problem. Go on."

Johnson frowned and shifted her feet. "Yeah. So she said she went about making her breakfast and getting showered and dressed and happened to glance back outside at around 11:35. New guy was there, so she figured they changed shifts. An hour later, he wasn't in the car, so she thought he was walking around, checking the property. After lunch, about 1:00 PM, she looked again and again he wasn't in the car.

"Ms. Marcks started to call Detective Curtis when she heard something outside. She hung up and went to the window, saw her neighbor running down the street. The woman was shrieking. Jasmine went out and discovered the officer's body, saw he'd been murdered. She found his body in a well-concealed planter between two shrubs. Jasmine grabbed her purse and tore out of here."

"The officer?"

Johnson pulled out her spiral notepad and thumbed to a couple of pages. "Arrived at eight, relieved the night watch officer. Gregory Greeling. Thirty-one years old, wife and son." She shook her head. "Anyway, he's got some strange markings on his body. ME's still here, with the body. You wanna see for yourself?"

"Hell yes," Vail said, and she and Curtis followed Johnson down the street.

Hurdle intercepted them midway and gave them a half-hearted salute. "I'm off."

"Off?" Curtis said. "We're going to look at the body."

"Already done. Weird shit, not sure what it means. But it's not important. Whoever did that's got some problems."

That might be the understatement of the year.

Hurdle backed away. "What matters is we got a bad dude out there on the run with a nice head start. On my way back to the command center. Gotta catch us a fugitive and every goddamn minute is precious. You find the daughter, let me know. I wanna make sure she knows to call us if she hears from her father. That's about all I gotta do here. Be back at the motor home at five, ready to roll up your sleeves."

"He's kind of abrupt," Curtis said as he watched Hurdle move off. He nodded at Vail. "Reminds me of you."

Johnson chuckled.

"Hey," Vail said, giving Johnson's shoulder a shove. "Don't encourage him. Besides, I'm nothing like Hurdle. I mean, he's a deputy. I'm a special agent. He's Marshals Service, I'm FBI. He's a man. I'm a woman. See what I mean? We're totally different."

"Okay. Whatever you say."

Vail continued walking toward the medical examiner. "I respect the guy. No nonsense. Knows what he needs to do and does it. Helps to have someone like that in charge."

They stopped a few feet from the body and Vail took in the scene. The ME turned and watched them approach.

"First homicide, your second day on the job." Curtis glanced at Johnson. "Welcome to Fairfax, *partner.*"

"Definitely not my first homicide," Johnson said. "I worked in New York, remember?"

"Karen Vail, FBI," she said to the ME, holding up her badge. "This is Erik—"

"I'm Lindy Dyson. I already know Detective Curtis. And Detective Johnson and I have met. Guess you want to hear about our victim. Time and cause of death?"

"That'd be a good place to start," Vail said.

"TOD looks to be within the last four hours, consistent with what Jasmine Marcks said relative to when she last saw Officer Greeling. Cause boils down to a laceration of the carotid. Massive hemorrhage. Clean margins, so your killer used a *very* sharp knife." She swung a hand around, gesturing off to her left. "As you can see from the amount of blood in the planter and the arterial spurt on the surrounding foliage, he was killed right here. And then there's this." Dyson moved the white canvas down to the officer's waist.

Vail swallowed. She had seen it before—but always in photos. The abdomen featured deep parallel slice marks carved into the skin, down to the muscle layer. "Not deadly, and done postmortem. Right?"

Dyson nodded slowly. "Correct."

"And I assume his penis and—" Vail cleared her throat. "The male genitalia have been excised?"

She drew back the sheet farther. "Right again." Dyson rose from her crouch. "You've seen this before?"

"Not in the flesh." She winced. "Sorry. Didn't mean that. Only in photos. But yeah, I'm familiar with the mutilation pattern."

Curtis licked his lips and turned away. "Okay, let's cover that baby up. Please."

Johnson was squinting, the back of her right hand covering her mouth. "That's pretty goddamn disgusting," she said, her palm rising and falling as her lips moved.

"Welcome to my world." Vail gestured to Dyson to recover the body. "We've got a marshals task force set up."

"Hurdle," Dyson said. "Just met him."

Vail gestured at Dyson. "You'll make sure we get all the reports ASAP?"

"Soon as I can, yeah."

"You think of anything, let us know. The guy who did this just escaped from Potter Correctional. Any detail could be crucial. You know the drill."

"Unfortunately, I do."

"LOOK," JOHNSON SAID as they walked back down the street. "I just want you to know it wasn't anything bad. The thing with the NYPD. You don't have to worry about me not having your back. It wasn't anything like that, nothing bad."

"So you said." Curtis continued on for a few steps. "No offense, but you lost your job. How can that be anything but 'bad'?"

They stopped at Vail's car. Johnson rested her hands on the roof and glanced around. Satisfied no one important was around, she said, "I got a good guy letter."

Vail nodded. "I figured."

Curtis looked from Vail to Johnson. "What's a 'good guy letter'?"

"A letter from the commissioner saying you've retired from the NYPD in good standing." Vail shrugged. "It basically lets you get another job in law enforcement so you can carry a firearm."

"So the good guy letter ain't actually a bad thing. But it's not sounding so *good*, either."

"Because there's more to it," Johnson said.

There always is.

"Remember the Martinez shoot about ten years ago?"

Vail jutted her chin back. "Yeah. Good shoot. You were cleared, no one had a problem with it. So what?"

"I had another shoot I don't think you knew about. No problems with that one, either."

"So what am I missing?" Curtis asked.

"I had one last month that was . . ." Johnson squinted. "Questionable. I was off duty. Actually, I was an off duty *lieutenant*, out for a drink with a friend in Jamaica. On the way back to my car I see this asshole, looks like bad news. Acting like he's high, carrying what I think is a handgun. He's harassing a couple homeless people. It's late, a few minutes before 1:00 AM. I follow him, call it in. He goes over to some woman trying to sleep in an alley and puts the gun to her head. I yell for him to stop, drop the weapon. He turns to me with the gun. I shoot him before he can shoot me. Only turns out it wasn't a real gun. Some fuckin' toy pistol. No red tip."

"Let me guess," Vail said. "No witnesses, no video."

"Right. Not to mention I'd been out with friends at a bar. And no, I wasn't drunk."

"Okay."

"And," Johnson said, "the guy was black."

"So are you."

"Probably the only thing that saved my ass."

"Again," Curtis said, "what was the problem?"

"Leslie was forced to resign in case it got out about the shooting."

"I didn't have a great relationship with my chief," Johnson said. "So he didn't have my back."

"*Someone* did," Curtis said. "If you got that letter from the commish."

Johnson laughed. "Trust me. That was done to help the department more than it was to help me. It was done to save face. If the media found out, another unarmed black guy getting shot by a cop . . ."

"Too many dicey 'issues' with the shoot," Vail said. "Once the media starts digging and finds the first two—they put 'em under the microscope. Remember, this is New York City. Big stage as it is. Stuff can get blown out of proportion. And you know how it is. Some good shoots can look bad. Depends on how you spin it."

Curtis frowned. "No shit."

"So we good?" Johnson looked at him. "Partner?"

Curtis pulled open his door. "We're good."

Vail pointed at Johnson. "I still expect a dinner." She gave her a broad smile, then got into the car.

12

After stopping by her office, Vail walked into the relatively small mobile command center and found it crammed with several people. Curtis was not present, even though it was straight up 5:00 PM.

She had guests coming over for dinner and Robby was taking care of the meal, so she hoped this did not drag on past 6:30.

The oblong room was considerably more crowded than the first time she had been here: with four more large bodies, there was not a lot of clearance to move about.

"Okay everyone," Hurdle said, a sheaf of papers in his hand. "Let's get this thing going."

The door swung open and Curtis walked in.

Hurdle made a point of checking his watch and then making eye contact with Curtis. He was a no-nonsense leader. If he told you to be there at five, he meant it. And he was making sure Curtis *knew* he meant it.

"Let's do some quick introductions." He nodded at the far end of the room and a short, stocky Latino man in his thirties began speaking. "Ray Ramos, DHS, Homeland Security Investigations. You can call me 'Rambo,' like everyone else does. Did three tours in Iraq, then hooked on with West Virginia State Police for nine years before scoring the gig with HSI. Been on CARFTF almost two years. I got no wife and no kids and no siblings so I'll be working this thing sunup to sundown. Pretty much."

In other words, he's got no life. Then again, I could almost be accused of the same thing.

"Ben Tarkoff," the middle-aged guy with bulldog features said. "Marshals Service. Been doing this fifteen years. Way I see it, you do the crime, you better be prepared to do the time. These assholes think the rules don't apply to them. I'm here to make sure they do." He turned to the man seated next to him, who took the cue and perked up.

"Jim Morrison, Secret Service." He was one of two wearing a suit—a black one with a red tie. "Yeah. Jim Morrison, like The Doors lead. I've been known to do some songwriting but I can't sing too good. Karaoke's about it. I'd say I'm no Jim Morrison—but I can't say that because I am." That got some chuckles. "Anyway, I got my degree in finance from Louisiana State and hooked on with the Bureau, ended up working the Violent Gang Task Force in northwest Louisiana doing financial analysis before hooking on with the service. So among other things, I can definitely help with tracking down and analyzing Marcks's financials."

"Suits aren't necessary here," Hurdle said. "Cargo pants, jeans, khakis, any of that is fine. Doing what we're gonna be doing, most of the time we don't wanna stand out and be tagged as law enforcement from a mile away. Be comfortable. Casual professional. Concealed carry shirts are good. When we go operational, we'll gear up with tactical clothing and vests. Got it?"

Morrison nodded.

"Good to have you on board. Whether or not you can carry a tune, your skills and contacts are going to be key. Next." He nodded at the man to Morrison's left, also wearing dress clothes—a tan sport coat that complimented his dark skin.

"Travis Walters. FBI."

They waited a moment for Walters to add something, but he did not.

"How long you on the job, Walters?" Hurdle asked.

"Two years. First task force posting."

Terrific.

"Same goes for you. No suits. Anything you want to tell us about yourself?"

"Not interested in discussing my personal life. I keep that separate from work."

Hurdle shook his head, then gestured at Vail.

"Karen Vail. FBI. Started with NYPD, made detective, then moved to the Bureau and worked as a field agent before my promotion to the Behavioral Analysis Unit several years ago. I've got a son in college and a fiancé with the DEA. And I curse too much and I get pissed off too easily. And I tend to work too much. Trying to fix all that, lead a more normal life."

"Good luck with that," Hurdle said. "Anything else?"

"I play well with others and I'm easy to get along with."

Curtis snorted.

Vail cut her eyes at him. "Fuck you."

Curtis threw his hands up. "My point exactly."

She managed to subdue her smile. "On a serious note, I handled the original Roscoe Lee Marcks case seven years ago when he was put away. Actually, the profiler who drew up the assessment that led to Marcks's apprehension was Thomas Underwood. I came in right after that when Underwood retired. So I'm familiar with Jasmine Marcks, the daughter, as well as the offender. Hopefully I'll be able to help with establishing his behavioral patterns and tendencies. We need anything from Jasmine, I've got a good relationship with her." She turned to Curtis.

"Erik Curtis. Detective, Fairfax County Police, Criminal Investigations Bureau. Served on CARFTF a bunch of years ago, so I'm familiar with the drill. Plus, I worked the Marcks case. I was the arresting officer so I know this douche bag pretty damn well. Two grown kids, a younger brother who's a detective in New Orleans, where I grew up. Oh, and I'm divorced. I'll leave you to draw your own conclusions about that. Because you will anyway, no matter what I say."

"Okay," Hurdle said. "You've all met me and know who I am. Got a teenage daughter I don't see enough and a wife I don't see enough. And a bunch of friends like you I end up seeing way too much."

Tarkoff and Ramos emitted a low groan of disapproval.

Hurdle reached over and gave Ramos a swat with the stack of papers. "We've got a bit of a new team here, so I'll walk us through some of the things we'll need to get up to speed. Think of me as the quarterback. We'll huddle, I'll call the plays, and you'll go out and run the routes. If I hand the ball off to you, I expect you to run with it. No fumbles.

"Speaking of which, I run a tight ship. No penalties. By that I mean we follow the rules. And the law. When we can. You know some ways to bend shit, fine—as long as it'll hold up in court. I don't want any asshole going free because of some dipshitly stupid thing one of us did while under my command."

"Is dipshitly a word?"

"It is now, Rambo. Know why?"

"Because you said it is, boss."

"Right. Now, with that out of the way, let's talk about this case." He glanced down at his papers, then set them aside in favor of an iPad. "Marcks was incarcerated at Potter Correctional in West Virginia." He stopped and turned to Curtis. "That's a federal prison. Aren't serials usually prosecuted by state or county?"

"Usually. But Marcks copped to two murders and one of them was done in a national park in Fredericksburg."

"And thus federal jurisdiction," Hurdle said. "Okay, well, our model citizen was involved in an inmate-on-inmate fight in the showers this morning at oh-eight-hundred. Looks like he instigated it against a known enforcer, a guy no one screwed with at Potter. Those two facts should give us reason to suspect that this was part of a preconceived escape plan. The fight was designed to put him in a bad way so he'd have to be transported to a nearby hospital."

"But prison hospitals are usually pretty well equipped," Morrison said. "How could he be sure they wouldn't just treat him there?"

"You familiar with Potter Correctional?" Hurdle asked.

"Potter's older than dirt," Vail said. "Should've been closed decades ago. I'm willing to bet their hospital has never seen the equipment they'd need to treat a serious injury."

Hurdle consulted the iPad again. "And he supposedly had a head injury and a wickedly fractured arm. That qualifies as a serious injury."

"So Marcks intentionally got his head beat in just so he could escape?" Walters asked. "A bit extreme."

"Hard to say how bad he was hurt. I'm told the nurse only did a cursory exam and said it was an emergency, that he needed to be transported to the hospital."

"Nurse could've been in on it," Vail said. "Not unheard of. That escape from Clinton Correctional in upstate New York wasn't the first time something like that happened. Woman becomes enamored with a good-looking inmate, he charms her, promises her the world if he can only get out, convinces her he's innocent and was framed, whatever. She hears what she wants, believes what she wants. Sometimes he'll reel her in, do the charm thing, and once he's made her do things that could get her fired or even arrested if they're egregious enough, he's got his hooks in her. He can up the ante under the threat of exposure. She feels like she's got no choice because if he talks she'll lose her job. So she does increasingly risky things to help him escape."

"Have they detained her?" Curtis asked.

"She's dead. Marcks slit her throat."

"Another man who makes promises and doesn't keep his word," Vail said.

Chuckles and muted laughter trickled through the room.

"That's one of the things we'll be looking at," Hurdle said, "to see if she was complicit. Back to the escape. He was taken in the back of a small correctional transport truck. Last communication was at oh-eight-fifty. Driver reported nothing unusual.

"When he failed to check in at the hospital at oh-nine-ten, Potter went into lockdown, we were notified, and an emergency bed book count was done."

"Bed book?" Vail asked.

Ramos answered. "It's a book maintained by the cell house correctional officer that contains a quarters card for each inmate. The quarters cards contain a mug shot of each inmate, his cell assignment and job assignment. This helps confirm that the inmate assigned to that cell is actually the inmate standing in front of you. If one or more inmate's not where he's supposed to be, it helps the officer quickly identify who's missing."

"Like I was saying," Hurdle continued. "Potter's off-duty staff was called in and interior and exterior searches of the prison facility were conducted. All buildings. All closets, rooms. The kitchen. Everything. Vehicles were accounted for. Once they confirmed Marcks was the only escapee, Potter staff was assigned to their escape posting in the immediate area inside the city and county limits around the prison. State troopers were dispatched to expand the search and on Route 48 they found the transport vehicle on the west side of the road, just across the border in Virginia, near Strasburg. It crashed and might've been moved further into a nearby stand of trees."

"The transport team consisted of two correctional officers," Tarkoff said. "Correct?"

"Yes," Hurdle said. "Driver was shot through the van wall, probably with the other officer's service pistol. Sanders, the guard who was in the back with Marcks, was stabbed through the eye with what was likely a scalpel. Nurse's throat was slit, no doubt with that same scalpel. Don't know who was killed first."

"What the hell was a scalpel doing on that truck?" Vail asked.

"Good question. Possible answer is that the nurse was a collaborator and gave it to him, assuming he'd use it on the guard, not on her. So we've got reason to question just how badly his arm was really injured." Hurdle tapped on his screen. "Name was Susan Olifante. If she was part of the plot, we'll have to reconstruct it. We can't sit her down. Obviously. Forensics is going through the van, the prison, the medical facility at Potter. Anything turns up, we'll know ASAP."

"Big picture," Ramos said, "is that if you escape from a max-security prison, you've gotta have help on the inside. Day in, day out, it's all routine, scheduled stuff. They've got it down to a science, a *proven* science that's designed to prevent escape. It'd be very difficult to get out of a facility without assistance—even an old one like Potter. We'll find out who it was, whether it's the nurse or someone else. Once we're clear on the process of how he escaped, it's just a matter of working backward: how did he have access to that location? Who had access to that location at this time? These three people? Bang."

"Rambo, you've worked with Prisons," Hurdle said, referring to the Bureau of Prisons. "Get on this. Let's look at everybody who's had contact with Marcks inside the facility. Medical staff, including that nurse—but don't stop there. We don't wanna miss anything—or any*one*."

"The COs, too," Walters said. "See if any have a spotty record."

"Not just the bad officers," Ramos said. "We need to look at all of them or we could miss something in front of our faces. Even the good ones can get roped in."

"How can you 'rope in' a good cop?" Walters said. "Doesn't make any sense."

Hurdle's face stiffened. "I'll tell you how. I've seen it happen first-hand." He dropped his chin and his gaze bore into Walters. "Let's say you're a legit officer doing your job the right way. You steer clear of all the pitfalls that come with the post. But you talk with your coworkers, right? 'Cause we all do. Stuff happens at home, in your personal life, and you talk about it at work. You get married. You have a baby. So take that example. You come back to work the next day and you're beaming. Why? Because your wife just had your first baby, Karina—a baby girl, six pounds eight ounces, and she's the most beautiful thing you've ever seen. So you show some pictures you got on your phone and others that you posted to Facebook. And you're ecstatic, you're so fucking happy. Everyone pats you on the back, tells you how gorgeous she is. But you don't know that one of the guys on your block is spilling your dirt.

"So next day, you're on the block doing your rounds, an inmate says when you walk by, "So how's Karina doing, dawg? Yeah, you want Karina to stay healthy? How about you get me a pack of Marlboros. Or I'll have some homies come over and take care of your wife and daughter."

Walters swallowed.

"That shit goes on all the time," Ramos said. "No one talks about it, but that's real life. Inmates as a group are very manipulative and they're always probing for weakness. Always trying to see what they can get from you. They watch your body language, your face. If they can find that weakness, that button to push, they're gonna use it on you. They teach each other how to do this shit. Because it's proven. It works. Because correctional officers are people working in a very dangerous environment. And not all of them are the sharpest tools in the shed. It's the easiest federal law enforcement career to get into, so who's it going to attract?"

"Seriously?" Tarkoff asked.

"Seriously," Ramos said. "Think about it. It's a dangerous fucking job. You know anyone who walks around saying, 'I wanna be a correctional officer when I grow up? I wanna walk a beat surrounded by violent criminals and not have a decent weapon on my hip?' No, man. If they want to go into federal law enforcement, they're looking at FBI, DEA, ATF, Marshals, DHS. Bureau of Prisons? Not likely on that list. But Prisons doesn't require a college degree. So if you can't pass the exam to get into one of the sexy alphabet agencies, you take what you can get: Prisons. And at some point you try to get a transfer out. You may think that's just my opinion, but I'm just tellin' it like it is."

"Once the inmates identify who the care bears are," Hurdle said, "it's game on."

"Care bears?" Walters asked.

"Guards they know they can manipulate," Hurdle said, "who'll do what you want and *get* you what you want, because you've got something on them. These inmates know how to twist your arm, manipulate you. Once they know your personal shit, now what do you do? They own you. Because you're a human being and you know their threats have weight behind them. And you know these bastards are the scum of the earth." He looked again at Walters. "*That's* how a good officer, with a good record and admirable intentions, gets dragged into the muck of prison life."

"And that goes to what I was saying," Ramos said. "It's a big reason why I've never heard of anyone who aspires to be a correctional officer."

Hurdle brought them up to speed on Gregory Greeling, the deputy murdered at Jasmine Marcks's house, then nodded at Curtis. "You two find anything out after I left?"

Curtis brushed back his hair, which was beginning to show gray streaks. "Based on Jasmine Marcks's account of when she last saw him and when a neighbor discovered the body, he was killed in a window that we can narrow down to between 11:35 AM and 1:00 PM. That fit with what the ME estimated from liver temp."

"That timeline also fits with what happened at Potter," Vail said. "If Marcks escaped from the truck around 9:00 AM, he had time to get into Virginia and over to Jasmine's house by the time the officer was killed."

"You think Marcks did Greeling?" Tarkoff asked.

Curtis turned to Vail. This was clearly her call.

"There were odd markings on Greeling's body, the abdomen specifically. Postmortem slices through the skin, adipose, and fascia to the muscle layer. Parallel lines. And his genitals were excised."

A few of the men winced.

"I'm not trying to be graphic," she said. "It's significant because we've seen this before. Most of Roscoe Lee Marcks's victims had this same pattern carved into them. Same with the genitalia. I know you're all intimately familiar with MO. But it doesn't really apply here relative to the previous Blood Lines murders because it's a different scenario, different situation. If we assume that Marcks is responsible for this deputy's murder, he was not selecting his victim based on the same set of criteria he used for his previous vics. This was an opportunistic kill, one out of necessity. He's presumably after Jasmine. Greeling was in his way and presented the biggest threat. So he took him out."

"But the markings," Walters said. "The 'blood lines.' It's a pattern, so more than likely it's the same guy. It's Marcks."

"In the Behavioral Analysis Unit, we call these 'patterns' ritual behavior. Bottom line is that it's things the offender does with the body, or crime scene, before *or* after he kills the victim. These are things that have nothing to do with succeeding in his crime. He measures success as murdering the person and doing it without getting discovered. The things he does to successfully kill his victim and get away with it make up his MO.

"These postmortem 'blood line' markings have meaning to him. We may not be able to make sense of what they mean, or why he's doing them—but all that matters for the moment is that he felt the need to make them. It feeds some inner desire. It's comforting to him in some way. Because of that, the offender does it on all his victims, or almost all, depending on the situation. He enjoys doing it and it becomes like a signature that allows us to link his kills."

"So," Walters said, spreading his hands apart, "what you're saying is that I was right."

"Do we know what kind of knife or implement he used to make those lines?" Tarkoff asked. "Kitchen knife that he found at the scene or—"

"Great question, Ben," Vail said. "No, this was something we're almost certain he brought with him."

"At one of the earlier crime scenes," Curtis said, "we found a karambit."

Tarkoff leaned forward. "A what?"

"One nasty weapon," Ramos said. "A guy in my unit in Iraq, he had one. He picked it up in Southeast Asia. Indonesia, I think. Curved blade, looks like an animal's claw. There are a lot of variations but the more modern ones have double-sided edges and are used for slashing and fighting. The original karambits are small and have a finger ring and extend down from the fist, attached to the pinky. When you punch your enemy, he never sees the blade and you do some serious damage. Like I said, if you know how it to use it, it's deadly in seconds with a minimum of effort."

"So where the hell did Marcks get one of these?" Hurdle asked.

"You can get 'em anywhere," Ramos said. "There are several manufacturers that put their own spin on the design. Just about any store or website that sells knives has them now."

Morrison leaned back in his chair. "You think Marcks left the karambit behind at that crime scene on purpose?"

"We didn't think so," Curtis said. "It wasn't anywhere near the body. It was in the grass, about ten yards away, like he dropped it on the way back to his van."

"Obviously he replaced it," Ramos said. "But why'd he choose such an unusual knife in the first place?"

"We never found out," Vail said. "We can read into something like this, and we did, but bottom line is it could simply be that a friend told him about it. Or he saw it used in a movie, or whatever, and he thought it'd fit his needs. Might not be any meaning to it at all other than it came across his desk, he tried it, liked the way it felt, and started using it on his vics, got excited by it. Or it related to something done to him as a kid."

"What he's doing with these cuts," Tarkoff said. "Is it like him leaving his signature on Greeling's body? Like, claiming it as his kill?"

Vail bobbed her head. "Kinda. Sorta. But it may not be something he's aware of to that extent. I mean, he was aware he was doing it, but he may not know why he needs to do it. And I doubt he realizes that it's helping us connect these murders to him."

"Where's Jasmine Marcks in all of this?"

"Fortunately, she got away," Curtis said.

"When the neighbor found Greeling's body and screamed," Vail said, "maybe it scared him off. We won't know until we can sit down with Jasmine. I'm going to call her on the way home, see if I can set something up for tomorrow."

Hurdle set his iPad on the worktable to his right. "Okay, here's our fugitive playbook. In the Service we call it a quality of life survey. A lot of you are familiar with some of this as your basic criminal history checks. We'll run his sheet. Sift through any court documents that list addresses, phone numbers, associations. Who posted bail? Social media—Facebook, Instagram, phone records. Who's he talking to?

"We'll assemble a top 10 list. Look at people who visited him at Potter and everyone he had contact with during the last three months before he was arrested."

"That's at least seven years old," Vail said.

"Doesn't matter. Marcks is on the run and he needs help. Shelter, food, money, sleep. And it's friggin' cold outside. Unless he goes to people he doesn't know—which is possible—it's only logical he's going to lean on those he *does* know, or knew. Some of them may owe him a favor, some of them may be afraid of him and help him out because they fear what'll happen if they don't. Point is, these are the people we focus on."

"We've got the names of three guys he's friends with, according to Jasmine."

"That's a start. Share those names with us. But from this top 10 list we assemble, we'll branch out and start looking at *other* people who associate with those people. Where they work, who *they've* had contact with, where they live, previous contacts and correspondences. Interactions they've had. So if they've been arrested with someone in a car, we want to look at them, too. Sometimes we find relationships we didn't know existed because these are all people in a loose nexus with the fugitive. Then we look at family members."

"What about hangouts?" Walters asked.

"That's next," Tarkoff said. "We'll look at where Marcks liked to smoke, or drink, or watch a ballgame. Places where he spent his time when he was a free man. Big picture, we'll be focusing on people, money, and residences."

"What about ex-girlfriends?" Vail said.

Hurdle pointed at her. "Yes. That's a biggie. A guy who's been behind bars for seven years wants his pussy. And he wants it sooner rather than later because he doesn't know which day is gonna be his last."

"Ex-friends, too," Tarkoff said, turning to Vail. "Those names Jasmine gave you will be important. Interviews with these guys sometimes nets us useful information. If Marcks is an asshole who burned bridges and was generally disliked, he won't have many. That obviously makes our job tougher. But if we've got three to start with, that's something."

"They're not gonna want to rat out a friend," Vail said, "so it has to be done surreptitiously. I can help design an approach if anyone's got a lead that's promising."

"Neighbors, too," Hurdle said. "Some may've moved since he was arrested, but it's worth a shot. Same with social media, as I mentioned before. Normally this can yield us some good intel, but I can't remember what year Facebook caught on." Tarkoff looked around. "Anyone know?" There were no takers. "Pretty sure Instagram wasn't around then. What about

WhatsApp? We need to see if he had an account with them. Twitter?"

"Doesn't strike me as a Twitter kind of guy," Vail said. "For that matter, he's not social to begin with. I'm not sure this is going to get us anything."

Hurdle leaned against a closet door to his right. "If it's a dead end, it won't be the only one we hit. But we do our job and see what we get."

"What about where they spend their money?" Morrison asked.

"Yes," Tarkoff said. "And that's your assignment because that falls under your purview with the Secret Service. Credit card bills, bank accounts. Look for patterns. We may get something from those old spending patterns. Maybe not. But we're all creatures of habit. He's a free man again. He may fall back into buying the same things. What he liked before he'll still like—maybe even crave. Could be the kind of thing he's been thinking about for months, obsessing over every night before he went to bed. The taste of beer, a movie, a football game. Shit he can't do in the joint, stuff he figured he'd never get to do again in his life."

Hurdle stood up straight. "We also need to look at what resources he has at his disposal. What cash he's got, in what bank accounts. Jasmine may be able to help with some of that, like maybe she knows what bank he was with. They've obviously been dormant, but she may've kept the accounts active for him."

"Doubt it," Vail said.

"Check it out anyway," Tarkoff said, "in case they're still open and he tries to get at the cash. Never know what we'll find.

If we filter things out because of our personal biases, we may miss something important."

"We're monitoring the phones that the CO, Sanders, and his partner had, as well as the one that Olifante left the prison with this morning." Hurdle consulted his iPad and typed something into the onscreen keyboard. "Curtis, I'm making you point on that. Could give us some valuable leads if Marcks took one of their cells when he left that truck. At the moment, I've been told all three numbers have been silent, no activity. Powered down—or the battery's dead. But anyone makes a call on any of those lines, you'll be notified immediately."

"I've assembled an Excel sheet with all our phone numbers," Tarkoff said, turning toward the computer to his right. He slid the keyboard out from beneath the countertop and started hunting and pecking. "Emailing it to each of you right now. Import the numbers and emails into your phone contacts."

Morrison gestured at Vail. "How about you give us a psychological profile of Marcks."

"It's not really a psychological profile," Vail said. "But I can give you Agent Underwood's assessment of the UNSUB they were looking for, what motivated him, elements of his personality that lent itself to serial murder, and so on. Actually, I'll focus more on what we learned about Roscoe Lee Marcks after he was apprehended because that's more relevant to what we're dealing with here. He's a known quantity, not an unknown subject.

"I tried interviewing him a number of times over the years but ironically it wasn't till a couple of days ago that he finally agreed. Probably because he figured it'd be his last chance to talk because he was planning to leave. He was engaging and glib, bright and threatening. Not to state the obvious, but it's not good news that he's out in the general populace."

"You think he'll get back into the rhythm of killing again?" Morrison asked. "Aside from the CO and nurse—which were part of his escape."

"I wouldn't exactly call it a rhythm, but I understand what you mean. And yes, he'll definitely return to his old ways. Count on it. Killing is something these guys enjoy. It fills a need, a hunger that builds over time. He's had seven years to fantasize about it. Not to mention that psychopaths get bored very easily. Being out in the wild, on the run, most people would be nervous. Not him. He's excited. It's one big challenge to him, one he's sure he'll win. So there *will* be more bodies—very soon— unless we can scoop him up."

Vail rose and rested her right hand on the chair back. "We're looking at an offender of greater than average intelligence. Other than his avocation as a serial murderer, he graduated from Indiana University with a degree in public administration. But in his sophomore year he was arrested for assaulting a dorm mate. Beat him pretty good. Kid didn't press charges and there were mitigating factors because alcohol was involved and a witness said the other guy started it. He eventually recovered fully and no formal charges were brought against Marcks.

"Until his senior year when he was again arrested, this time for armed robbery of a mini-mart. Problem is, the gun belonged to the store owner. Marcks claimed he was with a friend who was robbing the place and he had no idea what was going down. The owner pulled a .38 Special from the register and his friend punched the guy. The gun flew out of his hand and Marcks picked it up just when the cops showed. There was no video so they only had statements of admission from Marcks and his friend. Marcks dropped the dime on his buddy and a plea deal was reached. Case dragged on until after he graduated, so he got his degree.

"But he served six months and when he got out he couldn't land a job, let alone something in his major. No company would have anything to do with him—nor would any municipality. He walked around with a ton of student loans and a big chip on his shoulder. Got into a few bar fights and eventually moved back to Virginia. He found a gig driving a bread truck, which put him on the road at 4:00 AM and at home by 3:00 PM. That later became significant because it gave him a lot of time to troll for his victims.

"For those of you who don't remember, he killed a total of fourteen people, eleven women and three men. Back when Underwood developed his assessment, the BAU was still using the terms 'organized' and 'disorganized.' We've moved away from that terminology, but Underwood felt he was a classic organized offender, meaning he was intelligent. Thought out his crimes beforehand. Selected his victims, studied them, watched for lifestyle patterns. Once he spotted a weakness, he chose his spot and snatched them up. He came prepared. No weapons of opportunity. Whatever he needed, he brought with him.

"He kept his vics under lock and key at an undisclosed location—to this day we've never found it—and tortured them. Brought them to the brink of death and revived them before finally murdering them. And then . . ." She sighed. "Well, the same thing I described before. The sliced lines on the abdomen and the excising of the external genitalia. Male or female, the ritual was the same." She stopped and glanced around. They were listening intently, waiting for her to continue.

"How did he subdue them?" Morrison asked. "You said there were three men. Not as easy to control as women."

"He used an inhaled anesthetic to incapacitate them. Very effective." Vail turned back to the others. "The ME was able to determine that the vics were sodomized with smooth objects, probably plastic or glass, neither of which leave behind any kind of telltale signs or residues. But there was trauma to the tissues, as you would expect. Enough to conclude there was some anger behind it."

"Do we know why?" Tarkoff asked.

"I'd planned to ask him but never got the chance."

"I thought you met with him," Walters said. "From what I know of the BSU, wouldn't that be high up on your list, to understand what motivated him?"

"I'm in the BAU, and, yes, the BRIU would be interested in that. As would we. But you can't walk in and sit down across from one of these guys, especially the bright ones, and start asking questions like that without building a rapport—which takes a long time. If you don't establish some kind of relationship, they'll either tell you where to go, or they won't answer the question. Or they'll give you a bullshit answer. None of those scenarios are worth a roll of pennies."

"Is there anything to that? The sodomy? In your experience?"

"Yeah. I can guess, but I don't think that'll do us any good. We're not at that point where we've exhausted everything else and have to resort to educated guesses. There are numerous psychological explanations for sticking an object in a victim's anus and doing physical damage. The most obvious, which is why I mentioned it, is anger. You want to move farther out on the limb, you can make inferences. Maybe he's homosexual and isn't comfortable with his sexuality. Maybe he was sexually assaulted as a young adult by a male power figure. Maybe he was sexually assaulted during his stint in the joint when he was in Indiana. You see what I mean? Not going to help us find him."

"I think it could help us," Hurdle said. "If he's homosexual, rather than looking at prostitutes or trying to find former girlfriends, we should be looking at gay bars and other hangouts and neighborhoods where gays tend to congregate. I think it makes a huge difference."

Fair point. Vail bit the inside of her bottom lip. "I'll see what I can do. I'll dig through the file in case there's something I'm not remembering. I'll talk with Jasmine, see if she remembers seeing anything when she was a kid." She pulled out her Samsung to make a note and gestured at Curtis to continue. "Oh—I did notice something I hadn't seen before. When I interviewed him at Potter, he had what looked like a self-inflicted scar on his left forearm. We've learned that self-mutilation is often found in adults who were sexually abused as children. So there's that."

"We had definitive evidence tying him to only two of the murders," Curtis said. "He pled to those in exchange for avoiding the death penalty. We know he did the others but they're officially listed as unsolved. We were never able to tie him to them forensically."

"And that's not unusual," Vail said, looking up from her phone. "Being a smart offender, he's aware of the basic concepts of forensic evidence. Since we don't have a crime scene where he did the actual killing, we're left to examine only the dump sites where he left the bodies. And he knew to cover his tracks. So to speak."

"Officially," Tarkoff said, "those other twelve cases were never closed."

"Right." Curtis raised a hand to fend off a comment from Walters. "But the victims' families know the deal. They understand. Some accepted it and have closure. Others need all the i's dotted. I've asked my partner, Leslie Johnson, to get in touch with each of them personally to deliver the news of his escape and to assure them we're working to find him. Unfortunately, for them it's like opening an old wound."

Vail holstered her phone. "As I said, Marcks has a relatively high police IQ—he understands why we do what we do, and how we do it, and I'm sure he's gotten more of an education while at Potter—as well as the max facility at Florence in Colorado where he served out his first three years. So bottom line is we have our work cut out for us. We have a lot of avenues to pursue but I wouldn't be surprised if we end up with zeroes. We may need to think outside the box on this one."

"What did I tell you, Vail?"

She looked at Hurdle. "That we'll find him. It's only a question of when."

"Exactly."

"What kind of law enforcement support can we expect?" Morrison asked.

"It's a matter of managing resources. This isn't the same as the Clinton escape in upstate New York. They had intel those knuckleheads were going to skip into Canada, so they brought in the National Guard to secure the border and a gazillion cops to search a well-defined area. Here, we've got all of Virginia to deal with. Because Vail thinks he's going after his daughter, he'll probably stay somewhat close. But *he* knows that *we* know that.

"We've got more officers on the streets. But we can't go hog wild in terms of manpower. We don't want to blow through budgets with overtime and personnel—unless it's needed. Bottom line, escalation is based on necessity. Scale personnel to where you think the guy is, mass your assets in that area. If bodies start dropping, we'll start adding resources, get more aggressive with deployment. If we can be smart about it."

"Right now," Tarkoff said, "we've got a tip line set up. NGOs and GOs are involved, providing lookout," he said, referring to nongovernmental and governmental organizations. "Media blasts are going to start soon. We've got checkpoints set up at strategic locations along the Virginia border. Next in line would be highway billboards, but we're not there yet."

"We've got choppers up flying routes around and near the daughter's house," Hurdle said, "since we know Marcks was there when he killed Greeling. But that's not gonna continue 24/7 with a spotlight and thermal imaging equipment running one or two grand an hour. Not to mention that Marcks was probably long gone before we even arrived on-scene."

Hurdle stole a look at the time, which was spelled out in a red LED display above the computer workstations.

Vail's eyes ticked over as well and she cursed under her breath. She was late.

"Everyone get some dinner and be back here at 10:00 PM sharp. I'll hand out assignments and we'll get started. Vail thinks he's gonna kill again. I think she's right. We're a little handcuffed at night, but we can at least get organized so we can hit the ground running once the day starts. Keep your phones on and always nearby. I don't want to hear any excuses about not getting my texts."

Everyone got up and started shuffling awkwardly toward the door, slowed by the cramped quarters. Morrison had trouble with the handle but ultimately got it open, and they filed out into the frigid, damp night air.

"Where you headed?" Hurdle called after Vail.

"Home. I've got dinner guests and I'm already late."

"Just be back on time."

"Yes sir," Vail said as she walked briskly toward her car. "Heard you the first time."

13

Vail phoned Jasmine the moment she got into her car. The seat was cold and the steering wheel was colder. Snow was predicted, but she hoped it would fizzle out.

"You okay?" Vail asked as she pulled out of the police department parking lot.

"I'm fine," Jasmine said. "A little rattled—check that, a lot rattled—but I'm holding up."

"Where are you?"

"Safe. Which is more than I can say about being in my home. You told me I'd be okay there."

"I thought with the cop posted . . . we figured that if the guy wanted to hurt you the first time, he could have. Curtis thought he was just trying to scare you. I agreed."

"Well, I don't think the cop who was lying there dead on the side of the house would agree with that analysis."

Probably not.

"So you're not going to tell me where you are."

Jasmine hesitated. "I think it's best no one knows. Besides, I'll be moving around. Just in case."

"You need me to pick up some stuff from your house? Clothes?"

"That'd be great. I figured I'd just have to go shopping. I've got a suitcase in the hall closet."

"I take it you heard the news," Vail said as she navigated a turn on the dark street and accelerated.

"About my father? Once I saw that deputy lying there, I knew. That's why I'm not telling anyone where I am. And now that my father knows I'm not at my house, he won't be going back there. I'm still gonna stay away, though. Who knows if he's got someone keeping an eye out for me."

"Why do you think he knows you're not there?"

"Because he's smart. And because he knows me. And because he probably saw me drive away—or he searched the house and knew I'd left. It's the only logical conclusion. Cops have an officer stationed there to protect me, so I'm going to be there, right? He kills the cop and searches the house but I'm not there. Obviously I left when I realized something was wrong. Thank God for that neighbor. If she hadn't found the body and screamed, I probably would've ended up like that cop."

No one knows that better than me. "I don't know what more I could've done, but I'm sorry you had to go through that. And I'm relieved you got away."

"What's being done to find him?"

"Don't worry about that. We're working on it. Actually, a whole task force is working on it. Law enforcement is deployed all across the state." She glanced in her mirror.

No headlights. No one's following me. Jesus, Karen. Why would anyone be following you? This whole business with Marcks and the task force and Jasmine's paranoia—although well deserved—had spooked her. Not an easy thing to do.

"Let's meet tomorrow. I need to go through some things with you about your dad, things that may help us find him. And

I'll go by your place on the way. Okay? A quick breakfast. My treat."

"Only if you make sure you're not followed. Can you do that?"

"I've got some experience with that, yeah. Text me the time and location and I'll be there."

14

The Virginia winter was proving more brutal than Roscoe Lee Marcks had remembered. The sweaters and knit shirts that he had pilfered from a house owned by the Jensen family somewhere along the way between Strasburg and Cub Run had reached the limits of their insulating capacity.

The bottle of foundation he found in the wife's bathroom drawer helped cover some of the bruising on his face, while the car he had taken from the Jensens' garage—though nothing special—was proving useful. He had parked it a mile down the road in an area not visible from the street to prevent the cops from finding it and proceeded on foot in search of shelter. He had to stay hydrated and fed, and avoid the extreme overnight cold.

The flashlight he borrowed from the Jensens' kitchen, however, was not as serviceable. It was the type that used an old incandescent bulb, which produced a pathetically dim beam that had diminished significantly in the past fifteen minutes. Its yellow hue covered only a few feet in front of him.

However, at some point this afternoon, he lost the cell phone Sue Olifante had bought him. He had made the calls he needed to, so it was not a tragedy, but having it would have made life easier. Where it was, he had no idea—it could be somewhere along the side of a rural road or buried in a snowdrift where he had stopped to take a piss. He knew that in the hands of law enforcement—if they figured out it was his—it would provide them with some insight as to who he had contacted . . . and how to apprehend him. He hoped it would remain where he had left it, untouched.

But of course he could not take a chance. He had to alter his approach.

It was merely another obstacle he would have to overcome. Hell, he had escaped a maximum-security facility. Whatever lay ahead might be considered infinitely easier.

He now trudged along in a rustic, forested area that was dotted with occasional homes. Some two dozen yards in the distance, illuminated slightly by the faint moonlight that made its way through the barren tree branches, was a clapboard house and, more importantly, what looked like a large detached shed. A bedroom with a mattress, running water, and toilet was unquestionably better—and he had no compunction about doing what was necessary to the home's inhabitants—but the fewer breadcrumbs he left in his wake, the better. He could hide in the shed, get some sleep, and map out a plan of action in the morning.

The problem he had now—how to find Jasmine—was at the crux of all he had to solve. Everything else was a matter of survival . . . though he had to stop and take a deep breath of chilled air from time to time, smell the flowers, enjoy his freedom for as long as it lasted.

If he was careful, and a little bit lucky, he would have the luxury of taking his time working his way to Canada. Or Mexico. He would have to think on that. He had originally figured he would go south, to get out of the cold. But that was perhaps too obvious. He had to start thinking with a contrarian point of view . . . do the opposite of what he should, or would, do.

After what he had done—*especially* after what he had done—the authorities would be looking for him en masse. Like death and taxes, that much was a given.

As he approached the shed, he could see it was more like a small barn—and the main house was larger than he had thought. He broke the rusted lock and pulled open the wooden door only enough to slide his body inside.

He winced at the creak of the hinge as he drew it closed behind him.

There was equipment of all kinds from what he could tell. Although there was a light switch on the wall where he had entered, he would not dare turn it on.

The homeowner was a handy guy, it seemed: he had an extensive assortment of tools mounted neatly on pegboards, with workbenches, drill presses, ladders . . . and a variety of power saws.

Marcks gathered up an old tarpaulin, scattered straw, and rags he had found in a lawn bag by the door. As he assembled his bed, the cold now penetrating down to the bone, he tried to think of a way to get close to Jasmine.

First he had to find her. He was sure she would not go back to her house. He knew she had left her old job. But where did she work now? He had no idea.

That presented a problem. Just as he began to feel like he was looking for a needle in a haystack—appropriate given where he was—he hit on an idea.

Yes, he thought. *That'll definitely work . . .*

15

Vail arrived home thirty minutes late. After hanging up with Jasmine she called Robby and apologized, then told him she was en route. He took it in stride and was not surprised.

She ran into the house, looking frazzled, as if she had just come from a crime scene—which was not far from the truth.

"I'm so sorry," she said.

Aside from Jonathan and Robby, DEA Special Agent Richard Prati and his son Ryan were seated in the family room. She stepped around the ottoman and stretched to shake their hands when Hershey pushed his way in to greet her. They all laughed as she cuddled his head in her left palm while extending her right toward Prati.

"Good to see you again, Karen. Working a case?"

"You heard about the escape of Roscoe Lee Marcks?"

"It's all over the news," Prati said.

"That's mine. Working on a Marshals' fugitive task force." She turned to the nineteen-year-old. "Ryan, good to meet you."

"Same here, Agent Vail."

"Karen, please." She leaned left and gave Jonathan a kiss on the cheek. "How are you, sweetie?"

"Good. Just found out Ryan's a Beta."

Vail straightened up. "You pledged Beta too? What school are you at?"

"University of Florida. I'm in for a quick visit to see my parents, then it's back at it."

"I'm going to check on dinner," Robby said. "Let's go take a seat at the table."

As they gathered up their drinks and walked into the dining room—which was meticulously set—*Thank you, Robby*—Vail asked, "What's your major?"

Prati laughed. "Ryan has some pretty career-specific plans."

"Following in your dad's footsteps?"

"In a way. I'm going to join the Navy, see if I can hook on with the SEALs."

"That's a pretty demanding program. I know some former Special Forces guys if you want to talk to them. I'm sure I can get one or two to sit down with you."

"That'd be cool."

Prati placed a hand on his son's shoulder. "Ryan's already a certified advanced SCUBA diver, lettered in track, swimming, cross-country, wrestling, and lacrosse."

"You're kidding," Vail said.

Robby poked his head out of the kitchen. "Actually, he's not kidding. That's one impressive young man."

"No shit."

"He's also a licensed sky diver—"

"Dad," Ryan said. "They get the picture."

"I have the utmost respect for Special Forces," Vail said.

Robby stepped in carrying a steaming tureen and gave her a look.

Okay, fine. I better shut up. I'm not supposed to talk about that stuff. "Jonathan's taking fencing," she said, changing the subject.

"Really?" Jonathan asked mockingly. "I'm taking a class in fencing? That's supposed to be impressive?"

"Hey," Robby said. "Don't sell yourself short." He elbowed Ryan. "Jonathan's *very* good."

"It's something I've wanted to learn," Ryan said. "You like it?"

"You need a lot of lower body and core strength—obviously that wouldn't be a problem for you—and like any sport you've really got to practice a lot to be good. Things happen very fast, so you're reacting instinctively rather than thinking. The more you do it, the better prepared you are to respond. If you've got to take a split second to think, you're done."

Ryan was nodding. "Definitely would like to get into that."

"And how are things with DEA?" Vail asked as she took the casserole from Robby and set it in the center of the table.

"Never a dull moment," Prati said. "I'm sure Robby can attest to that."

"No kidding. Law enforcement's a tough career for a family." She picked up the bottle of wine and began refilling Prati's and Robby's glasses, then poured one for herself. "Between his work with DEA and mine with the Bureau, we have to work to make time for each other."

"And *I* can attest to that," Jonathan said. "Like today."

Vail blushed. "Sorry, sweetie. Not how I envisioned it going. But I really had no choice." She turned to Prati. "I was giving a talk to one of Jonathan's criminal justice classes when all hell broke loose. Marcks escaped, a police officer who was guarding his daughter was murdered—and both calls came through at the same time . . . about a minute or two into my talk." She placed a hand on Jonathan's. "We'll get it rescheduled, I promise."

He grinned slyly. "It *was* kind of cool, actually."

"Cool?" Robby asked as he set bowls of broccolini, sautéed spinach, and kale/beet salad on the table.

"Everyone could kind of figure out there was something serious going down. It was a bit dramatic. Especially when you dropped the F-bomb in front of the class."

Robby covered his eyes and shook his head.

"It sounds worse than it was," Vail said, giving Jonathan a disapproving glance. "Everybody, eat up." She started passing around the dishes and unfurled her napkin. "Robby tells me you guys went to the same college in LA?"

Prati swirled his wine glass. "When he called me to help you out on that domestic bombing case a couple of months ago, I googled him, just to see who I was dealing with. I realized we both went to UCLA. A few years apart, but we had some of the same classes. And instructors."

"From there you went into the DEA?"

"My degree was in chemical engineering. Then I did an internship with Dow and realized I didn't want a career in corporate or research work. Too boring for my taste. But someone at Dow mentioned there was a need for chemists in law enforcement." Prati set a spoonful of broccolini on his plate. "Started out with Florida Department of Law Enforcement, then hooked on with ATF."

"ATF," Vail said. "Impressive. What's the hire rate, 5 percent of applicants?"

"I think it's even lower. No question I was fortunate. The six years I spent with them was an *important* six years. Learned a hell of a lot about arson, explosives, firearms trafficking—and the criminal elements that play in those sandboxes. The most eye-opening experience was the training I got at the fire research lab in Beltsville."

"What's a fire research lab?" Jonathan asked.

Prati chuckled. "A place where people go to play with fire. Seriously, it's a huge facility dedicated to the study of fire. Fire scientists use every imaginable piece of high-tech instrumentation to measure heat release rate, burn rate, something called heat flux, and a bunch of other things important in forensic reconstruction of fire-related crimes. Only one like it in the world. They even construct actual buildings and re-create an arson scene that they videotape to demonstrate burn patterns for investigation and court testimony."

"I'd love to check that out," Robby said.

"I can probably get you a tour. Just stay away from the dead pigs."

"Is that a joke?" Vail asked.

Prati laughed. "Pigs have the same makeup of skin, fat content, and body mass as we do, so the scientists use them to simulate the burning of a human body. Those studies helped me break the last case I worked for ATF. A string of arsons that ultimately turned out to be crime concealment fires."

"We've got one of those right now at the BAU," Vail said.

"They can be tough, especially if the arsonist is good."

"Still getting info on the other crime scenes but it definitely looks serial."

"Can you pass the chicken?" Robby asked. "Which case is this?"

Vail lifted the serving dish to her left and handed it to him. "Not one of mine. It's Art Rooney's. But we've got those Wednesday presentations where we put our heads together, help each other out."

"I'll have some of that, too," Jonathan said, receiving the platter from Robby. "I assume a crime concealment fire is what it sounds like?"

"Pretty much," Prati said. "Killer sets fires to cover his tracks. It's a way to destroy any evidence they inadvertently left behind. Like if they touched things without realizing it. This way, they get rid of everything and don't have to worry about it."

"But they have to know a fire like that will attract attention," Ryan said. "Obviously the fire department's gonna be all over it."

"And the police," Prati said, "if not the ATF. But they're figuring that whatever evidence they've left behind linking them to the crime will be destroyed."

"And if they've killed someone," Vail said, "they're hoping they've completely removed the ability for investigators to determine that it's even a homicide. No body, you can't even be sure the person in question was home at the time."

Prati finished chewing and pointed his fork at Vail. "Yeah, but arson investigators are really sharp. They find all kinds of stuff the offender has no idea these guys can find. They can usually tell it's an arson."

"Art had a case where the body was pretty well gone but not completely consumed. They were able to tell that the cause of death wasn't the fire but some other kind of traumatic injury." She turned to Ryan. "Unless the offender's an insider, they don't know all the things we can do. Like the guy who kidnapped and killed that family in DC. While waiting for the ransom payment, he ordered pizza. We got DNA off the crust in the garbage, ID'd him, and nabbed his ass." Vail stuck her fork into another chunk of chicken. "Everything's really good, honey. Thanks again for taking care of dinner."

"Yes," Prati said, "everything's perfect. I appreciate you asking us over."

"I'm glad we got to meet Ryan," Robby said.

"How's GW?" Prati asked.

Jonathan wiped his mouth with the napkin. "I'm really enj—"

Vail's phone vibrated noticeably, crawling along the table. Her eyes drifted over to Robby's. He shook his head subtly, telling her not to look. But she had to. She was now working a case that was time sensitive. She had been warned about not missing a text.

Except that it wasn't a text. It was a phone call.

"Excuse me," she said. "I've gotta take this."

"No worries." Prati laughed. "Just goes to what we were saying before. And hey—any questions about fire, I'm happy to help."

She thanked him, apologizing again as she gathered up the Samsung and walked into the family room. It was Hurdle.

"I thought you said to be back at ten."

"Something's come up."

"Wasn't the protocol a group text message?"

"This is only for you and Curtis. Don't bother going back to the command post. You were right. There's a new vic. Tarkoff's texting you the address."

In times like these, I hate it when I'm right.

16

It was a county road a few miles off George Washington Memorial Parkway, pitch-black in all directions except for the rhythmic pulse of the law enforcement vehicles' candy-colored lights and their focused high beams, which bored directly ahead into the stand of pines.

Vail pulled behind the line of cars as snow flurries began to fall, twinkling in her headlights like wayward lightning bugs zipping this way and that. She got out and blinked away the snowflakes that stuck to her eyelids, then came up alongside Hurdle, who was standing at the perimeter puffing on a cigarette.

"Curtis'll be here any minute," he said, not bothering to turn to look at her. He blew smoke out the side of his mouth, away from Vail. "How'd you know he was gonna kill again so fast?"

"He'd been in the slammer for seven years. Most incarcerated offenders are able to turn off the instinct, the hunger. They don't have any choice, really. Marcks appeared to be one of them—but as soon as he was free, he was like a kid in a toy store. So many potential victims, all he had to do was choose one he wanted. And strike. This had been building inside for years."

"Like pulling a cork out of a champagne bottle."

"What was wrong with my kid in a toy store simile?"

"Like mine better."

Two headlights threw their shadows against the black tree trunks of the tall pines. Vail turned and saw Curtis get out of his car.

"Haven't even had time to digest my dinner," Curtis said as he made his way toward them.

Victim could've probably said the same thing.

"Let's go do this." Hurdle dropped the butt to the ground and squished it with his shoe into the wet asphalt.

They slipped booties on and ducked beneath the crime scene tape, where a patrol officer with a flashlight directed them to another cop, who was standing below ground level, in a slight clearing next to a body.

Lindy Dyson was there, her kit splayed open and a few portable lights standing on tripods surrounding the corpse.

"Do we know who she is?"

Without a word, Dyson handed back a Virginia driver's license.

Vail took it and used her phone light to read it. "Tammy Hartwell. Thirty-four. Corrective lenses." Vail looked up and scanned the body. "She's not wearing any glasses."

"Contacts?" Curtis said. "Or maybe she wasn't driving when the perp came upon her."

"Or maybe they fell off in the struggle." Behind them was Leslie Johnson. "Got here as soon as I could."

"We had a theory on MO," Curtis said. "He entraps them when they're driving, uses a ruse to get them out of the car, then gets close enough to easily and quietly disable them. Maybe he makes believe his car is having problems. They stop and come over to help him, and that's when he anesthetizes them. He takes them somewhere and tortures them, brings them to a secluded area, usually a park or a wooded area, and dumps the body."

"Well, that seems to fit," Hurdle said.

"Doesn't pose them," Vail said, "at least not overtly. He leaves them face-up, probably so we see the bloody lines. Abdomen's laid bare. As we discussed, those lines mean something to him. He wants us to see them."

"Well, he succeeded," Hurdle said. "We see 'em."

Curtis licked a few flakes of snow off his lips. "And the excised genitalia. Don't know about you, but that's just friggin' gross."

Vail turned to him. "Did you think we'd find that anything but gross?"

"How long's she been out here?" Johnson asked.

Dyson checked her watch. "I did a liver poke. I'd say about four hours. Lucked out that a hiker found her before some animal realized he hadn't gotten enough to eat today."

"Cause of death?"

"Severed carotid," Dyson said.

Curtis looked up into the falling flurries. "Like the others."

Like the others. Vail considered that. Except that this was not exactly like the other murders.

"Problem?" Curtis asked.

"Nah, just giving it some thought. It's like the other MOs, and yet it's different. He usually spent time with the body before dumping it. But he didn't do that here. He's not been out long enough to 'enjoy' his time with the victim. Why would he spend so much less time with this woman?"

Hurdle crouched to get a better look at the body. "What you said earlier. Maybe he was so excited to be free, to be able to kill again, that he couldn't contain himself. He was so eager to kill that he had to do it. He couldn't wait. Kind of like premature ejaculation."

"Not a bad analogy. I guess that's possible. But for him, it's not just the kill that he's after. It's the whole process, the interplay with the victim, the power he exhibits over her while he tortures her. He skips parts of his ritual, it won't be nearly as enjoyable for him."

"Makes sense to me," Curtis said. "But that still leaves us with the question of why he rushed through it."

"Could be something as simple as he had no place to bring the body," Vail said, "where he could take his time. He's been in prison and he's on the run."

"And he doesn't know how long he'll be out," Johnson said, "how long he'll be free, so he's doing his best to get in as much 'fun' as he can. Yeah, he takes less time with the body, enjoys it a little less, but he'll make it up in volume."

Vail filled her lungs with frigid, moist air. She exhaled and sent a robust cloud of vapor into the forest. "Hope you're wrong, Leslie. Because that would really suck."

HURDLE LEFT SHORTLY THEREAFTER, but Vail, Curtis, and Johnson remained at the crime scene another ninety minutes, passing theories back and forth. They decided that until they knew more about Tammy Hartwell—who she was, where she frequented, and what could have brought her into the crosshairs of Roscoe Lee Marcks—they were playing with a deck of cards missing all the suits: you didn't get very far and the game was not much fun.

Hurdle had excused Vail and Curtis from returning to the command post until the morning. Given their past experience with, and knowledge of, Marcks, their time was better spent working the new homicide—for the moment. When he got the call about the Hartwell murder, he had directed Tarkoff to hand out assignments to the task force members. They could deal with the "fugitive 101" items that they had discussed before they broke for dinner. And if there were things they needed help with, he could pull more men and women from the Marshals Service as well as the county police force.

When Vail walked into her house at midnight, she found Richard Prati sharing a glass of port with Robby in the family room. Jonathan had driven Ryan home, then gone on to his dorm because he had an 8:00 AM class.

"You two still at it?"

Robby sat up and drained his glass. "We were swapping stories about growing up in Los Angeles."

Vail wondered if he had disclosed some of the most significant ones, those he had told Vail a few years ago. His face was impassive and she could not read it—a rarity.

"We had some similar experiences," Prati said. "Why we got into law enforcement."

Vail picked up a pillow from the couch and fluffed it, put it back in the right place. "I'm glad you two connected. It's good to have those kinds of relationships where you work." *God knows it took me awhile to find them.*

"We've got each other's backs. Figuratively." Prati laughed. "I've got a good gig doing what I do. Something opens up in my unit . . ." He shrugged. "We'll see. Robby may be interested."

Vail studied him intently—but his expression did not reveal

anything. "If you had it to do over again, Richard, would you leave ATF for DEA?"

"I've been lucky to have spent time with two law enforcement agencies I admire and respect. I cherished my years at ATF. And I wouldn't trade my work with DEA for anything. So, tough decision. But yeah, I'd do it again."

Robby pushed himself off the couch. "I've gotta get up early." He gave Prati a man hug. "We'll have to do this again. Hopefully a time when your wife can join us and Karen won't get called away." He glanced at Vail. "Miracles have been known to happen."

Vail grinned. And clenched her teeth. *I love you, honey.*

"Maybe catch a Nats game next season," Prati said. "A buddy of mine has season tickets."

Vail gave Prati a hug and backed away. "Great seeing you again, even if it was only a short visit."

She had washed her face and pulled off her clothes when she heard the front door close. After she fell into bed, Hershey climbed in beside her and cuddled up against her body.

Off in the distance, she heard Robby talking to her. But that was the last thing that registered as she fell into a deep sleep.

17

"What do I do about the book tour?"

Jasmine and Vail were sitting in a McLean, Virginia, Starbucks. Vail had pulled the lid off her venti Americano and was stirring in a packet of raw sugar.

The snow had stopped during the night but the cold temperatures persisted. The café was warm and cozy, the inside of its windows dripping with condensation.

"That's going to have to be put on hold. I just don't see a way around it."

"If I can't promote my book, I might be in breach of my contract. My publisher—"

"Will be very happy with the press and media attention. They'll do fine. In a way, this is the best possible thing that could've happened for them."

Jasmine stared out the window, wrapping her hands around the coffee to warm them. "We'll see. If I'd known this was gonna happen . . ."

Vail took a bite of her egg sandwich as she waited for Jasmine to finish.

"You're going to say you never would've written the book?"

"Hell no. It was cathartic in more ways than one." She glanced around the café and lowered her voice. "It wasn't something I planned to do. It just sort of happened when I began reflecting on everything, how I'd lived with a man who had brutally murdered young women and men, how that man had kissed me and held me when I was afraid. The most important man in my life."

Jasmine started peeling away the corner of the cardboard cup jacket.

"*That's* how I came to write the book. Started with some thoughts, kept writing night after night after night. I realized I probably saved some lives by turning him in. Eventually the guilt subsided. But it's never completely gone away. And now he's out and killing again. Because of me."

"Look," Vail said. "No one could've foreseen your father's escape. Well, I guess *he* did—he's likely been planning it for a while—but there's no way you could've known what was going to happen when you wrote your book. I'm sure your publisher will understand that your safety has to be the top priority here."

"My agent is talking to them today."

"Hopefully we'll catch him fast and it won't be an issue." She snapped her lid back on the cup. "Speaking of which, is there anything you can tell us that would be helpful?"

"Like what?"

"Like his bank. Is his checking account still open?"

Jasmine laughed sardonically. "Like a dutiful daughter, maybe out of guilt, I've made sure it stayed open. Every so often I make a small deposit to generate some activity so they don't close it. Kind of stupid, isn't it? I mean, he's in prison for life." She shook her head. "Definitely guilt."

"I'm not judging you. Whatever the reason you did it, it's a good thing. That'll help us. But stop for now. We need to monitor it for activity."

"Okay."

"Which bank?"

"Sutter Savings. I'll text you the account number." She took out her phone and opened the messaging app. "What else do you need?"

"Those friends of your father, the ones you told me about. Anything more you can give me on them? Places he used to go when he wanted to unwind. A bar, a restaurant, anything you can think of."

Jasmine took a bite of her blueberry scone and chewed as she thought. "He did go out drinking. But I never knew where. It's not like he accounted for his whereabouts to me. Or to my mom."

"What was their relationship like?"

Jasmine's gaze wandered around the café, pondering the question. "It's hard. I keep trying to think about signs, things I saw in how they interacted, that could've tipped me off to the fact that he was . . . murdering people." She shook her head. "Their relationship was fine, I guess. They spent time together. Sometimes they fought, sometimes they didn't. He never hit her, at least not that I ever saw." Jasmine looked down at the table, no doubt replaying her childhood in her mind's eye. "They weren't very demonstrative."

"Demonstrative?"

Jasmine shrugged. "They didn't hold hands in public. I never saw them kissing. It's—it's almost like they were more friends than lovers." She stopped talking, then took a bite of her scone.

"Some couples are like that," Vail said. "I wouldn't read too much into it." *But it could definitely be significant.* "Do you think it's possible he's gay?"

"What?" Jasmine began rolling the edge of the cardboard jacket between her thumb and index finger. "Why would you ask that?"

"Just something we're looking into." Vail watched her a second, sensing there might be more to it than she was letting on. Now did not seem like the time to press it. "You going to tell me where you're staying?"

She hesitated a moment. "I think it's best that no one knows. For now."

Vail nodded slowly. "Okay. I'll respect that." *For now.* She drained her cup and dabbed her mouth with the napkin. "But I want you to promise me you'll stay in touch. I text you, I want you to answer me right away. I could have something important to tell you, for your safety, and I need to know you're getting my message. If I call, answer it."

"Got it."

Vail frowned. "I still don't like it. Who knows where your father is? You have habits you're not conscious of, things that he knows you do, places you go—and have gone."

"I'm doing my best to be aware of things like that." She placed a hand on Vail's. "I'll be okay, Karen. I may not be trained in this kind of thing, but I've got my intuition. And so far, it's served me well."

"You've done okay. Lucky?"

"Nope. Just being smart about things. Really, I'm going to be fine."

Vail crumpled up the wrapper and dumped her empty cup in the recycling bin behind her. "I have to get back."

They stood up and Vail gave Jasmine a hug. "I'll be in touch. Be careful."

Jasmine grinned weakly. "Always. Especially now."

18

Marcks awoke with a start. He had fallen asleep a short time after preparing his bed, which, when he settled into it, was more comfortable than he thought it might be when he gathered up the sundry materials. Then again, he had been sleeping on prison cots that dated back five or six decades. Anything better than that would feel like duck feathers.

He sat up, taking in his environment: he was in the barn and light was streaming in through cracks and spaces between the wood slats that formed the walls.

And there it was again. The creak of rusted hinges. It's what had jostled him from a deep sleep, deeper than any he'd had since his arrest—definitely not his intention when he put his head down last night. He did not have a watch but it looked to be late morning. He thought for sure he would be up at dawn, his routine at Potter. Now free, without the regimen of a highly structured schedule, he should have realized that his body might react differently.

And right now it had apparently let him down.

He relaxed, his normally razor-sharp senses going on vacation. He would not let that happen again.

Marcks glanced across the barn at the entrance, which was located to the right of an extensive tool rack. A man, silhouetted against the gray light, stood in the doorway.

"Hey! Who're you?"

Marcks stood up. "I needed a place to sleep. It was snowing, I was cold."

The man squinted, clearly trying to make sense of what was happening: Did he have a squatter? Was this going to be a problem? Or could he merely ask his house guest to leave?

"What's your name?" Marcks asked.

"William. What's yours?"

"Bart."

William appeared to be a bit over seventy. In decent shape but probably no more than a hundred and fifty pounds. Not much of a challenge for a violent criminal with multiple murders under his belt and seven years of hard time in a max-security prison to his name.

"You have to go," William said.

"I'm leaving, no worries." But Marcks knew that he could not trust William to keep quiet about his presence, especially when there had to be police reports detailing the brazen, bloody escape of a convict from Potter yesterday. Not just a convict, a convicted murderer.

William tilted his head, and in doing so his eyes caught the light. Marcks saw something there, perhaps recognition. Perhaps not. But he could not take the chance.

As William stood there pondering the situation, Marcks knew what had to happen. And if William could put two and two together, he would know it, too. But William looked like a simple man and he probably believed that if he talked tough, he would dodge a bullet and his unwelcome guest would be on his way.

Marcks held his hands up in surrender and walked toward the exit—which happened to be past William.

Before William realized what was happening, he was immobilized in a headlock, Marcks's left arm cutting off the blood supply to his brain and Marcks's right hand clamping over the man's mouth, preventing an errant noise or desperate scream.

William slumped into Marcks's hold, unconscious. Marcks set him on the ground and perused the workbench, ultimately finding his tool of choice: a wicked-looking keyhole saw. Long and narrow, with alternating teeth that were sharp as a knife, it was as imposing as it was lethal.

Marcks jabbed it into William's chest between the fourth and fifth ribs slightly left of center.

"No witnesses, Willie," Marcks said. "Just the way it's gotta be."

He then yanked out the saw and brought the man to his feet, bent his knees and folded William over his shoulder. With a quick contraction of his thighs, he lifted William and took him for a ride.

No one was going to find William's body parts for an awfully long time.

19

Vail walked into the command center at 1:00 PM and found Hurdle hunched over his keyboard, examining spreadsheet data. Tarkoff was seated across from him studying other documents.

"Long breakfast," Hurdle said without diverting his eyes.

"We had a good talk. She's worried about not being able to finish her book tour."

"I expect to get Marcks sooner rather than later. But either way, her sales and promotion are not my problem."

Vail sat down opposite him. "Of course. I think she understood that my sole concern was keeping her safe and apprehending her father."

"What about the bank account?" Hurdle asked.

"She's kept it open. And when I hit her with the question of whether or not her father's gay, she seemed . . . I don't know. Like there was something there. Guess I could've been reading into it."

The door swung out and Curtis stepped into the RV. "Just got a call from Warden Barfield at Potter. Wants to know if we're making any progress on the escape."

Tarkoff swiveled in his direction. "And you told him?"

"That we've got guys working on it."

"He accepted that?"

"He wanted details but I didn't wanna give him anything," Curtis said. "Until we know who's working with Marcks, we can't trust anyone there. Not saying the warden's a suspect, but he's a suspect. Know what I mean?"

Hurdle shrugged. "Can't think of a case where a warden helped an inmate escape—not counting incompetence. But there's always a first. You two gonna follow up on his three friends the daughter gave us?"

"Next on our list," Curtis said.

Good to know.

"For now, that's your priority."

"Well, that and investigating the Hartwell murder," Vail said as she got up from her seat. "You want us to check back here later?"

"I'll let you know. If not, see both of you tomorrow morning."

Vail and Curtis left the trailer, Vail offering to drive.

"Where are we on the three of them?"

"Johnson did some of the grunt work, looked into their whereabouts, and put together some solid dossiers. She did a nice job."

"I would've told you if she was going to be a problem. Leslie's a good cop. She'll have your back." Vail turned right onto Lincolnia Road. "Where to?"

"Hood bridge."

"What bridge?"

Curtis laughed. "Woodbridge, in Prince William County. What we call it, you know?"

"Because it's got some high crime areas?"

"Hey, I didn't coin the phrase. Fair or not, I wasn't surprised this joker lives there."

"Which one?"

"We've only got a twenty on Vincent Stuckey. Johnson's still working on Scott MacFarlane and Booker Gaines—the one Jasmine said was following her in the store."

"You got a phone number for Stuckey?"

Curtis squinted, then pulled out his cell and thumbed through his emails. "Yeah. You thinking of calling him?"

"Just want to make sure he's there. Don't want to make a wasted trip."

He read off the number and she dialed her Samsung. It rang three times before a male voice picked up the line.

"This is UPS and we've got a package for Vincent Stuckey. Is Mr. Stuckey available?"

"Yeah, that's me. But why are you calling? Don't you guys just show up?"

"This is our third attempt," Vail said, "and it's marked for signature. Our driver can't leave it at the door. You going to be around awhile so I can get you your package?"

"Be home for another hour, then I gotta take off. Who's it from?"

"Sorry, sir. I only have the tracking information. Would you like the number?"

"No. Jus' get here in the next hour."

Vail hung up, a grin thinning her lips. "He's there."

THEY ARRIVED AT DALE CITY APARTMENTS, a series of attached four-story red brick buildings with thick-trunked oak trees that lined the periphery.

Curtis had briefed her on the drive over, filling her in on the backgrounder that Johnson had assembled. Vail parked at the curb and leaned forward, her eyes surveying the complex.

"You're thinking he'll run if he sees us coming."

Vail sat back and faced Curtis. "If he's involved with Marcks's escape, yeah. There's a risk."

"You got a UPS box in the trunk?"

"Funny." Vail popped open her door. "Let's split up, take a quick look around, see how many ways in and out there are. A place this size, gotta be a few."

Vail made her way around the building exterior, then headed inside and found a map of the property. There were several exits, but based on Stuckey's apartment number, they would be able to approach his place with exposure to only one.

She called Curtis and told him what she had learned, and a couple of minutes later he met her on the fourth floor, down the hall from Stuckey's door. "Only way out is off the terrace. Right into the pool. He jumps, I'm not sure we'll have enough time to get down there and fish him out."

"Not a problem. We can handle it."

"With the task force," Vail said, "manpower isn't an issue. We can have a couple of guys here in twenty minutes."

Curtis checked his watch. "He's here now. I'm not interested in waiting. He goes off the balcony, I'll go after him. You can run around the building."

With the temperature hovering around thirty-five degrees, Vail could not find fault with that division of tasks. "Works for me."

They walked up to the door and Curtis drew back his coat, placing a hand on his SIG Sauer; he used Vail to shield Stuckey's view.

She knocked and focused her attention on listening for unusual noises emanating from the apartment. Seconds later she heard the footsteps of someone approaching. There was no peephole lens.

"Who is it? UPS?"

"Karen from next door. I think I found something of yours in the hall."

"What kind of 'something'?"

"A wallet with, like, two hundred dollars in it. It was right outside your apartment. Gotta be yours. I was thinking maybe you can spot me a twenty for turning it in."

The knob rattled and the door pulled open. Stuckey made eye contact with Vail and then bent left to get a view of Curtis—but Vail shifted right, catching Stuckey's gaze. "I didn't really find a wallet, Vincent. I'm FBI. Can we talk?"

He looked past her, taking in the hallway.

He's thinking about running.

"We've got seven agents outside in case you plan to jump off your balcony. And it's really friggin' cold outside, so that pool water's gonna go right down to your bones. So—how about we just sit and chat for a few minutes. And then we'll be out of your hair. Promise."

Stuckey chewed his lip a second. "There ain't no wallet?"

Vail blinked. *He's not smiling. That wasn't a joke.* "No wallet. Sorry."

"What's this about then?"

"Roscoe Lee Marcks."

"What about him?"

"How about we go inside?" Curtis asked.

"Yeah, all right." Stuckey turned and led them to a tattered couch, its cushions flattened and potholed with wear, its threadbare olive green material pocked with stains.

Okay, gross. Do I really want to sit down on that?

Stuckey sank into a nearby chair. Vail took the armrest of the sofa—as safe as she could get. Curtis floated in the background, casually glancing at items in the apartment—which was decorated much like the couch: thrift store reject.

"We know you're friends with Roscoe," Vail said.

"Since we were kids. What about it?"

"He contact you in the past couple of days?"

Stuckey looked away. "No."

"That was a trick question, Vincent." Vail waited for him to bring his eyes back to hers. "We know he called you." *Okay, that's a lie. But it usually works.*

"So?"

"So we want to know what he said. Where's he staying?"

"Didn't tell me. I told him he could crash here, but he didn't think that'd be a good idea."

No shit. Marcks is a smart cookie. Stuckey apparently didn't get any of the chocolate chips when they were mixing the batter.

"And? Where's he staying? Where's he been?"

Stuckey looked away again, his eyes examining the puke-green shag carpet.

"Vincent. Look at me." Vail tilted her head and gave him a one-sided grin when he brought his gaze back to hers. "It's against the law to impede our investigation. See, your buddy's been killing people again. And if you know where he is and you're not telling us, you could be an accessory to those murders. Do you understand what that means?"

"I think so."

"It would not be good." She paused, realized she had better elaborate. "You could go to prison. For a long time. A guy like Roscoe can survive in a place like that. But you . . ." She shrugged. "Be better if you just cooperate so you don't have to worry about that."

Stuckey thought a moment, his gaze wandering across Vail's face. "He wouldn't tell me where he is. He's moving around, that's all I know. Not staying in one place. Wanted me to bring him money."

"And? Did you?"

"Ain't got any to give. As it is I'm behind two months in my rent. I have a hard time keeping jobs."

"What about places he liked to go? Before he was arrested."

"Anyplace they served beer." Stuckey laughed, showing tobacco-yellow teeth.

"You're not being very helpful, Vincent. I need specifics."

The smile disappeared. "Coupla bars he liked in town. Don't remember which ones."

Vail nodded. "What about when you were kids? Did you like to go places, places you used to play, where you'd go to get away from things? From your parents?"

Stuckey started biting his bottom lip. He got up from the chair and turned, came face-to-face with Curtis.

"What's wrong?" Vail asked. "Something bothering you about a place you used to go when you were kids? Teens? Somewhere you weren't supposed to go?"

"No," Stuckey stammered. "Nothing like that." He started rubbing his left forearm.

We're onto something here. She glanced at Curtis and he appeared to be thinking the same thing.

"Tell me about what happened when you were younger. I want to know all the details."

"I—I'm not s'posed to talk about it."

Vail pushed off the sofa and put her left hand on Stuckey's shoulder. "C'mon, sit back down. I promise we won't say anything to anyone about what happened. You have my word."

Something's not right with this guy. He's not just lower IQ. There's something else.

Stuckey sank back into his chair. Vail knelt in front of him. "Something happened with you and Roscoe?"

"And Scott and Booker. And Lance."

Vail and Curtis shared a look. "Scott MacFarlane and Booker Gaines, right?" She got a nod from Stuckey so she pressed on. "Who's Lance?"

"Lance is the one who started it but Rocky's the one who took the blame. Well, Rocky did kill the kid."

"Back up a minute," Curtis said. "Who's Rocky?"

"Roscoe. That was our name for him. Because he was so strong. You know, like a rock?"

"And Lance's last name?" Vail asked.

"Can't remember. We used to hang out all the time, but I never saw him again after that. Something with a K, kinda like that old film, *Kodak*. But not Kodak."

"You said there was a kid involved? That Rocky killed?"

"That's the part I'm not s'posed to talk about."

"I understand," Vail said. "And we won't tell anyone. Your secret's safe with us, okay?"

Stuckey looked down. "I guess." He took a breath, then looked up and his eyes found the clock on the wall. "I gotta go. I have an appointment."

"We'll be done here very soon," Vail said. "Tell us about this kid Rocky killed and we'll be on our way."

He licked his lips and canted his head toward his hands. "Name was Eddie. He was just a kid who hung out at the playground. Talked shit, smoked reefer. I don't think he went to our school."

"How old were you?" Curtis asked.

"Fourteen."

"And what happened?"

"We'd been smoking. Rocky got us some angel dust and we was real wasted. Eddie came by and . . ." He shook his head, as if he had some water trapped in his ear. He slapped his forehead a few times. "And he had a gun. And Rocky took it from him and shot him. And me."

Vail recoiled. "Why?"

Stuckey looked up at her. "I don't fuckin' know, we was high. Rocky had a temper, even back then. Maybe Eddie was talkin' shit again, but whatever. It happened real fast. After the gunshots, I didn't hear or see nothin'."

"Where'd you get shot?" Curtis asked.

Stuckey pulled back a lock of hair and revealed a dime-shaped scar overlying his temple.

That might explain Stuckey. But . . . "And Eddie. He died?"

Stuckey nodded, his gaze again somewhere on the floor.

Vail ran a hand across her mouth. "What about the police?"

"Well, Scott told me him and Booker and Rocky left. The cops came and found me there, took me to the hospital. Next thing I know, when I woke up after they did surgery and I got out of the hospital, they found Rocky and arrested him."

How come I don't know about this? It's not in his file. Unless—

"But Rocky didn't do time," Curtis said. "In prison. Did he?"

"Booker was the only witness who remembered what happened. And he said it was Eddie's fault, Eddie came at him and pulled the gun on us and Rocky was trying to get it from him and it went off."

"Is that what happened?"

"That's what Booker said. That's all that mattered."

"But didn't you just say—"

"I don't remember!" He slapped a hand against the chair arm. "The bullet. It made a hole in my brain." His face was red and he had started to perspire.

"Okay, Vincent. It's all right, I understand." Vail stood up and pulled out a card from her pocket. "If Rosc—if Rocky calls you, I want you to let me know right away. I really don't want to have to arrest you and put you in jail. And don't mention we came to visit you because you'll never hear from him again. Can you do that?"

"But that'd be like telling on him. And Rocky's my friend."

"Look. Vincent." Vail gathered her thoughts. "Rocky did some bad things. He killed a lot of innocent people, men and women who were just living their lives. And he's doing it again. I know he's your friend, but he's a dangerous guy. It's our job to keep him from hurting more people. You can help us do that. That'd be best for everybody."

"You help us out," Curtis said as he came around to Vail's side, "you'd be a hero."

That's not his motivator. "I can even see about getting you some reward money." She pulled out her wallet, removed a twenty, and offered it to Stuckey.

He snatched it with the alacrity of a cheetah.

"Okay?"

Stuckey nodded sheepishly. "Yeah, okay."

AS THEY PULLED AWAY FROM THE CURB, Curtis looked back at the apartment building. "You think he'll call us?"

"More relevant question is whether Marcks will call *him* again." She was silent a minute, then said, "Poor guy."

"Drugs, guns, and stupidity are a bad mix."

"We've gotta find that juvie case. It's obviously sealed. There was nothing like that in Underwood's file—or in yours."

"Nope." Curtis looked out at the passing snow-covered foliage. "Think it went down like Vincent said?"

"Knowing our buddy Marcks, no. He probably killed the kid. No struggle necessary. But who knows. Maybe it was just a dumb fight between two kids who were high."

"Either way, probably doesn't matter."

Vail tilted her head. "Actually, it does. Because now we've got another friend of theirs to follow up on. This Lance joker."

"Vincent said he never saw him again after that."

"*Vincent* didn't see him again. Doesn't mean Marcks didn't."

20

Curtis hung up his phone. "That was the sergeant in charge of the records room. It's a bit of a quagmire."

"How so?" Vail negotiated a turn onto Chain Bridge Road, then slowed behind a line of cars. The temperature had dropped and snow had begun falling again.

"Fairfax County used to be on an old CAD—computer-aided dispatch system. Back in '97 or '98, we brought in Northrop Grumman and migrated over to new records management software. Idea was to go to a paperless reporting system. Problem was, the integration was a massive data dump. All sorts of shit happened, records got . . . well, not lost per se, but misplaced. Well, not really misplaced. They weren't compatible with the new system so they didn't transfer over."

"So does this Marcks file still exist or are we wasting our time?"

"It won't show up in the new CAD system, but the original paper reports were archived. Too expensive to digitize all the incompatible records because there are thousands of them. So generally speaking, when we access the database, it's as if these files don't exist."

"So if you don't know what you're looking for, you have no idea they're there."

"Exactly."

"But since we know that these records exist," Vail said, "we know to request them."

"And that's what I just did. I asked for all PD-42 initial reports and PD-42s, the supplementals. Basically, all ROIs," he said, using cop speak for reports of investigation.

"That explains why we didn't know about this case when we were looking into Marcks for the Blood Lines killings. Kind of an important thing not to be aware of."

"Shit happens in police work. Especially where records and technology are involved. You know that."

"Had a thing like this in New York. So yeah, I know."

They arrived at police headquarters, formally known as the Public Safety Center or the Massey Building, an aging 1960s-era structure with leaking pipes, malfunctioning air-conditioning, and its most endearing feature, asbestos.

They got out of the car and started trudging forward in the fresh layer of snow.

"The new HQ will be finished later this year," Curtis said, gesturing to a partially constructed eight-story edifice. "We move in next year. Gonna miss that old building."

"Really?"

"Nope."

They walked past the twelve-level public safety facility to the Massey Annex, the archive center commonly referred to simply as the "records room" by Fairfax County police.

They passed a sign that divided visitors into two categories: citizens and police. They headed right, down a short alcove to a twenty-year-old woman with her hair pulled back in a bun.

Curtis badged the clerk and explained what he needed. "Already spoke with the sergeant about it."

"He just called. Give me some time to find it."

As she walked off, Vail looked at Curtis. "She's kind of young, no?"

"Cadets. Prospective police officers. Gotta be creative with county budgets. Put the eager, low-cost bodies where you need 'em, where they can't do any damage."

The woman returned an hour later with a thin folder. "Copies of the Marcks file. It's a really, really old case."

"Not to worry," Vail said. "Marcks is updating his body of work as we speak."

Curtis elbowed Vail away and gave the clerk a disarming smile. "Thanks. Appreciate your help."

They went back to the warmth of Vail's car. She clapped her gloved hands together and looked over at Curtis as he pulled open the folder.

He gave it a quick once-over while Vail turned up the heater and defroster.

"So it looks like Stuckey was being straight with us. Assuming this Lance guy told the truth—and it's a stretch to make that assumption—it went down like Stuckey said. When they arrested Marcks, he was charged with improper discharge of a firearm and involuntary manslaughter. But once they found and interviewed Lance—" his finger tracked down the page— "Kubiak. Lance Kubiak. When they sat down with him, they accepted his version of events and null prossed it."

Vail knew that was a bastardized version of a Latin term

nolle prosequi, meaning they decided not to prosecute the case against Marcks.

Curtis harrumphed. "Forensics didn't exactly match up. Gunshot residue was inconclusive. There was residue on Marcks and a trace amount on Eddie Simmons, the deceased teen. But with Marcks in the wind for—" Curtis turned a couple of pages and consulted the paperwork—"three hours, that kind of ruined the evidentiary value. They expected to find more on Simmons's hands if they were struggling for the gun. But it wasn't enough to press forward with a case. Especially with their only witness corroborating Marcks's version of events, tainted as that accounting was."

"So where does this leave us?"

Curtis closed the file. "Not sure."

"Looks like Lance Kubiak knows what really happened. Assuming he's still alive, he's someone that Marcks put his trust in once before. Could be he does it again."

Curtis cocked his head.

"What?"

"I can't see Marcks making that mistake. Tracking down old friends . . . he's wise to that. He's too smart, too careful to let us to trap him like that."

"Is he? He contacted Stuckey."

"And what did that get us? Something on a thirty-year-old case. Nothing on where Marcks is in the present day."

"We'll see about that. For now, we follow the Marshals' recipe. And a key ingredient of that recipe is watching known associates, family, and friends. Let's find Lance Kubiak and see if he's had contact with Marcks. It's another bread trail."

Curtis checked his watch. "Speaking of bread, I'm starving. We totally blew past lunch."

"I'll drop you off at your car. I'm running late for a meeting at the Academy."

VAIL STRODE INTO THE ADMINISTRATION BUILDING and signed in at the front desk, then texted Art Rooney to tell him she had arrived.

He suggested that she meet him at the gymnasium. She passed through the magnetron scanner, then headed straight past the auditorium, library and classrooms, and on to the physical education wing. As she made her way down the hall, she saw Rooney opening the door to the pool area.

"Art!"

Rooney turned, nodded at her. "Trying to squeeze in a short workout before heading off to an appointment. You mind?"

"That's fine. I got hung up over at Fairfax County PD. Took the clerk an hour to pull a file from archives."

"Normally I wouldn't care but I've got a dinner appointment."

"Speaking of dinner, Robby and I had a guy over last night. Former ATF agent who did time in the fire lab."

He tossed a pair of swim goggles onto a railing and continued on to the stairs, which led down to the main level of the cavernous gym. "Anyone I know?"

"Richard Prati, now with DEA Special Operations."

Rooney pursed his lips. "Doesn't ring a bell."

"We had a chance to chat about Crime Concealment Fires. Anything new on that case?"

"Got back some forensics on the latest scene," he said, grabbing a basketball off a wheeled cart. "Come shoot some hoops with me before I swim laps."

Vail removed her shoulder holster and placed it around the

head of an oversize gray and black "Cuff Man" dummy, which was outfitted with Velcro and designed to teach the proper techniques for applying handcuffs.

"Anything surprising?"

Rooney took a shot and the ball swished but came off to the right toward Vail. She snatched it up and threw a bounce pass to Rooney, who caught the ball, dribbled left, then pulled up for a jumper. It hit the side of the rim and Vail again gathered it up, fed Rooney as he moved toward the basket and laid it in.

"Hey, you're good at this."

"I've played with Robby and Jonathan. They taught me well. Can't shoot worth shit, but I'm good at rebounding and passing."

"So, the forensics." He pulled up and took another shot. "I'll have to show you everything when you've got some time. Getting close to identifying the accelerant."

"I thought it was Sterno gel."

"That's the one we found but I knew he had to have used a more conventional, and effective, accelerant."

"And?"

"And I should have an answer soon."

"Keep me posted. Sounds like this is shaping up to be an interesting case."

"Definitely challenging." He dribbled once and took another shot. "But that's not what you came here to discuss, is it?"

"You had a case a couple of years ago. That homosexual serial. Padrova?"

"Yeah, what about him?"

"I wanted to pick your brain. I think Roscoe Lee Marcks might be gay. Something Thomas Underwood missed or overlooked. Or discounted. Nothing in his case file about it."

"Have you spoken to Tom about it?"

"Left a message. Hasn't returned my call yet. He could be traveling."

"Let's say you're right. The purpose of our assessment is to help identify the kind of person doing the deed. But we know who it is. He's not an UNSUB. So is this just curiosity on your part or is there some relevance that I'm missing?"

"If he is gay, then it could impact how the fugitive task force goes about looking for him."

Rooney nodded. "Okay. So then let's talk homosexual serial killers. A lot of the well-known serials were gay. But there isn't necessarily a predominance of gay serials relative to the general population. So it won't be unusual if he is homosexual."

"Right. Again, it's only significant in terms of finding him."

"If I remember right," Rooney said, "Marcks excised the male genitalia, right?"

"Correct. I'm thinking that could be his way of making the male body look more feminine. Cut away the penis and testicles, you've got a more female body type."

Rooney took a shot and it clanged off the rim, hit the backboard, and fell through the net. "And why would he do that?"

Vail gathered up the ball and bounced it while she thought. "He's uncomfortable with his homosexuality and he's trying to make the men, who he's attracted to, look more like women, who he feels he *should* be attracted to."

He held out his hands and she threw him a chest pass. "Could be. I'll accept that. But didn't he kill women also?"

"Yeah. It was one of the things I was going to ask him about. Before he escaped."

"Two different killers?"

"They found forensics at two crime scenes—one male victim and one female victim—that fingered Marcks."

"Okay." Rooney took a shot. "Well, there are some killers who don't have a preference for a particular type of victim, but most do."

The rebound caromed to Vail. "Right. So?"

"So for those who do, it's unusual for them to have more than one victim preference. But they can stray from that preference when their type isn't available. So if he likes white females and the night he has the urge, he can't find a white woman, he kills a Hispanic. Then he'll go back to whites." He gestured at her. "Go on, take a shot."

She dribbled and then launched a fifteen-foot jumper. The ball swished the net.

"I thought you said you can't shoot worth shit."

"I purposely set low expectations. See how impressed you were?"

"You mean you lied." Rooney laughed as he gathered up the ball and started walking toward the rack. "So you think that's what happened with Marcks? His type wasn't available so he went after a woman those times?"

"Not sure. But I think there's more to it. Someday soon I hope to ask him about it." Her Samsung vibrated. It was a text from Hurdle:

another marcks body

need you and curtis here asap

where are you

She replied and asked for the address.

"Problem?"

Vail realized she had suddenly gone quiet, focused on her phone.

"Another Marcks vic. Gotta go."

Rooney set the ball on the rack. "You want to talk some more tomorrow?"

"I think I'm good for now. Let you know."

She jogged out of the gymnasium, trying to reach Curtis as she ran. He answered as she hit the door. Ten minutes later, she was driving through the security booth at Quantico, headed for a wooded area near Cub Run.

21

SLEEPY HOLLOW ROAD
FALLS CHURCH, VIRGINIA

Marcks stood in the shade of a large black walnut tree, its trunk a good three feet in diameter and offering solid cover from oncoming cars. The snow had not packed down around the tree, but was only a few inches deep. Its dense canopy of branches had shielded the ground from any significant accumulation.

He was getting chilled again, which meant he could not remain here much longer. But his goal was not simply to find shelter for the evening. He needed cash and some decent food. A bed and a hot shower would be a good bonus.

Marcks had ditched the Jensens' sedan earlier in the day because there would be a stolen vehicle alert circulating among police officers. And with law enforcement patrols likely beefed up because of his escape, the risks of having the car now outweighed its benefits.

He had selected a wealthy neighborhood and was waiting for a luxury automobile: Mercedes, BMW, Audi, Porsche . . . he wasn't picky. When one came along and turned into a nearby driveway, that would be his first mark.

He would observe for a while, scout out who was in the house and determine if it was a feasible target. Since there was only one of him, he had to maximize his odds of a successful intrusion. No dogs was his first screening criterion. His second was a fair amount of foliage around the front door, where he would likely enter, to block the view of anyone from the street. Third was no males—or it had to be one smaller than him.

Good odds of that.

It was late afternoon, so he figured that most men had not left work yet. Yeah, that was a bit of an assumption—more women were breadwinners in families nowadays, especially in cities and sleeper towns for corporate centers—but playing the averages, he figured most of the people in this affluent area had a high-earning male in the household . . . and chances were the woman was at home raising the kids. Or a nanny was—in which case, he could make her summon the wife home.

As the minutes ticked by, he realized that the longer he stood there, despite the tree's cover, his odds of being reported to police as a suspicious person increased. A neighborhood like this, where property values were exceptionally high and the power halls of Washington exceptionally close, cops responded in short order. You never knew who would get pissed at a slow rollup of a patrol car: a CEO, a lobbyist, a congressional representative, a State Department executive. Safer for dispatch to jump on it when a call came in—and for the officers to hightail it over.

He bent his knees, attempting to get the blood flowing and restore sensation to his toes. As he flexed his fingers, a car moved down Sleepy Hollow, its xenon headlights a telltale sign that the vehicle was expensive. The turn signal flicked on.

Marcks moved against the rough bark and watched as the vehicle slowed and then hung a right into the long driveway that led up to the single-story brick house set back from the street and behind a rolling berm of snow-covered grass.

It was a Mercedes. Very good.

He shifted left, keeping his hands on the tree trunk, and peered into the gray distance. The garage door rolled up and the sedan pulled to a stop. There was space for two vehicles, meaning—hopefully—the other one was for the husband and he was not home yet.

Marcks moved out from behind his cover and walked toward the house, using the trees and hedges to shield himself from the neighboring home to his right.

He stopped and watched as a woman in her late thirties or early forties got out. It looked like a child followed her from the rear driver's side door.

Like a tiger salivating over his prey, he licked his cold, dry lips.

This was exactly what the criminal ordered.

22

Vail arrived at the crime scene almost forty-five minutes later. She knew Hurdle's car by now and slid in between it and Curtis's sedan. Vail figured that Johnson must be there too.

"Talk to me," she said as she approached Hurdle.

"Deceased is a resident of that house," he said with a nod of his chin west of their location. The gray, snowy sky was darkening, evening approaching rapidly.

"And that?"

"That," Curtis said, "is a barn. It's also our crime scene."

Vail lifted her brow. "Really. Let's go check it out."

"Already seen it," Hurdle said. "Want me to tell you what I think?"

"Actually, no. You're not a homicide investigator."

"Neither are you."

"I *was*," Vail said. "Been there, done that. So, yeah. I know my way around a crime scene." She snapped on gloves and struggled to pull booties over her wet shoes.

Hurdle squared his shoulders. "So do I."

"Let me back up," she said, straightening and stamping her foot to reseat her boot. "I want to walk into that barn and see it for myself, without your biases."

"My biases?"

Vail scratched a phantom itch along her right temple. "I don't want you to interpret things for me. Nothing against you or your investigative skills."

Hurdle held up his hands. "Fine. I'll keep my mouth shut."

As Vail and Curtis approached the barn, Leslie Johnson emerged, pulling off her rubber gloves as she exited.

"Hey," Vail said.

Johnson gave her a nod. "You might be disappointed."

"Is there a dead body in there?"

"Matter of fact, no."

"No?"

"Like I said, you might be disappointed."

"Do we have a body?"

"We do," Hurdle said. "Neighbor's dog dug it up. That's why Fairfax County PD got called."

Johnson handed Vail a flashlight and Vail entered, Curtis right behind her.

A couple of bare bulbs hanging from the canted ceiling gave off inadequate illumination, but Vail could make out a puddle of what looked like dried blood pooled on the cement, a few feet from a workbench where dozens of tools were mounted on a pegboard.

Vail shone her beam from left to right, sweeping the area. She stopped and focused on a spot ahead of her, then stepped closer. "Uh, what the hell?"

Curtis came up beside her. "What?"

"Blood smear. See?" Vail directed the light to the middle of a crosscut hand saw, its metal surface pocked with rust—and the remnants of dried maroon bodily fluid. She shifted her light a bit farther along the workbench and stopped on a long, round tool. "That's one nasty gizmo. What the heck is it?"

It had sharp, saw-like teeth but it was shaped like a screwdriver.

Curtis tilted his head, sizing it up. "Looks like something you stick into a hole to make it larger, like a reaming tool—but with a lot more teeth. Not sure what it is, but it makes for one wicked weapon."

She examined it and then turned to Hurdle. "Let's get the crime scene tech back in here, make sure she got some good photos of these bloody tools."

He nodded and whistled.

"Time of death?"

"Sometime this morning."

Vail turned and looked at the blood stain on the ground. "So I'm thinking he stabbed the victim with that long—whatever the hell it is—and killed him here. Then he moved the body."

"Who lived here?" Curtis asked. "Do we know who the vic is?"

"William Reynolds, seventy-three," Johnson said, reentering the barn. "Wife died last year. Lived alone."

"And why were we called?" Vail asked. "I mean, why did they assume Marcks is the offender?"

"Simple," Hurdle said. "We're notified of any violent crime in the region. With an escaped fugitive on the loose, let alone a murderer, the first assumption is it's related to our case."

Makes sense.

"There was also a report of someone matching his description here last night."

Vail drew her chin back. "Wasn't it checked out?"

"Cruiser came by." Hurdle chuckled. "But the officer didn't look in the barn."

"You're shitting me."

"What can I say? He knocked on the door of the house, looked around, didn't see anything out of the ordinary, walked the grounds, then left. They screwed up."

You think? Vail sighed. "I've seen it before. It happens. But it's always a head shaker."

"Did he take Reynolds's car?" Curtis asked.

"There's an old '69 Dodge registered to him and it's still in the driveway."

"That's interesting," Hurdle said.

"Maybe." Vail gave a glance around the barn interior. "I was Marcks, I'd think twice about taking Reynolds's car because it's a unique year and model and people in these parts know it's his. If they see a strange person driving it, they call Reynolds, don't get an answer, maybe stop by and see the blood."

"Riskier to flag down a hitchhiker," Johnson said.

Probably true.

Vail gave a final look around, her gaze settling on the pooled blood. *So he stabbed Reynolds right here.* She glanced back at the saw, then let her gaze drift a few feet to the left where a shovel leaned against the back wall. *Oh, shit. Don't tell me.* "Where's the body?"

"Well," Hurdle said, "I used the term 'body' loosely because—"

"He cut it up, didn't he?" Vail pulled her eyes away from the rusty tool.

Hurdle shoved both hands in his pockets. "He did."

"Didn't want it found," Curtis said. "Ever."

"So much for the best laid plans of men." Vail shook her head.

"You wanna see the body parts?" Hurdle asked. "You know, so you can form your own opinions. Without bias."

Smartass. "Let's go take a look."

Hurdle lifted his brow. "Detective, what about you?"

"I'm good," Curtis said.

"I got this." Johnson gestured with her chin. "Follow me."

Johnson led the way out back, trudging through the snow, which was still falling—though it had slowed to a flurry.

"You sure you want to see this? Or has the marshal gotten under your skin?" She glanced at Vail and flashed a wide smile.

Vail shared the laugh. "You know me too well, Leslie. Posturing aside, though, still a good idea to take a look."

They walked up to a temporary tent where three crime scene technicians were kneeling over a shallow grave, bright Klieg lights flooding the area.

Vail stepped up and introduced herself. "Find anything unusual?"

The lead crime scene detective was working with a grid, taking a photo of what looked like a hand. "You mean other than a hacked up body buried behind a barn?"

Okay, I deserved that. "Yeah. Other than that."

"He knew what he was doing. Cut through the joints. Shoulder, knee, hip."

"But why? I mean, what if someone sees him hacking away at the body?"

"We have to take a better look around tomorrow," Johnson said, "when we've got some daylight. He probably cut the body up somewhere safe, where no one would see. Maybe inside the barn."

"Fair enough. He probably enjoyed doing it, too. He's been under extreme stress since the escape. Could've been a pressure release valve for him."

Upon returning to the barn, Ray Ramos was there with Travis Walters and Jim Morrison.

Hurdle peered around Morrison when the door opened and found Vail. "I told them all to get their tails over here rather than sitting in the command center by themselves. We'll go through some things, then break for the night."

"I gave them all a quick and dirty rundown of what we're dealing with here," Curtis said.

"You get some good *impressions*?" Hurdle asked.

"I did," Vail said. "Body parts were severed at the joints, which was unnecessary. He could've buried a whole body just as well as one in pieces."

"Easier to dig a smaller hole," Ramos said.

"Correct me if I'm wrong," Vail said. "I'm no carpenter, but I'm pretty sure it takes a lot longer to use a wood saw to cut up a body than it does to dig a larger grave."

"Affirmative," Walters said. "I dabble in my spare time. With woodworking."

I didn't think you dabbled with severed body parts.

"But not only did he have to dig a hole," Ramos said, "he had to dig a hole in frozen ground—after he cleared the snow away. A smaller hole makes sense."

"All true," Walters said. "But it's still easier than sawing through multiple joints."

"Either way," Vail said, "he was taking a big chance. He had to stick around a substantial amount of time to dig the hole or sever the limbs—which is extremely messy and a lot of effort. Even if he did the cutting in a place where he wouldn't be seen, it's still taking a huge, unnecessary risk. It'd fit a smaller grave, yeah, but cutting it up doesn't make it harder to find."

"Meaning what?" Morrison asked.

"Meaning that this could be significant. If this was a new case where I didn't know the killer, I'd say this is part of his ritual. But we know who this offender is. I'm not talking about identity but his psychological basis for the behavior he engages in."

"And?" Hurdle said.

"And I can't say this makes a lot of sense. It *would* if it fit the ritual we've seen in his past murders. But it doesn't."

"So how do you explain it?"

Vail thought about that a moment. "This wasn't a typical victim. If I had to guess on the sequence of events, he was cold and hungry and tired. He came upon the house, saw the barn, and figured he'd take the path of least resistance. Spend the night there, keep out of sight, then in the morning stake out the house, wait for the owner to leave, then break in and get some food, maybe take a shower and get a change of clothes. Cash, if there was any in the house. If he was lucky, a firearm.

"But William Reynolds needed something in the barn and found Marcks sleeping."

"How do you know he was sleeping?" Walters asked.

"I don't. But if he wasn't sleeping, he probably wouldn't have still been in the barn. And based on the blood here, our vic was killed in the barn, not in the house."

"Your point?" Ramos asked.

"Just that this wasn't a planned kill. Probably the opposite. It was one of necessity. Once Reynolds stumbled onto Marcks, he was a goner. Marcks couldn't take a chance on Reynolds blabbering about his whereabouts."

"I thought this guy was smart," Morrison said.

"He is. But even smart criminals make mistakes. Just like smart cops make mistakes. And he's been on the run in the dead of winter—in a snowstorm. He's tired and hungry and he might not be thinking clearly. So he saw the tools and went to town on the body."

"He does have a history of cutting," Curtis said. "He just took it further this time."

"Okay," Hurdle said. "So we know Marcks was here last night and this morning. Anyone else have new information?"

"We do," Curtis said. "Karen and I tracked down one of his buddies, Vincent Stuckey. He's been in contact with Marcks but nothing that's gonna help us. Stuckey's a little slow, so we don't have a problem with the veracity of the information he gave us."

"Slow," Morrison said. "As in . . ."

"As in his bulb ain't too bright."

"He suffered a GSW to the head when he was a teenager," Vail said. "And that brings us to an incident with Marcks back when they were fourteen. Turns out Marcks's first murder was potentially involuntary manslaughter if you believe the lone witness—which was his friend, another guy we've gotta look into. Lance Kubiak."

"Kubiak," Ramos said. "You sure of that?"

Vail glanced at Curtis, who nodded. "Yeah. Lance Kubiak. He was a childhood friend of Marcks. Kubiak, Marcks, and Stuckey were supposedly hanging out, getting high, when this loner comes up to them, a kid they knew. Name was Eddie. He brought a gun to the gathering and Marcks and Eddie got into it, the gun went off, killed Eddie and wounded Stuckey. No charges were brought."

Ramos had his pocket spiral notebook out and was flipping the pages. "Kubiak. Lance Kubiak."

"Like I said. Yeah. Why?"

"Because Lance Kubiak also happens to be the name of a correctional officer at Potter."

23

Marcks stood in the backyard, which was well shielded from surrounding homes by dense trees and hedges. Even in winter, they provided more than adequate concealment.

He inched over to the back door and looked through the large picture window: leather sofas, stone flooring of some kind, indirect lighting that shone up toward the ceiling rather than down toward the floor.

A redhead, thirties, attractive, with a substantial diamond ring and matching tennis bracelet, flitted by. She was rushing about the kitchen putting together a snack of some sort as the child, maybe four or five, sat in front of a flat-panel television that filled the wall opposite the couch.

They had plasma TVs before he went away to prison, but nothing this big, this bright. He would not mind spending a few nights in this place. He would have to see how things transpired in the next hour or so to determine if that was feasible.

Marcks tried the doorknob, to no avail. He had learned a long time ago to always check because you never knew; people were funny that way, thinking that for some reason it was safe to leave their houses unlocked—while others just could not be bothered or did not give it a second thought.

No matter; it just made the intrusion a little bit tougher. One of his former cellmates, Orlando, schooled him in the best way to approach such a situation. He could have pulled it off without Orlando's tips, but why not learn from someone who had experience? Of course he asked Orlando, not so tactfully, if the reason for his ending up in the slammer was from a failed home invasion. It was not, so he felt confident that the counsel Orlando was meting out was solid.

Marcks checked the door one last time, evaluating it like his former roommate had described. Then he kicked it in, using just the right amount of pressure to pop the lock. Do it wrong and you could injure your knee and ankle, and he wanted no part of that.

The noise from the TV partially masked the bang. He was careful not to let the door swing open so hard that it struck something on the rebound and shattered the glass. That was sure to attract attention.

The woman turned, locked eyes with Marcks—and froze. Her body recoiled in fear, shoulders drawing forward, hands coming out in front of her—as if that would stop him.

She opened her mouth to scream, but Marcks was prepared. And faster. He leaped forward and clamped his large hand down on her fine-boned face.

"No need to make noise," he said calmly into her ear. "I'm not going to hurt you or your daughter. *If* you cooperate and do what I tell you to do. The opposite's true, too. Do anything that puts me in a bad way and I'll kill you both and worry about the consequences later. It's survival instinct, understand?" He leaned back, appraised her face. She was terrified, eyes glazed and straining left, trying to see her little girl. "Nod if you understand everything I just told you. No noise, no problems for me, you and your daughter live. Got it?"

She nodded vigorously, indicating that she had a grasp of the situation.

"I'm going to let go of your mouth. Tell me your name. Calmly. And quietly." He glanced over at the girl; she was still engrossed in her cartoon. It was an animated show featuring animals. Now there's a unique concept. "Here we go," he said as he released the pressure on her face.

"Victoria," she whispered.

"Good, Victoria." Orlando had told him to use their names as much as possible. "And your girl's?"

"Cassie."

"Very nice. I like Cassie. Now, in a minute you're going to introduce me to her as a guest and tell her that she should make me feel welcome. Got it?"

Victoria nodded.

"When's your husband due home?"

Victoria's gaze went wild: up, down, left, right. Orlando had told him to always read the eyes because they held the key to what the person was thinking.

"No, no, no, Victoria. A lie will only piss me off." He clenched his jaw. "And I'm getting kind of angry even entertaining the thought that you'd *think* of lying to me." He left his fury exposed, using it to show her that he could turn on her at any second. It was just like training a dog. Do as I say and I'll give you a treat. But do something bad, pee in the house, and you'll be very, very sorry.

He pointed his finger at her, put it right in her face, inches away from her eyes. "Tell me truthfully. When's your husband due home?"

"In—in—what time is it?" She blurted it and Cassie turned, perhaps thinking that her mother was asking her the question.

"Now, Victoria," he said under his breath. "I'm a guest. Tell her."

Victoria tried to make her face smile. "Cassie, honey, we have a guest. He's come by for . . . for dinner. Let's make him feel at home, okay?"

Cassie slid off the couch and walked into the kitchen. She leaned against her mother's right leg and wrapped her arm around her thigh, sizing up Marcks. "What's your name?"

"It's Lee. Nice to meet you."

Her gaze drifted around his body and face. He had not showered and his clothing did not fit well, so he probably looked a bit ragged.

He did as Orlando suggested: forge ahead, not allow them any time to think.

"So how old are you, Cassie?" He let his voice rise and fall like he did with Jasmine when she was young. Regardless of what she said about him, he treated her well.

She held up five fingers.

"Five's a good age." He wanted to get rid of her, to send her back to the television without doing it too obviously. "What's that show you're watching? I'm not familiar with it."

"Wild Kratts."

She was not saying much, which went along with her body language—fear, perhaps shyness around strangers. But he also had to be prepared to handle an unpredictable outburst, the wildcard in a situation like this.

He knew what Victoria was thinking: could he kill a child?

"I think Cassie should go back and enjoy the rest of her program, don't you, mom?"

"Yes, honey, go back to the couch and watch your show." She pushed her gently away from her leg and, using both hands on her daughter's back, guided her toward the family room.

As Cassie walked away—glancing over her shoulder at Marcks—he grinned at her and then said to Victoria, between his teeth, "When's your husband coming home?"

"Four-thirty. Any—any minute."

Marcks felt his shoulder muscles tighten. His mind went blank. He squinted, trying to recover, hide his sudden weakness. "Is there a gun in the house?"

"We don't believe in guns."

He turned and surveyed the kitchen. A Henkel knife block sat on the dark gray, black and white granite counter beneath the window. He stepped over and pulled out a couple, chose a serrated blade of medium length. "Very good. Recently sharpened."

"What are you—what are you going to do with it?"

"I'm not going to kill you with it, if that's what you're worried about. Or anyone else. If you cooperate."

"Then why do you need it?"

"Victoria. Really? It's in case you *don't* cooperate." And for control. But he did not tell her that. He slipped it into his back jeans pocket.

A low rumble vibrated by the far wall.

"Daddy's home!" Cassie said as she slid off the couch.

Marcks rushed across the room and took Cassie by the hand. "Shh. Hang on there, darlin'. Let's surprise him." He put his large hand across her belly and lifted her up in one motion toward his body. "I've got a present for him and I don't want to ruin the surprise. Okay?"

"What's the surprise?"

"Oh, it's a really good one. Wait till you see his face." Without taking his eyes off the family room door that led to the garage, he said, "Victoria. What's his name?"

Victoria put a hand over her mouth and mumbled, "Nathan." It came out as a muffled whimper, but Marcks understood what she said.

Marcks moved into the blindside of the door as it opened and Nathan walked in. Physically fit—but no threat to Marcks, who had about four inches and fifty to seventy-five pounds of muscle on him.

Nathan saw his wife's terrified face and stepped farther into the house as he swung his head left, toward Marcks. But it was clear his brain did not register the man's presence. His gaze was fixed on to Cassie.

"Who are you?" Nathan said, recovering.

Marcks kicked the door shut. He was not going to give Nathan a chance to escape back into the garage. Then again, he was reasonably certain that a husband and father would not leave his wife and daughter with an intruder.

"Just do what I say and no one gets hurt."

"Who the hell do you think you are?" Nathan repeated, anger and dominance permeating his tone.

And this was another moment where Orlando's guidance would prove useful. Nathan was likely a man of importance;

perhaps a vice president or even a CEO. Someone accustomed to being in charge, calling the shots. Directing people around.

Marcks reached into his pocket and drew the knife out. He held it up. He did not slap it against the girl's neck. He did not raise his voice.

Cassie began crying. She squirmed but Marcks held her against his body with a vise-like grip. He brought his right hand, which held the Henkel blade, against her mouth.

"I'm the man holding your wife and daughter at knife point. I'm the man you're going to listen to, the man you're going to be courteous to. Got it, Nathan?"

Nathan's eyes widened. His breathing became shallower, his bravado replaced by fear for his family's well-being. "Just—just put my daughter down. Let my wife leave with my daughter."

"Victoria and Cassie aren't going anywhere," Marcks said. He knew that using their names, thereby showing familiarity with Nathan's family, would be unnerving. Questions would be darting through his thoughts: what else did he know about them? Had he been stalking them? What was this about?"

"What jewelry and cash do you have in your house?"

"I—I, uh—"

"Do not lie to me," Marcks said. "Victoria and I have already been through this. Tell him, Vicky."

"Tell him the truth," she stammered. "And he won't hurt any of us."

Marcks turned back to Nathan and tilted his head. "And your answer is?"

"We've got some diamond rings here. Nothing big. And about two hundred in cash."

"That's it?" Marcks shouted it, scaring Cassie again. "Quiet," he said, squeezing the girl tighter.

"How much do you usually withdraw when you go to the bank?"

"I—I don't know, it varies."

"What's the most?"

Nathan looked to Victoria. Clearly she was the one who took care of the banking chores.

"Five thousand," she said.

Marcks shifted his weight and looked at Cassie. "I'm going to release my hand. You are not to cry or scream or yell. If you do, I'll hurt you. Understand?"

She began whimpering but did not say anything.

"Did you hear me?" he said firmly.

"Yes."

He removed his hand from her mouth and pointed the knife at Nathan. "Get over there with your wife."

Nathan complied and Victoria nearly jumped into his arms.

Back to Victoria: "How often have you withdrawn five grand?"

"I don't know," she said with a sniffle, her eyes riveted to Cassie. "Twice, maybe."

"Did it draw attention? Did they ask you about it?"

"Not on our account," Nathan said. "Five thousand isn't a big deal."

"I asked Victoria, Nathan. Keep your mouth shut."

Marcks looked at Victoria and lifted his brow.

"Like Nathan said. It's not a problem."

"Okay." Still holding Cassie, Marcks paced down the hallway, turned, and walked back. "Victoria, you're going to go in there and withdraw four thousand dollars."

She swallowed. "Okay."

"And why are you taking the money out?" Marcks asked.

"Why?" Nathan asked. "Because you're holding us hostage."

"Wrong fuckin' answer, *Nathan*. See, you say something stupid like that and cops'll come here and I'll kill you and your daughter." He turned to Victoria. "Now I'll ask again. And I want *you* to answer. Why are you withdrawing this money?"

"We—we're doing some landscape work and the contractor wanted to be paid in cash because he had to lay out the money for the trees he planted."

Marcks shook his head. "In the dead of winter, with snow on the ground? You planted trees?"

"I—I, uh, we had new carpeting installed."

Marcks grinned slyly. "Very good, Victoria. Very good. And how far away is the bank?"

"Fifteen minutes. At most. Probably twelve."

Marcks nodded slowly. "Let's both check the time." He gestured at the digital radio-controlled clock hanging in the kitchen. "You can get there and make the withdrawal before they close. Be back here in forty minutes."

"What—what if I'm late? It's rush hour. I can't control—"

"I'm a reasonable guy, Victoria. Tell you what. If you're late, I won't kill your daughter. Or your husband." He held up the knife. "But I will chop off one finger of Nathan's right hand for every five minutes you're past due. Fair enough?"

Victoria's mouth dropped open and tears welled up in her eyes.

"I'm talking to you, Victoria. Fair enough?"

She nodded quickly, words still too difficult to form in her hysterical state.

"Good. Give me your cell phone."

Victoria dug it out of her purse and handed it over.

"Now remember. If I smell anything wrong. If I hear anything out of the ordinary. If I see a car pull up anywhere it's not supposed to, I'm going to stick this knife in your daughter's stomach. Then—" He stopped himself. "Well, you don't want to know what I'll do after that, trust me." He gave her a reassuring smile. "Now take a deep breath with me." Marcks threw his shoulders back and filled his lungs. Victoria forced herself to follow suit. "That's it. Good. Okay now. Forty minutes. Starting . . . *now*."

Victoria ran for the garage door.

24

A chill rattled Vail's body. "This correctional officer. Kubiak. Have you interviewed him?"

Ramos stamped his boots against the barn's cement floor. "Scheduled for tomorrow morning, 11:00 AM."

"Mind if I sit in on that?"

"If you think it'd help, fine with me."

"What are the ramifications of this?" Curtis asked.

Hurdle folded his arms across his chest. "First thought is that this is no coincidence. Second thought is that Kubiak had a hand in the escape. And if he's willing to risk his career to break Marcks out of Potter, he may've arranged other things for his friend. Third and most important thought is that he may know something about his whereabouts."

"So you don't think we should wait till tomorrow," Ramos said.

"Hell no. Get over there now. I'll call Potter, see if Kubiak's shift is over. If not, I'll make sure he hangs out till you get there but I'll make it clear they're not to freak him out. We just have some questions. We're looking for help locating the fugitive. That's it. If he's gone for the day, I'll get his home address."

"This guy a flight risk?" Vail asked.

"Only if he realizes that we're on to him. Regardless, I don't want to get blindsided. Until we know what his deal is, whether he's helped Marcks or not—and I'm thinking he probably did—we treat him as a person of interest and a potential flight risk. Let him prove otherwise."

"We've got a wiretap in place for Marcks," Ramos said. "Since we're already up on that wire, let's see if we can get something from Kubiak."

Vail pulled out her phone to text Robby that she was not going to make dinner. "Looking for what?"

"I'm thinking we drop some bread crumbs, then watch him eat. If he does shit his pants when he hears we want to talk to him, he may call Marcks—or someone who's in contact with Marcks—which may ultimately *lead* us to Marcks."

"It's a slower approach," Hurdle said, "but I like the idea. And if we weren't dealing with a violent criminal who's just killed two people, I'd be on board. But I'm not sure we have time to wait and see if Kubiak *may* have a way of contacting him." He turned to Tarkoff. "Ben, what do you think?"

Tarkoff leaned back in his chair. "Try it for a few hours and see if he bites. A guy like that, if he really did put his career on the line to help Marcks get out, he's gonna want to warn him ASAP. I say if we haven't heard anything in three hours, we have another chat with him."

Hurdle rocked back on his heels a few seconds. "Okay. Do it."

"Does Kubiak have a wife and kids?" Vail asked.

"Married, one young son," Ramos said. "And he rents. Doesn't own his home."

"So if he is involved, his career's over anyway. He could take off."

"Let's make sure that doesn't happen," Hurdle said. "Yes?"

"Hell yeah," Ramos said as he gathered his keys off the worktable.

"Take Vail, get up there, and sell it good. Don't give Kubiak any reason to think we know he's Marcks's bud."

25

Marcks sat on the living room couch facing the front window. The curtains were drawn, but he could see through them whenever headlights turned toward the house. While that would give him some warning if police or tactical vehicles came up the driveway, if they set up shop down the street and approached on foot, he was screwed.

Of course, this whole escape was fraught with risks. Tonight was just one of many.

Nathan sat facing him three feet away. Not far enough to attempt an escape and not close enough to present a threat. Not that he presented a threat to Marcks. But it was better to follow Orlando's rules of engagement—and that meant keeping your distance.

Cassie was between them, crying.

"At least let me comfort her," Nathan said.

Marcks glared at him. "Stay right where you are. She'll get over it."

"She's just a little kid."

"I can see that."

"Why are you doing this to us?"

Marcks debated whether or not to answer him. "Because you had what I needed. I think you could just chalk it up to wrong place, wrong time. In other words, rotten fu—rotten friggin' luck."

"Are you going to let us go?"

Marcks looked away. "All depends on Victoria, Nathan. Simple as that."

Victoria had been gone for thirty-eight minutes. Nathan kept checking his luxury watch, no doubt stressing over what was going to happen to them.

"I'd like to see that," Marcks said, gesturing at the timepiece.

"See it or steal it?" Nathan asked.

Marcks gave him an icy stare. "What kind is it?"

"Tag Heuer. My fifteenth anniversary present."

"Very touching." He held out his left hand.

Nathan unhooked the latch and handed it over, then gave Cassie a brave wink. Trying to add a positive spin to the grim situation. If Dad was confident all would be okay, everything had to work out.

Marcks tried to put the watch on, but it was too tight. He slipped it into his jeans pocket.

"Where do you keep your medicine?"

Nathan turned away from Cassie. "What?"

"Your medicine cabinet. For the kid. Where is it?"

"Her bathroom, down the hall."

"Let's go. Lead the way. Cassie, take my hand."

She stopped crying long enough to shake her head, an emphatic no.

Marcks was not deterred. He gathered her up into his arms, bear-hugging her as they walked down the hallway.

"Don't hurt her," Nathan said.

"I'm not hurting her," he said as they passed the master bedroom. "Wait." He pushed Nathan inside, then went to the vanity that Nathan and Victoria used. "Where's your shaver?"

Nathan slid a drawer open.

Marcks removed a Norelco, a comb, and a pair of scissors. He saw a leather Dopp kit embossed with a George Mason University logo and inserted the grooming items, then took the bag with him back down the hall.

They entered Cassie's bathroom and Marcks set her down next to the sink.

"Open the cabinet."

Nathan did as instructed and Marcks perused its contents. There were a few over-the-counter bottles, a couple of homeopathic remedies, Children's Tylenol, and—Benadryl.

"Open the Benadryl and fill the little plastic cup."

Nathan struggled with the child protective top.

"Calm down, Nathan. Take a breath."

He did just that and steadied his hand long enough to remove the cap. He poured the red liquid, then handed it to Marcks.

"No, it's for her."

"For her—no. She doesn't need—"

"Don't fucking argue with me, Nathan." He clenched his fist. "It's not a good idea. Or *I'll* give her the medication and I might not be so gentle."

Nathan turned to his daughter and told her to open her mouth. She looked at him, showing some understanding of what was going on—that her daddy was being forced to do things he did not want to do. Still, he was asking her to take medicine, which didn't always taste good. But it was something her parents told her was good for her.

She opened her mouth and Nathan poured it in. She made a face but swallowed.

"Now you," Marcks said. "Same thing."

Nathan did as he was told.

"Now take that bottle with us back out to the living room." As they walked down the hall, Marcks said, "Where's your duct tape?"

"Duct tape?"

"Everybody's got fuckin' duct tape, Nathan. I'm not in the mood to play games."

"Garage."

They retrieved a half-full roll and went into the kitchen, where Marcks made Cassie sit in one of the seats. He went about securing her wrists and ankles to the arms and legs, then placed a strip across her lips and around her neck. By now the Benadryl was having its intended effect, and her crying had become soft, drowsy whimpers.

As he sliced the last strip of tape, Marcks heard the vibration of the garage door rolling up. In walked Victoria.

"Is—is everything okay?"

"We're all fine," Marcks said. "Thanks for asking."

She did not think that was funny. Her eyes found Cassie as she walked into the kitchen. "What's wrong with her? What'd you do to her?"

"You have something for me?"

Victoria handed over an envelope about a half-inch thick and went over to Cassie's side.

"Leave her alone, Victoria. She's fine just the way she is." Marcks gave a quick glance inside and saw greenbacks. "And now we've got something for you. Nathan, give your wife a dose."

"What?" Victoria turned to Nathan and watched as he filled the cap. "Benadryl?"

"Just looking out for your well-being. Drink it."

Nathan nodded and she tipped it back into her mouth.

"One more, Nathan."

"Two? But—"

"I said one more."

Victoria drank that as well.

"Great. Now, Victoria, did you say anything to anyone while you were gone?"

"Of course not. I did what you asked."

"Winter coats?"

Victoria looked at Nathan, then indicated the hall closet.

Marcks took hold of Victoria's arm. "Nathan, go get three wool hats."

"How do you know we've got three wool hats?"

Marcks stared him down. "Go get the hats."

Nathan's left eye twitched—but he apparently calmed his anger and did not make trouble. He trudged off and retrieved the articles of clothing.

Marcks took them and slipped one over Cassie's head, covering her eyes. He stepped over to Nathan and held out his left hand. "Car keys. What do you drive?"

"Mercedes."

"That'll do."

Nathan hesitated, then pulled them from his pocket and gave them to Marcks, who turned to Victoria.

"Seems kind of weird for me to say this, but thank you for following the rules, Vicky. Have a seat at the other end of the kitchen table."

Marcks secured her just like he had done with Cassie—except

that for her, he stuffed a rag in her mouth before sealing her lips with duct tape. He pulled the second hat over her head and, as with Cassie, brought it down to the level of the bridge of her nose.

"When does your cleaning person come?"

Nathan recoiled. "How do you—"

"By now you've gotta know I'm not some dumbshit criminal. Somebody with your kind of money doesn't clean his own toilets and mop the floors. Just answer the question."

"Wednesdays. Around noon."

Marcks absorbed that, thought a moment. The timing would work. He would be far enough away when the maid would discover her subdued boss. "Give me your cell phone."

Nathan fished it out of his jacket pocket, but before Marcks took it, he said, "Call your office and tell them you've got a stomach flu and you won't be in for a few days. Make it convincing."

When he finished, Marcks took the mobile from Nathan and switched it off, dropped it to the tile floor and smashed it with his heel. He then did the same to Victoria's.

He picked up the last wool hat and duct tape and turned to Nathan. "It's just you and me. Let's go."

"Go? I thought you were just gonna leave us alone. We did everything you asked!"

"Calm down, Nathan. I don't want to have to make you relax. Because I will."

"No. I've had enough. You want my car? Fine, take it. You want my watch? Take that too. But just leave—"

Nathan never saw it coming. The first punch struck him in the abdomen and the second fractured his left cheekbone.

Victoria and Cassie could not see what was happening but they could undoubtedly hear—and their imaginations filled in the rest. While their muffled cries expressed their emotions, they did nothing to reverse Nathan's fortunes.

Marcks hoisted Nathan over his shoulder and strode out to the Mercedes, chirped the remote, and was on the road thirty seconds later.

26

Vail and Ramos pulled into the Potter Correctional Facility parking lot at 6:00 PM. After securing their firearms they were led to the warden's office. Jimmy Barfield was sharing a laugh with an officer when Vail and Ramos were led in.

"Warden," Vail said with a nod.

The guard—doing his best to stifle his cackling—vacated the lone guest chair and made his way out of the small room.

Vail and Ramos remained standing, sending the message that they were there on business.

"You know," Barfield said, "when I told you to come on back real soon, I didn't really mean it. Figure of speech."

"Last time I was here, Roscoe Lee Marcks was still under lock and key. I was worried about his daughter, not him breaking out." *Nice work.*

"Well, things change. That's life, Agent Vail."

"Anything we should know about since he escaped?"

"Been fairly quiet. Any progress in your investigation?"

"Some things, yes. But we're not anywhere close to finding Marcks."

"Which is why we're here," Ramos said.

"I was wondering about that, Agent Ramos. I really don't see the need for you to interview my entire staff."

"We're not interviewing your entire staff. Not tonight, at least. But we will. Including you. If fact, I now have an opening in my schedule tomorrow. So how 'bout you put me down for 11:00 AM."

I like this guy.

Barfield ground his jaw. "I can do that."

"We'll hit the other executive staff every thirty minutes after that. Please see that it gets done."

Barfield's eyes narrowed.

"Meantime," Vail said, "we're ready to sit down with Officer Kubiak."

"And what's that about?"

"That's between us and Officer Kubiak."

"I'm the warden of this institution," Barfield said. "And—"

"And that counts for shit when we're talking about a federal manhunt for a fugitive who's already killed two people since his escape. Which—in case you hadn't noticed—happened under your watch."

Barfield's face shaded the color of blood. "Yeah, well, Kubiak's not available to talk to you."

Vail stepped closer to Barfield's desk. "And why's that, Warden?"

"Because I sent him away."

"Where, exactly?"

"That's for me to worry about." He stood up and hiked his pants. "Understand something, Agent Vail. I'm the boss here. If there's something you want to know, you go through me."

Vail glanced at Ramos. "That's not how this is going to work."

"Says who?"

Vail pulled her badge from her belt and slammed it on the table. "The FBI. You have ten seconds to tell us where Lance Kubiak is. Ramos and I don't have time for ego and testosterone."

Barfield sucked his teeth, mulling it over.

She made a show of checking her watch. "In five seconds we're going to place you under arrest for obstruction. You'll lose your job. And that means you won't get another position with federal law enforcement."

Barfield's face darkened. The vein in his right temple pulsed rhythmically.

What's this guy's role in the escape? His posturing was about to cross the line into self-preservation, where cooperating would be more detrimental than stonewalling them. Vail pulled a set of handcuffs off her belt. "James Barfield, you are—"

"He's here," Barfield said. "He's down the hall. I'll go get him."

"No," Ramos said. "Tell us where. You stay here. We'll go."

Following Barfield's instructions, Vail and Ramos filed into the corridor and hung a left at the end of the institutional-tiled corridor. Three dozen feet later, they turned right and walked into a room where a middle-aged man sat. His face was taut, his eyes glassy and fatigued.

"Officer Kubiak. I'm Karen Vail, FBI. This is Ray Ramos, HSI."

"I had an appointment with Agent Ramos for tomorrow morning. Why do we have to do this tonight?"

Ramos shrugged. "Because my boss said we have to."

"We're looking into the escape of Roscoe Lee Marcks. Are you familiar with Marcks?"

"He's an inmate here. Of course I know who he is."

Vail nodded. "Good, good. Agent Ramos and I serve on the Marshals fugitive task force so we're trying to track down any leads that may help us apprehend him. His daughter's been cooperating and we're *real* close, but it'd be great if you can help us speed up the process. People are at risk each day he's in the wild."

"How well do you know him?" Ramos asked.

"He's not on my block, but I've seen him around. I don't think I've said ten words to him."

Vail elbowed Ramos. "You got a picture of him?"

"Don't have one with me. Officer Kubiak, you know who he is on sight, right? You clear who we're talking about here?"

"Oh, yeah, of course."

"So where do you think he is? One of the things we try to do with this task force is compile information on who the fugitive might know, places he might go."

"No idea. Like I said, I've barely said ten words to him in four years."

You're up on exactly how long he's served at Potter? Someone you barely know?

"Why are you asking me about that? What about the other COs? We've got guards who were on his block, who know more about Marcks than I ever could."

"We've already spoken with some of them," Ramos said. "And I'm gonna be talking with others tomorrow morning. We'll be talking to everyone."

"You know the nurse who was with Marcks when he escaped?"

Kubiak's shoulders slumped. "Yeah. Nice lady. Always had a smile, good things to say about people here."

"So you were surprised that Marcks killed her."

"We all were. I mean, why bother? What kind of threat was she to him?"

"A guy like Marcks doesn't need a reason to kill," Vail said. "You're a correctional officer. I'm not telling you anything you don't already know."

Kubiak made a show of agreeing with her—a bit too overzealously, in her opinion. If she did not already know he was deceiving her, that would have tipped her off that something was not quite right.

"So you don't have any information that can help us locate him," Ramos said. "No one you think he'd contact, hang out with, ask for money, look to for help, that kinda thing."

"Wish I could help," Kubiak said. "But no. I just didn't know the guy. And since he wasn't on my block, I have no idea about his personal life, people he may trust or lean on when he's on the run."

"Do us a favor and call us if you think of anything that can help us." Vail and Ramos handed him their cards.

"Of course. I want this asshole caught soon as possible. Before he hurts anyone else."

Vail gave him a disarming grin. "Thanks so much, Officer Kubiak. We really appreciate your time."

THE COLD AIR HIT VAIL'S CHEEKS when they entered the parking lot, the breeze bringing the wind chill down to well below zero. At least the snow had stopped.

Although the sodium vapor lights illuminated the area well, the isolation of the prison building gave it an eerie feel, as if it were the only sign of life for miles in all directions. "So we've got people listening in?"

"If he makes a call," Ramos said, pulling out his car keys, "we'll know about it."

"Clock's ticking. We should go get a bite to eat, use the restroom while we can."

Ramos laughed. "What, are you going all Special Forces on me?"

"Special Forces?" Vail fought to keep a straight face. "I wouldn't know anything about that stuff."

27

Vail looked up at the racing flag-style sign, which read "BLUES" in red letters, protruding from a weathered vertical wood plank facing.

"I think the owners of this restaurant missed an opportunity."

Ramos sat forward in his car seat. "What are you talking about?"

"The sign says Blues and it's red. Shouldn't it be . . . I don't know, is blue too obvious?"

"All I care about is the food. Their barbeque pulled pork is awesome."

Fifteen minutes later, Vail was staring at Ramos's plate. "I'm not sure about those fried pickles."

"What?" Ramos leaned back and appraised the side dish, tilting his head. "Are you saying they look like a bowl of penises?"

"Kind of, yeah."

"Want to taste one? They're very good."

"I'll pass. But I will try one of those hush puppies."

"Go for it." Ramos gestured at her meal. "How's the crab cake?"

"Very good. Glad I listened to you."

"I don't get to Moorefield, West Virginia, very often. But when I do, I've gotta stop at Blues Smoke Pit."

She looked past his head at the framed Jackson Browne album cover on the wall. "I have that CD. People think it's called 'Saturate Before Using' because those are the only words on the cover. But that's just the label of a burlap bag that's pictured in the photo on the cover. The album's really only called 'Jackson Browne.' It was his first."

"Thanks for that bit of trivia," Ramos said. "I can now die happy."

"Not a Jackson Browne fan?"

"I'd rather talk about Roscoe Lee Marcks."

Vail stopped chewing. "Seriously? Hall of Fame rock musician or depraved serial killer and you'd rather talk about the killer? Over dinner?"

"I've got an iron stomach."

Vail lifted her brow. "Suit yourself. But if you lose it, lean left or right. Don't vomit all over me. Deal?"

"You think I'm some kind of wuss?"

"I'd never call you a wuss, Rambo. So what do you want to know about Marcks?"

"What makes him tick? What kind of asshole are we dealing with? If I can get a sense of who this guy is, maybe it'll help me think like him."

Vail pursed her lips and gave a nod. "I agree with your approach. So, I didn't do the behavioral assessment on Marcks. I inherited the file when I joined the unit. And I was learning, feeling my way. I had a sense of things, but compared to what I know now, well, as in anything, you get better the more you do something. So I'm starting to think I should give his assessment a fresh look."

"The profiler who had the case before you did, he wasn't any good?"

"Thomas Underwood? Shit yeah. He was one of the founding fathers, he made the BAU what it became. Ressler, Underwood, Douglas, Hazelwood. Those guys were visionaries."

"But."

"But maybe Underwood was distracted, thinking more about retirement than about his last case. I don't know. Maybe that's not fair. None of us are perfect. Maybe he missed something. I've got a call into him to ask him some questions."

Ramos picked up one of the fried pickles and took a bite. "So what are you seeing now that conflicts with the profile?"

"Can you not do that while I'm . . . just put that thing down. Given what I'm about to tell you, it's in poor taste. So to speak."

Ramos looked at the pickle, then dropped it on the plate and sat back. "Done."

"I'm working on the theory that Marcks is a homosexual sadomasochist."

"Okay. Is that unusual?"

"Not sure how to answer that. There've been a lot of them, relatively speaking. One of the legendary homicide detectives, Vernon Geberth, broke out the most common types of homosexual serial killers into three groups: those who target male homosexuals, those who go after both gay and heterosexual male victims, and those whose victim preference is young males and boys—pedophiles. Homosexual serial murders typically involve sadomasochistic torture and lust murders, as well as child and thrill killings.

"In one variation or another, you've got some of the better known ones. Jeffery Dahmer. John Wayne Gacy, Wayne

Williams. William Bonin. And two really sick bastards—as if the others weren't depraved enough—Robert Berdella and Larry Eyler. If we look at common features across a broad spectrum of homosexual serial killers, we see role-playing, domination and control, humiliation, sadistic sexual acts. They often commit lust murders, where the offender focuses his attention on the sexualized areas of the body, like cutting or excising the genital areas."

"Like a penis or vulva?"

Vail glanced down at the plate of pickles. "Yeah. And nipples, rectum, throat, or breasts. Evisceration is also common."

Ramos bit his top lip. "Okay."

"So Marcks exhibited some of this, as you know. But other key characteristics weren't present. He didn't engage in overt domination and control role playing—as far as we know. But another common feature, keeping a trophy of the killings, he did do. It's the one thing that tied together a lot of the murders after he was arrested, at least circumstantially. Some, but not all, of the vics were represented in this trophy stash. He kept them stored behind a false wall in his bedroom closet."

"Them? What kind of trophies?"

"The excised sexual organs."

Ramos contorted his face as if he had bitten into a lemon rind. He reached for his glass of water and took a long drink.

"Wanna hear more?"

Before he could answer, his phone rang. He snatched it up, no doubt to prevent Vail from continuing. "Rambo." He listened, his eyes darting left and right. "You sure?" He waited a second, then said, "Got it. Thanks."

"Kubiak?"

"Yeah. Made a call two minutes ago to—are you ready?—a guy named Booker Gaines. He's on our list."

"Haven't been able to find him."

"Kubiak obviously knows how to reach him. He told Gaines to get word to Marcks that he's in trouble, that the feds think they're closing in on him. And that his daughter's been cooperating with them."

"You said you were with West Virginia State Police, right?"

"Before HSI, yeah. Why?" He slapped the table. "You want to know if I still have any buddies on the force."

"In case we need to arrest Kubiak, we'll need a local. State warrant's gonna be a whole lot faster than going through an AUSA to get a federal warrant."

Ramos made the call and ten minutes later, Detective Terrence Linscombe was on board. "We'll take him in on state charges of obstruction, which'll give us time to get a federal warrant for aiding and abetting."

"Perfect." Vail wiped her mouth with a napkin, then rose from her seat. "Let's go get him."

"Is this the fun part of the job or what?"

Ninety minutes later, a warrant in Linscombe's figurative back pocket, Vail and Ramos rolled up in front of Lance Kubiak's home, a small ranch house six miles from the correctional facility. It was well maintained—as best as could be observed with the accumulated snow—with an American flag flapping in the cold breeze above the entrance.

"I'm pretty confident Kubiak helped Marcks escape," Vail said, "in one way or another. But I wouldn't consider him a violent threat. What do you think? Will he freak when he sees us here?"

"Maybe." Ramos pulled out his SIG Sauer P229. "Nothing a good gunfight won't solve."

Vail gave him a crooked smile. "Why don't I go in without you. Less threatening. Once I walk in, give me a couple of minutes, then knock."

"Fine, we'll do it your way. Not as exciting as busting in a door."

"Idea is to talk to him, Rambo, draw him out. We're not in Iraq."

"And thank God for that. You know I was just kidding, right? About the gunfight?"

Sure hope so. "How long till Linscombe gets here?"

Ramos checked his watch. "He's about ten out. He'll be ready to move in when I text him."

Vail shut her door quietly and headed up the icy concrete walk. She was about to knock when the door pulled open.

"Agent Vail."

"Officer Kubiak."

He was dressed in a bulky navy blue sweatshirt that bore a gold embroidered Bureau of Prisons logo over his left breast.

"Warden Barfield gave me your address. I forgot to ask you something and he didn't want to make you drag your ass back to the prison after a long shift." She laughed. "His words, not mine. Anyway, I'm headed home tonight, so he figured you'd rather I stop by on my way back to DC. Said he was gonna call."

"Oh, yeah?" He looked over his shoulder, then back at Vail. "He didn't."

"Probably got tied up with something. Can I come in?"

"Umm—" He turned again and looked behind him.

"Great," she said. "Thanks." She stepped inside, the signal for Ramos to follow.

"How about the living room?"

"Uh . . . well—"

Vail led the way toward the couch and took a seat on the chair. She detected the distinct smell of marijuana. And on the coffee table was a bottle of Budweiser—with a half-smoked joint beside it. *Now I know why he wasn't keen on letting me in.* "Your wife or kids here?"

"At my mom's house. Should be home soon."

A knock at the door made Kubiak jump. "Oh, that's Agent Ramos. Mind getting it?"

Kubiak stood up from the couch and hesitated, looked left—into the kitchen—and Vail stepped behind him, her hand on the Glock in its harness. Just in case. He swung his gaze back to her . . . and lowered it to Vail's weapon.

"Answer it, officer."

"Is there a problem?"

"You tell me."

He hesitated, no doubt trying to figure out what was going on, perhaps wondering if she was going to bust him on possession of a joint. "No problem."

"Then let's not keep Agent Ramos waiting."

Kubiak headed down the hall and opened the door. Ramos entered.

"More comfortable in the living room," Vail said.

Kubiak looked from Vail to Ramos. "Okay."

They sat down around the coffee table, Vail subtly gesturing at the joint.

"His wife and kids are due home soon."

Ramos nodded.

That was a variable that had to be accounted for. They needed to work fast. Depending on Kubiak's involvement, they might need to have Linscombe hook him up. But the timing was key; handcuff him too soon and he might ask for a lawyer. And it would be better if he was secured when the family walked in. Even better if they could be gone before the wife and son arrived.

They could legitimately get Kubiak for the marijuana, but it would be weak. She preferred something stronger. But at the very least, an arrest on state charges for obstruction—as well as possession—would buy them some time to dig deeper into Kubiak's interactions with Marcks, both before and after the escape. She would give it a few minutes to unfold and if nothing better materialized they'd go with what they had.

"So why'd you really come out here?" Kubiak asked.

"Just some things that we need to clarify," Vail said. "Like when you said you don't really know who Roscoe Lee Marcks is."

"That's right. He's one of two thousand inmates and he's not even on my block."

"But he was on your *block*. When you were kids."

Kubiak swallowed but did not answer.

"We know you're friends with him." Vail waited but Kubiak did not react. "We know about the incident with Vincent Stuckey and Eddie Simmons when you were fourteen."

"So what? Nothing against the law about having friends."

"You don't see the problem here?" Ramos snorted. "You're a correctional officer at a facility that houses one of your childhood friends. And not only didn't you disclose that, but you lied to us about it."

"I didn't lie about it."

"Really?" Vail said. "Lance, you're a law enforcement officer. Let's not play games. Now's the time to come clean. We need to know of anyone you can think of who'd have contact with Marcks after the escape. Or who might know how to get word to him."

"Don't know anyone like that."

"You must have a shovel here," Ramos said, "Because you're doing a good goddamn job of digging your own grave."

Vail reached forward and gathered up a small, framed photo of what was likely Kubiak's son. "We know you talked with Booker Gaines. You were trying to warn Marcks that we're getting close. And that his daughter's cooperating with us."

"So now you're going to answer some questions for us," Ramos said.

Kubiak worked his jaw, staring straight ahead. "I want a lawyer."

"You're not under arrest, Lance." *Yet.* "Miranda doesn't apply. But even if you were, and you went that route, we wouldn't be able to help you."

"I don't know what I should tell you. I—I don't want to lose my job."

That train's left the station, bro. "Let me make this as simple as possible for you, Lance: You should tell us anything that would help us find Marcks. You do that, I'll see what I can do about keeping you out of the system. We're not talking about you keeping your job. Your law enforcement career is over. But I'd hate to see you end up in a prison cell with the general pop, especially as a former CO. That'd be a death penalty without having to go through all the years of legal appeals. You know I'm speaking the truth."

"Yeah." Kubiak took a long, uneven breath. "So what do you want me to do?"

She held up the frame. "Good-looking boy. Think of him while you answer these questions."

His Adam's apple rose and fell sharply.

"So we want you to cooperate with us. Call Gaines and leave a message for your buddy *Rocky* that you can help him, that the feds came around asking questions and you know what they're looking for. You want to meet him. You've got money and a fake passport so he can get into Canada because you told us that you'd heard that he planned to go south, to Mexico. So that's where we'll be looking."

"You want me to lie to my friend?"

Vail's jaw tightened. "Look. Instead of being with my fiancé tonight, I'm sitting in a house in West Virginia trying to track down a goddamn serial killer who's already murdered three people since he escaped—an escape you helped facilitate. Then you had the balls to lie to us by saying you hardly know the guy when you're friends going back forty years. And let's not forget about Eddie Simmons and what happened to Vincent Stuckey. You lied about that, too." *Probably.* "And you're concerned about lying to a convicted killer?"

Kubiak's right leg began bouncing as his eyes darted left and right.

"Nothing to think about, dipshit," Ramos said. "Do the right thing here and maybe you save your skin."

"I'll do it. I'll make the call. But Rocky's real smart. He's not gonna fall for that."

"You might be right. We'll see soon enough. For your sake, I hope he buys it. Which means you'd better do your best to sell it."

Vail called Hurdle so he could triangulate the call, then Kubiak phoned Gaines and left the message they discussed, providing a location to meet.

"Tell me how you ended up at the same prison as Marcks," Vail said. "That's a stupidly convenient coincidence."

"I don't know," Kubiak said, rubbing the palm of his left hand against that of his right. "I'm telling you the truth. One day he shows up there in a transfer. We just took it to be luck. I got to see my buddy and he knew I was looking out for him. I'd slip him some cigarettes, spices, cookies, anything he could sell on his block."

"What about the escape?"

"I wasn't involved in that."

Vail chuckled. "You believe him, Rambo? 'Cause I sure don't."

"Not for a second."

Kubiak's knee began bouncing again. He thought a moment, then sighed. "I knew it was going down but I didn't do anything to help. All I did was introduce him to a few people who might be . . . good targets, care bears. But that was a long time ago. If it's connected to his escape . . ." He shrugged. "Can't tell you. Ask Rocky."

"We will," Ramos said.

"What about the nurse? Sue Olifante?"

"She was one of them people I figured would help him. She was having a tough time in her marriage and she seemed to be looking for a sympathetic ear. Depressed, needing validation. She'd gained ten pounds and didn't feel good about herself."

"So you told Marcks this."

Kubiak nodded.

"And he went to work, complimenting her, making her feel good, telling her what she wanted to hear. What she needed to hear."

"I guess so," Kubiak said, his voice flat.

"You *know* so."

Kubiak shrugged and dropped his gaze to the floor.

"What else did you help him with?" Ramos asked.

"Just giving him the lay of the land when he came over. Who to stay away from and, like I said, which COs were care bears. I may've given him some personal information on a couple of officers."

"Great colleague," Vail said. "Really had their backs, didn't you?"

Kubiak looked away. "My friend needed me. I didn't see it as doing anything wrong. I just told him about people. He did everything. And those people he approached, *if* he did, well, they're adults, you know? They make their own choices and decisions."

Already lining up his defense. Impressive. "Is Marcks gay?"

Kubiak seemed to recoil into himself. "Why are you asking me that?"

"*We* ask the questions here," Ramos said.

He sighed. "It wasn't something he talked about. But yeah."

"Then how did you know?"

"I—" He slumped and let his head drop. "Do we really need to discuss this?"

"What do you think?" Ramos said.

Kubiak closed his eyes and, after a long moment of thought, looked at Ramos. "It was a long time ago. After his wife died. He said he had a meeting and asked me if I'd pick his daughter up and take her to a soccer tournament she was in. I said sure. So I did, except that Jasmine—that's his daughter—had forgotten her cleats, so we ran home to get them."

"And you walked in on him?"

"They were in his bedroom. But Jasmine heard the noise and went in. And she found her dad . . . uh, well, you know."

"I can guess," Vail said, "but guessing won't cut it. We need to know."

"He was fu—he was having anal sex with this guy. The other guy was on his hands and knees and Rocky was behind him."

"Okay. And what was Jasmine's reaction? How old was she?"

"Ten or eleven, I think. She was, well . . . I don't know. She ran out of the house and back into my car."

"And then what happened?"

"Nothing. I followed her to the car and we went back to the field. The coach got on her case a couple of times for not hustling, but nothing really stands out."

"Did you talk to her about it? On the car ride over?"

"I tried to, but I mean, I didn't know what the hell to say. I didn't know what Rocky'd want me to say. I asked her if she had any questions. She didn't answer me. I told her to talk with her dad about it."

"And? Did she?"

"No idea."

"Did you ever ask him about it?"

"Once. He said to forget what I saw and if I told anyone about it, I'd be sorry."

Some friend.

"Obviously," Vail said, "you didn't forget about what you saw. Did you ever tell anyone about it?"

"Rocky's a pretty scary guy. In case you haven't noticed."

"That's a no?" Ramos asked.

"That's a *hell* no."

"Right." Vail set the frame back on the coffee table. "Did you ever know him to have a heterosexual relationship?"

"Nope. I mean, he was married, you know that. Other than that, no."

"How'd his wife die?" Ramos asked.

"Accident."

Ramos tilted his head. "Car accident?"

Vail knew the details surrounding Rhonda Marcks's death but would let Kubiak answer—sometimes you learned a morsel of long-withheld information that was not reported to the police.

"She slipped on a skate in the garage and fell backwards, hit her head on the concrete. Smashed it in pretty good."

"Well, that sucks." Ramos glanced at Vail.

Vail knew what he was thinking: he was not convinced that's what really happened to Rhonda Marcks.

"Any witnesses?"

"No," Vail said. "Patrol officer checked the scene, didn't think it looked like anything but an accident so he didn't call detectives. He wrote a standard one-page report. Body went to the ME for an autopsy because it was an unwitnessed death—and the ME categorized the method of death as an accident."

Ramos swung back to Kubiak. "Did Marcks have any other homosexual encounters after that one you . . . described?"

"No. I—I don't know."

"Your old school buddy Vincent Stuckey said that there were a couple of bars that Marcks used to go to."

"Yeah. Rock 'em Hard was one of them."

"That's a gay bar," Ramos said.

Vail gave Ramos a quick glance. "And the other?"

"Yellow Lantern. We'd just go hang out, drink after work. Watch the Redskins on Sundays."

"You know Marcks is out to kill Jasmine," Vail said.

Kubiak turned away. "I told him to think long and hard about what he's doing."

"What did he say?"

"Nothing. He doesn't really talk about her much."

"Do you know why he wants to kill her?"

"Pretty damn obvious. What she wrote in her book really pissed him off. But we didn't talk much while he was at Potter. We couldn't."

"You ever ask him about the murders?"

"You crazy?" Kubiak chuckled. "I didn't dare. But like I said, he wasn't on my block. I mostly just passed him short notes, sometimes taped to an envelope with shit in it—spices, cigarettes, that kind of stuff—things I could toss into his cell as I passed."

Not sure how much I believe that, either.

"What about Booker Gaines?"

"What about him?"

Vail lowered her chin, her face drooping in disappointment. "Lance, you know what we're after. We're looking for Gaines because we've got questions, same ones we've asked you. He may know where we can find Rocky."

"Don't know where he is. Was living in Richmond but I dropped by his apartment once and he'd moved."

"Anything you can tell us?"

Kubiak examined the ceiling. "Not really. That's all I know. Haven't heard from him in, I don't know, maybe a year."

"What about Scott MacFarlane?"

"Mac, man, I haven't talked to him in a long time. He and I grew apart."

"Why's that?"

Kubiak tapped his right foot on the floor. "He accused me of being the enemy. Couldn't believe I'd go into law enforcement."

"The dark side, eh?"

Kubiak looked hard at her. "Not funny. Wouldn't talk to me after I got my badge. Wouldn't even *look* at me."

She turned to Ramos to see if he had any other questions. He shook his head. "Okay, Lance. Thanks for your help. I'll let the prosecutor know you were cooperative. *And I won't even tell her I had to threaten you.*

"Prosecutor? Couldn't we just let it go?"

"Like a speeding ticket?" Ramos asked. "Wink, wink to the officer, ask for a warning."

Kubiak shrugged. "Something like that."

"Yeah," Vail said. "But no. That never works, anyway, does it?"

"Only if you're a knockout blonde with a nice rack," Ramos said.

Vail looked at him.

"Just sayin'. It does happen."

"I'll be right back," Vail said. "Which way to the restroom?"

Kubiak hesitated a second. "Uh—"

"Got a long drive back."

His gaze met Vail's, which was intended to convey something like, "You're actually thinking about telling me I can't use your bathroom?"

I can tell him I have my period, which would really make him squirm. His shoulders rolled forward slightly in acquiescence—body language that told Vail there was something in the house worth hiding from her. *But is it in plain sight?*

"Second door on the right."

Vail stood up and glanced at Ramos, letting him know she was going to take a look around in case there was anything connected to Marcks lying out along the way.

Instead of taking the second door on the right, however, she turned left, into the kitchen. Checked the refrigerator for a phone number, a name, anything that might indicate where Gaines was living. Several magnets advertised a local insurance agent, a pizza parlor, and a dentist. Another held a reminder note from Kubiak's wife to her son to take the trash out on Wednesdays.

Other things that had no obvious connection to their case were scattered across the countertop. She glanced around but saw nothing of value.

A small oak rolltop desk sat in the corner with a corded phone on its left edge. She examined the spiral pad beside it and read the scribbles: a doctor's appointment, by the look of it. Car repair reminder for tomorrow afternoon.

And—something sticking out of a drawer. Vail leaned closer and saw a small plastic bag filled with white powder. Sugar? Flour? In a desk? She pulled her phone and turned on the flashlight and shined it inside. From what she could see, there were several others.

She found a dishwashing glove draped over the sink's drying rack and removed the protruding packet and held it up to the light. *Won't have to bother with a weak marijuana charge.*

When she returned to the living room, Ramos was sharing a laugh with Kubiak—something to do with their first teenage girlfriends.

Vail held the bag up in front of Kubiak. "You supplying coke to the convicts? You a dirty officer, Lance? Are you getting paid to move this shit in and out of Potter by the inmates?"

Kubiak was on his feet. "No way, that's not me. I don't do that shit."

"Then explain this. You've got a lot of packets like this in your desk drawer from what I can see. You saying this is your personal stash?"

Kubiak's dilated eyes danced from left to right, trying to fight through the beer and marijuana haze to reason a way out.

"I'm tired," he said, turning to Ramos. "I worked a full shift. I just wanna go to sleep. Can we talk about this tomorrow?"

Ramos pulled out his phone and started tapping out a text.

"Yeah," Vail said. "We'll definitely pick this up tomorrow."

"So let me get this straight," Ramos said. "This cocaine is yours?"

"Yeah, it's mine. I'm not dealing."

Arresting him on a charge of cocaine possession was the better play here. The locals would not hold him long, Vail knew, but it would accomplish their goal: give them time to call an AUSA and make a case for rolling on a federal warrant for obstruction of justice and aiding and abetting a fugitive. That was where their real leverage was. If something was going to make Kubiak talk, that would be it.

Seconds later, there was a knock at the door.

"Who's that?" Kubiak asked.

Ramos shrugged. "Your wife?"

"She's got a key."

"Let's go see."

Kubiak pulled the door open and a suited man was standing there, badge in hand.

"Lance Kubiak, I'm Terence Linscombe, West Virginia State Police."

Vail held up the packet.

"That what I think it is?" Linscombe asked.

Kubiak looked from Vail to Ramos to Linscombe. "What's going on here?"

Linscombe pulled out a small black and white box marked "NIK Narcotics Identification System." He opened it up and added some of the kit's powder to a modified Scott Reagent tube. He looked at Ramos and nodded, then turned to Kubiak. "This is cocaine, sir."

Kubiak rolled his eyes. "I know it's cocaine."

"Can you 10-15 him?" Ramos asked.

"I can indeed. Lance Kubiak, you're under arrest for possession of cocaine."

"Looks like there's more in the kitchen," Vail said. "Desk drawer. Plain sight."

Linscombe finished mirandizing him, then secured the handcuffs.

"Cooperate with us regarding Marcks," Ramos said, "and we'll see what we can do about the coke."

Vail took a throw blanket from the couch and draped it over his wrists. "In case your wife and son pull up as we're getting into the car."

Kubiak teared up. "I'm sorry."

Linscombe gave him a tug, leading him toward the door.

"I'm sorry for your *son*," Vail said. "This is going to be hardest on him."

28

Vail's Samsung buzzed as she navigated the interstate. She handed the phone to Ramos, who was on his own call. "Who is it?"

"Hang on a sec," Ramos said into his handset, then glanced at Vail's caller ID. "Thomas Underwood."

"Shit, I've been waiting for that. Answer and tell him to hold for a second."

As Ramos complied, Vail slowed and pulled onto the right shoulder. "Be right back." Ramos returned to his conversation and Vail turned off the engine. She walked in front of the sedan, the headlights illuminating the immediate vicinity.

"Agent Underwood, thanks for calling me back. I don't know if you remember, but we met a few years ago, on the Richard Ray Singletary case."

"I do remember. And please call me Thomas. Sorry it's taken me so long to return your call. I'm in Hawaii shooting an episode for my new cold case show. We're on lunch break."

"Didn't realize you were out of town. I've got some questions on the Roscoe Lee Marcks case."

"I heard he escaped. Been following the news alerts on my phone."

"I'm standing on the side of the road in West Virginia and you've gotta get back to shooting, I'm sure. Is there a good time to talk in the next couple of days? I've got some questions."

"I'm shooting for another week but I'm buried. Up against a deadline for a serial case I'm testifying in in Philly. So when I'm not filming I'm on trial prep conference calls with counsel."

"I saw that interview you did with NBC after the offender was arrested. Right in front of your house."

He grumbled. "Wasn't my idea. I try to keep my work and personal lives separate. But they showed up at my door."

"You did a great job. Really nailed it. But I'm surprised they're letting you testify."

"I'm actually appearing for the defense."

Um . . . okay. Not sure what to make of that.

"Let me see what I can do when I get back. If I can't meet with you before, definitely after I get back from testifying."

"Appreciate it. But can I ask you a couple of questions over the phone?"

"I've got two minutes. Max."

Vail glanced at Ramos, who was still jabbering into his phone. "I've got a theory on Marcks—that he was homosexual. If I'm right—and we just got a witness account that, if credible, supports that—it'd give us a better line into finding him. But if I'm wrong, I don't want to send the task force in the completely opposite direction."

"I had the same thought. Keep pursuing that theory."

"You did? There's nothing in your assessment about it."

"I got a lot of pushback from the unit and my partner in particular. In the end, he talked me out of it. There are always exceptions to the rules, obviously, but I couldn't ignore his arguments."

"But you were the senior profiler in the entire unit at the time. You were—are—well, a legend. Why would you allow yourself to be talked out of something like that?"

"Because there were female victims as well as male. And because there were too many unanswered questions regarding the homosexual angle that couldn't be supported in court if and when they found the UNSUB and the case went to trial."

"Good point." A sharp defense attorney could pick apart a single weakness in the profile—and in doing so, discredit every conclusion Underwood reached, essentially rendering the entire assessment useless. It would not be worth the risk, especially in this case, where the circumstantial evidence ended up being relatively weak and only two of the cases had an actual connection to Marcks.

Vail heard someone in the background through a muffled handset. "Who was the profiler you were working with? The one who changed your mind?"

"He was with you when you came to talk with Singletary on the Dead Eyes case. Frank Del Monaco."

Vail couldn't help but drop her jaw. *Frank? If I tell him I know that he schooled Thomas Underwood, I'll never live it down.*

"Gotta run." Underwood again covered the phone with a hand, telling them he would be right there. "I'll be in touch soon as I can and we can sit down with the case files, give everything a close look, try to poke holes in our theory."

"I'd love that." Vail thanked him, then got back into the car.

"That name, I know it," Ramos said.

"Thomas Underwood? A pioneer in my unit, one of its founding fathers. You probably know him as an author. He's written seven books on serial offenders. All bestsellers."

"I think I read one. *Anatomy of a Killer*?"

"Never read it but it's supposed to be riveting."

"I've got another one on my shelf, called . . ." He looked at the ceiling of the car. "*UNSUB*. Yeah, I think that's it. Haven't gotten to it yet. So many good books to read." He turned to her. "You think you'll write one when you retire?"

Vail laughed. "Who knows? I'll worry about that when the time comes. But I've got plenty of material. That Dead Eyes case could fill a book all on its own. Then there's the John Wayne Mayfield case in Napa, which was unlike anything the unit's ever handled. That, too, would make an awesome book. And one I handled on Alcatraz." *Then there are the cases I can never tell anyone about, let alone write about.* She turned the engine over. "Yeah, I think I will write a book or two."

"So was Underwood helpful?"

"He's out of town so I'll need to meet with him when he gets back. But at least he confirmed that we appear to be on the right track." She pulled back out onto the interstate and continued toward Fairfax.

29

Vail had just arrived at the command post and dropped Ramos off at his car when her Samsung buzzed violently in her pocket.

So much for going home. She drove off toward I-66, headed for a wooded area that surrounded the banks of the Potomac River: Great Falls National Park in northern Fairfax County, where a dead body had been found.

It did not sound like the deceased male was related to their case, but the task force was obligated to look into all area murders that could be associated with their escaped violent felon.

While en route, her phone rattled again. She did not recognize the number.

"Vail."

"Karen, it's Jasmine."

"Hey girl, I was beginning to wonder about you."

"I've been following the news reports," Jasmine said. "He's been killing people again."

"As I expected," Vail said. "That's why I want you in protective custody."

"Karen, please. Let's not go through this again. You saw what happened to the last cop you posted outside my house—*to keep me safe.* No thanks. I'm doing just fine. I'm moving every couple of days to a different place. Although I *am* eating away at my book advance."

"Look on the positive side. It'll give you material for book two." *Ouch. That's not fair.* "Sorry. I didn't mean to make light of this."

"Of all people, you don't have to explain your motives. I know you have my best interests in mind. But for now, I feel safer where no one knows who I am. Or where I am."

"I don't like it, but I get it."

"Plus, it lets me be absolutely sure no one talked, voluntarily or involuntarily. My father's not above torturing someone for information on my whereabouts. This way, no one can give me up. And no one gets hurt."

"That's admirable, but—"

"And I'm wearing a disguise."

Vail stifled a chuckle. "A disguise?"

"Nothing elaborate. Just enough to keep people from noticing me. Maybe it's silly. I was only on TV a couple of times. But I figured it can't hurt. You any closer to finding him?"

How do I answer that? "Closer? I think so, yeah. But I wouldn't say we're close. I'll keep you posted. And you stay safe."

Vail hung up as she turned onto Route 738, then took Old Dominion Drive to the closed National Park Service entrance shack, where she was admitted by a posted law enforcement officer.

In the parking lot sat Curtis's Chevy sedan and Hurdle's Toyota SUV. She pulled alongside them and saw a group of men huddled thirty yards away that looked like it included her task force members. Vail made her way over to the knot of personnel and joined the conversation.

"So who and what do we got?"

"No ID," Curtis said. "Fit white male, early forties and wearing what looks like an expensive shirt and shoes. Nordstrom and Allen Edmonds, according to the ME."

"Nice wardrobe. But why are we thinking the vic is one of ours?'

Hurdle shrugged. "That's what we have to determine. Might not be."

"Cause of death?"

"Strangulation. There's bruising, pressure marks on the throat, neck, and behind the ears, consistent with a large hand. Hyoid bone may be broken. Petechial and subconjunctival hemorrhages. He said it's likely to assume the assailant was a male because, judging by the bruises on the neck, those are two sizable paws."

And women don't usually have the strength to strangle a man. "Anything else?"

"Looks like he was raped," Curtis said.

A woman approached with a flashlight in hand. From the gait, Vail knew it was Leslie Johnson.

"Raped how?" Vail asked.

"There's anal penetration," Curtis said. "ME thinks he used a condom. He'll know more later, but he's fairly certain."

"Important to know ASAP," Vail said.

"Why?" Curtis asked, keyed in on her enthusiasm.

"Something that came up in the last few hours. Remember I mentioned my theory that Marcks is gay? His murders may have something to do with that. I'm still working it through." She turned to Hurdle. "But for purposes of the task force, I think we should put some guys at known gay bars throughout the county, even in the district."

"Okay," Hurdle said.

Even in the relative darkness, Vail could tell his facial expression was one of skepticism. "Look, I realize that'll take a lot of manpower, but I'm confident enough in what I'm seeing to think it's worth it. If I'm right, and we put undercovers at known gay bars and he shows, we may get our man."

"He's gotta know we'd be looking for him there," Johnson said.

"I don't think so, Leslie. Even before he went to prison, he kept his sexual orientation close to the vest—under the threat of violence. And his vics weren't pure homosexual plays. He killed both men and women—which is unusual for homosexual serial killers. Well, for any offenders. They have their victim type and generally don't deviate unless they have to—but they always go back. That could be what happened here, but I don't think so."

Johnson tilted her head in thought. "So you're saying that because he was careful about hiding his sexual preference, he won't think we're hip to looking for him at known gay establishments."

"Right. And straight people don't hang out at these places. So for him, these may be safe havens. Where he doesn't have to worry about law enforcement hanging out there and picking him up."

"What makes you think he's homosexual?" Curtis asked.

"Victim selection. The lust murder flavor to what he does to the bodies, the cutting of the genitals. Most of the vics were anally penetrated. And the correctional officer, his childhood friend, Lance Kubiak, walked in on him once many years ago when he was having sex with another man. Assuming he's telling the truth—which might be a stretch for this guy."

"We should ask Jasmine about it," Curtis said.

"I did. She didn't really answer me. And she sure as hell didn't mention the incident Kubiak described, but I had a feeling there was something she wanted to tell me. Let's face it, it's a sensitive subject for some people. I'll revisit it with her when the time's right."

Hurdle shrugged. "Let's work this angle. I'll get some undercovers deployed at key places."

Vail told him about the two bars that Kubiak mentioned.

"Those'll be at the top of the list."

"Who found our new vic?" Johnson asked, lifting her feet to get the blood flowing.

"Park's open till half an hour after dark," Hurdle said. "Guy with his dog got lost, didn't get out before it closed. About 7:30 PM he came across a man who seemed to be lugging something heavy over his shoulder. He stopped and watched. It was dark and obviously there were trees in the way, but there was some decent moonlight. He was finally able to see that it was a body draped over the guy's shoulder.

"The dog saw it too, because he started barking. Perp dropped what he was carrying and fled. No phones in the park and damn near no cell service. So the witness couldn't call us. He went over, saw the body, then had to find his way back to his car. But he couldn't get out because the gate was closed. After realizing the guy he saw could still be in the area, he plowed through the barricade and drove till he had a signal, called 911."

"Did he give us a description?"

"White guy, big and strong. Had no trouble maneuvering the body."

"Certainly sounds like Marcks," Vail said, looking around. "Only been here once. Aren't there waterfalls around here somewhere?"

"You mean because the park's called Great Falls?" Curtis said.

"I see I'm not the only one who can do sarcasm."

"There are three," Hurdle said. "They've got overlooks not far from here. Five to ten minute walk. Aren't any roads that lead there, so only way in is by foot. Why?"

Vail thought a moment. "It fits in that he seems to gravitate toward parks."

Curtis stamped a foot. "We found one of his earlier vics in a national park."

"Yeah," Vail said, glancing around. "That could be it. He's comfortable in less densely populated, wooded spaces. And after hours they offer definite advantages."

"There are a gazillion square miles of parkland in Virginia," Hurdle said, "but I can put out an alert to Park Police."

"Can't hurt." Vail shook her head absentmindedly. "But he came here, to this one, for a specific reason. Maybe he was going to dispose of the body. Dump it into the falls. Be a long time before we'd find it, if ever."

"Why dump only this one?" Johnson asked.

"Remember he hacked William Reynolds to bits and then buried him?" Vail shrugged. "I don't think he wants to leave any traces of where he's been. He wants us to think he could be half-way to Mexico by now. Or Canada. Or even Arizona or Montana. Harder, if not impossible, for us to focus our resources to find him if it's a nationwide manhunt."

"But because we've found these bodies," Hurdle said, "we know he's staying local. So we don't have that problem."

Johnson held out both gloved hands, palms up. "Wouldn't we know that anyway, if the object is to kill his daughter?"

"We don't know for sure his objective is to kill her," Curtis said. "We think he wants to do that. I wanted to be president at one point. Thinking changes, goals shift."

"You wanted to be president?" Vail asked. "Can't see that."

"Thanks," Curtis said, then gave her the finger. "Can you see *this*?"

She suppressed a laugh. "Point is, he could dispatch someone to take her out. Depends on whether or not there's anger behind his desire to kill her. If there is, *he* needs to do it because it's personal. If shutting her up is a means to an end, and his real goal is to escape imprisonment, he's probably looking to leave the country. I mentioned this to Rambo on our drive to Potter. Homeland Security and Border Patrol, that's his playpen. He alerted his people. But right now, until Marcks can secure a way across the border, he's hanging around Virginia. Which could mean he's out to do Jasmine. Or not."

"So are we thinking this is Marcks?" Hurdle asked.

"What about the vic's genitals," Johnson said. "Intact?"

"Yeah. And no knife marks on the abdomen."

"But he was interrupted by that dog." Vail rubbed her arms to get the blood moving. "I'm gonna go take a look at the body. Leslie, want to take a hike?"

They walked about fifty yards to the area that was lit up by Klieg lights powered by a portable generator that was making a considerable amount of noise. At the center of all the commotion was the medical examiner.

Vail and Johnson exchanged pleasantries with him, then Vail knelt over the body, taking a long look at the face and torso. She snapped a few photos.

What are we looking at here? Why this victim? He doesn't fit the males who were killed during Marcks's active killing period.

"What are you thinking?"

Johnson's question pulled her out of her reverie. "Let's head back, give me a few minutes to mull this over, then I can share it with everyone all at once."

The task force members had retreated to the warmth of their vehicles. Upon Vail's and Johnson's return, they emerged and complained about the cold. Tarkoff and Morrison had arrived in the interim.

"What do you think?" Hurdle said. "This our guy?"

"If this is Marcks, the victimology doesn't fit the men he targeted in the past. They were younger, blonds. Not educated, not successful. Easily controlled. I doubt a guy like this, with his expensive attire, is easily controlled. He's probably someone accustomed to giving orders, not taking them."

"Marcks has been in prison for what, seven years?" Tarkoff said. "Things change. Preferences change."

Vail cocked her head. "There are always exceptions, but generally speaking, that's not how it goes. These preferences are hardwired. They're innate, it's part of who we are—just like homosexuality, or heterosexuality, is not a choice we make. But how you decide to commit your crimes, and what you do with the victims, what you do to—and with—their bodies, how you treat them, that's personal; that type of development occurs in adolescence, in that abnormal fusion of sex, violence, and arousal. It's different for everybody."

"I always thought what these assholes do to their victims is a conscious decision," Curtis said.

"Offenders don't understand why they're doing it; they just know that it's what they like. So yes, they're aware of what they're doing. They're doing it because they like it; they fantasize about these things and start by acting out their fantasies with inanimate objects, pets, compliant partners like prostitutes. The ones that go on to become killers, they take it to the next level because playacting is not enough. It doesn't satisfy the need. They cross that line because they need a victim that resists, one that forces them to exert control.

"So while what they do with the bodies varies, victim preference is fairly consistent. Some offenders prefer elderly women; some want children; some want young men, like Gacy. Some want young men in their late teens or early twenties, like Dahmer.

"Now, what these offenders do with that victim is up to them in terms of what excites them; Dahmer wasn't interested in a living victim but a dead one. All of his interaction with the victim, everything that he did to the body—which was very important to him—he did after the victim was dead. For other offenders, it's all about what he can do while the victim is alive. The torture is the key. Gacy was aroused by the torture aspect. But once the victim was dead, he had zero interest. At that point, he got rid of the body. So while Dahmer and Gacy both had a preference for young males, they were completely different in how they went about their business. Their psychopathology was different."

"So why does Marcks cut off the genitalia?" Tarkoff asked. "Part of his fantasy?"

Vail rubbed her gloved hands together. "I can give you a number of potential reasons why he does that. Same with the lines he carves in their abdomens. An important thing to remember is that killers who mutilate make up a very small subset of offenders. First off, they're just about *always* men. Second, most of the men who mutilate do it for utilitarian purposes: they dismember so they can get rid of the body parts and prevent identification.

"Then you've also got offenders who are offensive mutilators. He's pissed and gets his revenge by attacking the genitalia, the sexual areas of the body. The smallest group of this already small subset are the guys who do it because they get some sexual satisfaction out of it. Some wear the vulvas they cut away. Others play with them."

"Thanks for that," Hurdle said. "I haven't eaten dinner yet."

"Honestly," Vail said, "for the purposes of catching Marcks, why he's doing these things to his victims is not as important as our observations. And that brings us back to his sexual orientation being a key to finding him."

"Because that's where he'll be finding his new victims?" Morrison asked.

"Or it could just be a place of safety and comfort for him, where he doesn't think we'd look for him. Before he was arrested, he did not get his victims from gay hangouts. And not all of them were gay."

Hurdle took a moment to bring Tarkoff and Morrison up to date on their new undercover op involving gay bars.

"We were never able to determine *how* he found his vics," Curtis said. "And he wasn't exactly forthcoming about it—or anything else—when we had him in the box."

"Let's get back to victim preference," Hurdle said. "Because that holds a lot of promise for catching him. If we know the victim population, and we can narrow the geography where these people congregate, we can use that to our advantage. Morrison, get with Walters. That'll be your focus." He turned to Vail. "When do you think you'll have an answer on whether or not this victim is one of ours?"

"Let's see if we can get an ID. That might help."

"If the vic's gay, would you think it's more likely a Marcks kill?"

"Not necessarily. It could've been opportunistic. Guy stumbles on Marcks—who might've been planning to stay in the park overnight—and he has to kill him to keep him quiet."

"Or," Morrison said, "maybe the vic and Marcks knew each other years ago and this was a retribution kill. Way he's dressed, could be a lawyer. Let's see if the vic matches one of Marcks's defense attorneys."

"Whoa," Vail said, holding up two gloved hands. "Before we go running in a million directions with a ton of assumptions, let's pull back a second. I think there's a real good chance this was Marcks. We've got a general witness description that matches well and we've got a fugitive killer on the loose in the area. For now, I'd call it ours. But by morning we should know more definitively." Her phone vibrated. She struggled to get it out with her gloves on, so she pulled one off and answered. "Art. Kind of late to—"

"Got another crime scene. Arson case. Fresh. If you're not busy, thought you'd want to take a look."

Busy? Nah, just sittin' around watching mindless reality TV.

"Where?"

"In the sticks. I'll text you the address."

"On my way." She hung up and asked Hurdle if there was anything further he needed her for tonight. "Crime scene one of my colleagues wants me to take a look at. We good here?"

"Got it covered. Have fun."

Oh, yeah. A blast.

30

Vail arrived at the address the GPS directed her to—but aside from a mass of emergency responder and law enforcement vehicles, she would have sworn she was in the middle of nowhere. Thick stands of Hickory, Cottonwood, and Hemlock trees obscured the residence from the road, and there were no neighbors for quite a distance in any direction.

She pulled up behind the fire marshal's truck and found Art Rooney moments later, walking alongside a man and a woman dressed in fire department uniforms.

Rooney excused himself and met her about twenty yards from the burned-out structure, small flare-ups of fire still visible here and there, firefighters quashing them as soon as they sprouted.

"Is it definitely arson?" Vail asked.

"Affirmative. I'll show you what we've got so far—but let's not forget that it's below freezing and damp out because of the snow, which makes an accidental fire less likely to do such dramatic damage—without some very substantial help."

"Same guy?"

"Hard to say just yet, but my gut says yes. If nothing else, look at a basic fact: the arsonist we're looking for chooses his targets in rural areas where there's distance between the houses—which means it delays discovery, allowing it to burn longer before the fire department can get to it. More importantly, rural areas are served by volunteer fire departments."

"Not as experienced?"

"Potentially—but they have to go to the station first to get the trucks. And *then* they go to the fire. That obviously allows it to burn longer. That extra time means less evidence left behind for investigators to find. Our arsonist has done this in every single instance. That alone is an identifiable MO."

"But there's more."

"Yes," Rooney said, "there is. Follow me."

They walked around the scene and approached the area where the front door had been located. Rooney pulled out his phone and turned on the flashlight. "See this?"

Vail crouched, got close to the spot where Rooney was pointing. "Tool marks on the strike plate."

"In other words, evidence of forced entry. The fire also extended beyond the perimeter of the house in an unnatural manner. Plus, there's extensive damage, there are no V-shaped patterns, and the fire looks to be low burning."

"V-shaped patterns. That's when a naturally occurring fire burns up and out," she said, bringing her hands together and separating them as she gestured toward the sky.

"Correct. Usually the *v* is burned into furniture and/or walls. We checked the lightbulbs, too, because they're often a natural point of origin in fires. They'd be melted and flat on one side, like an arrow pointing you to where the heat source was greatest. Again, nothing. So without all that stuff, we've got enough to call it arson. But that's not all."

"Unusual burn patterns?"

"And high heat stress. Come inside."

Rooney led the way into what Vail guessed had been the living room.

He knelt again. "Know what this is?"

"Sterno can."

"And that's part of our UNSUB's signature, right? Sterno's a bizarre, and inefficient, way of starting a fire. But it's not the only thing that's strange." He rose and swung his body, and his light, 180 degrees.

"What am I looking at?"

"That, Karen, is ritual behavior for this arsonist."

Vail stared at the detritus in front of her, some of which was surprisingly intact: more Sterno cans and lids, burned remnants of a wood match, wax, and a small fragment of what looked like a rag. "Can you be more specific?"

"Not yet. But generally speaking, this is his way of setting the fire. This is the point of origin. There's some kind of elaborate setup he constructs that gets the fire going using these items you see at your feet."

"Why go through all that?"

"Think, Karen. Why do any of our offenders do the shit they do? This isn't any different."

Vail nodded slowly. "None of this is necessary to start a really hot fire that'll kill the inhabitants, destroy evidence, and take down the structure. It can be done a lot more efficiently. But for some reason, doing it this way has meaning to this guy. He likes it, fantasizes about it."

"Right. I'm not sure how all these pieces fit together, but I'm gonna work on it, go through the prior crime scene videos and photos to see if I can reconstruct what he does. And why."

A chilled wind blew across the landscape and a shiver racked

Vail's body. She stood up and began flexing her fingers. "Will you keep me posted on what you find? I'd love to keep expanding my knowledge base, know what to look for in a scene like this. I've got the basics of arson but—well, there's a lot to know."

Rooney rose from his crouch. "Soon as I get some more forensics back, you'll be the first to know."

31

The morning came with one redeeming characteristic: the temperature had risen to thirty-five degrees. Well, two: it was not snowing.

Marcks had a third reason to celebrate: he had spent the night in a secluded area in Greenbelt Park inside a very comfortable Mercedes S-series sedan outfitted with plush napa leather seats and the heater running most of the evening. Before retiring, he had sought out the hot showers described in the brochure and map he had taken from the self-serve receptacle upon entering the grounds.

He spent only about ten minutes under the water but it was like being home, before his incarceration. He could close his eyes and not worry about being shanked in the side. Out in nature, no dim-witted idiots in his space . . . for the first time in years, he was at total peace.

Afterwards, he retired to the car and enjoyed the most restful sleep he had experienced for as long as he could remember. He awoke at first light feeling refreshed and ready to take on whatever obstacles he would face today.

And given what he had planned, there would certainly be some significant challenges.

However, he derided himself for not learning his lesson at the barn. He should not have slept so soundly—he should have been on alert for threats that approached the car—but the hot water, fatigue, and constant stress won out over self-preservation . . . at least for seven hours. He needed to regain his edge—or he was going to get caught.

Marcks checked around outside. Trees stretched in all directions, some fallen and others canted at forty-five–degree angles to their brethren. Snow blanketed the landscape as far as he could see. As he sat there, he ran his hands over the supple leather and thought he could get used to this. He could not recall a time when he felt so relaxed.

And it was going to end *now*. He had work to do. He leaned forward and craned his neck, looking left, right, ahead, and behind him.

No one was in sight. He took Nathan's Dopp kit and used the reflection off the tinted exterior side windows of the sedan to trim up his new beard, which was still mostly black with a touch of gray around the chin. He combed his hair, snipped a few stray strands with the scissors and made it as presentable as he could. He had gone to sleep while it was still wet and that never turned out well. However, hidden beneath a wool knit hat, that would not matter.

He brushed the trimmings off his clothing and appraised the reflection.

Not bad for an escaped felon on the run. But was it good enough? While the sleep did him a world of good, did he look presentable or would he scare away an unsuspecting passerby? He could not be objective—and he did not know what picture the police were using in their Wanted notices on TV and online.

Probably his booking photo, which was now several years old. Wait, no. They had shot another one when he was transferred to Potter.

Nothing he could do about it. Except . . . he popped the trunk release and rummaged through a road hazard toolkit, which contained nothing of use. But he found a Nationals hat in a backpack—a more disarming look and better coverage than the beanie—along with a sweater and a bottle of sunscreen. He searched inside the car and pulled a pair of aviator sunglasses from the glove box. Not a good look on him, but the idea was to hide his identity, not pose for *GQ*. With the hat, shades, and nascent facial growth, it was a decent start.

He parked the Mercedes up the road several spots from his discarded beard and hair clippings, then wiped down the interior and abandoned the vehicle.

Marcks made his way on foot toward Kenilworth Avenue and found a Chinese takeout restaurant. After crossing the street, ten feet from the door, he saw two police cars cruise by, the officers' heads rubbernecking in both directions. Looking for him, no doubt.

He ducked into the storefront and quickly moved away from the windows. By the time his order of Chow Mein was ready, the cops were gone, off to another part of their patrol grid.

He asked to use the phone and called a cab. Twenty minutes later the taxi was dropping him half a mile from where he really wanted to go: a used car dealership that had been around since he was a teenager. He never bought a car there but his friend Booker had.

When he walked into the office, it was pretty much as he had remembered it: a shithole of a business. The elderly man lounging behind the counter was camped out in a lawn chair watching some insipid TV show on an old compact VCR/television propped in a corner on a pile of yellowed phone books.

"Help ya?"

"Looking for a car. Something old, real cheap. Got cash."

"How much cash you got?"

"What's the cheapest car you got?"

The man put a beat-up clamshell cell phone down on the counter, swung his feet off an orange overturned bucket and stood up—not quite erect but enough to shuffle his way out the door. Marcks realized the guy was older than he had initially thought.

"Name's Oliver. You?"

"Bud. Friends call me Buddy."

"Can see why." He didn't turn but kept walking another dozen or so yards.

"Anyone else work here with you, Oliver?"

"Nope. Juss me. Ain't got no kids, neither. Don't make enough to hire no employees. Why?"

Marcks took a look around, trying to appear nonchalant. "Oh, just lookin' for a job."

"Can't help ya there, son." Oliver stopped in front of a sedan to catch his breath and leaned his right hand on the hood. "But I can help ya with a car. Got something for a hundred twenty-five bucks."

"Still run?"

"It runs. How much longer, who knows."

"How many miles?"

"Lots." Oliver straightened up a bit and started trudging along again, working his jaw, then said, "I take it out every now and then. Engine purrs, runs real smooth. Not burning oil, so that's good." He stopped in front of an ancient Buick LeSabre, its tan finish long faded into a hazy gray suggestion of its former luster. "Sixty-four. Nothin' fancy. Gotta roll down the windows with a crank. Automatic transmission, but no headrests, none of them airbag doohickeys, no ee-lectronics. Just your basic car."

"Can I take it around the block?"

Oliver reached over to a carabiner hanging from his pants belt loop and selected one of several dozen keys. "Just around the block. And don't get lost. Police'll track you down if you try to stiff me."

Marcks took the ring from Oliver and said, "Yes sir. Be back in five."

He returned in three. It had decent pickup, the engine was in surprisingly good condition, and the tires were not bald. It needed an alignment but it was a sturdy car built like they made them back in the sixties.

"So?"

Marcks pulled out some of the cash that Victoria had given him—which he had counted before getting out of the Buick—and made a show of slapping each Andrew Jackson into Oliver's hands. "One-twenty work for you? All I got with me."

"One-twenty works. Enjoy your car, Buddy."

Marcks adjusted the aviator glasses on his nose. "I'm sure I will, Oliver. I'm sure I will."

32

Marcks settled himself in front of the cyber café PC. He entered the code the guy at the register had given him and was granted access.

He took a moment to look over the desktop, which was a lot more flashy since the last time he had used a computer, over seven years ago. But once he started clicking, he realized that Windows still worked pretty much the same way: there was a start button and the task bar contained a big blue E for Internet Explorer. Except that when he launched the program, it said "Microsoft Edge" with something called "Bing."

Whatever. It worked and he was able to get onto the internet. He first searched for FBI profiler Karen Vail. It brought up dozens of articles and a number of references to her in the form of press releases on the FBI website.

There was even one in the search archive related to her work on his case, when he was arrested. He found an article in the *Post*, quoting her on how important an arrest this was for Fairfax County Police because "Roscoe Lee Marcks is the worst of the worst and getting him off the street made the county a whole lot safer."

Marcks clenched his fist. *What bullshit. And how clichéd.* "What the hell do you know?"

He realized he had said that aloud. A woman two seats over glanced at him. He shrank a bit in his seat and smiled sheepishly. "Sorry."

He turned back to the monitor and continued reading: a quote from Erik Curtis, the detective on the case, saying how they could not have captured Marcks without the assessment provided by the FBI's Behavioral Analysis Unit.

He paged back and clicked on another link. And another. And another. Vail had been one busy friggin' profiler. And successful. If an organized society for serial killers existed, they probably would have taken out a contract on her by now.

He searched for the address of the Behavioral Analysis Unit but could only find "FBI Academy, Quantico" in a couple of press releases. Finally he discovered an announcement from a local real estate firm touting the contract they had scored in leasing 12,000 square feet in Aquia, Virginia, to the FBI for an expansion of its Behavioral Analysis Unit. Marcks grinned— only this time it was genuine. That was exactly what he had been looking for.

He scribbled down the name of the complex, then looked it up and found the address. Bing asked him if he wanted to map it, and he said yes, clicked the link, and it showed him exactly where the building was located. It even gave him an aerial view. And an interactive look at the surrounding streets. Very helpful. *Thank you very much, Mr. Bing.*

With that in his back pocket, he typed in his daughter's name. Could he be so lucky to find some kind of reference as to where she would be hiding?

No. Articles on her book—that damn book—and a list of signings and speaking events on her tour. But cancellation notices appeared next to all of them.

He clicked a link among the Bing results and landed on Jasmine's author webpage. The photo of her was professionally staged and designed to invoke a sense of pity. At least that was what he took from the picture. Most fathers look at images of their daughters and see beauty and innocence. But he was not *most fathers*. He paged through her website and found the "Contact the author" page. He chose to send her an email.

His fingers paused over the keys, rage building as he composed his thoughts. He banged out an angry message—but then deleted it. Shorter, simpler was better:

I'm going to make you pay.

Yes, that would do.

He hit "send," then glanced at the clock on the taskbar. He had to finish up. He typed his name into the search field and—whoa, lots of results, including his mug shots and photos he did not even know were public, pictures of himself he had long since forgotten about. He suddenly became very self-conscious. He leaned closer to the screen. Looked left, then right.

A patrol car rolled by slowly outside. Marcks nonchalantly turned away from the large windows. Several people were in the café, all doing their own thing, tapping at their keyboards or reading the monitors. Oblivious to the police outside. Oblivious to him inside.

Marcks returned to his task and found a *Post* article dated yesterday. His gaze moved across the page so fast he realized he was not absorbing the impact of the information. He slowed down and took a deep breath. There was a US Marshals fugitive task force working his case. They had interviewed officials at Potter. And dammit—they had found William's dismembered body and were attributing the murder, and subsequent defiling of the corpse, to him.

His eyes zeroed in on one name: Karen Vail. The thorn in his side, the one apparently as responsible for his incarceration as his goddamn daughter, was noted by an FBI spokesperson to be a key member of the task force who had thus far made invaluable contributions.

Marcks clenched his jaw. He should've strangled her in the interview room when he had the chance.

He shut the browser and paid for his time . . . time more than well spent.

33

Marcks drove into the Aquia Commerce Center parking lot, surprised there was no security presence of any kind. Not even a guard booth.

He had stopped at a crafts store in Alexandria and purchased a pair of fake eyeglasses, which would look less suspicious than shades. While they cut down on glare, few people wore them on a dark, overcast winter day. His first goal was to not get caught, and his second was to avoid anything that would make him stand out in any way—which directly impacted goal number one.

Marcks chose a parking spot that gave him a view of the front entrance of the building on the left. Its counterpart on the right could easily have been the one in which Vail worked, but he had to start somewhere. If he was lucky, no matter which one she entered, he would still be able to see her.

One of his fellow inmates, a more recent addition to Potter, told him about the security cameras that a lot of businesses and government institutions had begun installing in and around their buildings. Because he had seen them at Potter, Marcks knew what to look for.

He checked when he entered the lot but only saw a few devices closer to the facility, far enough away from where he was parked that he doubted they could see him. They were a little different and did not exactly look like cameras, but they had a round bulbous covering that was conspicuously out of place and did not seem to perform any other function. He decided to play it safe and assumed they were the surveillance devices his colleague had warned him about.

Because it was winter—and in the midst of a cold spell—he figured that agents and visitors hanging out near where he was parked would not be a concern. In fact, no one lingered after leaving the buildings or the warmth of their cars. That lowered the risk that someone would stand around long enough to notice he was sitting in his vehicle for an extended period of time.

Ninety minutes passed when a blue late-model Honda pulled into the lot and parked two rows over, close to the left building's entrance. A redhead got out—and Marcks rose to attention. He had to wait for her to turn her head a bit to get a good look.

It was Vail.

He watched as she walked briskly to the Behavioral Analysis Unit external staircase and then entered the facility.

His goal was to follow her when she returned to her car. Sooner or later she would lead him to Jasmine. Once she did that, he might have the option of killing both of them.

Now that would be quite a deal: two for one.

And if he did it right, it would not cost him a thing.

34

Vail headed to her office, where she had to drop off a report to Lenka, who planned to distribute copies to Gifford and DiCarlo. Vail could have emailed it, but she had one boss who preferred to do things the old-fashioned way and one who was not tech savvy and wanted hard copies with a "wet signature" whenever possible.

She printed off the document and signed it, checked her messages and inbox, FedEx and UPS deliveries, and left the paperwork on Lenka's desk.

"Karen!"

Vail turned to see DiCarlo walking toward her.

"Saved me a call. Where are we on Marcks? How close are we to finding him?"

"Doing our thing. I think it's taking longer than the Marshals Service thought. But he's an intelligent offender and he seems to be a few steps ahead of us."

"You're not still spending time on Jasmine, are you?"

"Of course not. Haven't seen her since before the officer assigned to protect her was murdered."

DiCarlo gestured at Vail's back. "Turn around."

"Turn around?"

"What are you wearing?"

"A knife. Head of the Joint Terrorism Task Force gave it to me."

"I don't care who gave it to you. I care about you carrying it. Only your Bureau-issued Glock is authorized."

Here we go. "Actually, Knox authorized it."

"Director Knox?"

"Yes ma'am."

"Now why the hell would he do that?"

Take the easy way out of this, Karen. Be smart. "Probably best if you ask him yourself." Vail backed away, down the hall. "I've got to get over to the command center. Lenka's got a copy of my report."

With that, she turned and walked briskly toward the exit.

VAIL HAD JUST SLID onto the Honda's cold leather seat when her phone vibrated. It was Curtis.

"Got a line on Gaines. Kubiak came clean while a Detective Linscombe with West Virginia State Police was booking him at the county jail. Could be good intel."

"Where are you?"

"About to leave the command center. Meet me there. I'll wait for you."

Curtis was sharing a coffee with Tarkoff, Ramos, and Walters when Vail arrived. She walked over and filled her travel mug. "Where's Hurdle?"

"On his way over," Tarkoff said, rolling his chair to the left to give Vail some room.

She dumped a packet of sugar in the java and stirred it. "So what'd Kubiak give us?

"Gaines's got a house in Lake Ridge."

"Lake Ridge," Vail said. "You serious?"

"Not like it sounds," Curtis said. "Best we could tell, it's abandoned. Owners nearly went belly up during the housing crunch. They negotiated a deal with the bank and kept the place, but the wife has cancer so they're living with one of their kids in Ohio while she gets treatment at the Cleveland Clinic's cancer center. House has been empty for about eleven months."

"He's squatting in a vacant house?" Vail asked.

"Free rent, nice place. What could be bad?"

She moved over to the computer by the side wall and sat down. "We have an aerial?"

Ramos worked the keyboard and brought up a satellite image.

"What do we know about Gaines?" she asked as she studied the screen.

Tarkoff pulled his handgun from a locked drawer and holstered it. "Not exactly a model citizen. Did three years for assault when he was twenty-one. Some drug-related offenses in '07, charges dropped. Couple of drunk and disorderlies, another assault—charges dropped again. Picked up for soliciting, paid a fine. And a dom vio eighteen months ago," he said, referring to a domestic violence complaint.

"What are you thinking?" Curtis asked.

Vail pulled her gaze away from the monitor. "Just that we don't know what to expect. We're only going there to do a knock and talk. Sit him down, see if he'll answer some questions. But—"

The door to the command center opened and Hurdle and Morrison entered.

Vail looked again at the satellite imagery. "It's a big house. I think we should all go. Gives us numbers without overkill."

"Talk about overkill," Walters said. "You're just going to question the guy. About *Marcks*, not something he himself's done wrong."

"Marcks could be there."

Walters squinted. "Not likely. We've got an undercover sitting on his house. Gaines's there. No sign of Marcks."

"How long has our guy been there?"

Tarkoff checked his watch. "About ninety minutes."

"Do I have to state the obvious?" Vail turned to Hurdle. "He could've gotten there before our undercover set up shop."

Hurdle bent over the countertop and peered at the screen, examining the bird's-eye view of the neighborhood. "This cul-de-sac off Wainscott? What's the problem?"

Vail put the lid on her coffee mug and leaned back against the wall of the RV. "We need more men than just me and Curtis. Even if we're confident Marcks isn't there, it's a big house in a heavily wooded area. Gaines could easily slip out the back. He gets away, we may never find him."

"You think he's gonna try to run?" Hurdle pulled his gaze away from the computer. "Why?"

"Gut instinct," Vail said. "Really depends on whether or not he's involved with Marcks. But even if he's not, this is a guy who's had some run-ins with law enforcement. He's living in a house that doesn't belong to him. He sees us coming, yeah, I think his predisposition is gonna be to take off. He's not going to hang around to answer questions."

"I'm with Vail," Ramos said.

Hurdle mulled that over, then said, "Okay, the seven of us go. We'll treat him like a hostile."

Walters glanced over at the screen. "Any firearms-related offenses?"

"Nothing in the system." Tarkoff shrugged. "Doesn't mean much, if you ask me."

"I agree," Hurdle said. "Wear your vests."

They took two cars and half an hour later they were sitting at the mouth of the cul-de-sac, a few houses away from Gaines's location.

"Nice homes," Morrison said. "Three or four thousand square feet, probably half a mil apiece. Maybe they've got another vacant place nearby?" He saw Vail's look and gave her a half grin. "Just saying—wouldn't mind spending a weekend, or a month or two, here."

Vail removed her Glock and got out of the vehicle, joining Hurdle at the front bumper of his sedan. "How about you and Walters deploy around back while I go up and knock? Woman, less threatening. Curtis and Rambo can take up positions by those trees about ten and fifteen yards from the door, Morrison and Tarkoff can take the sides of the house in case he jumps out one of the first-floor windows."

"I like it." Hurdle nodded at the men. "You heard Vail. Let's do it."

They moved into place swiftly, using the cover of bushes and thick tree trunks. As Vail approached the front lawn of the Colonial-style home, a car horn began honking.

What the hell?

Vail swiveled and tried to locate the vehicle. *This is deliberate. A spotter, watching out for Gaines, warning him someone was approaching the house?*

She was sure everyone heard the signal and realized what was happening. Before she could turn to make eye contact with Curtis and Ramos, gunshots burst through the front door. Vail dove to the grass, nearly dropping her Glock.

Seconds later the assault stopped.

"You okay?" Hurdle asked over the radio.

As Vail and Curtis ran a zigzag route toward the front of the house, Vail keyed her mic. "We're fine." *But the homeowners are not gonna be happy when they get back to Virginia and find their house shot to hell.*

"This is just great," Curtis said. "He's obviously not coming out and we can't go in."

Ramos positioned himself on the opposite side of the doorway behind a large planter. "Why the hell not?"

"No reason to. This is now a barricade situation."

Vail stood up and pressed her back against a pillar on the wood deck. "We should have SWAT deal with this."

"Good call," Curtis said. "Can't argue with that."

"*I* can argue with that," Ramos said as he peeked over the planter to get a better look.

"There's no exigency," Vail said. "No reason to go in. No one in harm's way. He's not even threatening to kill himself."

"I'm calling it in, making the request," Curtis said as he drew his radio.

The three of them heard the reply: SWAT was seventeen minutes out.

Vail texted the rest of the team, who also heard SWAT's ETA, and requested a SITREP—situation report—from each of them.

Seconds later, their responses came through: the rear of the house took gunfire as well. The sides were quiet.

Second gunman in there with Gaines? Marcks? Or was Gaines just standing in the middle of the residence and firing in both directions?

"We need to go in," Ramos said.

"Were you not listening?" Curtis asked.

"Booker Gaines," Vail yelled through the door. "This is the police. SWAT is en route. Throw down your weapon and come out with your hands on your head. We just want to talk." *Well, now I want to kick you in the nuts. But officially, we just want to talk.*

"Go away or I'll kill everyone in here!"

Vail and Curtis exchanged a look.

Vail keyed her radio. "Hurdle, you hear that?"

"I did."

Curtis elbowed her. "You got him to talk once. Keep the dialogue going."

"We certainly don't want that, Booker. Can I call you Booker?"

Gaines's answer was decisive: more ear-shattering gunfire.

Then silence.

Guess that would be no.

Ramos moved beside Vail and keyed the radio. "Boss, this guy ain't comin' out. And he may have hostages. We need to go in."

Hurdle, back at them over the two-way: "Give it a minute. Everyone hold your position."

At the sixty-second mark, Hurdle's voice crackled over the speaker. Vail lowered the volume: "We have zero confirmation he's got anyone in there. We're gonna wait and let SWAT handle it. They're making good time. Updated ETA, nine minutes."

"Let's use the time to our advantage," Vail said. "Rambo, you're with me."

"With you where?"

"We're gonna do a quick canvass. Maybe a neighbor's seen Marcks—or someone else—in there. We need to know if Gaines's really got hostages. C'mon," she said as she started a strategic retreat from the property. In truth, she wanted to take his mind off Gaines, let him cool down—and get him away from the house.

As they made their way along the sidewalk, Vail glanced over her shoulder at the street behind them, checking for the lookout—if he was still there—who had honked a warning to Gaines when they arrived. She saw only two cars, and both appeared unoccupied.

"Curtis," she said into her radio. "Head over to those vehicles parked at the curb. I don't think there's anyone in them, but be careful." She explained what she was looking for, and why.

"I'll ping you right back if I find anything."

Vail thanked him and continued on to the two-story to the east. No one answered, but at the residence to the west, an attorney who worked out of his home office—and who had to be persuaded to come to the door in view of the automatic gunfire—said he thought he had seen another man enter the residence.

"When was this?" Vail asked.

He glanced past Vail and Ramos nervously. "You sure it's safe to stand here?"

"The gunman's inside the house," Ramos said, "and we've got it surrounded. If you'd just answer the question, sir."

"A few days ago. Maybe Wednesday."

"How old was this guy?" Ramos asked.

He shrugged both shoulders as he thought. "Twenty, at most. A teen, maybe. I'm not even 100 percent sure it was that house. I think it was."

"Any other activity?" Vail asked. "People going in or out, cars or trucks that don't belong?"

"I've been tied up with a case I'm litigating. I haven't really paid that much attention."

"You know that your neighbor's been out of town?" Ramos asked.

"I only moved here five months ago. I haven't had time to go door-to-door meeting people." He made a show of checking his watch. "If you don't mind, I've got a conference call in five minutes. Assuming the shooting doesn't start up again."

For all our sakes, I hope that's the case.

"And do us a favor? Stay inside until we get the situation under control."

He gave a nervous laugh. "You don't have to ask twice."

They thanked him and started back toward the house just as SWAT arrived. The armored Bearcat—it looked like a cross between a tank and a truck—pulled in front.

Hurdle and Vail used the vehicle as a shield as they briefed the commander, whose uniform tag read "Morales."

"We did our best to put together a breach plan on the way using Google Earth images and what we could pull up on county records for the house's blueprints. What can you give us on the occupant?"

"Suspect's a squatter," Vail said. "Owners have been out of town for several months."

"Far as we know," Hurdle said, "there's no one else inside."

"Check that." Ramos waved a thumb over his right shoulder. "Neighbor back there saw a young male enter a few days ago."

"He *thinks* he saw," Vail said.

"So there could be two occupants," Morales said. "A hostage?"

"Potentially. Suspect said he had people in there and was going to kill them. But it could've just been bullshit to keep us from going in."

Morales absorbed that, then said, "What do we know about your guy?"

"Buster Gaines," Vail said. "He's got a sheet, in and out of trouble with the law. Domestic violence, drugs, assaults. Nothing over the top. His buddy's the fugitive serial killer Roscoe Lee Marcks, so it's possible Marcks is also inside."

An officer emerged from the SWAT vehicle with a K-9, who was outfitted in a black tactical vest, leading the way.

"That's Rex," Morales said. "Belgian Malinois."

"SEAL Team Six used one of those on the bin Laden raid," Hurdle said as he and Curtis joined them behind the Bearcat.

"Affirmative." Morales glanced around at the cul-de-sac. "Other than that one neighbor you talked with, have you done a canvass?"

"Only had time to hit a couple houses," Vail said. "The rest of us were holding our positions, all entrances and exits."

"You guys going to breach?" Curtis asked. "Or are we looking at a barricade?"

Morales chewed his bottom lip. "You think he's a talker? A negotiator?"

Ramos laughed. "No sir. Definitely not."

"Tried that," Vail said. "He answered with a burst of automatic rounds."

"Okay. He may have a young male in there, he's shown extremely violent tendencies, and he's volatile. I think we've got exigency. Better to assume that's the case than do a time/talk/tactics approach and have a hostage get killed."

"Time, talk, tactics?" Curtis asked.

"Methodical approach. We try to negotiate by phone, bull-horn, throw phones, anything that'll get him to communicate with us. If that doesn't work, we shift to annoyance tactics. Breaching windows, shutting off utilities, deploying flash bangs to get his attention and eventually tear gas to try and drive him out. We might even get a robot in there to get eyes on or send Rex in. All else fails, our team goes in. Very time-consuming. Could be an all-day—or more—affair."

"We've got Marcks out there," Hurdle said. "We can't afford to dick around with this guy."

"I've got other considerations," Morales said. "But I understand the pressure you're under." He gave the structure a once-over. "Gaines's not the homeowner, so I doubt he has authority to deny us access. We're going in. I'll deal with the consequences. If there are any." He then turned and conferred with his mission leader, a younger man with a crew cut. Morales brought the radio to his lips and issued orders to the other ten officers, who had already taken up their positions.

"Can we follow you in?" Ramos asked.

Morales gave Ramos a look that bled disbelief. "No."

Hurdle checked his watch. "How long?"

"I know you guys want to get in there ASAP. We'll do our best. But you gotta understand, it's a slow, systematic process."

As Morales moved off, Ramos frowned and said something to Hurdle. Vail did not hear it but she picked up Hurdle's response. "It was the right call, Rambo. If we knew for sure there's a hostage in there? We would've gone in. But he's got a semiauto and we had no good reason to enter."

"Seven of us and one of him," Rambo said. "That's all I'm saying. We could've handled this."

"I can do the math. Let it go." Hurdle kept his focus on the SWAT team as it deployed. "Take a breath. And stay on your toes."

Vail watched as Morales did a knock and notice—he banged on the door, announced who they were and that they were going to enter. Almost immediately, an officer released a couple of flash bangs on either end of the house. The mini-explosions were concussive, designed to induce fear and overwhelm the occupant—lead him to believe that an army was about to storm the place.

And that was not far from the truth, because in the next instant a breach specialist swung his battering ram and blasted the front door in. They tossed in a gas canister and entered.

A few minutes later, Curtis came up alongside Vail. "I don't hear anything."

"You won't. They're looking for a barricaded suspect, so they're not gonna be shouting to one another as they clear rooms like we do. Everything's done with low whispers and hand signals. That way they can also pick up any movement from the suspect—or hostage. Sometimes when they enter a room, they cover the angles and hold for several minutes in silence. Listening for movement."

Curtis eyed her. "How do you know so much about it?"

I'm part of a black ops team. "Read an article."

She checked her watch and waited. It was going to be awhile before they could get their hands on Gaines.

RAMOS, CURTIS, AND VAIL ENTERED FIRST, followed by Hurdle, Walters, Morrison, and Tarkoff. Hundreds of brass shell casings littered the granite floor and the smell of munitions hung in the air.

"Where's our suspect?" Hurdle asked.

Morales shifted his MP5 to the left, across his shoulder. "No one was in the house."

"No one—" Vail swung her gaze around the main floor. "We had the entrances and exits covered. How the hell did he get out?"

"Follow me."

Morales led Vail, Curtis, and Hurdle down to a finished basement, a large open room with sports loungers and a sixty-inch LED television with surround speakers mounted on the ceiling and walls.

"Got his assault rifle, though."

"He left it behind?" Curtis asked.

"Found it down here," Morales said as his tactical boots gripped the tile floor. "When we breached the door, he needed to get out fast. As soon as you see what I'm about to show you, you'll understand."

They moved left past a pool table and stopped at a closed door. Morales pushed it open and they filed in.

"Laundry," Hurdle said.

What gave it away? Washing machine? Or the dryer? Vail walked in farther and examined the long and narrow area, which seemed to run at least half the length of the house. Above her were two windows. One of them was unlocked. "You saying he went out through here? We had guys on both sides of the exterior."

"First clue was that we found the rifle right where you're standing. Second clue was—well, take a look."

She climbed up onto the washing machine and peered into the yard. Stands of pine, hemlock, cedar, and cypress stared back at her, a melting layer of snow blanketing its floor. *It's like a friggin' forest back here.* "What am I missing?"

"Over here." Morales moved several feet deeper into the room. "I think the unlocked window was a ruse. Or it could've been accidently left like this by the homeowner and Gaines had nothing to do with it." He pulled open a cabinet door and gestured them over. "I was referring to this. Rex sniffed it out."

Vail jumped down off the appliance, turned on her phone's flashlight, and peered in. "Gaines made a tunnel? Are you kidding me?"

"Wish I were. I've only seen this twice before, in all my years with SWAT."

Vail stuck her head in. "Where does it lead?"

"Go in, take a look."

Vail snorted as she drew back. "Uh, no thanks. I don't get along well with tight spaces." *And this is one time when I can say no.*

"I'll go," Curtis said as he turned on his iPhone light and climbed in. "I've gotta see this."

He got in about five feet before he backed out. "Okay, I've seen enough. Nothing elaborate, barely enough room to fit a body. Tell ya, if I wasn't claustrophobic before, this could definitely make me catch it."

"It's not a contagious disease," Vail said.

"Whatever. I'm not going all the way through."

"No need," Morales said. "One of our guys took off all his gear and went in. There are some wood planks to shore up the walls. Comes out just past the property line, twelve feet north-west, in the dense trees."

"That's why he didn't take the rifle with him. Hard enough to get a *body* through." Hurdle crouched down and took a look for himself. "He really built a tunnel?"

"He's been here for—who knows. Several months?" Curtis said, dusting off his hands. "Maybe he got bored."

Hurdle shook his head. "Think like a criminal, Curtis. He must've known Marcks's escape plans and he dug the tunnel because Marcks was planning to spend some time here. We come knocking, he'd have an escape route."

"Probably took him . . . what, a few days? A week? To clear twelve feet of dirt?" Curtis said. "But he'd need help, someone to haul off the buckets of soil as he went."

"Could've been Scott MacFarlane," Vail said.

Morales turned and headed out of the laundry room. "Bottom line, your guy—or guys—are gone."

I can do the math as well as Rambo. Seven against one, or two, and we still lost. "So no hostages."

"Doubt it," Morales said. "But with the tunnel, hard to know. Forensics may help you on that one. Meantime, we're casting a wide net, see if we can prevent Gaines from leaving the area. I've got more men on the way. They'll be here in five or six minutes. Police are mobilized, too. But I'm not hopeful. Acres of densely wooded land, lots of residences, a park."

Vail looked out the windows and saw the boots and legs of SWAT officers searching the woods. "A school. I saw one nearby. On the aerial view. They need to go into lockdown."

Morales stopped and pulled his two-way and chattered into it, passing on Vail's suggestion.

She heard someone descending the basement steps and saw Ramos approaching, followed by Tarkoff and Morrison.

As Curtis filled them in, Vail turned to Hurdle. "We blew this about as badly as it could be blown."

He glanced around, taking in the laundry room and Gaines's escape route. "Self-recrimination's not gonna help us catch this knucklehead. Yeah, had we known he was going to come at us with guns blazing, we would've done things a little differently. But given what we knew, he was not an extreme threat. And there's no way in hell we'd think he built a tunnel. It didn't work out the way we wanted, but I don't think we blew it. Sometimes shit happens. Way I see it, no one got killed—on our team or innocents in the area. Only bad thing in all of this is that one of our prime witnesses is not in our custody answering our questions."

Vail put her phone away. "Then I suggest we turn our attention to getting a warrant and tossing this place, see what we can learn about Gaines and Marcks and their relationship. Maybe we'll get lucky and find a cell phone he left behind with Marcks's number in it."

"Don't count on it," Curtis said. "Too goddamn easy."

"Plain sight stuff," Hurdle said to everyone. "We need something that'll give us probable cause for a warrant."

They fanned out, all of them but Vail and Curtis heading back upstairs.

Vail shoved the Samsung in her pocket, pulled on a pair of gloves, and wandered around the room. There was not much "in plain sight," so she made her way over to the living area—the entertainment cabinet and loungers—while Curtis checked out a nearby walk-in closet.

She noticed something wedged into the side of the recliner—
a DVD case with a handwritten note in Sharpie marker:

7 y/o

Vail bent her head and read the spine from a different angle.
Seven-year-old?

She pushed down hard on the leather seat and the cush-
ion parted from the armrest, revealing part of the DVD's cover.
"Uh, got something."

Curtis joined her just as she held up the disc. "Are you shitting me? Child porn?"

A photo of a naked boy had been inserted inside the clear
plastic sleeve of the case. She pulled it open and found a burned
DVD marked in the same black handwriting:

Jimmy

"Yo, Hurdle," Vail called out.

A few seconds later he came halfway down the steps.

"We've got our probable cause. Not exactly what we were
looking for, but it'll do."

Given Curtis's firsthand knowledge of the scene and police
department procedure, he drove back to Fairfax to videocon-
ference with a magistrate. If all went smoothly, he would have
the warrant in hand in about an hour.

"Makes me want to vomit." Hurdle tossed the disc onto the
recliner. "At least it'll get us the warrant. Good job."

"I'm afraid to see what else we'll find. This cabinet could be
filled with more of that shit." She sat down on the lounger and
thought a moment. "Can I ask you something?"

"You're asking me permission to ask me a question?"

"No. Yes." She glanced around and saw that they were alone. "I want to know what's up with Rambo. I mean, you know him. Pretty well, I take it."

Hurdle pulled out a pack of gum and folded a stick into his mouth. "How do you mean?"

"Kind of chomping at the bit."

"His time in Iraq, urban warfare. Changes you, your outlook. Asked him about it once. He said, 'You can't be afraid to go after the baddies or you shouldn't be carrying a badge. Risk is part of the job.'"

"I'm okay with smart risk. Even desperate risk. But not foolish risk."

"Every circumstance is different. You never did something that, in the moment, seemed like it had to be done, but in retrospect was a foolish risk?"

Hmm. Let me count the times.

Hurdle did not wait for a reply—or he read Vail's face and got his answer. "I guess one man's smart is another man's foolish."

"Not sure I agree with that."

"I take Rambo for what he is. A good cop, solid task force member. He just needs some policing at times." He headed toward the stairs. "I'm gonna get up there and finish looking around."

Vail checked her watch, then called Jasmine to see if she remembered anything about Gaines, whether or not she might have an idea as to where he would go, places he used to hang out. She doubted Jasmine could offer anything of value, but it was a logical question to ask.

The call went to voice mail and Vail left a message. *Maybe she turned the ringer down while she was in a movie and forgot to fix the volume.*

As she sat down to clear her mind and think, Walters and Tarkoff joined her with reports of what they had seen in the bedrooms, most of which seemed to pertain to the homeowners. However, it did appear that two beds had been slept in recently. They would need a more thorough evaluation with forensics to know for sure.

Hurdle followed moments later with his assessment of the caliber and type of weapon Gaines had used. Based on the spray pattern and shell casings, it looked to him to be .40-caliber rounds from a semiautomatic weapon. "Not very helpful—we pretty much knew that when we were under attack. But I think there's evidence of two shooters, one of whom only had a handgun. We really need to wait for crime scene and their analysis. And no sign of that teen the neighbor told you about."

"Could be we were right before," Vail said. "About finding Scott MacFarlane. Just a guess, but it's an educated one. That group seems to have been together since middle school, if not before. No reason to think MacFarlane was an aberration. And it would explain why we haven't been able to find him."

By the time they finished their discussion, Curtis texted her that the warrant was approved.

They all returned to their floors and Vail began by rummaging through the basement closet, picking up where Curtis left off. It doubled as a second pantry and storage room. She saw winter clothes, ski equipment, and other assorted items a family stuffs into available spaces.

Vail saved the entertainment center for last, partly out of avoidance. She already knew what she was going to find.

When Curtis returned with the warrant, she briefed him on what he missed, including the potential second occupant in the house. She then moved on to the cabinet beneath the television. They were full of old DVDs and tapes of family videos from the last twenty years or so.

Well that was a pleasant surprise.

Until she opened another drawer. "Here we go. More DVDs. And not the G or PG rated kind. Except . . ."

Curtis crossed the room and knelt beside her. "Gay porn?"

They looked at each other.

"Wonder if Gaines—is he, *was* he, Marcks's lover?"

"Interesting question. Or MacFarlane, if it was him who was shacked out here with him. Let's keep looking."

Vail returned to her area and found sex videos with handwritten labels. She put one into the DVD player and fired up the TV.

"Oh shit," Curtis said. "More child porn."

Vail wanted to turn away but could not—she needed to see who was in the video; specifically, which adults, if they revealed themselves to the camera. "There's Gaines. Right?"

Curtis, his eyes narrowed as if to lessen the impact of what he was viewing, tilted his head.

Vail hit rewind on the remote, got the spot she wanted, and hit pause. "Only got a portion of his face in the frame."

"The lab can do a better job with this, but I'd say, maybe. Maybe not. Don't know, could be him."

Based on what she was seeing, she thought again about that teen the neighbor mentioned. But the age was not right. These were not young men, they were boys. "When's crime scene due here?"

"They're here. Started on the main floor." He held up one of the DVDs with a gloved hand. "If it is him in these videos, or some of them, we've got him dead to rights."

"Either way," Vail said, doing her best to keep the bile from rising in her throat, "really wish we had this bastard in custody."

"We'll get him," Curtis said, averting his eyes from the screen. "Turn that shit off. We'll let the guys at the lab analyze it, see if we can get some other faces and IDs. Maybe we'll get lucky and get MacFarlane in it, too."

"Hopefully they can pull some metadata off the DVDs that can tell us where they were made, shut them down. Vail returned the disc to its holder and pulled out her radio, told Hurdle what they had found.

"I'd like to get some agents in the Cleveland FBI field office over to the house where these homeowners are staying. Break the news to them about their property and unwelcome guest. Leave out the part about him shooting up their place. But we need to cover all the bases and ask if the husband had a secret collection of child porn. And if he's gay."

Hurdle snickered. "That's gonna be a fun conversation."

"Got a better idea. Have them arrange for a Skype session when they get there. I want to see their reaction. No—I want to interview the husband, away from the wife. If this is his shit, he won't admit it in front of her."

"Will he admit it even in private? It's a federal offense."

"I'm not expecting a verbal admission. That's why I want to Skype. I need to see his reaction."

"I'll have someone arrange it. Over."

Vail continued looking through the collection. "Assuming this stuff belonged to Gaines, I can see why the asshole ran.

Might have nothing to do with Marcks. You got anything over there?"

"Male porn. Bondage stuff. Nothing like what you found." Curtis tossed a stack of magazines to the ground. "Like you said, maybe this is just noise."

"If we catch Gaines, this isn't noise, Curtis. It's leverage."

35

Marcks sat in his '64 Buick, windows closed and the Nats hat pulled down low over his forehead. With the sunglasses and beard, he hardly looked like himself. Which was the point, of course.

Once the car he had been following turned into the Lake Ridge neighborhood, he knew where Vail and company were headed. It allowed him to drop back and keep a discreet distance.

Unfortunately, because he no longer had a cell phone, he could not warn Booker and Scott who was on the way to their place. So he did the next best thing.

Blaring his horn from over a block away would be heard—but he could not be seen because of the trees and the curved angle of the streets.

There was no way for him to know for sure, but he was reasonably certain that they had gotten the message. He moved farther down the road and parked on a side street while waiting for Vail to leave—assuming his buddies did not kill her.

But when the SWAT truck rumbled past him, his shoulder muscles tensed and his level of apprehension clicked up several notches.

Almost four hours later, Vail and a couple of other cops drove by, headed away from Booker's house. Though he wanted to double-back and check on his friends—were they in body bags or had they gotten away?—he started up the Buick and followed Vail's vehicle, keeping as far back as he could without losing her.

Thus far, she seemed to have no idea she was being shadowed . . . which was exactly what he hoped.

IT WAS NEARLY 8:00 PM when Vail pulled into the driveway of a residential neighborhood. Marcks coasted down the street, several car lengths behind her, and came to a stop against a curb. Idling, observing.

He killed the engine and sat there, wondering what his next move would be . . . what it *should* be.

One thing was certain, however: he was building his book of intelligence, and now he had a key piece of information, one with potential leverage: he knew where Karen Vail lived.

36

Robby slid into bed beside Vail and touched her foot with his.

She jumped. "Oh my god, that's cold."

"Sorry. I'm freezing. Warm me up."

The down comforter had trapped her body heat and banished her own chill ten minutes ago. Now toasty warm, she cuddled up to him and wrapped her arms around him.

They slept without interruption until a noise startled Vail. She sat up, the cool bedroom air snapping her mind to attention. Or the most attention it could muster at 3:00 AM.

She put a hand on Robby's shoulder and shook him. "Hey, honey. Wake up."

He groaned. "Tell me it's not morning."

"Yeah, it's morning. Three in the morning."

He rolled over and faced her. "What's wrong?"

"I heard something." She reached over to her night table and unholstered her Glock, then threw the covers back and stepped onto the cold wood floor.

Robby swung his legs over the side of the bed and likewise grabbed his handgun. In a low voice: "What did you hear?"

"Not sure, but it woke me."

"Maybe you were dreaming."

And then she heard it again: a thump. She glanced at Robby: he nodded.

They advanced toward the bedroom door.

"Where was it?" he whispered.

Good question. "Kind of sounded like it was behind the house or—"

"In front of it."

Vail nodded. "Which doesn't make sense. How could it be in both places?"

They walked down the hallway, lights off, their eyes acclimated to darkness and wanting to keep it that way. The second they turned on a lamp, their night vision would be shot.

Another thump. Vail stopped.

"Could it be your aunt?"

"She sleeps like a rock," Vail said. "Never gets up in the middle of the night."

"Still, we want to be absolutely sure before we pull the trigger. You know?"

"Yeah, fine." She moved to the front window and peeked through the curtain. "I see a late model pickup halfway down the block and something behind it, looks like an old sedan."

"Anything else? You see anyone?"

Vail swung her gaze left and right. "No."

Again. A thump.

"This way. Definitely out back." He led her to the rear door and they took up positions on either side.

"Ready?"

Robby tilted his head. "I guess so."

Vail pulled on the knob and Robby pivoted into the yard—

where he came face-to-face with a raccoon creeping out of the crawlspace beneath the house. It saw him and got up on its hind legs.

"Are you serious?" He stepped toward the animal. "Get out of here. Go on!"

It turned and scurried off.

"A raccoon ruined our night's sleep?"

Robby yawned. "Apparently. Either I'm sleeping like a log or you're sleeping lightly."

"This Marcks case has me a little jumpy. With him out there somewhere, it's a perpetual feeling of unease. I'm worried about Jasmine."

He led Vail back into the bedroom, where they reholstered their weapons. "Look, it was her decision to go it alone, without your help."

"Only because we failed her. The cop paid with his life, which sucked big time. But I can't fault her. I might've done the same thing."

Robby groaned as he pulled the covers back over his body, shivering from the now-cold sheets against his now-cold body. "You'll catch him soon."

Vail sat up in bed, her mind a tangle of competing thoughts on the case. "Yeah," she said absentmindedly. But it didn't matter because Robby was already asleep.

37

Vail spent the morning at the BAU planning the interview that she had requested with the owners of the Lake Ridge home and setting up a secure Skype connection with the Cleveland field office agents.

"Knock, knock."

She looked up from her desk and found Art Rooney standing there.

"Got a minute?"

"I've got five."

Rooney grinned. "Good. I only need two. Want to know what I just found out?"

Vail lifted her brow. "Let me guess. Forensics on that new arson scene."

"The accelerant."

She leaned back in her desk chair. "What was it?"

"Kind of interesting. So you know the common ones: petrol, kerosene, mineral turpentine, diesel. Complex mixtures of hydrocarbon molecules."

"Yeah, that much I remember."

"Well, my guy didn't use any of these—which are all pretty

much readily available. For some reason, he used a non-halogenated ether."

"Ether." Vail drew her chin back.

"I know, not something you're familiar with."

"No, that's not it. I came across it. Recently, too."

"Well, it's not rare or anything like that. It's a chemical used in all sorts of things. When I was a kid they sprayed a variant of it, ethyl chloride, on baseball players who got hit with a pitch to freeze the area and reduce the swelling."

"No, I mean I saw it in a case of mine." She snapped her fingers. "That's what Marcks used to subdue his victims. He soaked a cloth with ether and then held it over their mouths and noses." Vail thought a second, then said, "Wait, you said your arsonist used it as an *accelerant*?"

"The kind he used is very volatile. Extremely flammable. Gives off irritating or toxic fumes—or gases—in a fire when exposed to open flames, sparks, that sort of thing. Gas/air mixtures are explosive. So when combined with what we found there—a Sterno flame—it'd work pretty damn well. Unconventional, but effective." Rooney handed her a folder. "Copy of the forensics reports for you to read while you're eating breakfast."

"Can't wait."

"Unfortunately, we've got laboratory proof of how well that chemical works as an accelerant. It's the same non-halogenated ether used in this UNSUB's other arsons."

"That's weird, though, don't you think?"

"That he used an unusual accelerant? It's not unheard of."

"No. I mean, on a basic level, he had reasonable access to common accelerants, but he used an uncommon one. *Why* would be a key question. But I was referring to the fact that the accelerant used in your arson cases is the *anesthetic* used in my serial killer cases. Bizarre, don't you think?"

"Not necessarily. Coincidence, if that. Now if you traced the chemical to a specific manufacturer and batch number in your case that matched the manufacturer and batch number used in my case, yeah, then I'd say it's obviously related. But that's not what we've got here."

Vail shrugged. "If you say so."

"Don't take my word for it. Tell me what relevance you think it's got—to either of our cases."

"I'll have to think on it. At first glance, nothing. The arsons started after Marcks was behind bars, right? So we know he didn't do those. Just the last two fires are suspect, I guess, because Marcks was in the wild. *If* Marcks is responsible. And *if* the other fires are truly related to your more recent ones." She thought a moment. "Unless Marcks knows the arsonist."

"All the arsons *are* related," Rooney said. "Same UNSUB for all of them. I'd stake my reputation on it. Which means none of them are Marcks's handiwork."

"I'll buy that." Vail shoved her hands into her pockets. "Hey, we all need to be humbled once in a while, right?"

"You admit that?"

"Of course not." She gathered up her purse and the copy of Rooney's case folder. "But it sounded good, didn't it?"

VAIL SETTLED HERSELF into the ergonomic conference room chair in front of a secure laptop, the Skype interface opened. Curtis entered and sat down, a visitor badge clipped to his shirt pocket.

"You ready?"

Curtis took a seat. "So we've got the homeowner. Stuart Sheridan."

"Right. His wife's Nancy, the one with cancer. So we should go easy on him."

"Unless Stu's a child pornographer."

"Then we go for the jugular." Vail clicked "video call" and the familiar Skype ring filled the external speakers.

A suited agent answered the call. "Agent Vail, I've got Stuart Sheridan here with us, as requested." He pivoted the laptop and revealed a man in his forties, graying at the temples.

"Good morning, Mr. Sheridan."

"Agent Vail, is it? I'd like to know what this is about. I haven't been told anything. But anytime the FBI shows up at your door it's not good news."

"No, Mr. Sheridan, it's not. I mean, it's not horrible, but it has serious implications. Let's put it that way."

"I don't care how you put it. Just tell me what's going on."

"You own the home in Lake Ridge?" She read off the address.

"Yeah, about ten years now. Why?"

"Can you tell us what you've got in the basement, in the entertainment center?"

Sheridan cocked his head to the side. "How do you know about our basement? What the hell's going on?"

"We had reason to enter your home. It has nothing to do with you, I assure you."

"That's not an—"

"Mr. Sheridan, this will go a lot faster if you just answer my questions, and then I'll explain everything. Okay?"

Sheridan took a deep breath and sat back in his chair. "Fine."

"The entertainment cabinet. You've got DVDs in there."

"Yeah, movies my wife and I bought back before Netflix and HBO Go started streaming. And we've got some videotapes of our family trips, stuff like that. Why?"

"Can you describe some of the types of movies you've got there? Not the ones of your family."

He shrugged. "Some romantic comedies—*When Harry Met Sally. You've Got Mail.* Thrillers and suspense, some dramas. *Hunt for Red October. No Way Out.* We've got a little bit of everything. Some foreign films. *Chocolat. Edward Scissorhands.* Oh, and a bunch of Disney films, the animated classics, the early Pixar ones—*Toy Story, Monsters*—really, can you tell me why that's relevant?"

"Any adult films in your collection?"

"Adult? You mean like—X-rated? Porn?"

"Like that, yeah."

"No." He shook his head. "My kids play Xbox down there, they watch TV in the basement. It's our playroom. Why would you even ask that question?"

"We found some movies of . . . of that nature. And I wanted to know if they're yours."

"Definitely not mine. Now—Agent Vail, I have to insist you tell me why you've been in my house without our knowledge. And—and how those X-rated movies got there."

Vail squared her shoulders. Based on his reaction and body language, she was reasonably certain that Sheridan was telling the truth. "You had a squatter living there for the past several months."

Sheridan's mouth dropped open. "You're not serious. We've been here with my wife, she's in an aggressive cancer treatment program. With the kids and everything, I haven't had a chance to fly home. My neighbor's supposed to be checking on things, taking in any mail that's not forwarded here."

"He or she isn't doing too good a job."

"This squatter. What's he been doing in my house?" Sheridan shivered, twisted his face with revulsion. "This is disgusting. I feel . . . violated."

"We had reason to question him and we had an informant tell us where he could be found. Your house. There was—well, he had some automatic weapons and your front door is, um, it needs to be replaced. As soon as possible. It's been snowing here. Our crime scene unit should be finishing up today."

"Crime scene unit." He covered his face with both hands. "Jesus Christ."

"Mr. Sheridan, did you bring a laptop or tablet with you to Ohio?"

He looked up. "Both. Why?"

"Would you consent to having the FBI do a search of them?"

"What for?"

"We just need to confirm what you told us. Bottom line, if we don't find any child porn, we'll leave you alone."

"How long will that take? I've got a bid that needs to be completed by this afternoon. Do you have to take it with you?"

"I don't think that'll be necessary. An hour should be sufficient. Give or take. But if I need to follow up with something regarding your house, can I call you?"

He looked at Vail with weary eyes. "Of course."

"Sorry to be the bearer of bad news. I wish you and your wife luck with her treatment." Vail finished up the call, then disconnected Skype and turned to Curtis. "I think he was being honest with us."

"Yeah, he looked very surprised. And genuinely pissed off."

"So Booker Gaines will now have a warrant out for his arrest for possession of child pornography."

"I'll see if CSU can get us a list of items found in the house sometime today or tomorrow."

Vail pulled out her phone and looked at the display. *Shit. Still nothing from Jasmine.*

"Problem?"

"Jasmine's not answering her phone and didn't return my call. Left a voice mail, still haven't heard back."

"Try her again. Maybe she didn't hear it ring and doesn't realize she has a message."

When she called last time, it was a number I didn't recognize. Vail dialed it and waited, got a generic computerized greeting, then hung up.

"You want to go looking for her?" Curtis asked.

"Not really. Already got two people we're looking for. I'll put out a BOLO."

Curtis rose from his chair. "I'll let you handle that. You coming back to the command center?"

"If you can hang out a few minutes, we can take my car over, pick up yours later."

38

As Vail pulled out of the parking lot, she chuckled. "Did you see that old Buick?"

Curtis swiveled his head back to the right. "Missed it. Why?"

"Mid-sixties. I think it was a '64 LeSabre. My friend's mom had one of those. She drove carpool to ballet lessons every Wednesday night."

"You?" Curtis laughed. "Ballet lessons?"

"What's so funny?"

"Can't see you wearing a tutu, that's all."

"Anyway," she said, "those cars, they didn't have seatbelts in the back. Guess it was before it was the law. But when my mom found out, she wouldn't let me go with them unless I rode in the front, where there *were* seatbelts. Which was a problem because my mother had a class on Monday and Wednesday nights, and if I sat in the front, her friend's daughter had to sit in the back without a seatbelt."

"Lemme guess. That next week they had rear belts installed."

"Yeah—and a couple weeks later, boom. Real bad rear end accident. Crushed the trunk, pushed us into the car in front of us and shot it across the intersection into a telephone pole.

That seatbelt saved my life. I would've flown right through the windshield."

"Fate, you know?"

"Don't tell me you believe in that."

"Hey, when it's your time, it's your time. Seatbelts, no seatbelts, vest, no vest . . . your number's up, you're done in this life."

"So why do you have a seatbelt on right now?"

"Really, Karen? Because it's the law. And *I'm* the law."

THEY ARRIVED AT THE COMMAND POST, where all team members were present. They spent the next hour reviewing their status on the case: Marcks, Kubiak, Gaines, Stuckey, and their efforts to find Marcks's last known associate: Scott MacFarlane.

"While I was in town," Ramos said, "I sat down with the inmate Marcks got into the fight with at Potter. Patrick O'Shea. Wanted to be sure he wasn't in on the escape. You know, like the fight was a ruse designed to get Marcks into the medical transport."

"It *was* a ruse," Hurdle said. "Only question was whether O'Shea was complicit or just used. Even though he got the better of the fight. By design."

"And let me guess," Vail said. "O'Shea wasn't talking."

"Actually, he did. He basically said he had nothing to do with it. Marcks insulted him and he beat him to a pulp."

Vail nodded. "Guess male bravado trumps looking like a stoolie."

"This guy's huge," Ramos said. "It's like they put Marcks on a copier and hit 'enlarge 10 percent.'"

They all laughed.

"Point is, no one's gonna get in his face, stoolie or not. And that's what made me think he was telling the truth. No way Marcks would pick a fight with this guy unless he had other motives."

"I think I should mention that I haven't heard from Jasmine."

"Should we be concerned?" Morrison asked.

Vail shrugged. "I am. She's never ignored my calls before."

"Try her again," Hurdle said. "Over what period of time?"

"A day, give or take."

"We should put out a BOLO, see if we can get our army of eyes around town looking for her."

"Already done."

"Keep us posted."

"Something else I wanted to mention," Vail said. "Not sure if it's relevant or not, but a weird forensic finding came up in another case I thought I should make you all aware of, just in case it becomes significant—or somehow suddenly becomes meaningful to our pursuit of Marcks."

"And that is?"

"A series of arsons that have been going on for a while now, first one a year or two after Marcks started doing time in North Carolina. Last two were set after he escaped."

"And why are we discussing this?" Tarkoff spread his hands. "What's it got to do with Marcks?"

"Marcks used an anesthetic-soaked rag to subdue his victims. That same chemical was used as the accelerant in the arson cases."

Tarkoff leaned forward, as if closer proximity would bring greater clarity. "The anesthetic is also an accelerant?"

Hurdle shook his head. "I don't see the connection."

"Hang on a second," Morrison said. "What chemical was it?"

"Something unusual as far as accelerants go. I mean, it's a fairly common chemical, a form of ether. Begins with an *n*, I think. I'm blanking on it. Or an *h*. Hydrogen or halogen something." She rose from her chair. "Let me just get the file."

"Where you going?" Hurdle asked, checking his watch.

"It's in my car."

"I've got a meeting in twenty minutes."

"We can do it later," Vail said. "It's not urgent."

Hurdle chewed on his lip. "Nah, let's do it now while we've got everyone here. Double time it."

"Be back in thirty seconds."

VAIL STEPPED OUTSIDE and jogged over to her car, which was two rows away in the Mason District Station parking lot, pulling out the key fob as she approached.

She opened the back door, retrieved the file, and chirped the remote. As she turned back toward the command post, her eye caught sight of the '64 Buick parked just ahead of her, about twenty yards away.

That's the second time I've seen that car.

She tucked the folder beneath her arm and advanced on the sedan, which had been backed into a row of spots that fronted a stand of trees.

Has the driver been following me? An undercover? For what reason?

As she wondered if it was in any way related to the covert work she had done for the Pentagon—something she would not dismiss out of hand—she got a better view of the vehicle and could see that it was vacant.

Vail noted the plate and pulled out her phone to ask for a registration check.

She peeked in through the window, cupping her face against the glass to cut the glare, when something sharp and hard struck her in the back of the head, slamming her cheek into the doorframe.

Vail tried to turn toward her attacker but he kept her face and body pinned tightly against the car. She tried to grab her Glock but could not get her hand up to the holster. She writhed and twisted, trying to dislodge the man's grip on her.

C'mon, Karen! Fight!

The car keys and file folder hit the ground and her handcuffs slipped off her belt as she again tried to wriggle out of his grasp—

Until he grabbed her hair and slammed her face one last time into the car window.

39

"She's not answering." Hurdle lowered the phone from his ear and checked his watch. "This is the longest thirty seconds I've ever lived through. Curtis, do me a favor and go see what's keeping her. Otherwise we'll just do it tonight. Or tomorrow."

"On it." Curtis pushed open the command center door and walked down the two steps to the asphalt pavement, then glanced around. Vail was not in sight. He went over to where they parked, circled her car, looked in the backseat and did not see the folder.

"So she already got it." He swung his gaze left and right. "Then where the hell did she go?"

He pulled out his cell and called her. It rang three times and—he stopped and looked to his right. Listened. Thought he heard something, but it stopped. The call went to voice mail.

He tried her number again, moving in the direction of what he thought sounded like a ringing phone. Straight ahead and a bit to the left. It was very faint, which made sense: Vail kept her volume turned down most of the time.

Again, voice mail clicked on.

He hit "redial" and started walking faster. About ten yards away he saw Vail's Samsung lying on the ground alongside a set of handcuffs, a manila folder, and a stack of stapled papers riffling in the breeze.

He knelt down and looked it over, then swiveled on his heels and checked for blood or other signs of a struggle. But there was nothing.

Curtis dialed Hurdle and swung his head in all directions while he waited for the call to connect.

Hurdle answered on the third ring. "Look, I've gotta get going. Just forg—"

"You're not going anywhere. Get everyone outside. We got a big fucking problem."

40

The team huddled in the area where Curtis found Vail's phone. Curtis's cell was pressed to his ear as he requested that Crime Scene be immediately dispatched to their location. The only good news was that the forensic technicians were not far off. While there was a local unit in the Police Department's Mason District station, they did not handle complex violent crime–related cases. However, they would only need twenty minutes to make the drive from the Massey Building headquarters—adjacent to the records room where Vail and Curtis retrieved the PD-42 regarding the Marcks's teen shooting.

"This is exactly how I found it," Curtis said as he snapped some pictures with his iPhone. "That folder there is the one she came out for."

Hurdle put both hands on his hips. "So she got it from her car, which is what, about twenty, twenty-five yards away?"

Tarkoff, who was walking along the stand of trees, stopped suddenly. "If she had the folder, why wouldn't she just come right back to the RV? She knew you didn't have a lot of time."

"She saw something that intrigued her," Hurdle said. "Or

someone called her over and she thought it was important enough to stop. Maybe somebody in distress?"

"Or pretending to be in distress." Curtis turned in place and looked at the large brown, sand, and turquoise single-story building behind him. "The police department has cameras. Wait here for Crime Scene, I'm gonna go grab a look."

"I'm with you," Hurdle said.

They jogged into the station's lobby and up to the large bulletproof glass-enclosed half-moon front desk where two PCAs, or Police Citizens Assistants, were seated.

"Richie's here," Curtis said to Hurdle as they approached. "He's a cop, on light duty after blowing out his ankle." Curtis stepped up to the speaker by the pass-through slot. "Yo, Richie!"

A man in his thirties turned and gave Curtis a nod.

"I need the video feed from the parking lot, the past hour."

Richie put his coffee mug down and hobbled over to the window. "Parking lot?"

"Officer was abducted. Move fast, Richie. Her life depends on it. We're coming around. Jane," Curtis said to the closest PCA, "let us in."

When Curtis and Hurdle entered the horseshoe-shaped administrative space, Richie was clicking his keyboard and downloading the footage to a flash drive.

"Pull it up on that screen," Curtis said, gesturing at the one closest to him and Hurdle. "Can I have the mouse?"

Richie handed it to Curtis, who began fast-forwarding, watching the seconds cascade by until it got to within fifteen minutes of the current time. Then he slowed it down and hit "play" when he reached the spot he wanted. They watched as Vail, barely visible in the distance, exited the Marshals' RV.

"Okay, so she's walking toward the camera," Hurdle said.

"Toward her car. We parked in the first row of spots."

"She disappeared." Hurdle turned to Richie. "Camera lost her. We have another angle?"

"I can check."

"Don't need it," Curtis said. "She's back in the camera's field of view. Walking away from her car. And the folder's under her arm."

They watched Vail's back another few seconds as she headed toward the task force command post—but veered to her right, the spot where they found her phone.

"Fuck me," Curtis said under his breath.

"What? What do you see?"

"Just a sec."

Curtis pulled out his pad and jotted down a note as Hurdle took over the mouse.

They watched as Vail bent over to look inside the car window—and a large male figure with a ball cap pulled low on his forehead emerged from the row of trees that stood along the parking lot's perimeter.

He struck Vail from behind, her head hit the door, they struggled, and then he slammed her into the car again. She dropped—but the man caught her before she struck the ground. He pulled open the back door and pushed her inside.

Curtis shifted position. "This is tough to watch."

"He's doing something—taking her Glock. Of course. And . . ." Hurdle tilted his head as he studied the screen. "Looks like he's tying her up."

The assailant got into the front seat and drove out of the lot.

"Hold it." Curtis stabbed at the monitor. "Back it up."

Hurdle clicked pause and the image froze, rewound frame by frame.

"There," he said, pointing at the best view they had of the man's face, behind the glare of the windshield as he started the car.

"Richie, I need that cleaned up. See if you can get us a decent still image of that asshole's face."

"Doubt it, too far away. But I'll do my best."

"And get a screen grab of the license plate, see who it's registered to. Probably stolen, but let me know. A cop's life is on the line. We need everything fast."

"I'm on it," Richie said as he picked up a phone on the desk and began dialing.

Curtis removed the USB flash with the downloaded footage and turned to Jane. "Can you tell the sarg I need a BOLO on this car? I think it may be a '64 Buick." He pulled out his phone and googled 1964 Buick. Images popped up on his screen. He scrolled and spread his fingers, enlarging the photo. "Affirm, it's a '64 Buick LeSabre." He read her the license plate.

"Got it," Jane said.

"That what you were talking about earlier?" Hurdle said. "You seemed to realize something."

They walked briskly back toward the knot of task force members in the lot. "Yeah, that Buick. Vail saw it in the parking lot of the Behavioral Analysis Unit when we left there this morning. Bastard must've followed us here."

"Why was she suspicious of it when she saw it?"

"She wasn't. It was just a car she knew during her childhood. Brought back some memories."

"You think it was Marcks?"

Hurdle glanced at Curtis. "I keep hoping it wasn't—but I'd bet money that it was."

41

Vail opened her eyes. Everything was blurry. She fought to focus and tried to move—but her hands were bound behind her with rope.

What the hell?

She was lying on her right side, facing the backseat of—*Holy shit, I'm in the Buick!*

It all now came back to her. She struggled to sit up and saw the back of a head—and the unmistakable face in the rearview mirror—of Roscoe Lee Marcks.

He did not glance back at her, did not divert his eyes from the road, which were scrolling left and right, no doubt looking for law enforcement. He had to know that if you kidnap an FBI agent, there would be an alert put out immediately. Then again, there were already alerts issued for his apprehension.

Vail leaned forward in the seat to ease the pressure on her wrists. "So, Rocky, what do you have planned for me? Gonna slice lines in my stomach and cut off my genitals?"

"You think you're so smart," he said. He did not raise his voice. His tone was not one of anger. It was matter of fact. "But you're fuckin' clueless."

"Am I? I know all about your murder of Eddie Simmons when you were fourteen. And I know about your love affair with Booker Gaines."

He swung his right arm around and slugged her in the face, a quick, powerful, fisted backhand that stunned her. It hurt. A lot. She saw stars and she lost consciousness for a brief second. At least she thought it was a brief second. They were still driving and her head was extended, resting against the back of the seat.

Obviously that's a sore subject. Certainly for me. She stretched her mouth open to make sure her jaw still worked.

"You asked what I have planned for you. I'm going to take you somewhere and then we're gonna talk. You're going to tell me what you know about the search for me, what approach your task force is taking. Then you're going to tell me where Jasmine's staying. When you've told me what I want to know, well, we'll see. I'm very angry for what you did to put me behind bars."

Translation: he's going to kill me.

"You've got it all wrong. I wasn't—"

"We're done talking. For now. When we sit down, that's when we'll clear the air."

Vail could not let it come to that.

She desperately wanted to hear what he had to say—her years-long curiosity was screaming at her to press forward, to ask him the questions she'd wanted to ask . . . the ones she hoped she would get the opportunity to ask back at Potter.

But that desire to know the answers did not outweigh her wish to live a long life.

She could feel that her Glock was no longer in its holster. No surprise there—it was now probably in Marcks's waistband. But

Tzedek, the dagger-like tanto she kept sheathed in the small of her back, was still there. And that was not surprising, either: Marcks was a career criminal but he was not a law enforcement officer trained in the proper ways of frisking an individual for hidden weapons. He likely checked her for an ankle holster—she was not wearing it today—but he had no reason to suspect she had anything other than standard-issue police weapons: a service pistol and perhaps a smaller backup piece. Vail was not aware of any FBI agents who carried such atypical weapons—well, other than she and her friend, Aaron Uziel.

Her bindings were tied tight but she was able to get her fingers on Tzedek's handle. She worked the knife out of its scabbard a quarter inch at a time, keeping her eyes on the rearview mirror, watching Marcks to see if he checked on her. He had not as of yet. Clearly he did not see her as a threat so his concern was focused on the more likely immediate danger: cops who by now could have a description of the vehicle. And him. And her.

He's going to either ditch the Buick soon or we're close to his secret interrogation site. Hurry up, Karen.

Vail cleared leather and had the tanto in hand. Now she had to turn it blade side up and start slicing. But manipulating it into position with her fingertips was more difficult than she thought—and she almost dropped it . . . which would've been disastrous.

She got the tip reoriented and started working on the twisted fibers of the rope. Even not restrained it would take some effort to cut through this material. But there was no choice. She had to do it.

"Do you really intend to kill your daughter?" she asked, hoping to distract him.

"I told you. We'll talk later. On my terms."

"She's your daughter. How can you do that?"

For the first time, Marcks looked at her in the rearview. She saw intense anger folded into the creases around his eyes and across his brow.

"Fine," she said, "I'll drop it." A moment passed. "When we sit down to talk, will you at least answer some of my questions? The ones I wanted to ask you at Potter?"

"Yeah," he said, leaning forward and peering down the road. "Why not?"

Vail followed his gaze and saw a police cruiser on the right.

Marcks slowed. "Don't try anything, Vail. Or I may have to slug you again."

More fibers gave way.

"Once was enough," she said. "Oh, wait, you hit me twice. I lost count." *And consciousness.*

They passed the cop. She watched as he sat in his car, looking at his radar gun, apparently more concerned with catching speeders than apprehending fugitives.

"Maybe third time's the charm."

Vail flexed her neck left and right. "No thanks."

Marcks turned onto a secluded side street—no houses in the immediate area—and no other vehicles.

Shit. Now or never.

Vail pressed harder and felt the fibers of one of the loops of the knot give way.

Keep going!

A minute later she felt the rope loosen. *Got it!* Her wrists popped apart and she grabbed the knife's handle firmly in her hand, then rotated it to get it into position.

She whipped it around and slapped it against Marcks's carotid, then grabbed a handful of hair protruding from beneath the hat. "Pull the fuck over! And keep your hands on the wheel where I can see them."

He laughed. "Go ahead. You don't have it in you to slice my neck open."

She pressed the blade into his skin and a thin line of blood oozed. "You wanna test me? You think you know who I am and what I've done, but you've got no fucking idea." She knocked his hat off and gathered up a full-fisted clump of hair, yanked back hard. He winced. "No one's going to question me killing you. No one. Because it's *justice*. Understand, asshole?"

He closed his eyes, the only acknowledgment, the only victory, he was going to allow her.

Vail knew she had to bully him because it was the only language Roscoe Lee Marcks understood. Show weakness and he would go for the jugular. Literally.

"You've got three seconds," she said. "Two."

Marcks lifted his foot off the accelerator and the car slowed. He angled the vehicle toward the right shoulder of the two-lane roadway and brought it to a stop.

"With your left hand, using two fingers, remove the Glock and hand it back to me. No fast moves."

He did as instructed and she released his hair to grab the pistol's handle, keeping the tanto's pressure constant against his neck. She wanted to check the handgun's chamber but needed two hands—and there was no way she was going to remove the knife from Marcks's neck.

"Now give me the keys."

He pulled them out of the ignition and handed them back—but moved them away when she reached for them. She dug the knife further into his skin, drawing more blood. "I swear, you fucking try anything—anything—and I'll kill you. Now give them to me!"

He handed them back and she took them.

She wanted to handcuff him but there was nothing to secure him to: no headrest. Nothing except the steering wheel. If she had him lean forward and put his hands behind his back, there would be no way for her to reach over the seat to fasten them.

Vail set the Glock on her lap and reached for her cuffs—but they weren't there. She patted the area around her, felt around with her shoes, taking care to keep firm pressure on the tanto—but they were not there.

She felt for her phone—gone as well. *Shit.*

"Pop your door open, then put your hands on the dashboard. Splay your fingers. And push your chest against the wheel."

As he leaned forward, she removed the knife from his neck and got out, pointed the Glock at his head as she came around to the front seat—

But Marcks accelerated hard and the Buick lurched forward, the rear door slamming into her side and spinning her into the asphalt.

Vail got to her knees and squeezed off three rounds at the retreating vehicle, pinging the metal and doing nothing to stop Marcks as he once again fled.

Into the ether.

VAIL STOOD UP and watched the LeSabre disappear down the road. She had forgotten that older cars did not have ignition locks that prevented the removal of the keys unless the engine was off—both an anti-theft and safety measure enacted by the federal government.

Sonofabitch. He knew what he was doing. She kicked at a rock in the road and sent it skipping down the pavement. *How could I miss that? Because I've taken three blows to the head. Probably have a concussion.*

Vail slipped the tanto into its sheath, realizing that Tzedek had once again saved her life. She had to remember to thank Uzi—the knife was turning out to be one of the best gifts anyone had ever given her.

She turned and looked in both directions but saw no one, no houses, no cars. And she had no phone . . . she could not even look on a map to see where she was.

Vail turned and started back from where she came, reasoning that she knew approximately how far it was to get back to the main road. There would be people and cars there—and a way to reach someone on the task force.

She holstered her Glock and palpated her swollen face, opened and closed her sore jaw, and felt lucky to be alive. She took a deep breath as she trudged forward, tried to ease her stress, to decompress after all that had occurred in the past hour or so.

And then she realized that she still had not heard from Jasmine.

42

All right, what've we got?" Hurdle was pacing near the spot where Vail's phone was found, vapor puffing from his mouth like steam from a locomotive. The other task force members stood in a circle nearby, while crime scene technicians processed the area behind them. More snow was expected, so they erected a temporary tent.

"BOLO's out," Walters said.

"The license plate came back to a used car lot in Fairfax," Curtis said. "I've got a uniform on his way there to talk with someone, see if the Buick was stolen or purchased and if so, by whom."

Ramos held up his phone. "We just got an image of the perp. A frame capture." He played with the screen and threw his head back. "Looks like Marcks. Sonofabitch."

Hurdle clenched his right fist. "I'm really beginning to hate this guy."

"He kidnapped one of our own," Morrison said. "From a goddamn police department—fifty yards from where we were all sitting."

"He's got a big set of balls, I'll give him that," Tarkoff said. "Or a death wish."

"Let's look at this a minute," Curtis said, holding up his hands. "Remove the emotion. It's not easy, believe me, I get that. Seeing him take Karen on the surveillance video—" His voice caught. "That was tough to watch. But we gotta push that out of our minds. We've gotta think clearly." He said it as if he were trying to convince himself.

His eyes settled on the photo of Marcks on Ramos's phone. "He found out about our task force. He knew about Vail's involvement in the case and somehow figured out where to find her. Assuming that was the Buick Karen saw when we left the BAU, he went to a goddamn FBI office—a ten most wanted fugitive—and hung out in the profiling unit's parking lot until she left and then followed us here. Drove into the police department, parked his car half a football field away from the hounds trying to track him down, and grabbed one of us up."

"If I didn't want to put a bullet between his eyes," Ramos said, "I'd have to call it impressive."

"Just making us earn our paychecks," Hurdle said. He stopped pacing and turned to face them. "We can't let this go unanswered. What have we missed?"

"Nothing," Tarkoff said. "Marcks is smart. He knows what he's doing. We feed off the dumb ones, catch them doing shit they need to do to stay alive. But Marcks, he knows our playbook, how we track fugitives. And he avoids doing that stuff. Makes our jobs that much more difficult."

"Yeah, well right now, one of our own is depending on us to work smarter. Work harder. Because if we don't—"

Curtis's phone rang. He glanced at the caller ID, did not recognize the number, and was about to ignore it when something told him to answer. "Curtis."

"Hey, it's me."

"Karen? Where are you? You okay?"

"Marcks grabbed me from the parking lot and—"

"That much we figured out. How'd you get away?"

"I'll tell you when I see you. Right now, all you gotta know is that Marcks left me about twenty minutes ago still driving the tan '64 Buick LeSabre." She gave him the location and requested that someone pick her up.

"On my way. And hey—really glad to hear your voice."

Vail laughed. "I could say the same thing."

43

"What are you doing here?" Hurdle asked as Vail and Curtis walked through the command post door.

"I work here," Vail said. "Unless you guys voted me off the task force while I was away on vacation."

"Not what I meant," Hurdle said. "Shouldn't you be at a hospital?"

Vail sat down at one of the workstations. "You mean because my head's spinning? I'll be okay. No time to sit in an ER."

"You're a mess. Your face looks like hell."

"Thanks. Not what a woman wants to hear, ever. Remember that, Hurdle, and it'll save you years of grief when you get married."

"I'm divorced."

"See what I mean?"

"Karen—"

"I'll get some ice later. It's just swollen."

Hurdle looked at Curtis, who held up a hand. "Already tried talking sense to her, boss."

Hurdle took a breath and cocked his head. "Suit yourself. Ramos and Tarkoff are on their way, just ran something down for me. Be here any minute. You should at least drink some water."

Vail shrugged. "Okay. Why?"

"Stop arguing." He poured her a glass from the refrigerator spout and handed it to her, then pulled out several ice cubes and dropped them in a Ziploc baggie. "Put this on your nose. And your jaw. And your eye."

Vail took it and gently pressed it against her skin. "This feels worse."

The door swung open and Ramos, Tarkoff, and Morrison entered.

"Great. Three of you. Grab a seat, let's get caught up."

They gave Vail a pat on the back as they passed her chair.

"So that Buick," Ramos said. "It was sold from a used car lot on Fairfax Boulevard in Fairfax. Owner's Oliver Aldrich. Old guy, pushing ninety-five. Pretty good memory, though. Remembers selling the car to a guy matching Marcks's description. I showed him the mug shot and yeah, we got a positive ID."

"We already knew that, more or less," Vail said, moving the ice over her swollen jaw.

"Right," Ramos said. "Paid a hundred twenty bucks, cash."

"Did he seem stressed?" Hurdle asked.

"Marcks? Not at all."

"Took it for a test drive," Tarkoff said, "if you can believe that."

"Marcks took the car for a test drive?" Curtis shook his head. "Jesus. That's one cool dude. Not a worry in the world."

"With me," Vail said, "he was alert and in control, even when I had the knife against his carotid." *Too bad we didn't hit a bump.* "It's like he's steps ahead of us."

Hurdle slammed his hand on the table. "Yeah, well, that's our goddamn fault! We're not doing our jobs."

"All due respect," Morrison said, "he's had time to think this through. Years to plan it."

"Bullshit. Bottom line is that he's a felon on the run with limited resources. He's just more resourceful than we are, apparently."

Vail fought off a wave of vertigo and got up from her seat. "I think I should go lie down."

"Finally, some common sense," Hurdle said. "Curtis, drive her home."

"I can make it. Just a little dizzy."

"So much for common sense."

"I don't want to take any more resources away from the task force. I'll be fine. I'm not that far. I'll drive slow."

AS SOON AS THE DOOR SWUNG CLOSED, Hurdle's phone rang. He listened a moment, then said, "Text me the address."

He hung up and gestured to Curtis. "You're with me. They got an ID on the guy we found in Great Falls park. He lives—lived—in Falls Church. They went by his house and found his wife and daughter bound and gagged. They're at Fairfax Hospital."

THEY WAITED AN HOUR until the emergency room physician, David Pryor, came out to speak with them.

Hurdle badged Pryor and they identified themselves as federal agents on the fugitive task force tracking Roscoe Lee Marcks. That got the man's attention.

The doctor swung his stethoscope around the back of his neck. "You think Mrs. Anderson and her daughter know something about Marcks?"

"That's why we need to talk with them," Curtis said. "Might be something they can tell us that'll help find him. How are they doing?"

"They came in moderately dehydrated. Another day for the girl and a couple of days for the mother and you wouldn't have had anyone to interview."

"Are they well enough to talk? We'll keep it short."

Pryor made a mark on the chart. "You can talk with Mrs. Anderson. Cassie's still undergoing treatment. Maybe tomorrow."

"We'll take what we can get," Hurdle said.

Pryor led them to a curtained-off area and explained to Victoria who the men were.

"Thanks, doc," Curtis said. "We'll take it from here." In fact, Curtis and Hurdle had agreed to have Curtis do most of the questioning, since this was his forte and they did not want to overwhelm Victoria.

"Five minutes is all you get," Pryor said as he slipped out of the treatment area.

"Mrs. Anderson, I'm Erik Curtis, this is Lewis Hurdle. We—"

"Are you the ones looking for my husband?"

Curtis shot a glance at Hurdle. Apparently no one had done the death notification. But if they told her now, they would likely be unable to question her.

"No, the Fairfax police are in charge of that. Can we ask you some questions about the man who held you hostage, who . . . tied up you and your daughter?"

"He came in through the back door. Nathan wasn't home yet."

"The man who did this to you is Roscoe Lee Marcks, the escaped convict from Potter Correctional. We know that much."

"Oh my god. I heard about that. That—that was him? A

serial killer?" She shuddered and turned away, looked at the far wall, as if reassessing her contact with him.

"What did Marcks want?" Hurdle asked.

Her eyes canted up toward the ceiling. "Money. Jewelry. And our car."

"What kind of car?"

"He took our Mercedes. Nathan's. It's one of the S-class models."

"Did he hurt you?"

"No—no, he was very threatening but he didn't hurt us. He—he made us drink some medicine. Benadryl."

Curtis looked over at Hurdle, who was a foot to his right and slightly behind him—letting Curtis control the conversation. "Sounds like he was drugging them."

"Makes sense," Hurdle said. "Very smart. I'm getting kind of tired of saying that."

Pryor walked back in. "Okay, that's good for today."

"Excuse us for a minute," Curtis said to Victoria, then moved to the corner of the room with Hurdle and Pryor.

"How long will you be keeping them?" Hurdle asked.

"Mrs. Turner, another day for observation. Should be able to release her at that time. Cassie—at least one more day, maybe two, depending on how she responds."

Curtis leaned in closer and whispered in the doctor's ear. "Her husband was found murdered. She hasn't been notified. I think I should do it now, if you think she can handle it."

Pryor sighed. "Not ideal, I have to tell you," he said, matching Curtis's volume. "Mental state is crucial to recovery. But it's important for her to know, and it's probably best to tell her in the hospital, where we can monitor her."

Curtis turned around and faced Victoria. To say that this

was his least favorite part of the job was an understatement. But he would rather do it with compassion than have some rookie patrol cop dispatched to handle the duties.

He walked to her bedside and placed a hand on hers. "Victoria, I've, uh, I've got some news on your husband."

She read his face, and in that instant Curtis knew that he did not need to say anything further.

44

Marcks got out of the cab a few blocks from the used car lot. He trudged through the freezing snow, doing his best to keep his balance and avoid slipping on the slick ground. The last thing he needed was to hit his head, lose consciousness, and be taken by ambulance to the hospital. The stupid cops may just get lucky and realize that the guy in the ER was the escaped prisoner they've been looking for.

He arrived a few minutes past six. Oliver was approaching with a key in hand, no doubt to lock up for the evening. But Marcks stepped inside with seconds to spare, the edge of the door nearly catching Oliver in the nose.

"Looks like I got here just in time." Marcks stuck out his right hand. "Buddy. Remember me?"

"Yeah," he said, his eyes open wide. "I remember you." He returned a weak shake as his gaze traveled Marcks's face. He stepped back a few stuttering steps, jawing absentmindedly, his shoulders tense.

Marcks knew his secret was out: the Buddy cover was not going to work. Had Oliver seen a news report? An FBI bulletin with his photo? Or had Vail or the police connected that old Buick to Oliver's used car lot?

He swiveled and took a quick look at the street. No cops. If they had been watching the place he was sure they would have been on him by now.

However the old man found out, it meant he was going to have to get rid of him. He did not want to have to do that, but Oliver left him no choice.

"Didn't 'spect to see you again."

"I know, but the Buick you sold me, well, it had a limited useful life. It was real old and we both knew it didn't have much time left. Served me well, though. Worth every dollar I paid."

"What can I do for you?" Oliver asked, his gaze settling on the phone as he turned and walked toward his desk.

"Well, I need another car."

"Uh-huh." He stood behind his ratty chair, holding the back as it rolled a bit left and right with his shaking hands. "Well, I'm about to close. I was on my way to lock the door. I usually get out of here by 5:45 but I fell asleep at my desk. How's about you come back tomorrow, 9:00 AM?"

Marcks pursed his lips, as if he was considering Oliver's suggestion. "Well, being that I'm here now, and it only takes a few minutes, I sure would appreciate it if we can take care of this right now. I'll give you a few extra bucks. You'll be on your way and I'll have a set of wheels."

Oliver jawed his lips but did not reply.

Marcks studied him a moment. "So the cops paid you a visit, huh? That it?"

Oliver looked away, shuffled his feet a bit. "They came by, yeah. Said you were dangerous, escaped prison. Seemed angry I sold you a car."

"Well, how were you supposed to know?"

Oliver's gaze swung back to Marcks. "That's what I told 'em."

"What else did they say?"

He shrugged. "Just, you know, to let 'em know if I saw you again."

"And? You gonna do that?"

Oliver danced a bit, looked around the room—everywhere but Marcks's face.

"I'll make this easy on you, Oliver. Because you've been good to me. You sell me a car and I'll be on my way. Give me a ten-minute lead. Then, if you see fit to call the cops . . ." He gave a casual shrug as if it were no big deal. "I'm good with that. You have to do what you have to do. Your civic duty. I get it."

"Fought in the war, you know? Killed some Germans. Now them Nazis, *they* was bad guys. You, you don't look so bad."

Marcks laughed. "Things get blown out of proportion in the news. Half the stuff they say about you isn't true. The cops exaggerate. Lie. I'm not tellin' you anything you don't already know. Now—" He held up a hand and dipped his chin—"I'm no saint, I gotta tell you. But who is?"

Oliver nodded, his jaw working out the nerves.

"So why don't you and me take a walk outside and I'll pick a car that works for me?"

"Don't have no more that cheap. They're all more expensive."

"That's okay. I brought some more money with me tonight." He gestured with his left hand, waving Oliver to follow him to the door.

The man complied and they walked onto the fairly well-lit sales lot. Marcks did not want to stay under the lights too long for fear a passerby would recognize him and call it in.

Not to mention the circulating police cars, many of which he was sure were added to a round-the-clock patrol to search for him.

He ducked his head down and tried to angle his face away from the avenue that fronted Oliver's Used Cars.

He grabbed hold of Oliver to prevent him from slipping on the ice that coated the asphalt. "Just trying to keep you from falling. You hit your head at your age, could be fatal."

"Need to put salt down, melt this stuff."

"You want, I'll throw some down after I pick out a car."

"'Preciate that." He lumbered along a few feet then asked, "How much you lookin' to spend?"

"I need something newer. Leather interior, air-conditioning, traction control. Maybe a Mercedes or BMW."

Oliver stopped shuffling and turned stiffly to face Marcks.

"I'm kidding, Oliver. A guy can dream, right?" He laughed—and got a cigarette-stained smile from the proprietor. "How about a sedan, late 1990s or early 2000s?"

"You still dreaming? Because you're talking a lot more money, like two or three thousand. You got that much?"

"I can spend about three. Show me what you have."

Oliver turned left down a row of cars, passed a dark gray Chevrolet Impala and shuffled up to an adjacent Toyota. "Now there's this here one, or down the next—"

"This one's perfect, actually. The Chevy." It was better than Oliver could know because it was parked in a darker area of the lot, and farther from the avenue. More importantly, the vehicle had tinted windows, which would reduce the risk of being seen—and identified.

Oliver turned and glanced at the Impala—he knew the price

without looking at the sign in the window, which read $3800: a little more than his customer's budget. "But this is an '05."

"And it's perfect for my needs."

Oliver, either knowing the first rule of sales that you did not try to talk your customer out of a more expensive product, or realizing it would be better not to argue with Marcks, nodded his head and upper body, which moved stiffly, in unison. "Okay." He reached to the bulging carabiner on his side and selected the correct key and unclipped the quick release. Tried it in the door and it worked. He left it hanging out of the lock and turned to Marcks. "I can give this to you for $3500. Cash price."

"That'll work."

He moved behind Oliver, as if he was examining the car, then put his forearm around the man's neck and pulled, held it firm. Oliver squirmed and grabbed at Marcks's meaty limb, but a moment later, Oliver lost consciousness and stopped resisting.

Marcks supported him while he opened the Chevy's back door and pushed his limp body onto the seat.

He walked around to the front, turned over the engine, and drove Oliver to the office. After making sure no one was watching, he shut off the dome light and offloaded the body. He carried him to the desk and set him in the chair, Oliver's head resting on the blotter. He found a length of rope and strung it around the man's neck, tied it tight.

He grabbed Oliver's winter hat, black calfskin on the outside with a lamb's wool lining and large ear flaps, and pulled it over his own head. Warm, yes, but it also obscured more of his face than the ball cap. And given the temperature, no one would question it.

Marcks stopped and considered his course of action. If they

found Oliver's body, they would know he had returned and taken another car, then killed him. Maybe Oliver kept an inventory of vehicles. Maybe he didn't—but Marcks could not take the chance. The cops did, after all, track the Buick back here, so there were records of ownership somewhere. Of course there were.

If Oliver had family and reported him missing, it might be a day or two or three. And the police might just think Oliver was scared about Marcks coming back, so he disappeared for a while. That uncertainty was better than his body being found—which if he left him in the office would happen in the morning as soon as the first customer came knocking and saw him through the window, unresponsive at his desk.

Taking Oliver with him was definitely the better way of going about it.

Marcks looked around the office and found Oliver's old cell phone in the bottom of the cash drawer—which contained $900—and shoved both the money and the handset in his pocket. He found the charger dangling from the wall outlet and took that as well.

Marcks lifted Oliver off the seat and put him in the car. He would find someplace to discard him later tonight, when potentially inquiring eyes were fast asleep.

Problem solved. All in all, a productive evening.

But body disposal aside, he was not finished.

45

Jesus Christ." Robby tossed the messenger bag off his shoulder and ran over to Vail, who was sitting on the couch, a gel pack by her side. "What happened?"

"I got slugged a few times by Roscoe Lee Marcks."

"You caught him?"

Vail chuckled sardonically. "More like he caught me."

Robby squinted confusion. "He kidnapped you?"

She sucked her bottom lip and nodded. "Yep."

"Where?"

"Mason District Police Department parking lot."

Robby sat there a long moment staring at her, apparently realized she was serious and said, "How the hell does that happen?"

"He's a smart son of a bitch."

"Are you okay? Your face—"

"Is swollen. But it looks redder than it really is because I've been icing it."

"Did you see a doctor?"

"No fractures. Mild concussion." *Or maybe two.*

"Headache?"

"Oh yeah."

"So you're off work for a few days?"

Vail harrumphed and grabbed her temple. "Ow, don't make me laugh. But before you give me a speech on following doctor's orders—"

"How'd you know that's what I was gonna do?"

She looked at him. "Did you really just ask me that?"

"Fine. But you really should listen to the doctors."

"It looks worse than it is."

"Does my father know?" Robby asked, referring to Vail's boss, ASAC Thomas Gifford.

"Negatory. And neither does my unit chief." Vail placed a hand on Robby's. "And it's going to stay that way. I didn't go to one of the Bureau's medical facilities. I just went to a doc in the box, told them my fiancé punched me around a bit. A cop should be by in half an hour to talk to you."

Robby shook his head. "This is not funny, Karen. You need to take care of yourself."

"I'm not having any problems thinking, concentrating, or remembering. But if you notice me getting angry or emotional, that could be a bad sign."

"I'm not sure I could tell the difference."

Good one. "Look, this could all be better by the morning. And I'm taking the rest of the evening off."

"It's 7:30, Karen. There's not much left of the evening."

"As long as Marcks is still out there, none of us can let up. Because *he's* not going to let up. He's going after Jasmine, I'm sure of it. And I haven't heard from her in almost two days."

Robby sighed. "It's hard to argue with you when I'd do the same thing in your place."

"Come lie with me on the couch."

He kicked his shoes off and unhooked his holster, then snuggled up to Vail.

She had just gotten comfortable when her phone rang.

"Leave it," Robby said.

Vail groaned. "I can't." She fished it out and sat up quickly. Too quickly.

"Sorry I went off the grid."

"Jasmine?" Vail glanced at the number. "You using a different phone?"

"I think I saw my father. He was a block away, but if it was him, that's too close for my taste. I freaked, holed myself away. Tossed my phone again. Sorry."

"I want to meet with you, tell you what's been going on. Ask you some questions." *And ask you one more time to accept police protection.*

"How about now? Have you had dinner?"

Vail closed her eyes. *Shit.* "Uh, actually I haven't." She glanced at Robby, who was now sitting up as well, shaking his head no. "If you don't mind me bringing my fiancé along, I'd love to have dinner."

"I don't know, Karen. I—"

"I've got a concussion. I'm not supposed to drive, especially at night."

"What happened?"

"Your father happened. A couple of right hooks." *Or backhands. Who remembers?*

"You serious?"

"Robby's a federal agent. You can trust him. Where should we meet you?"

"There's an Indian restaurant on New Hampshire at M

Street. Rasika. It's a wedge-shaped building and the bar sits in the corner with walls that are all windows. I can keep an eye on both streets, make sure my father's not coming. And he's not likely to look for me in DC."

Does that mean she's been staying somewhere in DC? Or maybe she is now.

"On our way. Give me some time to get out there."

Vail hung up and dialed her compatriot in her other life, FBI Supervisory Special Agent Aaron "Uzi" Uziel, head of the Washington Joint Terrorism Task Force—and fellow black ops team member.

"How's my favorite redhead warrior princess?" Uzi asked.

"At the moment, you don't want to know. But I need your help and I don't have a lot of time."

"You know all you've gotta do is ask."

"I need some kind of tracking device," Vail said. "Something tiny that I can put on someone, something they won't know is there. It has to give me the ability to find them if I need to—and without them knowing."

"I've got just the thing."

"You do?"

"No. I just thought that's what you wanted to hear."

"Uzi, I'm not really in the mood."

"Yes, I have something you can use. You really doubted that I'd come to your rescue? I'm your knight in shining armor."

"Robby's sitting two feet away."

"Right. Tell him I said hi. And that I didn't really mean the knight thing. Just a figure of speech."

"I'm headed into the city to meet the target. Can you bring it to 23rd and M?"

"I will cancel my dinner plans and meet you there."

"Oh—sorry."

"Just kidding. No plans. I'll be there in . . . twenty?"

"That'd be great. I do miss working with you, Uzi."

"I know."

ROBBY DROVE AND PARKED in front of a bus stop on the corner. Uzi pulled in behind them and Vail and Robby got out. It was a relatively dark street, with only a couple of streetlamps on the entire block.

Uzi kept his headlights on and, judging by his expression, immediately noticed the condition of Vail's face.

"What happened?"

"Don't ask," Robby said as he gave Uzi a shoulder hug.

"Seriously. You okay?"

"Nothing a little time, Tylenol, and ice won't cure."

He gave her a long look, then reached into his leather overcoat and pulled out a small case and popped it open, revealing a tiny device. "GPS tracker. Stores locations internally but also transmits and triangulates a signal using local Wi-Fi networks. It's not 100 percent accurate but it'll get you pretty close—assuming there are active Wi-Fi networks nearby."

Vail took it from him. "Does it need a power source?"

"All electronic devices need a power source. But this is a low power unit and it's fully charged, so it'll last about a month."

"Plenty of time." *Better be.*

"One last thing. Give me your phone."

She handed over the Samsung, and he tapped a few times then handed it back. "Open that Find/Me app I just installed."

Vail did as instructed. "Okay, now what?"

"It has to initialize and communicate with the tracker. In a few seconds you'll see a string of coordinates. GPS coordinates. If you ever want to see where that device is, or where it's been for the past week or so, open the app and let it download the data from the server. If it takes a long time to connect, there's something interfering with the signal. Could be any number of things. You can try moving to a different location, but it may not be you. It could be where the tracker is."

She saw the numbers populate and then tapped them and a map loaded, showing their current location. *Perfect.* "Thanks, Uzi."

"This is a beta, but it's performed very well so far. Next version will have cell capability so tower pinging can be used for positioning as well as burst updates to the server. We'll be able to tell if its signal is being interfered with and determine the interference type."

She turned to Robby. "I love it when he talks techy. So sexy, don't you think?"

"One last thing," Uzi said, ignoring her dig. "It's technology."

Vail tilted her head. "Yeah. What does that mean?"

"It means it gives you awesome capabilities. But it can also be the scourge of your life. Shit happens. It's not foolproof and sometimes these things have glitches."

"Is that your way of apologizing before it goes haywire?"

"Didn't say it would. But I know you, you'll want to put a fist through a wall when it doesn't work the *way* you want it to work, *when* you want it to work."

"I'm not like that."

Uzi looked at her, his lips thinning. Holding back a smile.

"Fine. But I have confidence in you. Your last gift paid dividends again."

"My last gift—the tanto?" He grinned fully. "Tzedek?"

"It saved my life today. I mean that."

Uzi's face went slack. "I'm—" His eyes again found the bruises on her face. "I'm glad you're okay. That knife has some serious mojo forged into its steel."

"Thanks for sharing some of it with me."

"How are things with you?" Robby asked. "Good?"

"Yeah." Uzi pulled his eyes away from Vail. "All things considered. The way things are headed, counterterrorism will keep me gainfully employed until I'm a frail old man. How's the drug business?"

"Unfortunately, I can say the same thing." He gave Uzi another hug. "Stay safe."

"You too, brother." Uzi looked at Vail. "I'd tell you to stay safe too, but judging by the looks of you, I think that train's left the station."

46

Robby turned onto New Hampshire and came to a stop in front of the restaurant to let Vail off. "You sure you want to do this?"

"Meet with Jasmine?"

"The tracking device. That's a bit over the top, no?"

"Absolutely not. Look what happened to me today. There's no way she would've gotten away from Marcks. I have no idea what he has planned for her—other than death—but I'm guessing he'd keep her around for a bit, to prolong her suffering—give her what he perceives she gave him. With this thing, if she goes missing, I'll be able to find her. Hopefully in time."

"Hey, this is your case. I'm just giving you some unsolicited feedback."

"I'm still going to try to convince her to let us put her in a safe house. I felt helpless these past two days. I feel responsible for her."

"That's ridiculous."

"It may be ridiculous but it's how I *feel*."

"Okay."

Vail gathered up her purse and wrapped her fingers around the door handle. "You think I'm wrong?"

"About putting a tracking device in someone's purse without her knowing?"

Vail frowned. "About wanting to move her to a safe house."

Robby looked out at the street. "I don't know, Karen."

"You don't know?"

"On the one hand, I do think it'd be smart. As a law enforcement officer, yeah, that's what I'd say. But I also know what goes on behind the scenes. Sometimes cops don't do their jobs, shit happens, and in the end—if you know what you're doing—it might be safer if you took care of yourself. But that's only if you understand the criminal mind and the principles of staying off the grid and keeping safe."

"Yeah, if it was you or me, maybe that'd make sense. Maybe. But in this case?"

"From what you've told me, she's done okay caring for herself. She seems self-aware and security conscious."

Vail scoffed.

Robby turned to face her. "Look, you tell her what you feel is best for her. Like I said, it's your case."

"Noted." Vail opened her door. "Go park. I'll meet you inside."

She passed by an outdoor dining area—vacant because of the cold weather—and entered through the glass doors, stepping into a dimly lit contemporary restaurant abuzz with patron chatter. Vail checked in at the hostess station on the left. The woman grabbed a couple of menus and led her past a wall of stacked wine bottles that led to the main dining rooms and into the bar's lounge, which, as Jasmine described, was shaped like a wedge and bounded by tall windows.

Jasmine was seated at the corner table with a view of both 23rd and M Streets.

Vail pulled her chair away and gave Jasmine a hug, then took a seat. She studied her blond wig and dark-rimmed glasses and cocked her head. "Nice disguise. I think."

"Hey, if it keeps him from recognizing me, it's worth it."

"You really think that's enough to hide from your own father?"

She looked away. "Maybe *he* feels that bond. I just feel betrayed."

Oh, he feels betrayed, too.

"You look awful," she said, leaning forward and appearing to notice Vail for the first time.

"I don't *feel* so great, either." Vail forced a smile. "Robby's parking. He'll be here in—"

"I think he just walked in." She gestured over Vail's left shoulder.

"Ladies. Jasmine, good to meet you."

"Same here."

Vail saw her eyes flicker wider for a moment. "Down, girl. He's mine."

Jasmine giggled. "Lucky woman."

Robby sorted out the cramped space in front of him. "Would you like something to drink?"

"I would," Jasmine said, "but I can't. I need all my faculties."

Vail waved her off. "You're here with us. You can relax for an hour, we've got your back."

She sighed. "Karen, that's the point, isn't it? I don't want anyone having *my back*. I can't do it that way. I tried that once and—"

The waiter interrupted with a "Welcome," and proceeded to talk to them about the menu and specials—and then asked if they needed more time.

"We just got here," Robby said, "so—"

"You asked me to trust you," Jasmine said. "Will you trust me to pick out the dishes?"

Vail and Robby shared a look. "Okay."

After asking about dietary limitations and dislikes, Jasmine ordered Calamari Balchao, prepared with Kashmiri chilies; Tawa Baingan, eggplant with spiced potato and peanut sauce; Lamb Kashmiri, set with caramelized onions, ginger, and fennel powder; and a couple sides of chili olive naan.

"You just made me very hungry," Robby said. "And thirsty. I'll have a Bengali Tiger IPA."

"So how've you been holding up?" Vail asked as she handed her menu to the waiter.

Jasmine lifted her water glass. "Let me answer that with another question: how close are you to catching him?"

Vail palpated her swollen jaw. "Not close enough."

"What happened? You said he hit you? If he hit you, you were . . . *with* him?"

Vail recounted the events of the day.

Jasmine shook her head. "I'm sorry you got hurt. At least you fared better than his other victims."

The waiter brought Robby's beer and told them the appetizers were en route.

"My ordeal aside," Vail said, "I wanted to ask you about Booker Gaines, your dad's childhood friend. Know much about him?"

"He's a bad guy. Lots of run-ins with the law. I didn't like it when my dad hung out with him."

"Anything else?"

"They were really good friends. Spent a lot of time together."

"What did they do when they hung out?"

"What did my father do most of the time when he wasn't killing people or working? Bars. He spent a lot of time at bars."

"What kind?"

Jasmine drew her chin back. "What kind of bars? What do you mean? Where they serve alcohol and—"

"Were they gay bars?"

Jasmine's face stiffened.

Robby glanced at Vail, lifted the beer to his lips, and refrained from interrupting.

"You okay?"

"Yeah," Jasmine said with a laugh. "I just—I just wasn't expecting that. So you think my father is gay?"

"I know about the incident with Vincent Stuckey when you came home unexpectedly from your soccer tournament."

The waiter brought the calamari and eggplant with spiced potato and set them in the center of the table.

Jasmine reached for the calamari and put some on her plate.

"Do you remember that? When you came home with—"

"Yes." She stuck a piece of food into her mouth, as if that would relieve her of the obligation to say anything further.

Vail scooped some eggplant onto her plate to give Jasmine a minute to answer.

"He was gay or bi," she finally said. "He was married, remember?"

"Yeah. Although there are gay men who marry because they don't want to come out and it gives them cov—"

"I know," she said, conceding Vail's point. "We never talked about that night, about what I saw."

"Is Booker Gaines also gay?"

"No idea."

Vail nodded slowly and accepted her answer, moved on. "Is that a sensitive subject for you?"

"My *father* is a sensitive subject. My *childhood* is a sensitive subject. I'm sorry I wasn't completely forthcoming with you earlier. I thought I had a normal father who loved me. No, check that: I thought I had a normal *father*. Period." Jasmine took a long drink of water, as if composing her thoughts—or herself. "I could write a book about it," she said with a derisive chuckle. "Oh wait. I did."

Vail decided to drop that line of questioning as well. She observed the tension in Jasmine's face as she brought the glass again to her lips.

The waiter set the remaining plates on the table.

"I think you should consider letting us protect you."

Jasmine stopped drinking suddenly and set the water down. "He sent me an email, you know."

Vail threw a glance at Robby. "When? What'd he say?"

Jasmine kept her gaze on the food. "That he was going to make me pay."

"For turning him in?"

She shrugged. "And for what I wrote in the book, probably. I don't know. It was just that one sentence. He didn't sign it, but I knew it was him."

Vail set her fork down. "This is why we need to protect you."

"No."

"We'd move you to a safe house, guarded by the Marshals Service. They do this every day, Jas. Your case doesn't present anything new or different for them."

"Do they protect witnesses from serial killers?"

Vail sat back. "No."

"Have they *ever* protected a victim from a serial killer?"

"Their specialty is *witness* protection."

"That doesn't answer my question."

"Well," Vail said, "not to my knowledge, but—"

"I'm not a witness who's waiting to testify. My father isn't your ordinary criminal, some mafia thug who pulls out a sub-machine gun or sets off a bomb. So this is different on just about every level." She turned to Robby. "You're a federal agent. Tell me what you think I should do."

Robby glanced at Vail in mid-chew, a flick of the eyes to tell her she had better bail him out.

"I don't think we should put Robby in the middle of this."

"What exactly does that mean?" Jasmine asked as the waiter brought the lamb and naan and set them by the edge of the small table.

Robby swallowed. "It means that I think you should listen to Karen. No one understands the criminal mind better than she does. No one understands a *serial killer's* mind better than she does. So if she tells you that staying in a safe house guarded by US Marshals is the way to go, that's what you should do."

Jasmine looked at him a long moment.

Robby broke her gaze and started dishing out the lamb. "This smells great."

"You're just saying that," Jasmine said. "Because you have to. I can tell."

"If I had a witness like you and it was my case," Robby said, "that's the advice I'd give her."

"And if it were you? Or Karen?"

"Different. And irrelevant. We're trained law enforcement officers."

Jasmine did not say anything further about it—nor did Vail.

And if she was not going to accept protection, that meant Vail needed to put the tracker in Jasmine's purse at some point fairly soon—without her noticing. *I should've given it to Robby, then asked her to go to the bathroom with me.*

Vail thought of slipping it to him under the table, but if Jasmine—whose powers of observation were sharp in her heightened state—happened to notice her secretly passing something to him, she would become suspicious. And if she discovered it was a device meant to report on her location, she might never talk to Vail again—even if the tracker was meant for her benefit.

Vail thought about lovingly taking Robby's hand and placing the microchip in his palm. But it was small and if he was not expecting it and dropped it . . . *Shit.*

Robby checked his watch. "Almost lost *track* of time."

"Yeah," Vail said, "I know. The night's flying by. But that was yummy. Great picks, Jas." She folded her napkin and set it on the table. "I've gotta use the little girl's room." *Maybe if she sees me go, she'll think of following. If I can get back to the table before she does . . .*

But Jasmine did not bite. She stayed at the table, chatting away with Robby.

When Vail returned, Robby had already signed the credit card bill. *Jesus, that was fast.* Panic crept into her chest; her heart rate increased and she cursed herself for not thinking it through better. Then again, she had a concussion. She had to cut herself some slack. *Since when?*

"Thanks for dinner," Jasmine said. "And thanks for your help, Karen. And for caring. I know you mean well. I just think I'm better equipped to handle this than you give me credit for."

"I get it. I'll back off. I've said what needed to be said. I just . . . I came face-to-face with your father today and honestly, if it was you instead of me, you wouldn't be here to talk about it." She looked deep into Jasmine's eyes and let the comment penetrate.

Jasmine twisted her lips and gathered up her jacket and purse. "Obviously, I hope you're wrong about that."

"Here," Robby said, "let me help you on with your jacket."

Vail reached out and Jasmine instinctively handed her the purse as Robby held out the coat and Jasmine slipped her right arm into the sleeve. But Robby had squeezed the material in his fist and her hand got stuck.

"Oh, hang on. Sorry. I—" He shook the material and then guided her fingers into the opening. "There you go."

She shrugged it into position and buttoned it as they walked to the exit. They hugged and Jasmine promised to reply when Vail texted or called her.

As she got into a cab, Robby turned to Vail. "Did you do it?"

"I did. Thank you—that was quick thinking. I didn't plan it out very well."

"It's okay. I saved the day."

Vail stood on her tiptoes and gave him a kiss. "Yes, you did."

47

Marcks sat in the dark sedan, wanting to turn on the radio but preferring not to risk running the battery down on a frigid evening. He did not know how much life it had left and the fewer people he had contact with, the better: even a tow truck driver responding to a jump-start call could identify him.

So he chose quiet solitude, moving his feet and pumping his calves to keep the blood flowing. While he was tired and cold and hungry, he tried to keep it in perspective. He was free, calling his own shots, and directing his own destiny—and that was worth cherishing.

Earlier in the evening, while parked down the block from Vail's house, Marcks had seen her husband pull into the driveway—and ten minutes later they were back in his vehicle, headed into DC.

That he and Vail were meeting Jasmine was an unexpected bonus. It was what he had been hoping—and planning—for because he had no other way of finding her. What's more, the timing could not have been better: the darkness would serve as an accomplice to what he intended to do.

Now, as his buttocks began to go numb, Jasmine exited the restaurant, followed by Vail and her husband. When Jasmine climbed into the back of the taxi, Marcks started the Impala's engine and pulled the gearshift into "drive" as the cab pulled out onto M Street.

The sedan continued on to an area in the outskirts of the city, passing alongside the Potomac on the George Washington Memorial Parkway and into Alexandria. Snow started falling again and he switched on his wipers.

Marcks grew increasingly cautious, as the longer he spent on the road following the taxi the greater the likelihood that the driver would notice and mention it to his passenger. Or he would keep looking in the rearview mirror, which his daughter would inevitably note. She was sharp, like her mother. Too sharp for her own good.

As the area turned residential, Marcks began to wonder if he should break off pursuit and think of some other way of finding out where she was staying. But how would he go about locating her when he could not risk contact with anyone?

Just as he pulled the Chevy against the curb, the taxi stopped and let Jasmine off. She glanced around and then continued on foot, plodding through the snow.

After watching Jasmine trudge along for another block, Marcks wondered aloud what the hell she was doing. Why did she get out of the car? Was she short on money and had to walk the rest of the distance? In this biting cold? In the snow? On the ice? No decent cabbie would let a woman off at night, in this weather, just to save a few bucks.

Maybe she got out so no one would know where she lived—not even the taxi driver. A bit extreme . . . but then again, she had to know he would keep coming after her until he found her—and killed her. Viewed that way, it made perfect sense.

He pulled back into the street and drove slowly after her. But how long could he follow her at a low speed before she caught on? Jasmine would notice such a thing.

Just as he was mulling that question, Jasmine stopped. She turned and faced him. And she knew. She took off running, slipping and trying to stay on her feet, then turned right down a side street.

Marcks accelerated, then swerved around the corner and slammed his wheels against the curb. He cut the lights and engine and got out, running after her, falling twice but getting to his feet and keeping a bead on her. In fact, he was gaining. He was taller than she was, so his strides covered more ground than hers.

The residential area was relatively dark and because of the snow and cold, no one was out. At nearly 10:00 PM, many were no doubt already asleep.

He pushed the last fifteen yards and tackled her, brought her down hard. She tried to scream but he got his large hand around her mouth. She kicked and squirmed, the slippery snow making it harder on both of them: neither could get enough purchase to gain significant leverage.

But his right knee suddenly slid out from under him and Jasmine landed a direct blow to his groin. It took his breath away and he sprawled facedown, snow infiltrating his mouth and nostrils.

Marcks groaned and struggled to his feet—but Jasmine was already running away, awkwardly slipping and sliding, going fast enough that he knew she was going to get away before he would be able to give pursuit.

He dropped to his knees and waited for the pain to subside, then hobbled back to his car and drove away.

48

The next morning, with snow flurries continuing to fall, Vail awoke to an improving but persistent headache.

She called Richard Prati and asked if he had time to answer a few questions about the arsons they had previously discussed. He agreed to meet her near the National Counterterrorism Center in McLean, Virginia, in half an hour—which was perfect, because Vail was only ten miles away.

While en route, a thought occurred to her. She called Robby and he answered immediately.

"Everything okay?"

"The car. I may've seen it parked out front."

"What car? What are you talking about?"

"The raccoon. We looked out the window, I saw an old car. But it was down the street, behind a truck. It may've been the one Marcks was driving when he grabbed me. What if it was him? He'd know where we live."

"How would he figure that out? I mean, that information isn't secret but—"

"If you know what you're doing online, twenty-five bucks can get you access to county records."

"Yeah, but he was imprisoned, what, seven years ago? He probably doesn't know you can do that."

"Wait—there's an even easier way. He knows I work at the BAU. Assuming he can find a listing for it—it's probably out there somewhere—he goes there and waits for me." *We've always wondered if something like that could happen. Now we know.* She slapped the steering wheel. "I saw that Buick in the unit's parking lot right before he kidnapped me."

"You sure?"

"I'm sure I saw it in the parking lot. Not so sure it was the same one outside our house. But it would make sense. We need to stay somewhere, move my aunt. Unless we stay, lure him there."

"Use you as bait?"

"We could install surveillance cameras outside the house, small ones that can't be seen. Park a Marshals Service undercover van a few blocks away, monitoring the feed."

"No."

"It might work. And we'd get to test your theory."

"My theory?" Robby asked.

"Forgo a safe house, look after ourselves."

"It's not the same and you know it."

"Yeah, I know it. But I've gotta give you shit anyway."

"I see you're feeling better."

She called Hurdle and asked him to get it set up—quietly, in case Marcks was in the area. Whether or not they actually slept at the house was unimportant. She would figure that out later. But if Marcks showed up, they would capture him on camera— and maybe capture him in the flesh.

She walked into Greenberry's Coffee at 9:45 AM, a few minutes before Prati, taking the time to peruse the two shelves of pastries—the large black and white cookie tempted her—and settled on a carrot muffin and two cups of the decaf Guatemalan coffee of the day.

Prati entered in a dark suit and stamped the snow from his dress shoes.

"I got you decaf."

"That works, thanks."

He sat down at the square wooden table and dumped some sugar in the cup.

"What happened to your face?"

Vail snorted. "You don't want to know, trust me."

"Nothing I need to talk to Robby about?"

She laughed. "No. If he raised a hand to me . . ." She decided to skip the joke because, given her history with her ex-husband, it really was not funny.

"So you've got some questions about one of your cases?"

"Not one of my cases, exactly. About those fires."

"You're not commandeering that arson case, are you?"

Vail laughed nervously. The Bureau had been accused of such tactics—but that was a long time ago. "No, I'm looking at it because it's got some common elements to my fugitive serial offender case."

"I'm listening."

"The offender uses ether as the accelerant."

"Ether?" Prati bent his head to the left. "Seriously? I don't know if I've ever heard of a case like that. I mean, there are so many efficient, low-cost accelerants. Why use that one?"

"Are you familiar with it?"

"Yeah, ethers are well-known chemicals, been around forever. In various forms, they've been used as a refrigerant, anesthetic, antiknock gasoline additive, solvent—I think it's even used in paints. In 5 to 10 percent concentration it causes shallow breathing and loss of consciousness. But it's not used as an anesthetic anymore."

"Why not?"

"It was discovered about a hundred years ago. We've got more efficacious modern chemical compounds now, with better patient risk profiles—and most importantly, they aren't flammable." He laughed. "If the anesthetist weren't careful, he'd either cause a blue flame that'd singe wool and hair or actually blow up—exploding the patient's lungs, killing both him and the patient."

"Art Rooney, the profiler who's working the arson case, said there are also better, more efficient, more common *accelerants*. Why use this one, which might draw more attention? And why use one that can connect the serial murders to the arsons?"

"You're assuming someone would make that connection. Sounds like, until now, no one has."

"How easy is it to get hold of?"

"Not hard at all—for nonmedical uses. You can even buy it on eBay. It's also fairly easy to synthesize."

So much for that.

"Why?"

"As with anything criminals use, if access is broad and not too restrictive, it's harder for us to track down the source or supplier."

"Right." Prati pulled the lid off his coffee and added another packet of sugar. "Unfortunately, I don't think that's going to help you much here."

"Anything else I should know about it?"

Prati swirled his drink with the wooden stick. Steam spiraled up from the hot liquid. "Years before ether was put into service as an anesthetic, it was used as a recreational drug, sniffed from towels or handkerchiefs. I think it was called ether frolics. Nowadays, it still has a secondary market as a recreational inhalant drug, kind of like amyl nitrite, or poppers. It's popular during sex, especially for homosexuals, because it facilitates anal intercourse. It relaxes smooth muscle—including the ones in the anal sphincter."

Vail was staring at him, her mind suddenly racing.

"Did I say something wrong? You're spacing out on me."

"No—no, that might be incredibly helpful. My case, the offender's gay, so that would make sense as to why he'd use it. If he had it around for sex, why not use it for an anesthetic, to subdue his victims?" She nodded. "That answers the question Art had."

"Did the killer deploy the anesthetic on a soaked rag?"

"How'd you know?"

Prati took a drink of his coffee. "The inhaled concentration would be very high, so a couple of breaths would stun the victim for several minutes. Very effective."

"We found a soaked rag at one of the crime scenes."

"Did you also find a glass container?"

"Not that I remember. Why?"

"Part of what made ether so effective, aside from it being fat soluble, is that it's a solvent. It'd dissolve most plastic containers—or anything else that's not inert, so he'd have to keep it in amber-colored glass. Most likely scenario is he soaked the rag somewhere else ahead of time—because ether has a distinct chemical smell—then put it in the vial, which had a silicone seal. He'd then bring it with him to the crime scene and remove the rag at the last minute and hold it over the victim's nose and mouth."

"So the question is, How does that connect to the arsons?"

"Ah, well," Prati said with a grin, "that's for you guys to figure out."

"No kidding." Vail blew on her coffee, which was still throwing off steam. "The earlier fires were set while Marcks—my offender in the serial murders—was doing time in North Carolina and West Virginia."

"Any chance he had a partner in crime?"

"Yeah, there's a chance. Thomas Underwood, the profiler who worked up the original assessment years ago before he retired, he thought there could've been an accomplice." *And I think I may know who to look at first.* "I've got some homework to do." She took a long drink but did not even taste the coffee. "Still, why take the risk?"

Prati lifted the cup to his lips. "How do you mean?"

"Well, let's say he did have a partner. Marcks gets caught, he goes away. If his partner keeps killing with the same MO, we'd know there's a problem—we'd know that we got the wrong guy or he had an accomplice. So the partner keeps killing and he modifies his MO so we don't connect the dots, or—"

"Or he sets crime concealment fires so you can't see what he's done to the body, which is his calling card."

"Right. Because what he does to the body is much more difficult for him to modify—it's a big reason why he's doing it. But why take the risk of using the same chemical to set the fires that he uses to anesthetize his victims?"

Prati set his cup down and removed the lid. "Because as I

said back at your house, killers don't know we can put these things together."

"I get that, for sure. But Marcks is a smart guy. Smarter than most offenders we've encountered. From what I can tell, he's law enforcement wise."

Prati again stirred his coffee. "But you're not talking about Marcks, you're talking about his accomplice."

Right. Vail rose from her chair. "I've gotta go. I need to look into this other guy, the potential partner."

Prati stood up. "So I was helpful?"

"Richard, if this theory proves out, you may've just saved our asses."

49

Vail texted Art Rooney that she had some pertinent information on his case, then stowed her phone and popped open her car door.

She looked around the Mason District parking lot and flashed on her run-in with Marcks. *Not a run-in. An ambush.*

She surveyed the area as she headed to the Marshals' RV, determined not to be caught unaware again.

Vail walked into the command post to a crowded room—which was not saying much considering its compact size. Everyone was present.

"I've got some stuff to discuss," Vail said as she maneuvered her way to a seat.

"We've all got a number of things to address." Hurdle set his coffee mug down and rested his foot on a nearby ledge. "As I was saying, we've now got a second jerkoff in the wind. And since we were having so much success with the first one, I'm pleased as punch to have to add another to our plate." He nodded at Morrison. "Jim, you've got something on the Buick?"

"We found it in a ditch by the side of the road not far from Great Falls Park. Covered by brush, well camouflaged."

"So he's probably got new wheels," Walters said. "Let's make sure local agencies notify us of all stolen vehicles."

"Already being done," Hurdle said, "but I'll make sure they're on top of it.

"You don't think he'd go back to that same used car lot," Vail said.

"He'd be an idiot to do that," Ramos said. "And we know he's a smart sonofabitch."

Unless he figures we'd think he's crazy to go back there. "We should put an undercover there."

"I think it's a waste of time, but easy enough to do," Hurdle said. "Rambo, set it up. Ben—what'd you dig up on Scott MacFarlane?"

"Long sheet, but nothing that landed him in prison for more than two or three years at a time. A couple drug felonies for possession and an ADW that was pled down," he said, using law enforcement parlance for assault with a deadly weapon. "Did ten months at county. Oh, and an attempted rape that was thrown out."

"He's obviously got a good defense attorney," Vail said.

"He was living in Richmond, moved to Roanoke, then supposedly lived out of a trailer on some property he inherited from his uncle."

"He still have that land?" Ramos asked.

"Nope." Tarkoff flipped a couple of pages in his notebook. "There was some weird thing with the title and he lost it. I didn't have time to look into the problem, but bottom line is he doesn't have that property or the trailer that was on it. But when they took the deed over, they found evidence of firearms storage and what appeared to be an underground bunker."

"Bunker," Walters said. "What kind?"

Tarkoff pulled up some photos on the PC at his station, angled the screen toward the group, and then clicked through the pictures. "Freeze-dried food, six dozen liter water bottles, LED tactical lights, shortwave radio. That kind of stuff."

"Looks like MacFarlane is a survivalist," Curtis said.

"At best." Ramos leaned in for a closer look. "A militia member at worst. Preparing for the government apocalypse where the black helicopters descend and declare martial law. Could be why he was prepared with a submachine gun. In case we came knocking."

"We did," Vail said. "And he came up shooting."

"That does go along with stuff we found in the Gaines residence," Curtis said. "Guess I should refer to it as the house he commandeered." He reached over and pulled out packets of stapled sheaves of papers. "Good lead-in to what I wanted to discuss. Got a printout of preliminary forensic findings, including an inventory of items found throughout the Gaines house." He handed copies to Vail, who took one and passed the rest to Morrison, seated behind her.

She began looking over the report, stopping at the list of DVDs. "So it wasn't Gaines's face in the video we watched."

"No," Curtis said. "Either way, that's got no impact on our ability to catch Marcks or Gaines. Cyber team's evaluating the metadata on the discs to track their source."

Walters folded back a page. "Might help us catch the scumbags who create and distribute this trash. And maybe the ones who commit crimes against children. But it's not gonna help net us our guys. Directly, at least. Unless there's a local connection."

"I agree," Hurdle said. "We've got child pornography charges on him, but that's an administrative matter, way I see it. First we gotta find these knuckleheads. We'll worry about prosecuting them after the fact." He paused, no doubt realizing that both were concerns. "Whatever. You understand what I'm saying."

"We don't have any confirmation yet on MacFarlane?" Vail asked as she glanced over the itemized inventory.

"I was told DNA's being run. Problem is, we don't have any exemplars on file. I asked the lab to reach out to MacFarlane's sister, who lives in New Jersey. Not perfect, but it'll give us a real good idea if he was staying in that house with Gaines. And before you ask, yeah, we've got her under surveillance. Phone calls, email, text, all being monitored in case he contacts her."

As Vail's eyes moved down the page, she got stuck on two words: diethyl ether. *That's a chemical and it's got ether in the name.* She pulled out her phone and tapped out a quick text to Prati.

"Karen. Yo, Vail."

She hit "send" and looked up. All eyes were on her.

Hurdle lifted his brow. "You said you had some things to discuss."

"Yeah, I, uh, I do." *And depending on what Prati says, I may have more.* "Yesterday, before Marcks got the drop on me, I mentioned an arson case the BAU's handling. I wasn't sure if it had anything to do with Marcks. But I found out some stuff that leads me to think there's a connection. What, who . . . I'm not sure yet."

"Don't keep it to yourself," Morrison said.

"I think I was telling you about the chemical—" Her phone vibrated. She glanced at the display. Prati responded to her text. "Hang on a sec."

diethyl ether is the chemical name.

ether is the common name for the

chemical like water is the common

name for h2o. so--same thing

Vail looked up from her cell. "And it just got a little more interesting. So the anesthetic that Marcks used to temporarily subdue his victims was also used as an accelerant at the arson scenes, for the crime concealment fires." She explained why such an approach was unusual. "But we know that Marcks is gay. And ether is sometimes used by homosexuals during sex. So that explains why he'd have it, why he'd be familiar with it and its effects. And I'm willing to bet that the label has a warning on it about its flammability."

"Does look increasingly likely there's a connection," Hurdle said.

"And," Vail said, holding up the forensics inventory from Gaines's house, "there's a six-pack of Sterno cans listed here. The arsonist used Sterno as well. Thomas Underwood, one of the founding profilers back in the late seventies who drew up the original assessment on Marcks, initially thought there might be another UNSUB, an associate. But he abandoned that theory. Now it looks like he might've been right."

"Gaines?" Curtis asked. "Or MacFarlane?"

"Don't know. I would've said Gaines—but given what we're hearing about MacFarlane . . . we don't know enough to say yet. That said, on this inventory of items taken from the Gaines house, there was a small bottle of diethyl ether, which my expert tells me is the chemical name for ether."

They chewed on that a minute.

"So, what does this mean?" Ramos asked. "That the guy who was Marcks's accomplice on the serial killings is also setting these fires? He's an arsonist?"

"Looks that way."

"How does this help us?"

"It gives us another avenue of investigation," Hurdle said. "Let's get up to speed with the investigating agency on these fires, see if there are any forensics we can track that'll give us a lead on where to look for these guys. If this accomplice is getting his chemicals locally, maybe it dovetails with something we've got on Marcks."

That'd be helpful. If we actually had *something on Marcks.*

"You mentioned there were a couple of fires set after Marcks escaped," Tarkoff said. "Any chance he's involved?"

"Hard to know," Vail said. "But now that there looks to be a tangible connection I'll look at this case differently. I have a message out to Art Rooney, the profiler—" Her Samsung vibrated again and she held up an index finger while she answered the call. "Art. Just talking about you. Got something interesting on your case."

"Saw your text. And I've got some things to tell you, too, on the arsons."

"I'd like to share that with my task force. Can you Skype? We've got a setup here at the command post." Vail glanced at Hurdle, who nodded. She got the user ID and passed it on to Rooney.

Two minutes later the Skype tones were beeping and bopping over the RV's speakers. Rooney's face filled the forty-inch flat screen that was mounted at the front of the room. They huddled around the TV as Vail made quick introductions.

"You first," Vail said.

"Arson is no different from any other serial offender," he started, giving the other agents and detectives a quick and dirty primer. "He has a particular way of operating that is identifiable to him. MO just like a homicide."

"Behaviorally," Vail added, "we look for those things that are unique to that offender. Things he does a certain way because it's familiar to him and because it's got meaning to him. Forensically, obviously, we can also look at fingerprints he may've left on the items he uses. But the items he uses gives us something else, too."

Rooney picked it up. "If an arsonist has a certain way of setting the fire, it can provide linkage among the cases we've got where we're not sure if they're related. And if we can find a relationship, a forensic or behavioral trait from one case, added to something from another case, it might make the difference in whether or not we find the UNSUB.

"In this case, we had six fires that all appeared to be set by the same arsonist. In the most recent one, the investigators found remnants of a wooden match—and, most significantly, a small dollop of wax that chemically matched one from a case he remembered handling about six years ago. In that case, the offender used a candle with a hole drilled a quarter inch below the wick. He stuck a wooden match through the hole, then soaked the match in the jellied substance they use for chafing dishes."

Morrison turned to Vail. "Sterno."

"Sterno," Rooney said. "So this offender placed the match very close to the wick. The candle started to burn and when it hit the wood, the flame traveled down to the head of the match where there was jellied string. It lit up and went down to the Sterno can, which had the rest of the jellied substance—and a rag doused in gasoline that hung down to the floor."

Rooney clicked and crime scene photos appeared on the screen. "Can you see these okay?"

"Affirmative," Hurdle said almost absentmindedly as he studied the image.

Successive pictures showed a flame-scorched Sterno can, remnants of a match, a candle.

"So this fire was not successful," Ramos said.

"Right." Rooney's voice was off-screen, the crime scene photos still visible. "Which is the beauty of linkage. We now know that this earlier crime scene may in fact be the UNSUB's first attempt. And he screwed it up. The fire didn't really take off. We found a partially burned body, too."

"Very elaborate setup," Curtis said. "What's the point? Is this just something he enjoys?" He turned to Vail. "What do you call it, ritual?"

Rooney answered. "No, this is part of his MO. At first glance, it sounds like this guy's a nutcase. Why such a far-fetched contraption? It's a simple explanation, really."

"A delay mechanism," Curtis said. "To allow him to leave and get away. Once he lights the candle, he leaves. It gives him plenty of time to get a fair distance from the home before it goes up in flames."

Rooney clicked away from the photos and back to his face. "Exactly, detective. We thought he chose houses in the boonies because they're served by volunteer fire departments, which have longer response times. But there's another reason."

"He takes a long time at the scene setting up this elaborate candle and wood match contraption. If he's in the middle of nowhere, there's a greater chance he's left alone. Fewer visitors, less chance some neighbor or friend is going to drop by or walk in on him. Theoretically."

"Right again. This delay mechanism is another purposeful, well-thought-out scheme."

"Smart offender," Vail said. *Just like Marcks.* And then something Rooney said hit her. "They found a body at that crime scene?"

"That's what I was told. I just got this information from the investigator and I called you first. I'll have to get more details on that early case."

"I'd be very interested in seeing if that body had parallel lines carved into the abdomen. And excised genitalia."

"I don't think there was that much left intact. But you're still thinking these arsons are related to your case?"

"That brings me to what I've got for *you*." Vail explained how she had discussed the case with DEA agent Richard Prati and his background as a chemical engineer. "And the diethyl ether you found at your recent crime scene. We found it at Marcks's buddy's house, along with Sterno cans."

"I need the forensics report on that, see if those cans match mine."

"I'll make sure you get a copy," Curtis said.

She mentioned the homosexual use of the chemical and reminded him that Marcks had used it to temporarily disable his victims.

Rooney leaned back away from the camera. He rocked in his chair a few seconds, then said, "Okay. You've convinced me.

I think you're on to something. We should compare files, share info. Have you discussed this with Tom? It was his case way back when. He may have some insight, given time and distance. We all mull our cases, let them percolate over time, right?"

"He's in Hawaii shooting his new series."

Rooney chuckled. "That guy. Books, TV shows. Retirement's been good to him."

"I'm going to sit down with him when he gets back. But I'll try him again, see if I can pull him away from the cameras for a few minutes." She thanked Rooney and signed off. "I'm gonna call Stuart Sheridan and cross my t's, make sure that stuff isn't his."

She pulled out her phone and dialed, identified herself, and reminded him who she was. *As if he would forget.*

"Mr. Sheridan, we found a few other items at your place that I just want to make sure aren't yours. They're not illegal, but it has great importance to our case."

"When can I get into my home?"

"We're almost done with our investigation. I can ask someone to call you with a better answer. But did you or your wife have a bottle of ether in your laundry room? It's also known as diethyl ether."

"What the hell is that?"

Guess that's my answer.

"A chemical."

"Not ours."

"You want to check with your wife?"

"Hang on," he said with the enthusiasm of a turtle. He muted the phone with a hand and called to Nancy, asked her something, then returned to the call. "No. She has no idea what I'm talking about. And of course now she wants to know why I'm asking."

Oops. Guess he didn't tell her about the squatter. "Sorry about that. What about Sterno cans?"

"You mean the fuel they use for catering? Chafing dishes? No, we haven't had any events or major dinners at the house in years. Certainly nothing that we'd hire caterers for. And I'd never store chemicals or flammable fuel in my basement. Asking for trouble."

You have no idea.

"That's what I thought. Sorry to bother you with—"

"Why would this guy have that stuff in my house?"

"Nothing I can discuss right now," Vail said. "But it may have connections to another case we're looking at." She thanked him and hung up before he continued asking questions she would not be able to answer.

She then called Underwood and was left chuckling at his voice mail greeting: "Shooting in Hawaii. The TV series kind, not the handgun kind. Leave me a short message and I'll call you back." She told him what they discovered regarding the offender using the same chemical as both an anesthetic and an accelerant and that it was important she speak with him before he left Hawaii. She had just hung up when several of their phones went off simultaneously.

"Goddammit," Hurdle said as he read the text from Leslie Johnson:

another body
def a blood lines vic

Vail locked eyes with Curtis. "Terrific."

50

Marcks sat in the backseat of his new car, where the rear windows were darkly tinted. During his adventures last night he had slit open the right pant leg of his jeans so he decided to risk going into a twenty-four-hour Walmart in Fredericksburg. He picked up two pairs of jeans, a pack of underwear and socks, a few shirts, more toothpaste, and hair dye.

Even though it was pushing 1:30 AM and there were few people in the store, he felt self-conscious walking around, even with the hat on and the beginnings of a full beard. At the same time, while there was danger in being out in public, the challenge, the *rush*, of pulling it off was worth it—far better than the boredom of being stuck in a prison cell day after day.

He walked by a clothing display showing a blonde model and he flashed on his reunion with Jasmine. It did not go as he had figured it would. A part of him felt something for her. It was more than familiarity. A connection, perhaps. He had difficulty putting his finger on it because he rarely experienced such emotions. Anger, fury were more his speed. Love? Family? He wasn't sure he truly understood those constructs.

All he knew is that when he was face-to-face with Jasmine, touching her, he wanted to break her neck. End her life.

That was the rage he was accustomed to.

All in all, his encounter with her was not a complete loss. He showed her he could still find her, which was undoubtedly unnerving. If it made for anxious, sleepless nights, so much the better.

But he no longer had a bead on Jasmine, and unless he could follow Vail again it would be difficult tracking his daughter down. Since Vail had to have her guard up now, tailing her carried a lot more danger. He had done it successfully once, but attempting a repeat performance might be going back to the well too many times. While he was skilled at not getting caught, he knew when to back off. His ability to outsmart, to outthink, the cops was what had gotten him this far.

One thing being locked away in a prison cell taught him was how mind-numbingly tedious life could be. Staying free presented its challenges, for sure, but they were *good* challenges.

He might have difficulty feeling certain types of emotions, but excitement was not one of them.

51

Vail stood at the entrance to the apartment and pulled on a pair of booties while watching members of the crime scene unit ply their trade. Curtis was parking the car as Vail stepped inside and found Johnson in the bedroom, right hand on her chin, studying the victim's body from several feet away, as if trying to make sense of it.

"I'm here," Vail said.

"Yeah. I can see that."

"Are we sure this is a Blood Lines kill?"

Johnson did not move. While still staring ahead, she said, "Oh yeah, I'm sure. Go on, take a look for yourself."

Vail snapped on a pair of gloves. "Who is this?"

"Aida Cerulli. Thirty-nine-year-old pharmacist. Roommate, a factory worker who has the overnight shift, discovered her this morning. Best I can tell, Aida finished up at the drug store, an independent in Manassas, around 6:30 last night. I can't account for her whereabouts after that. A neighbor thought she heard her come home around nine, but wasn't sure."

Vail advanced on the bed and saw the familiar dried blood pooled, soaked into the sheets and mattress pad. "Do we have a time of death?"

"ME said last night, probably between 11:00 PM and 1:00 AM. There are tool marks on the front door lock."

"Really. Forced entry." *That's new. Why? Is this merely the evolution of MO? Or is it because this kill was done by Gaines or MacFarlane and we had his bottle of ether, so he couldn't use it to subdue her?*

"What are you thinking?"

"Hmm?" She turned around and saw that Curtis had entered. She told him what her thoughts were. "Take a stealth entry, get into the apartment while the vic's asleep. Surprise her, no screams."

"This is so different," Johnson said. "The guy we found in the barn, hacked up and buried. William Reynolds. Greeling, the cop. Tammy Hartwell, Nathan Anderson. All different."

"Not all are different," Vail said. "And in some cases the change in MO was logical and purposeful—and situational. In many ways the kills are reflective of the offender's instability. He's on the run, homeless. He's adapted his MO to ensure success and meet his needs. William Reynolds is an example. Nathan Anderson was opportunistic. I don't think he planned to kill Nathan. But once he used him to get away, he became an asset—for sex—and then a liability because he'd be taking a risk in letting him live."

"So you think this fits with the other kills?" Hurdle asked. "Is Aida one of Marcks's victims? And Gaines's?"

"I think it's consistent with Marcks's ritual. The difference in MO can be explained. Now, whether Gaines is involved, we may need to rely on forensics. And I need to go back and look at this entire case, rewinding to his first kills, to see how I'd assess him—and see how I'd look at the case if he had a partner. I basically worked off Thomas Underwood's assessment because I was new. I'd never do that now. So I think it'd be good for me to step back and take a fresh look at it, from the beginning."

"How long is that gonna take?" Hurdle said.

A lot longer than you'd like. "There were fourteen murders, not to mention all the recent ones. And the fires. Normally it'd take weeks, but we don't have weeks. I'll do it as fast as I can. Meantime, let me take a better look at Aida." Vail started a few feet away from the bed, taking it all in. She moved closer and resisted the desire to study the "blood lines" first, looking over her face. No unusual markings.

What's that?

She pulled out her phone and turned on the flashlight, shined it into the mouth, which was minimally open, teeth parted. "Hey, we got tweezers?" She moved into the hallway and called to a crime scene technician. "Tweezers?"

The woman reached into her kit and handed a pair to Vail, who rushed back into the bedroom. Curtis saw her and said, "What's going on?"

"Found something, I think."

Vail maneuvered the prongs between the lips and slowly extracted a piece of paper. She flashed on a prior case where she had found notes hidden in a victim's orifice, a case that caused her a great deal of pain in more ways than she cared to think about.

"What is it?"

Curtis's voice drew her attention back to the present. She set the tweezers down and unfolded the note.

"What the hell?" Johnson asked. "A blank piece of paper?"

"Maybe," Curtis said. "I think I told you Jasmine got one of these from Marcks. Turned out it had indented writing."

Vail brought it over to the window and held it at an angle to the gloomy, glary daylight. "It does say something." She kept moving it, trying to catch the shadows just right. "Next in line."

"What?" Curtis said.

"That's what it says. 'Next in line.'"

"Is that a reference to his blood lines?" Johnson asked. "A tongue-in-cheek reference to himself?"

Vail thought about it a moment. "Maybe." *He's never done something like this before. Why start now? Because we know who the killer is and he knows me? Is this note meant for me? Is he telling me I'm next in line?*

Her phone trilled. She slipped the note into an evidence bag and pulled out her Samsung. It was Rooney.

"Just found something," he said. "Where are you?"

"At a new murder scene. Since our cases appear to be related, want to stop by?"

"Text me the address. Might as well tell you what I've found in person."

"Tell me now."

"It can wait till I get there. You've probably got your hands full."

"Can't argue with that." Vail hung up, tapped out the info to Rooney, then faced Curtis and Johnson. "Art Rooney's on his way. Meantime, I'm gonna take a look around. Maybe I can see this from a new point of view."

HALF AN HOUR LATER, Rooney walked in and exchanged brief pleasantries with Curtis, Johnson, and Hurdle. "Good to meet you all in person. So where's our body?"

"Follow me." Vail led him into the bedroom.

Rooney stepped up to the victim and surveyed her from head to toe. Vail had never seen him at a fresh crime scene. Then again, given his military training, it made sense that he would conduct his business in an organized, systematic fashion.

He finally stepped back and looked over the room. "Okay. Brief me."

They gave him a summary of what they had had learned and explained their theory of why there was a difference in MO.

Rooney nodded. "Very good. I agree."

"We're looking into Aida's whereabouts after she left work," Johnson said. "It's possible she crossed paths with the killer at some point during the day."

"Could've come across her yesterday. Or the day before that. Not saying you shouldn't do your due diligence. But I'm not sure it'll bear fruit."

Johnson acknowledged Rooney's comment. "Might be right. Might be wrong."

"And then there's the issue of this note," Vail said, "which is new. Has nothing to do with MO."

"May just be a tweak," Rooney said, "at us. Not like we haven't seen that before."

"Where are we with the homosexual bars?" Curtis asked.

Hurdle frowned. "Let's go into the living room. I just feel weird discussing this in front of the . . . victim. I mean, I know she's dead, but it doesn't feel right."

They moved into the elaborately decorated space, where Hummel collectibles were meticulously laid out in a display cabinet whose shelves had been recently dusted.

"We've got the two bars under surveillance," Hurdle said,

"and several others in DC and Virginia. Undercovers come and go, mingle, and report back. We've given them an old mug shot of Gaines. Waiting on the DMV to send us what they've got—which is hopefully more recent. So far no sign of Marcks." He turned to Vail. "Where are you on your 'reassessment'?"

"You serious? You think I can snap my fingers and come up with something on the fly?" *Not like I've never done that before. But he doesn't know that.*

"What reassessment?" Rooney asked.

As Vail explained, Rooney sucked his teeth. "I think that's smart. You want some help?"

"From you? Hell yes."

"Let's talk it through for a minute. Start at the beginning. What do we know about Marcks?"

"Less than ideal childhood. Our knowledge is limited and based on interviews with relatives and neighbors because he refused to talk with us after his arrest. What we were told is that he was sexually abused as a child. My guess is that it stopped as he grew older because he was probably a big teenager and could defend himself and challenge the person who was abusing him. Likely a close relative. Father, maybe his mother. Hard to know unless he tells us. Not something he's probably shared with anyone. And not something he'd have shared with me even if I'd been successful in sitting down with him."

"He's a sexual mutilator," Rooney said, "if I remember correctly from Tom's Wednesday briefings."

"Good memory. He cuts the vics, parallel lines in the abdomen, and then severs the genitalia."

"The genitalia seems pretty straightforward. What about the lines?"

"Hard to know. Comforting for some reason." Vail thought a moment. "But why he did it may be less important now than the fact that he needed to do it. Especially since we know who the UNSUB is."

"True."

"Except," Curtis said, "that now we're looking at the possibility that Marcks may've had an accomplice."

"Yeah." Vail rested her arms on her hips.

"Let's explore that," Rooney said. "There's strong evidence that Marcks is gay. And we know there are a number of gay serial killers who worked in pairs. Was there anything in the behaviors that might indicate there were two different offenders at work?"

Vail mulled the files in her mind, thinking through each of the killings. "Nothing that Underwood specifically called out. He did think, at one point, that there were two offenders. I saw notes in the margin of one of his reports. But he obviously abandoned that concept in his final assessment."

"And what about you? Forget Tom's work on the case. What do you think?"

"It might answer a few questions I had in terms of things I couldn't account for. It was early in my career. I wasn't about to second-guess a legend."

"But now you've got the chops to do just that." Rooney folded his arms across his chest. "So tell me. What questions did you have?"

"On the ninth victim there were cut marks on the body that were different from the slices we'd seen on the previous victims. They were shallower, and on the back, between the shoulder blades. I couldn't explain that. It might indicate a second killer."

"Anything else?"

Vail's gaze drifted off, up to the ceiling. "Victim ten. There was something in the way he was penetrated that was different. Linkage to Marcks by the specific way the vics were killed is correct—except that the subsequent sexual interaction is different. More anal tearing. Underwood interpreted it as more anger on the part of Marcks, but it could indicate a second offender."

Curtis shook his head. "Without forensics, how do we know for sure?"

Vail and Rooney shared a cynical look.

"It's very difficult," Rooney said, "because with a pair of killers there's usually one alpha and one beta—the follower. And most, if not all, of the behavior that's expressed at the scene is from the alpha."

"The subordinate watches or has a minimal role," Vail said. "It could be because he's learning, or he doesn't have the confidence he needs. Or he's just naturally a beta and doesn't have it in him to lead. Or he doesn't have what it takes to kill but he enjoys interacting with the body afterward."

"It's much easier to evaluate if there are two victims," Rooney said. "The behaviors exhibited with each victim would likely be very different—and more recognizable to us. For example, let's say both victims are sexually assaulted. Offender A kills his victim first and then has sex with the body, but Offender B first has sex with the victim and *then* kills her."

"I'm not sure which is more sick," Hurdle said.

Vail tucked some hair behind her right ear. "The different cutting pattern on victim nine could indicate that Marcks, the alpha, was letting the beta, Gaines—if we're buying into his involvement—have his turn after doing the kill." *But then there are the fires.* "That said, if we consider the arsons, most of them occurred while Marcks was in custody. But the others were set after he escaped." She nodded. "If the arsons were done by the same guy, that'd mean we're definitely dealing with two offenders."

Hurdle walked over to a window and parted the slats of the miniblind. "What kind of thing would we look for in Gaines's background to know if he's a 'candidate' for this kind of violence? Assuming Marcks has a partner, how do we know if Gaines is the guy? How do we know it's not someone else?"

"Without standard forensics," Vail said, "it's tough. We have to make reasonable inferences based on the behavioral and physical and forensic evidence, as well as some assumptions. But if the second set of cuts are indeed what I think they are, then they're both mutilators."

"You mentioned mutilators earlier," Curtis said. "What exactly does that mean, other than the obvious—that he mutilates?"

"Robert Ressler was the lead author on an article about murderers and mutilation. They defined mutilation as the deliberate cutting of the sexual areas of the body—breasts, genitals, and abdomen. Almost 70 percent of murderers who were sexually abused as children mutilate their victims after death—and the number rises to almost 80 percent for those who were sexually victimized as *adolescents.*"

"So if we're playing the percentages," Rooney said, "we'd expect to see sexual abuse in Gaines's childhood and/or adolescence. Obviously, just because someone was sexually abused as a child or youth doesn't mean they grow up to become sexual sadists who murder on a vast scale and mutilate their victims."

"We know Marcks was sexually abused as an adolescent," Hurdle said.

"Don't know much about Gaines yet," Vail said, "other than what's on his sheet."

"I'll ask Johnson to look into it." Curtis took a few steps toward the bedroom. "Yo, Johnson!"

She entered with a contorted face. "You rang, sir?"

Vail stifled a smile as Curtis explained what they needed.

"Can you handle that?"

"I can handle that. Now can I get back to what I was doing?"

As she walked out, Vail said, "Sexually abused offenders are also highly likely to have sexual conflicts, sexual dysfunction of some kind, and sexual incompetence. Those would be harder to determine without actually interviewing Gaines himself, unless he confided in someone at some point."

"We can try finding that person," Curtis said, "if he or she exists. But I don't think we can count on that."

"Hang on a minute. Just a hunch, but Gaines was picked up on a solicitation charge, right?" Vail pulled out her phone and started dialing. "I'm gonna see if Tarkoff can dig a little deeper, find out who the prostitute was. If we can locate her, she may be able to give us something on their interaction."

"Find a prostitute?" Hurdle asked. "Bit of a long shot, no?"

"Maybe not. If I'm right, the prostitute will be male—in which case we can put our undercovers on this, the ones who're working the gay bars. But if it's a woman, we might be able to get something from her. If Gaines's conflicted about his sexuality, he might've gone to a female prostitute to prove to himself he was heterosexual. Maybe he had a hard time performing."

Rooney pursed his lips. "Worth looking into."

Vail elbowed him. "I think you've kept me in suspense long enough. What'd you want to tell me? When you called."

Rooney chuckled. "Sorry. This morning I ran a search in VICAP for offenders who used anesthesia during the commission of their crimes," he said, referring to the Violent Criminal Apprehension Program database. "And I found something rather surprising. There was a case where the UNSUB used ether."

Vail shrugged. "That offender isn't the first, or only, one to use an anesthetic."

"Ah, but it's the only one that Thomas Underwood handled. Before he was a profiler. Right before the BSU was started, in fact."

"That was Underwood's case?" *Where's he going with this?* "There's more, isn't there?"

"There *is* more. That same offender was later found to have started plying his trade as . . . anyone?"

Vail halfheartedly raised a hand. "An arsonist."

"An arsonist."

"And did he use ether as an accelerant?" Vail asked.

Rooney pointed at her. "Indeed he did."

And now I can't get in touch with Underwood. He said he was in Hawaii. But was he really? What are you thinking, Karen? Don't be ridiculous.

"So where does this leave us?" Hurdle asked. "Sounds like you think Underwood might be involved in this in some way."

"That's not what I'm saying," Rooney said. "But I'd be lying if I didn't tell you that I didn't start thinking what you're all thinking right now. For a fleeting moment. Because there's no way that Thomas Underwood is a killer. Serial, arson, or any other kind you can imagine."

"You sure about that?" Hurdle asked, fixing his gaze on Rooney. "I think we need to ask him about it. Don't you?"

Vail looked from Hurdle to Rooney, whose face remained impassive.

Hurdle spread his arms apart. "Let me put it another way. Can you guarantee me that Underwood is not part of this?"

Rooney snorted—but did not answer.

"Art?" Vail said.

Rooney looked away. "No. I can't. No one can guarantee something like that. But—"

"Plain and simple," Hurdle said. "Better not to assume. One of us needs to sit him down. Curtis, you worked with him."

Curtis drew his chin back. "Well, yeah, but it's not like I know the guy. We worked the case, what, ten years ago? We exchanged some ideas. I didn't exactly hang out with him."

"*I'll* talk to him," Vail said. "I left him a message earlier today but he's out of town and hasn't returned my call yet."

"There are other explanations," Rooney said. "That case with the ether is in one of Tom's books. His first, *Killer Instincts*. Never read it, but when I googled the offender and victim, Tom's name came up in a *Miami Herald* article. A quote from the detective who handled the case. He made a point of saying something like, 'Agent Underwood's thoughtful analysis of the arsonist's motives put him on the right path.'"

"Why was the FBI involved?" Curtis said. "You said this was before the BSU started consulting on serial cases."

"After quickly incapacitating the vics with the ether, the offender threw them in his car, injected them with a drug, and drove them from Florida—where he got his victims—into South Carolina, where he killed them. Crossing state lines."

"And why is this relevant?" Hurdle asked.

Rooney spread his hands. "At the very least, if we look at the most logical or most likely scenario, it tells us that Roscoe Lee Marcks and/or his partner, assuming he has one, read *Killer Instincts* and took the idea for himself."

"It also may explain why Marcks is wise to what we do and how we do it. Maybe he did read these types of books. True crime, case studies, that kind of thing, to learn how, and why, we do what we do."

"Should we look over Underwood's books," Hurdle said, "to see if there are other things the killer—or he himself—is mimicking?"

Vail chuckled. "I think he's written seven. It's gonna take a while. I only read his third one, *Profilers Unmasked*, which focused on the history of the BSU and its split into the research unit and what became the BAU. He gave some great insight into the thinking of the early profilers. But Douglas has written a few books, too, and so have Ressler, Hazelwood, and Safarik. We've got no reason to think Marcks was limiting his reading to Thomas Underwood."

Rooney shook his head dubiously. "Might not be a good use of our time."

"We can expand the task force as needed," Hurdle said. "We've got assets at our disposal. Vail, I want you to track down Underwood. Leaving voice mails is not enough. I want him in a room."

Vail shifted her weight, uncomfortable with that prospect.

"If you can't do that, let me know and I'll have someone else handle it."

"We've got these books at the Academy library," Rooney said as he pulled out his Samsung. "I'll arrange to have them brought to your command center."

"And I'll arrange to have several agents put on reading duty," Hurdle said.

"The one with the ether," Vail said. "*Killer Instincts.* I want to read that one myself. Art, can you have the library hold that one for me?"

Rooney shrugged. "Of course."

"I'm heading there right now."

52

Vail walked into the Academy library, a bright, modest-size square room with adjoining reading areas and a two-story atrium that gave it an airy grandeur.

Vail identified herself to the assistant behind the administration counter, and the woman handed over the near-pristine hardcover of Underwood's first book. *Either this is a new copy or it's not seen much activity among agents.*

She could not pass judgment, given that she had not read it herself. Then again, with the Bureau's intense pivot toward counterterrorism, and now cybercrime, agents'—and new agent trainees'—time was better spent on reading law enforcement periodicals and books covering those topics.

Vail glanced at the jacket and saw Underwood's bio on the rear flap. The snapshot was not the usual, posed FBI picture, taken in a suit against the backdrop of the American flag. This was designed to project the individual's humanity—a man with his dog; in this case a golden retriever.

As she looked at his photo, she recalled her one and only meeting with him, a few years ago. *Is that the face of a killer?*

She skimmed his professional accomplishments and had to

resist comparing her own career to Underwood's. Pulling her eyes away from the cover, she opened the book and perused the table of contents.

A moment later, Vail found the case Rooney had mentioned: Michael Neal Coleman, an UNSUB dubbed The Planner, was an engineer who began by killing colleagues he worked with at a nonprofit agency. He was methodical and calculating and plotted his kills with the precision of an NFL coach's game plan. Contingencies were mapped out. He studied his potential targets for weeks, watching for patterns, determining weaknesses, and then striking with alarming efficiency.

To hear Coleman describe it later during interviews with Underwood in 1979, killing became boring because he was so good at it—too good. It lost its appeal and no longer presented a challenge. That's when he began starting fires. It was something new to master, and in the process he discovered the tremendously destructive power of a well-constructed blaze. It triggered a long-buried fascination with fire that he had passed over in favor of killing. It was only then that he realized he could do both.

It was like learning a new skill and then perfecting it. For most people, the hobbies they took up included woodworking. Photography. Baseball. And then there were the deviants, who enjoyed discovering new and interesting ways of dominating other human beings, ending their lives and defiling their bodies.

The use of ether as a means of securing his victims and as an accelerant for setting the fires received only cursory mention by Underwood—more as an example of the UNSUB's cunning than as an exceptionally different MO not previously encountered.

Well, regardless of how little significance Underwood gave it in his book, it made an impact on our offender.

But something was not quite right. That note left in Aida's mouth was a departure in ritual. *Why? A threat? Or was it a clue, since I took over Underwood's cases, and I was "next in line" at the unit?*

Vail told herself not to overthink it. She pulled out her phone and texted Hurdle.

anything on the surveillance cameras outside my house

His response came almost immediately:

youll be second to know

Vail tried Underwood again and left another voice mail. "Got a question on one of your old cases. I know you're swamped, but it's time sensitive. Can you give me a call as soon as you get this?"

She opened the browser on her phone and looked up Underwood's television show, to see if there was information on where they might be filming. If Underwood was not answering his phone, she needed to track down someone who worked on the production, who would.

Ten minutes later, Vail came up empty—so she decided to call the network. After being transferred multiple times, she scored the producer's mobile number. Figuring she would get a better response if she used the library's landline—which displayed "FBI Academy" as its caller ID—the man answered on the second ring.

Vail explained that it was vital that she speak to Underwood. "We talked a few days ago and he told me he'd be filming until next week."

"I'm sitting in a café in Hollywood, Agent Vail. We wrapped two weeks ago."

A chill shuddered through her torso.

Why would he lie to me?

"Do you know where he is now? Have you had any contact with him since you finished?"

"No and no. Sorry I can't be of any more help."

"Did he seem to be himself? Was he stressed or acting strangely?"

There was a pause. "What's this about? I thought you had questions on a case you've got. Sounds more like Thomas Underwood is a suspect."

"No offense, but I'm the one who needs to be asking the questions here. Can you just save us both a lot of time and trouble and answer me?"

"He seemed to be himself. We film three episodes at a time, then we take a month break, and then he comes back and we do another three episodes. Nothing was unusual this time out."

Vail thanked him and sat a moment thinking it through. Then she went back to his book and finished reading about The Planner. Half an hour later, her phone rang.

"Karen, sorry for not returning your calls. We wrapped filming later than scheduled and I didn't even have time to go home. Had to prep for the trial on the flight from Oahu and buy a suit at the airport during my layover in LA. Headed off to Philly."

"I've got some questions about The Planner." *I've got other questions, too, but those will have to wait.*

"Yeah, I'm about to board my flight so I'll have to get back to you on that."

"Well—can you at least answer a few—"

"Okay," he said sternly to someone nearby. "I'll be right there." Back to Vail: "Look, I've still got a lot of trial prep to do. Email me your questions and I'll reply when I get a break in testimony. Couple of days, maybe sooner. You know, I did a pretty comprehensive write-up on that case in my first boo—"

"I'm reading it now."

"Then you're not reading carefully enough. Read it again." The phone was muffled a second, then: "Wish I had more time. Send me that email."

"No, wait. I need you to come—" But she realized he had hung up. She called him again and it went straight to voice mail.

Vail felt like slamming the handset down. She took a breath and went about composing her message, keeping it as short as possible while touching on the salient points of her analysis. And questions. Questions that were carefully constructed to potentially glean information as to whether or not he could be involved—without tipping him off. Not an easy task with a skilled profiler who literally wrote the book on interview techniques.

Vail sent it off, then stared at Underwood's book.

She opened the browser again and searched for the Philadelphia court case that Underwood was testifying in. After picking through a dozen links dealing with everything from jury selection to recaps of each of the murders, she found an article from two weeks ago mentioning that the trial had been continued for three *months* because of new evidence.

Another lie. Shit, could Hurdle be right? One of us, a partner in crime . . . a mutilating serial killer? An arsonist?

If she called Hurdle and briefed him, he would likely shift substantial assets to Underwood. Was that the right move? Was it her call to make?

Vail phoned Tarkoff and told him to have officers start contacting the airlines to determine if Thomas Underwood was booked on a flight—domestic or international—and if he was, to find a reason to detain him.

Vail sat back and played the case through her mind. *Start from the beginning.*

Marcks's wife's death was ruled accidental. But what if it wasn't? What if it was his first kill? Well, his first intentional *kill.*

She pulled out her laptop and opened the audio file of the 911 call that Jasmine had made:

OPERATOR/WOMAN'S VOICE: Nine-one-one, what's your emergency?

JASMINE: It's my mom, she slipped on a roller skate, she hit her head and--and she's . . ."

OPERATOR: She's what, darling? Where's your mommy now?

JASMINE: She's on the floor, she's not moving.

OPERATOR: Are you okay? Anyone there with you?

JASMINE: My daddy's here, he's holding my mom. He's very upset. [Garbled] I'm--I'm scared.

OPERATOR: Is your mom breathing?

JASMINE: No. I--I don't think so.

OPERATOR: I have your address. I'm going to send an ambulance. Meantime, tell me what happened.

JASMINE: We were in the other room, me and my daddy, we heard a loud noise, like a bang

```
and we, we ran in and she was on the floor.
[Garbled] And she's not moving. She's not
moving!
```

The sound of a child wailing nearly drowned out the operator's voice. The woman stopped talking and waited for Jasmine to compose herself, then continued:

```
OPERATOR: Can I talk to your daddy?
JASMINE: [Garbled] I--I think so.
```

There was muffled noise as Jasmine called out for her father, a disturbing hysteria permeating her voice. Frantic movement, more crying. Tears welled in Vail's lower lids. It was tough to listen to, the pain in Jasmine's voice. She could not imagine what she was thinking, looking at her mother's unmoving body lying on the floor. Her life forever changed.

In the parentage of a soon-to-be serial killer.

Vail shuddered. *I've gotta find Marcks. This has gone on long enough. I have to find him.*

```
MARCKS: My wife's dead. What do I do? I mean,
   what am I supposed to do with the body? Are
   you sending an ambulance?
```

Vail shook her head. *Calm, cool, collected. Clinical.*

His wife just died. He should be distraught. But he referred to her dispassionately—*the* body, not *her* body. While it was possible he was in shock, the most obvious conclusion, given what they now knew of Marcks, was that he killed her.

Did Jasmine see what happened? She said she was with her father in the other room. Was she just covering for him? Little girls love their daddies. Maybe he told her what to say. Did he threaten to kill her, even back then when she was a child, if she told anyone what really happened?

If that were the case, one would assume she would have covered that in her book. But there was very little on her mother's death—largely what was in the police report and on the 911 tape, as well as the medical examiner's conclusions.

Vail pulled out her Samsung and called Jasmine, but it went to voice mail. "Jas, it's Karen. I've got a couple of questions for you. It's important. I hope you're okay." She tried the other cell number Jasmine had used and left a similar message.

Vail set her phone down on the desk beside her laptop and went back to Underwood's book. She thumbed through the next case, and the one after that. Then her eyes caught something: an offender who left a note in the victim's mouth.

It was blank. Except that indented writing was discovered.

Vail felt a chill run from her shoulders to her legs. The hidden message the UNSUB left was, "Next in line."

She paged back to the beginning of the chapter and started reading: the offender was Desmond Robert Branson, also known as the Atlanta Strangler.

None of the behaviors Underwood discussed had any obvious connection to the Blood Lines case. There were no similarities she could find other than the note. Branson had killed seven prostitutes by asphyxiation. He was almost caught by the detective—but Branson got the upper hand and disabled the cop and took him hostage.

Vail sat there thinking. There was nothing, other than the communication with law enforcement, via the concealed message, that bore any resemblance to her current case.

You're not reading carefully enough. Read it again.

She sat staring at the page—but not seeing anything. *Why would he say that? What am I missing?*

Unless he was saying that to throw me off.

Vail took a breath, then returned her attention to the book, speeding through some of the subsequent chapters before forcing herself to pull back and slow down.

Focus, Karen.

An hour later, she checked her watch, then dialed Jasmine again. Voice mail. *Dammit.* She got up, rubbed her forehead, paced a few times, then launched the app Uzi installed on her phone.

A red error message appeared: it was unable to establish a connection with the tracking device. Just as Uzi had warned her might happen. A window opened asking if she wanted to enable an alarm that would alert her when the connection was reestablished. It warned her that constant searching for a signal would affect her battery life. *Fine. Do it.*

She clicked "yes" and was about to put her phone away when Ramos called through.

"Where are you?"

"FBI Academy library. Why?"

"Got a twenty on Gaines."

"No shit?"

"He's in the mountains. We were monitoring his cell phone in case he turned it on. And he did—less than a minute, but it was enough to get a fix."

"What's the plan?"

"Hurdle's deploying SWAT. They need their Bearcat, so it'll take them a bit to get up there. Tarkoff and I have four-wheel drive SUVs."

"On my way." Vail rose from her seat, the books still splayed open. "Leave that stuff as is," she said to the librarian as she headed out of the room. "I'll be back."

"How are you gonna get there?" Ramos asked.

"Figure out a place to rendezvous and I'll meet you there."

TWENTY MINUTES LATER, Vail was climbing into Ramos's Toyota 4Runner. The undercarriage was caked with a mixture of mud splatter and salt from his winter driving.

"I take it you do a lot of off-roading."

Ramos chuckled. "I live in the hills. And when it rains, this thing's the only way I can get home."

They were half a mile from the ping they had gotten when Ramos's phone rang. He put it on speaker. "Boss, you got me and Karen."

"How close are you?" Hurdle asked.

"Be there in a minute," Ramos said. "You?"

"Not far behind. And SWAT's about twelve behind me. Take a look around, see what we're dealing with."

"Got it. We'll take care of it."

"Best views we could get from Google Earth show an old trailer of some kind. But the dense tree cover made it tough to see. If we triangulated on the signal right, it's sitting on land owned by someone else, seventy-two-year-old Jack Welker. No priors on the guy, not even in the system. You'll see what looks like a large log cabin on the property. No idea where Gaines is exactly—cabin or that trailer. Be careful. We don't know what we're dealing with, if Welker's a hostile or if he's got no clue who Gaines is."

"Roger that," Ramos said, and disconnected the call.

A moment later, they approached the coordinates. It was indeed an old trailer—but not the kind usually used for habitation. This was a large forty foot cargo container that was traditionally attached to a long haul eighteen-wheeler. The tires were removed and the axles had been sunk into the ground so that its undersurface was flush with the hillside, leveled with cinder blocks.

Ramos pulled to a stop about sixty yards away. "Is that it?"

"If it is, we're too close. We should go back down the road a bit, get some cover from the trees where he can't see us."

"We're just here to take a look around." Ramos shut the engine and pulled a compact pair of binoculars from the armrest compartment. "SWAT's gonna do the heavy lifting of flushing the jackass out."

"I got that," Vail said. "But I think we should pull back."

Ramos frowned and squinted, as if to say Vail was speaking nonsense. "I think we're good right here. We're sixty or seventy yards away. Safe distance."

"How do you define 'safe'?"

"That trailer bugs me."

"Did you hear me?"

He peered into the woods. "I heard you. But I'm driving. And it's my truck. My call."

"We've got a guy who's already tried to kill us with an automatic weapon. If he's got an assault rifle—"

"He doesn't. He left it at that house in Lake Ridge, remember?

Shit, after all the ammo he blew through, he may be out of that, too."

"How can you be sure?"

"How can you be sure of *anything* in life?"

How did this turn into a philosophical discussion?

"We don't even know if he's *here*." Ramos popped open his door. "Let's go."

"Go?"

"Take a look around. Those are our orders." Ramos studied her face. "You can wait here if you want." He brought the binoculars to his eyes. "I was expecting a small, you know, mobile home. That people live in. What do you think?"

"Tactical challenge, for sure. No windows, no idea what's inside. *Who's* inside. Harder to breach."

"The blindness works both ways," he said. "Assuming Gaines's here, he can't see us, either."

"Good point."

He pushed open his door. "I'm gonna take a look around. If he's here and watching, at this distance, I won't pose much of a threat."

"I think we should pull back or wait for SWAT."

"I heard you the first two times." He dropped a leg out and slid his ass off the seat. "So wait."

Ramos closed his door and passed in front of the SUV.

Shit. I feel like a goddamn coward.

He continued another ten feet when Vail cursed under her breath and joined Ramos as he trudged through the frozen snow and mud.

"Thanks for having my back. I knew you'd come around."

"You did."

"I can tell what you're made of. You wouldn't leave a team-mate to do the dirty work while you cower in the safety of a car."

"I wasn't *cowering*. I just don't have a death wish."

"I don't think anyone's inside," he said, ignoring her comment. "Why live in a rectangular metal box when there's a cabin with all the comforts of home a few yards away? That trailer could just be storage." He handed her the binoculars.

Vail surveyed the structure. "Don't think so. Look at the electrical lines that run into it. Thick cables. More than you'd need to light up a storage room."

He glanced over his shoulder at her. "Listen to you, Ms. Electrician. Do you actually know what you're talking about?"

"No. But it sounded good, didn't it? If you really want to know, the satellite dish on top is what tipped me off."

Ramos squinted into the distance and said, "Oh."

"Not 'oh.' Uh-oh. There are cameras." Keeping the binoculars against her face, Vail pointed. "One o'clock and eleven o'clock. More toward the back. He might be watching us right now. I'm not getting a good feeling about this."

She handed him the glasses and he slowed as he studied the trailer.

Vail stopped suddenly and grabbed Ramos's arm. "Hang on." She crouched and gestured at something. "Trip wire."

Ramos growled. "Sonofabitch."

Is he watching us? Vail rose up. "I think we should get back to the truck."

"We're not a threat, especially if he's heavily armed. What are two cops gonna do with pistols?"

"I thought you were sure he didn't have any more assault rifles."

"I said we can't be sure of anything." He shoved the binoculars against her shoulder. "We keep our distance, we'll be fine."

She took another look. As she let her gaze roam over its metal skin, she saw cutouts, narrow slots, almost like gun turrets—

Vail pulled the glasses away from her face. "I'm going back." The crunch of tires on the frozen ground drew her attention. She turned to see Hurdle's SUV pulling to a stop. Walters, Tarkoff, and Morrison were visible in the passenger and rear seats.

As she continued on to Ramos's car, she saw another booby trap a few feet to her left. She stopped and turned toward Hurdle, who was getting out of his truck.

"Hold it!" she said. "Place is rigged. Trip wires. Could be mines."

Hurdle froze in mid-step, his boot hovering above the hard-packed terrain. "You shitting me?"

"What do we do now?" Walters asked.

"Retreat," Vail said, "a hundred yards back down the road."

"And wait for SWAT," Hurdle said. "Back in the truck—now."

That seemed like a sound plan.

Until automatic gunfire erupted.

Rounds struck the ground by Vail's feet and the tree trunks nearest her head. Lacking any cover, she and Ramos fled back toward his car.

Holy Jesus. What a choice. Do I want to get shot or do I want to step on an IED?

They made it back to the Toyota, its sides and windshield now pocked with large holes.

"Sonofabitch!" Ramos said as they got into the truck. "I'm still making payments!"

"Keep your head down," Vail said over the cacophony of gunfire. "Stay behind the engine block."

"And pray he doesn't hit the fuel line."

"I'd pray that none of the rounds hits *us*. Much more likely scenario."

"Aren't you the optimist," Ramos said, struggling to stay low.

Vail was doing the same. She had twisted her body and was now facing the back of the Toyota, kneeling on the floor, elbows on the seat. "You have the cell for the SWAT commander? We've gotta warn them they could be driving into a minefield."

"Text Hurdle, he might have a way of contacting them."

She did just that and got an immediate reply:

already done

Two minutes later, the armored SWAT truck slowly crested the hill and pulled in well behind Hurdle's SUV. They activated the PA system and directed Booker Gaines to throw down his weapon and come out with his hands on his head.

Gaines responded by treating the SWAT vehicle to the same bodywork that Ramos's Toyota received—but with a far different result. Designed to stop .50-caliber ball ammo, the Bearcat's half-inch steel shell and four-layer bulletproof glass absorbed the pounding well.

A moment later, the SWAT commander ordered them forward. They did not stop in front of the trailer, however. With a sniper in the Bearcat's turret and officers at the ready in the gun ports on its sides, they deployed the ram at the front of the Bearcat and punctured the short end of the cargo container, ripping off the metal siding as if it were the lid of a tin can.

Now exposed, Booker Gaines was standing there, assault rifle tucked against his shoulder, looking very much like a man at a crossroads in his life: challenge the SWAT team, which had just proven it was not going to be bullied, or surrender and spend arguably the best remaining years of his life behind bars.

He moved left and another man was visible in the dust fog: Vail believed it to be Scott MacFarlane.

The officers launched penetrating rounds of CS gas, a riot control agent that causes a burning irritation of the eyes, nose, and throat. They tore into the open end of the barricade, a dense, smoky haze filling the interior.

Vail counted the seconds, expecting to see Gaines and Mac-Farlane driven from the trailer, hands interlinked behind their necks. Instead, they ran forward in tandem, through the gaseous cloud, weapons blazing.

That was the last action the men took, as two SWAT officers opened fire.

"WAIT HERE," the SWAT commander said as they got back in the Bearcat and then drove up to the log cabin.

"Maybe you should run after the truck," Vail said to Ramos. "Through the minefield. Seems like your kind of gig."

He looked at her but did not reply.

"You could've gotten us killed."

"You didn't have to follow me," Ramos said. "You made your choice."

"You made it an impossible choice. I couldn't let you go alone. Anything happened, I would've had a really tough time living with myself."

"Whatever. Rationalize it any way you want."

"You know what, Ramos? You really disappoint me. Partner with someone else." Vail walked away and joined Hurdle behind his SUV.

"Everything okay?"

Vail kept her gaze focused on the Bearcat as it pulled up in front of its target. "Everything's great."

"Didn't look like it. You and Ram—"

"I said everything's great. We just had a disagreement."

"Fire!" Tarkoff started toward the open end of the trailer—then stopped, no doubt remembering the potential mines. "Anyone got an extinguisher?"

Vail pulled out her phone. "Calling it in. Doubt FD will get here before the blaze takes out everything in that sardine can. But they can prevent it from spreading to the forest."

"The trees and flora are draped in snow and ice," Hurdle said. "I don't think there's much of a risk."

She reported their location and then watched as SWAT encircled the cabin.

"You think Gaines or MacFarlane set that fire?" Morrison asked.

"Not necessarily. It can happen from SWAT's gas canisters." As she started to reholster her phone, it buzzed in her hand. A red alarm icon was blinking, informing her that Jasmine's tracker was back online.

She opened the app and a moment later, a string of GPS coordinates appeared: Jasmine's current location. *That doesn't mean she's safe, just that the unit's working and transmitting a signal.*

She thought of updating Hurdle on Underwood, but the sounds of gunfire snatched her attention. Her head snapped up and she saw the windows of the cabin shatter, gas filling what she figured was the main room.

The officers entered and seconds later Hurdle's phone rang.

"All clear," he said. "Let's go. We'll follow the tire tracks of the Bearcat to avoid any trip wires or mines."

Vail tapped the numbers and walked toward the cabin while the map loaded with a beeping dot. She zoomed in and the device's location came into focus.

I know that address. Is she crazy?

"I need your car," Vail yelled to Hurdle.

He turned and stopped, hesitating a second, then tossed her the keys. They landed at her feet and she retraced her steps to the SUV, revved the engine and made a tight circle, headed down the hill.

As Vail drove faster than she should have been going, bumping violently on the potholed road, one thought kept running through her mind:

What the hell is going on?

53

Vail waited until she reached the main road, which was smooth and flat. She took a second to get her bearings, then dialed Curtis. He did not pick up.

What is it these days? No one answers his phone?

"Meet me at Jasmine's house," she said to the voice mail. "We might have a problem. I mean, another problem."

Vail arrived in Bethesda at 4:35 PM, the clouded sky resembling a deep bruise: charcoal with hues of blue-gray and swirls of black.

She pulled to the curb and walked up to the front door.

The tracker had said that Jasmine was at home—but there's no way she would go there because of the risk involved. If there was one place her father would know to look for her, it was there. Jasmine knew that. Had she gone there to pick up some clothing? An ATM card? Risky, but maybe she thought she could tell if he was surveilling the place, waiting for her. That was something Jasmine would do—her enormous sense of self-confidence, however misguided, often led her to believe that she could adequately assess dangers as well as a trained law enforcement officer could.

Or perhaps she thought that Marcks had already determined she was not living there and would not take a chance on returning. There would be no need for him to watch her house—in which case it would be safe for her to go there. Still, it was a gamble, one that Jasmine had been careful to avoid.

Vail knocked. Waited. Nothing.

For that matter, Jasmine's car was not out front. *In the garage?*

Vail tried the doorknob. Locked. She pulled out her phone and called the home line—heard it ring in the kitchen—but it went to voice mail. Opened the Find/Me app and waited for it to obtain the signal. But the spinning dial kept rotating. She waited fifteen seconds, then twenty.

What am I going to do, stand here like a fool? She went around to the back and tried the knob but had the same result. *Kick it in?* She checked the app one more time but that wheel, or whatever it was, was still spinning.

Before she could talk herself out of it, she lifted her leg and struck the jamb squarely with her boot. A second later she was standing inside the house.

"Jas! It's Karen. Where are you?"

No response. In fact, there were no lights on, and with the setting sun, it was dark. She flicked on a lamp and glanced around, then walked to the foot of the staircase. "Jasmine!"

Vail ascended the steps, did a search of the second floor and found nothing: no Jasmine and nothing out of order. The downstairs looked much as she remembered the last time she was there.

She started for the garage when she saw the basement door. She pulled it open, turned on the light, and descended. "Hey, Jas, you down here?"

It was a finished room, fairly basic with a tile floor and a large area rug. An old sofa bed, washer and dryer. And no one down there. "C'mon, Jasmine," she said under her breath. "I know you were here."

As she turned to leave, a dog barked.

Jasmine doesn't have a dog. After what her father did to her stuffed animal, she would never have a pet of any kind, especially a dog.

Where is it?

Vail whistled. It barked again, a deep baritone. *It's got some size to it.*

"Hey guy. Where are you?"

More barking.

Vail moved closer to the far wall, put her ear to it, and listened. Called him again. "How's my doggy doing?"

Crying. Friendly, excited growling.

Vail looked at the paneling and ran a finger over one of the seams. And then she saw it, a break, from floor to ceiling. She had some experience with these. After pulling out her handcuff key, she dug it into the ridge and pried it open. There was a concealed door—with a room beyond it.

And a dog.

54

Hey boy." Vail gave his face and neck a rub as she turned on her phone's flashlight. "What are you doing down here?" She checked—he was, in fact, a male. And he was not wearing a collar.

Her phone rang. She answered it immediately, without checking caller ID.

"You here somewhere?"

It was Curtis.

"In the basement. Come in the back door. I opened it for you."

A moment later, she heard Curtis's heavy footsteps descending the stairs.

"You *opened it* for me? You broke in. What the hell's going on?

She did not want to tell him about the tracker, so she simply said, "Jasmine wasn't answering."

"Of course she's not answering. She's not stay—" He appeared in the doorway and noticed Vail's new companion. "What's a dog doing here?"

He went up to Curtis, tail wagging, and licked his hand.

"I was wondering the same thing. And here's another mystery. This is a concealed room."

He drew his chin back, then turned and looked at the doorway. "I don't get it."

"Makes two of us. Let's have a look around."

"Why are you here?"

"That requires a bit of an explanation." *And I guess now's as good a time as any.* She told him about the device Uzi had given her.

"I don't even know where to begin with that—but we'll save it for another time. Right now, we need to make sense of what's going on. And apparently that starts with a hidden room and a strange dog. Is it Jasmine's?"

"No. She can't have pets." Seeing Curtis's confused look, she said, "Because of what Marcks did to one of her stuffed animals as a kid."

"Shit, that's right." Curtis pulled out his iPhone and started dialing. "We need animal control. Until we figure out who this guy belongs to, someone's gotta look after him."

While he made the call and gave them the address, Vail started taking a quick inventory of the room: it was roughly ten by twelve feet, with a futon, shelving on one wall, and a cheap laminate armoire.

"You get anything from reading Underwood's book?" he asked as he hung up.

"Yes. Maybe. I mean . . ." She sighed. "I've got some problems with Underwood. I finally reached him. And he lied to me. Twice."

"How so?"

"He'd told me he was in Hawaii. But I reached the show's

producer and they wrapped filming weeks ago. He finally called me back—we spoke for less than a minute—and he said he was boarding a plane to Philly to testify in a case. But I looked up the case. The trial was postponed for three months."

Curtis looked at her. "What the hell?"

Vail turned back to the room. "I know. I didn't want to say anything to Hurdle. He seemed to want to go hard after Underwood. And I don't know . . . I guess I feel like we owe him more than that."

"We can't let emotions get in the way of doing our jobs."

Am I doing that?

"There's food here," Curtis said. "A water bowl. And . . . some dog crap. No collar. But he's definitely cared for. By whom? No way Jasmine would risk coming back here on a regular basis."

"Add it to the list of things I can't explain." She crouched down and—*Oh, shit.* "Uh . . ." Vail got up and spun around, her gaze darting from one wall to another. "We've gotta get out of here."

"Why? What—"

"I'll explain when we're in the car. Leave the dog. Follow me."

"Leave the dog? We can't just—"

"Do it. Did you touch anything? Move anything?"

"I don't think so, no."

"Then let's go." She passed through the door and closed it behind Curtis, her heart dropping at the sight of the pooch's sad eyes.

Vail ran up the steps, her gaze moving from one wall to another, one corner and shelf to the next. They exited the back door, where they had entered.

"Karen, what the hell's going on?"

They came around the side of the house and Vail pressed the remote for her Honda.

"Move your car. A block away, at least. Quickly. Meet me at the corner. And call animal control, tell them not to come."

"Why can't you just t—"

Vail started the engine and drove down the street, then parked in front of Curtis and got into his Ford.

He gave her a hard look. "Now what the fuck's going on?"

Vail sat there a long moment, trying to work it through. "I'm not completely sure—and I'm afraid that what I'm thinking won't make any sense."

"Just tell me, we'll work it through together."

"I'm pretty sure that's Thomas Underwood's dog in there."

"Underwood's dog. What are you talking about? How—"

"When I spoke to him this afternoon, like I said, it was a short conversation. But right before he ended the call, he told me to read his book, carefully, and that I'd find some of my answers there."

"Okay. Why is that weird?"

I'm not sure.

"You were reading one of his books."

"Yes." She dug two fingers into her temples and rubbed. "And I found a case where there was a note found in a victim's mouth that said, 'Next in line.'"

"Which could be explained by Marcks reading Underwood's book and he and Gaines are copying the killer. What's the problem?" He studied her face a moment and said, "You think it really *is* Underwood who's been setting these fires?"

"Things weren't adding up. *Aren't* adding up."

"Again, we know that. Spit it out. Was Marcks reading Underwood's book or is Underwood involved too?"

"I don't think that's what really happened. I think that . . ." Vail gathered her thoughts.

Curtis waited a moment, then said between clenched teeth, "In a second I'm gonna start shaking you."

C'mon, Karen. Think clearly. She took a deep breath. "Did you see what was in that room in the basement?"

"I was just starting to look it all over when you freaked and said we had to bug out."

Vail stared ahead at the descending darkness, at the headlights that were driving down the road toward them. "There was a camera mounted in the corner of the wall. I'm guessing it's a wireless camera. So that someone could watch it over the internet from another location."

"Lots of people have those."

Vail closed her eyes. She did not want to say it but she had to. "One of Underwood's cases involved the kidnapping of a detective. I don't think Underwood's a killer. He's been lying to me because I think he's been snatched up. And his call was being monitored so he couldn't tell me what was really going on. But he tried to give me a clue."

"A clue about what?"

"That he's been kidnapped. And how to find him. Or who's got him."

"I'll humor you for a minute. Let's say you're right. *Who's* got him?"

Vail bit her bottom lip. "I think we screwed up." She turned to Curtis. "There were books down there, too. Thomas Underwood's books."

"Someone's camping out in Jasmine's house? Marcks is living in that basement and he's got Underwood holed away somewhere? And he's watching the dog remotely? That makes no sense."

"It makes perfect sense. Except that you've got a few things mixed up. Roscoe Lee Marcks isn't holding Underwood hostage. Jasmine is."

"Jasmine. Why the hell would she do that?"

Vail found it hard to form the words. She hesitated and tried to clear her mind, tried to reason it out.

"Karen," Curtis said. "What the hell's going on? What am I missing?"

Vail turned to him and found the words tumbling from her lips before she could make sense of it. "Jasmine is the Blood Lines killer."

55

Are you feeling okay?"

Vail closed her eyes. "No, I'm not. I have to think this through. I just know what I'm seeing here and now. And it doesn't add up."

"There could be other explanations."

"There could be."

"Gaines could've come looking for Jasmine and she wasn't here so he broke through the wall and put that stuff in there."

"Why would he do that? He had his own secluded place in the hills. No need to build a fake room. That trailer was pretty well hidden. Besides, planning went into creating that hidden area. A false wall had to be constructed." Vail was still working it through her mangled thoughts.

"Fine. But there has to be another answer."

"Maybe. But I don't think that's what's going on here."

"Karen, I worked this case hard. Thomas Underwood, one of the BAU's best and brightest, one of the founding fathers of the profiling unit, drew up the behavioral assessment. Neither of us had any doubt Marcks was our guy. You didn't either. You may've been a rookie profiler but you were a veteran cop and detective. You knew your way around a murder case as well as me. We had definitive forensics at two scenes and Marcks pled to both those murders. Right?"

Vail nodded. "I know."

"Why the hell would he do that if he was innocent? And we know he's killed several people since breaking out. That was Marcks, no question."

"And there haven't been any murders with that MO and ritual since he's been incarcerated."

"Right," Curtis said. "They started again after he broke out."

"I know that." *I need time to think.*

"And the diethyl ether at Gaines's place. And the homosexual connection."

Vail slammed her hand against the dashboard. "I know! It doesn't make sense." *I've gotta clear my head and reason this out.* "Anything at Gaines's trailer?"

"Whatever was there, the fire finished it off."

Vail pulled out her phone and reloaded Uzi's Find/Me tracking app. *Please give me a good connection.* "Right now our objectives are to find Jasmine. Find Underwood. And find Marcks. We'll sort it out later."

GPS coordinates appeared—and Vail took a moment to peruse the numbers. Judging by her frequent visits to this location, it was a significant place for Jasmine. Finally Vail popped open her door.

"Where you going?"

"I'll follow in my car."

Vail tapped, the map rotated, and . . . "Got it. Arlington."

She texted Leslie Johnson and asked her to get land records on the address she was including in the message.

"Talk to me," Curtis said.

"I have a location on Jasmine. Call Hurdle. Tell him we need the task force and SWAT at the residence I'm sending everyone." She tapped it out and hit "send."

"SWAT?"

"If I'm right, Underwood's being held at that address."

"But you could be wrong about all of this. This whole thing with Underwood, it's just a guess."

"Look, none of this makes any sense. I don't know what to think. But we've got no idea who's waiting for us there: Jasmine? Marcks? Someone else? Who knows. After what just happened with Gaines—"

"Fine. I'll make the call."

56

Marcks had exhausted all means of locating Jasmine, having repeatedly driven up and down the streets in the vicinity where he had left her after she had disabled him—to no avail.

He thought of wearing some form of disguise and going door-to-door, but the risks were too great. It only took one observant and law-abiding citizen who had been watching the news to dial 911. The police were everywhere as it was, with roadblocks and swarming patrols. He did not need to do anything to make their job easier.

Left with no other alternative, he returned to her place in Bethesda, hoping she would eventually come back—if for no other reason than to pick up a change of clothing.

Jasmine finally showed up around midnight. She did not turn on any lights when she entered the residence and was inside barely four minutes. Before he could decide if he should go in after her, she came out and headed for her car.

He followed the vehicle at an extreme distance of about fifty yards, deciding that it was better to lose her than be discovered. If he did fall too far back, he could always sit on her house again the next night.

And that was precisely what happened. The following evening, much earlier this time, she returned, entered covertly, and left very quickly.

But this time, figuring—correctly, as it turned out—that she was headed to the same destination, he was better equipped to hang back and still stay with her.

After making it all the way into Arlington, he had to close the gap—because she would likely be making turns down side streets. If he was too far back, there would be no way for him to keep up with her.

Following a few course changes, she headed straight for a line of row houses. Marcks slowed, then watched as she hung a left and made a quick U-turn. He continued on down the block and parked. Lights went on inside a corner townhome.

He sat there for a while, getting his bearings, watching who came and went—when a vehicle pulled up in front of the place where Jasmine had entered. Marcks leaned back in his seat, away from the window, when he saw who got out: Vail and that detective, Curtis.

This presented an interesting opportunity. If he acted swiftly and flawlessly, he could take out his three primary nemeses in a matter of minutes.

But could he pull it off?

As he mulled that thought—he would have to wait and see if they separated for any length of time—he noticed that Vail suddenly had a gun in her hand. Marcks clenched his jaw. Could he take her on with a weapon at the ready? What about Curtis?

The street was relatively dark, so perhaps he could make it close to her, using the bushes, until he was upon her.

He leaned forward and watched.

57

Vail arrived first, followed a second later by Curtis. Vail drove past the house, an older three-story brick colonial attached on the left and fronting a side street on the right. A dozen concrete steps with a wrought iron railing led up to the front door about two dozen feet away. Cars lined the curb and residual snow blanketed the lawns and sidewalks.

They got out of their vehicles and perused the area.

"Let's grab a look around the perimeter. Low key, evaluate entrances/exits, see if we can get a peek inside."

"That's *all* we do," Curtis said. "We're not going in alone."

"Not unless I'm right and Underwood's a hostage."

"And his life's in immediate danger."

"Fine."

They unholstered their handguns and moved covertly toward the townhome, Curtis heading to the back and Vail taking the front.

Vail used the thick hedges, their yellowing leaves intact, as cover to get as close as possible before moving into the open. She ascended the stairs and stopped behind the last bush and surveyed the eaves and other hidden areas where a camera could have been concealed. She saw nothing.

She continued to the last few steps closest to the entrance, which were made out of metal grating, presumably to prevent pooling water from becoming sheets of ice during the winter months.

The door featured an ornately carved gold leaf–embossed glass window. But Vail avoided it, keeping her head below eye level as she approached. An American flag flapped noisily in the breeze fifteen feet to the left, fighting for her attention as she tried to make an accurate assessment of the premises.

She descended a few feet and moved right toward the windows, fighting through the branch-dense bushes. The curtains were drawn but unlined, so Vail should have been able to at least see forms if anyone was inside. Although the lights were on, the living and dining rooms appeared to be empty.

She was unsure where Curtis was, but until she heard from him, there was nothing for her to do but wait, listen, and observe.

Until a noise to her right snagged her attention.

CURTIS TOOK A CIRCUITOUS ROUTE to the back door—along the perimeter, looking for a point where he could either climb over the white cedar lock board fence or locate some kind of easement that would give him access.

He found a well-camouflaged gate, but it was securely latched. He tried to reach over the top and feel for a release lever, but it was too high off the ground. He shoved his right shoulder against it to test its integrity and found that it gave a bit more than he would have thought, considering the healthy condition of the wood.

Curtis stepped back and brought up his foot, slammed it against the planks, and knocked it open. He immediately regretted the noise; if Jasmine was in fact a kidnapper—or a killer—and if Underwood was inside with her, the last thing he wanted to do was tip her off to their presence.

Ten steps in, he curved around the rear of the house and along the path that led to the back door. He approached cautiously, not knowing who, besides Jasmine, was inside.

He surveyed the yard, which was longer than wide with planters on either side of the inlaid masonry path. A large wood double gate was built into the fence, fronting the side street. He walked over and took a closer look; tire marks in the grass and dirt were barely discernible. Whoever lived here drove their car into the yard. To park it? Because there's no garage?

He moved back toward the residence and saw something in the corner, a few inches taller than he was, covered with a black tarpaulin. He could feel a metal frame and a base with wheels, but had no idea what it was without removing the cover. First, however, he had to stick to the task.

He leaned up against the brick siding, then peered into the nearest window. The kitchen was empty, and as far as he could see, the other rooms were likewise vacant, although a lamp burned across the way in an area that was not visible to his line of sight.

He pulled back and retraced his steps, headed toward a rendezvous with Vail.

VAIL STOOD STILL, Glock raised, peering into the darkness. Her breathing had quickened and she puffed vapor into the frigid night air.

Before she had time to investigate, Curtis appeared, coming around the side of the house. She started down the stairs toward the street and met him at the curb one house over.

"Anything?" she asked.

He shook his head. "Lights are on inside, didn't see anyone."

"Same here. Heard something right before I saw you. Not sure what it was."

"Might've been me. I snapped some twigs on the way around. And that was after I kicked the gate in. Not my stealthiest moment."

He told her about the yard, the wide gate and covered metal contraption he had found, as well as the tire tracks. As Vail started to comment, a text hit her phone at the same moment a call came through. She glanced at the message first:

swat 9 min out

She brought the handset up to her face. "Vail."

"This is Lawrence Vickers. I'm working with your task force, reading the books written by Agent Underwood."

"Right. Find anything?"

"Not sure. In his latest book, uh, *The Masked Mind*, there are two cases that could be relevant. First involved a male killer whose daughter accidentally witnessed his first kill. Then he used her to help him get the vics in a vulnerable position so he could snatch them up. Second one's from Brazil. Killer grabbed up a child, held him for ransom, and even though the family paid, he killed the kid. He did this four times until he took a detective's son, the cop who was working the case. Oh, and there's a third one. Two male killers go—"

"Karen! Hey, heads up." Curtis nudged her arm hard and indicated the passing car. "Woman driving, kinda looks like Jasmine. Came from around back, the side street."

"Gotta go," Vail said to Vickers. To Curtis: "You sure?"

"Yeah," he said, running toward his Ford. "Didn't see Underwood. Check the house. I'm goin' after that car."

Vail ran up the steps but pulled out her phone to locate the Find/Me tracking beacon before breaking down the door—just in case Curtis was wrong. The Samsung started vibrating and the alarm was flashing, indicating that the connection had been reestablished. The coordinates populated the screen and the map showed Jasmine in motion. She was nearby—but not in the townhome.

Curtis was right—that was her.

Vail holstered the cell and kicked in the door, then moved swiftly, but carefully, through the house. Rather than checking the upper floor, she figured the basement was the most likely place Jasmine would be keeping Underwood—if she had left him behind.

Had Jasmine seen them, or was it a coincidence she was leaving soon after they arrived?

Vail descended the basement steps, turned on the lights—and her breath caught.

58

Thomas Underwood was lying on the floor, a tourniquet tight around his neck, his veins distended, his color more purple than flesh-toned.

Vail was on him in a split second. She tugged at the sheet-like noose, but it was too tight against his neck. *Tzedek.*

Vail pulled it from its scabbard, pressed the dull edge against Underwood's skin, and sliced through the cotton. "C'mon Thomas. Are you with me?"

She felt for a pulse. *Alive but unconscious.*

He was tied behind his back, but Vail nevertheless succeeded in rolling him into a supine position. She elevated his legs, then bent them repeatedly at the knees, helping to force blood back toward his heart and brain.

"Thomas, wake up!" She searched the basement for something that could help revive him—and found a jug of bleach on the laundry room shelf. It was not smelling salts, but it should work.

Vail soaked the cotton tourniquet, coughing and struggling to see through the heavy tearing from the intense fumes—and waved it underneath his nostrils. He jerked his head away, groaned, then slowly opened his eyes.

"That's it, come on. You know who I am?"

"Karen . . ."

"Do you remember what happened?"

"Help me up."

Vail got behind him and pushed him into a seated position, then freed his hands.

He took a deep breath and wiped his clammy brow with a sleeve. "I was wrong. I got it so wrong I'm embarrassed to admit it. My last case, I thought I was going out with a bang. But apparently I went out with a resounding thud."

"So Jasmine is the Blood Lines killer?"

"Yes."

Vail sat down beside him. "We both got it wrong. But how—"

"She's a cold-blooded, violent psychopath. There's very little literature on predatory or hunting behavior—as it's seen with psychopathy—in females. I know of only a few cases, and they're not well documented. Women prefer poisonings. Far down the list is guns and then knives." He turned to her. "Sorry. I know you know this. But—but physical attacks like this by a woman are almost unheard of. Especially female on male, if for no other reason they lack the strength to disable."

"That's why she used the ether."

"She probably seduced them to get close, then anesthetized them just long enough to restrain them and 'play' with the body, then do the kill. She had as much time as she wanted to have her fun. And between the tree cover and tall fences, no one would see her loading a body into the car at night."

"She'd still have to be able to lift a body, even if she did it a little at a time. A dead body is . . . well, dead weight."

"Ever see one of those hydraulic patient lifts? They use them in nursing homes and dialysis centers. Small yet very efficient, kind of like jacking up a car. Minimal effort, but it can lift a hell of a lot of weight. You put a sling on the patient—or in Jasmine's case, the victim's body—and then hook it to the device. A few easy pumps of the lever and you can set the body in the trunk. A child could do it."

"Curtis saw something like that in the yard, covered with a tarp."

"Where there's a will, there's always a way."

"So she got the vics here, where she killed them, and then used her car to deposit the bodies at the dump sites wherever we found them. How'd she get them out of the trunk?"

"She's very strong." His hands went to his neck and felt the bruise from the tourniquet. "But if she's not worried about hurting the body, which she wouldn't be, she'd definitely be able to pull it over the edge and let it fall to the ground."

Vail heard a noise outside: SWAT had arrived. She called Hurdle—who she suspected was with them, or could reach them—and told him about finding Underwood and Curtis's pursuit of Jasmine.

"Curtis lost her," Hurdle said. "We've got a BOLO out. He got her plate, so it's just a matter of time."

"If you talked with Curtis, you know about Jasmine? About why he was tailing her?"

"I do."

That was all he said, but she felt there were volumes behind those two simple words.

"We'll talk about it later."

"Yeah," he said, "I guess we will. I'll be at your twenty in two minutes."

She hung up and turned back to Underwood. "Marcks was not involved in any of the murders?"

"Not the Blood Lines kills. But he had at least two to his credit—years before his arrest. There was a gas station attendant he shot when Jasmine was twelve. Indianapolis. They were on their way back from watching the race—Marcks and Rhonda, his wife, and Jasmine. He went to fill up while Rhonda used the restroom. Marcks got into it with the attendant about something and the guy pulled out a gun. Marcks took it off him and shot him, point-blank, right in the face."

"And Jasmine saw this?"

"She said she did."

"And the other kill?"

"Rhonda."

"So she didn't slip on a skate in the garage," Vail said. "I just listened to the 911 tape today. Jasmine really sold it. She was completely believable."

"Impressive. A psychopath at a fairly young age, who can act."

Vail's mouth dropped open slightly. *Shit.* "She's good."

"Yeah she is. And I'm not saying that to be self-serving. But she fooled us. All of us. She even altered her ritual on vics nine and ten to throw us off track, to suggest there were two killers. That's beyond good, that's an awareness we don't often see."

"There was another murder you probably don't know about. Marcks supposedly shot a kid during a struggle. Other teen brought the gun. But given everything we now know, I'm not sure anything we were told was true. I doubt there was a struggle at all. He probably just killed the kid."

Underwood frowned. "Quite the family."

"But Marcks really is trying to kill Jasmine," Vail said. "That much I'm sure of. I saw the anger. I mean, Marcks is a violent man. And a killer. I agree with your assessment—he exhibits only some of the psychopathic cluster. And since there's a genetic predisposition, it makes sense that Jasmine also has these traits—but to a greater extent." She shook her head. "How could I not have seen it? I mean, I didn't know her well, but I had a fair amount of contact with her over the years."

"Because she was grooming you, manipulating you for her benefit."

Vail thought about that. And felt like putting her fist through the wall. She had to take the personal affront out of the equation. She forced her thoughts back to the case. "Why would Marcks plead guilty to the Blood Lines kills?"

"He only pled to two murders." Underwood chuckled wryly. "And he only did *that* because Jasmine was going to rat him out on Rhonda and the gas station attendant. This way, if he pleads to the two Blood Lines kills, he's famous, he's talked about forever in serial killer lore, and it's no difference to him. He was probably going to go down for the murder of his wife, without question. There was a witness. A compelling witness who could turn on the tears of how her father bullied her and threatened her if she didn't lie for him. No one was going to believe the hulking thug over the beautiful blonde when those tears start flowing."

"And I'm guessing she planted the evidence at those two Blood Lines scenes. Her father's hair and blood. To frame him."

"Right," Underwood said as he slowly rose from the floor and sat down on the couch. "And he knew that. He knew there was no way he was going to get acquitted for those two murders. We had his DNA at the scenes. Not a chance in hell they'd believe his story."

Vail joined him on the sofa. "That's why he took the deal. Plead to the two, no death penalty."

"He was going to do life no matter what. If he didn't agree to the deal—the one Jasmine presented him with—she would tell the police a convincing story she'd cooked up about how her father planned Rhonda's murder for weeks. Maybe she even planted some evidence for us to find as well in case it became necessary, in case we went looking. Bam, you've got premeditation. Special circumstances and the death penalty."

"She's one smart, evil bitch. But why does *he* want to kill her? Because she was going to rat—" Vail's ears perked up at the sound of footfalls on the steps.

"Vail, you down here?"

"Yeah."

Hurdle appeared seconds later. His eyes found Vail's colleague. "Thomas Underwood, I take it."

Underwood held out a hand and they shook. "Karen here saved my life."

Hurdle smirked and nodded. "Good for her. Might be the only thing she got right in this case."

"Hey." Vail rose—but Underwood grabbed her arm.

"I don't know what agency you're with, but—"

"Marshals Service," Hurdle said, subtly moving his jacket aside and revealing the badge he was wearing on a chain around his neck.

"He heads up the Capital Area Regional Fugitive Task Force."

Underwood absorbed that, then nodded. "Marshal, I don't

want to sound condescending, but this was a very complex murder case, perhaps the most difficult in my career, which spans four decades. It's wholly unfair to find any blame with Karen. Or me. Or Erik Curtis. We were all duped by two people who had motivations and a set of circumstances we've never encountered before. I'd even say no police force in the world has come up against something as elaborate as this, featuring two very disturbed psychopaths."

Hurdle frowned. "I'll debrief you tomorrow. Assuming you get it all figured out." He faced Vail. "And assuming we catch your buddy Jasmine."

"I feel bad enough about this. Thanks for rubbing it in."

"My pleasure. Really. It is." He turned to leave and spoke as he walked out. "Now I've gotta go catch *two* goddamn fugitives."

"He'll get over it," Underwood said as Hurdle ascended the steps. "He's pissed. But he doesn't have a clue what was really going on in this case. I do, I lived it. You do, because you lived the tail end of it. Just know that it is what it is. We do our best and sometimes that's not good enough. But know that you gave it your all. You did, didn't you?"

"Give it my all?" Vail studied his face. "Always."

Underwood smiled. "I have no doubt."

Vail's phone vibrated with a text from Leslie Johnson:

townhouse owned by edna heasley age 94

curtis told me why you were looking at this place

ss checks still being cashed

no children no known friends still alive

curtis thinks edna is another jasmine victim so to speak

I think he's right. "Sorry, just got the 411 on who owns this house." She typed a quick thanks to Johnson, then turned back to Underwood.

"Jasmine's had it for nine years," he said. "This is the place we searched for and never found. There are supposedly trophies here. Somewhere."

"How do you know? How'd you know all this other stuff about Jasmine?"

Underwood chortled—and coughed. He cleared his throat, then said, "I asked her. She told me. When I started to put it together, she laughed at me for getting it so wrong. I felt so humiliated. It's not just you. I'm good at dishing out advice, but don't think I didn't beat myself up over it, too. Which was, of course, what she wanted. She wanted to feel like she was in control, which meant beating me down. Me, the *expert*. Plus, she figured there's no reason not to tell me."

"Because she was going to kill you."

"And when she saw you at the door, she—"

"She saw me? There was a camera?"

Underwood gestured across the room where a small monitor showed a view of both the front and rear of the house.

Vail kicked a stool that was a foot to her left. "I looked. I didn't see anything." Above that monitor was another screen—of the dog she had found at Jasmine's. "That's yours, isn't it?"

"Rusty, yeah. I saw when you found him. You made him—and me—very happy."

"I take it Jasmine wasn't here when I was there."

"You missed her by two or three minutes."

"Sorry I had to leave Rusty behind." She took out her phone

to text Curtis to tell him to send an officer to pick up the retriever—and bring him to her house for the time being.

"I saw what happened," Underwood said. "You realized what was going on and you got your asses out of there in case Jasmine hadn't already seen you. How'd you find her?"

Vail explained the device Uzi had given her.

"So you know where she is now?"

"Maybe. It's subject to interference, so there are times when I don't get a real-time location." She opened the app. It showed a static signal. *Did she stop somewhere?* She texted the coordinates to Curtis, who said he and Tarkoff were not far away.

Underwood gave her a dubious look. "Either she's found what she thinks is a good place to lie low for a while or—"

"She found the device and ditched it. As soon as I showed up here, I was worried she'd realize I had some way of tracking her. She was careful to use burner phones to keep from being found by Marcks—as well as, apparently, by me. So there'd be no way for me to find this place unless I followed her."

"I'm sure she was extremely careful about that."

"I need time to rethink all my contacts with her, both recent stuff and in the past. What things did I tell her when my guard was down? What kind of information did I divulge about the investigation?" Vail closed her eyes. *What a mess.* "You were about to tell me why Marcks wants to kill her. Before Hurdle showed up."

"Right. Jasmine said he agreed to take the fall for the murders because he had no choice. But to have it rubbed in his face, to see her get all the glory of the abused and suffering little girl, was too much for him. That's according to her—and there's likely some truth to that.

"My take is that he probably treated her well growing up. We know that some violent male offenders have good relationships with their children, especially their daughters, who have no idea what their father does. They don't see that side of him. The fathers work hard to keep it concealed, for obvious reasons. This is just conjecture, of course. We'll probably never really know."

"And in Jasmine's case, she *did* know who and what her father was. But obviously it didn't matter because of what *she* is."

"Yes," Underwood said. "And if I'm right, and Marcks is capable of feeling a certain range of emotions, he probably felt used, betrayed. He held his tongue because he had no choice. And to some extent it was to his advantage. But to have it rubbed in his face, to have his reputation smeared, nationally smeared on talk shows, on a *personal* level, with lies about how horribly he treated his little girl, it just cements him in the public consciousness as a bigger monster than they already thought he was. The difference is the other stuff didn't matter to Marcks—fine, call him a serial killer. Whatever. It brought him notoriety, which fed his narcissism. Fact was, he *had* killed multiple people.

"But how he treated his daughter, that did matter to him. He probably couldn't take it anymore."

Vail thought about that. "At some point, before Jasmine's mother was killed, I have to think she realized her daughter was different, that she didn't form bonds, that she had little to no emotion—certainly no feelings for her, no more attachment to her than to a piece of candy."

"You're right. Rhonda knew something was wrong."

"How do you know? Jasmine said that?"

"Rhonda said it. There's a diary." Underwood stood up, steadied himself for a second, then took a couple of steps across the room and pulled a small bound notebook from the shelf. "I found it one day after Jasmine left. I don't think she realized I read it. But I doubt she'd care." He opened it, and as he thumbed to the right page, said, "Jasmine had turned twelve and Rhonda—her own mother—wrote something that, in retrospect, is chilling."

He handed Vail the five by seven inch notebook.

"She wrote about some behaviors she found 'disturbing,' and 'strange for a young girl.'"

Vail read the neat handwriting:

I came home this afternoon to find that Jas had gotten out of school early. When I walked in I saw her in the backyard. She didn't realize I was there. I watched her pulling Tabby's ears until the poor kitty shrieked. I stood there in shock. She then picked up a stick and chased it around the yard, trying to hit it. I ran outside and screamed at Jasmine to stop. I asked her what she was doing and she looked at me with this, I don't know. I can't describe it. This . . . these eyes . . . it was a cold stare. She just looked at me and didn't answer. I punished her, told her to go to her room and if I ever saw her do anything to hurt an animal again she'd be grounded for a month. The next day I walked into my bedroom and found Sparky, her favorite stuffed animal, the one she slept with every night, cut into pieces. His arms and legs stacked in a pile on top of his body, which had a deep slit across his stomach. I know it was

just a toy but I felt like throwing up. What if it represented something else? Me?

Vail looked up and met Underwood's gaze. Nothing more
needed to be said. If there was any doubt as to who and what
Jasmine Marcks was—and there wasn't at this point—this pas-
sage sealed the deal. Classic psychopathy.

"Read this one," Underwood said, turning the page and tapping it with his right index finger.

Today I went into the yard to take the garbage out and
found a hamster dead, tossed on top of a dead raccoon.
The coon's stomach had been cut open. I asked Jasmine
what she knew about it but she refused to make eye
contact. She claimed she didn't know anything about it.
I talked with Roscoe when he got home. I told him I
thought Jas was responsible, a tough thing for a mother
to admit. He said it's just a phase she's going through, to
just leave her alone and she'll grow out of it. Truth is, I'm
sick to my stomach. I don't know what to do.

"And this one."

I confronted Jas about it today, told her I was going to
take her to a doctor. Just to talk, maybe there's something bothering her that she needs to get off her chest.
She picked up a hammer and threatened to hit me with
it if I made her see a doctor. I told Roscoe I'm going to
go to the police tomorrow, to ask them what I should
do. He said he would talk to her to see if she'll tell him

what's bothering her. But she's his little girl, his perfect little girl who can do no wrong. He doesn't say it, but I think he thinks I'm overreacting. Or making these things up. I don't know what else to do, how to reach my daughter. It's tearing my heart out. She's my little girl, but she's turned into . . . she's turned into a monster. There, I wrote it. I couldn't bring myself to say it out loud. But I'm not doing her any good by ignoring what I'm seeing. It's only getting worse. And I now fear for my safety. If Roscoe's not taking this seriously, I need to do it myself.

Vail looked up. Tears pooled in her eyes. "This is . . ." She cleared her throat. "This is heartbreaking. There's nothing Rhonda could've done for Jasmine."

Vail turned the page but that was the last entry. "Is there another notebook?"

"That was the last entry, Karen. Rhonda Marcks was found dead the next morning."

Jesus Christ.

"It's hard to know for sure, because we're only making reasonable assertions about the degree of Marcks's psychopathy, but it's possible he would've eventually looked at his daughter as a lost cause, too. Jasmine shocked him, I'm sure, when she threatened to go to the police and rat him out for killing Rhonda. When exactly their relationship totally deteriorated, I don't know. Even though it probably happened over time, that's the point when he started to see who his precious daughter really was. But you're only looking at one side of the equation. Jasmine wanted her father dead, too. In the worst way."

"Why?"

"Who's the only person who knows the truth about what she's done? That she's the Blood Lines killer?"

"Her father." Vail thought a second. "Jasmine knew how he'd react. The only thing that could spoil her time in the limelight would be her father coming forward with a story that his daughter was really the Blood Lines killer. Who knows if anything would have come of it. He'd have little to no credibility.

"Curtis would've had to reopen the investigation to dot the i's, but really, unless Marcks could provide key evidence that would definitively prove that his daughter was the killer and that she framed him, it'd be just a lot of noise from a convicted killer who's trying to save his ass and use a get out of jail free card."

"All true," Underwood said.

"So she hired the biggest, baddest dude at Potter to attack him? To kill him?"

Underwood frowned disapprovingly at Vail. She suddenly felt like a rookie profiler being schooled by the mentor.

"No," Vail said, correcting herself. "This is personal. And having someone else do the kill wouldn't be fulfilling."

He winked at her. "You got it."

Vail stood up and paced, thinking it through. "So the only thing that makes sense, then, is that she would somehow try to facilitate the escape."

"Right again."

"Did she tell you this?"

"In so many words. I had hours to piece it together. But from what I was able to gather, she did, indeed, help Marcks escape."

"What could Jasmine possibly do to—"

"She worked at the Department of Corrections as—"

"Oh shit." *Numbers.* "She worked in the back office. She had access to their computer systems." Vail brought a hand to her forehead. "She studied computer science."

"She hacked into the system," Underwood said. "She said she replicated a judge's transfer order for another prisoner, forged it to read as a transfer for her father to be moved to Potter."

Vail sat down hard. "Where Marcks's childhood buddy, Lance Kubiak, was a correctional officer."

"I didn't get the full story, but Kubiak was involved on some level."

"She did that *before* the book came out, before he wanted to kill her."

"I bet she regretted that move."

Vail shook her head. "Don't think so. She couldn't be sure he'd attempt an escape, but she knows her father and felt he would try to exploit the situation. The book, and the media attention it'd bring, would drive the nail in further, baiting him, getting his ire up and motivating him to attempt an escape. She manipulated him, just as she manipulated me. And she gave him the tools he'd need to break out."

"So he played right into her hands."

"For her, it was a no-lose scenario. He'd either get killed in the escape attempt or he'd make it out and come after her. And she'd be ready for him. She's not afraid of him—but it had to be on her terms, when she could control the circumstances. Being larger and stronger, he's dangerous—so she's got to be smarter."

"She's definitely smarter. Formidable. She manipulated all of us. Did such a great job that no one saw what was really going on."

Vail pulled out her phone and called Curtis. "You guys find her?"

"Almost there. You still have a reading on her?"

Vail pulled out the device. "No. Shit—even if she ditched it, it should still be transmitting, right?"

"How the hell should I know?"

Dammit. Vail ground her molars. "I'm gonna have a friend of mine—Aaron Uziel—email you a link to download the app to your phone so you can track it in real time in case she hasn't found it. Hang on a second."

Vail pulled her Samsung away from her ear and texted both Uzi and Curtis, making the request preceded by the word "URGENT" in caps.

"Install the app," she told Curtis. "And let me know what happens when you get there." She hung up and began pacing, trying to clear her mind, refocus on Underwood. "Why kidnap you? Why keep you alive?"

Underwood was quiet a long moment.

Vail stopped, then turned her head slowly to face Underwood. "Because you helped her."

He looked away. "Not willingly."

"Of course not." Vail glared at him, waiting for him to elaborate. "But you did help her."

"She took Rusty and put him in her basement, hooked up that internet camera and put it on the screen in my 'prison cell.' Constant inducement to do what she wanted."

"Or she wouldn't go over there and feed him."

"Worse. She'd make me watch while she killed him. And I fully believed her when she said she'd do it. After reading Rhonda's diary entries, after realizing who I was dealing with, I had zero doubt she would follow through on that threat. After my wife died, Rusty's been . . . he's been my life. I couldn't let her hurt him in any way."

Vail thought of Hershey. She could not fault Underwood.

"I told her things to do that would shield her from your scrutiny," Underwood said. "Ways to stage the crime scenes. But I didn't give her everything she wanted."

"The clues you left me. To read your books so I'd figure out what she was up to." She shook her head. "But I didn't catch on, not fast enough."

"You eventually got it. You read the cases."

The cases. Vail thought a moment, then stood up as she replayed a conversation in her mind.

Underwood watched her a moment. "This isn't over, is it?"

She turned to face him. "Not by a long shot."

59

Vail started for the door, trying to work it through her mind.

Underwood was right behind her. "What's wrong?"

"There was a case—one of the agents I assigned to read your books called me before I came looking for you. The killer went after the cop's kid."

"Fernandez. He'd killed four children. The fifth one he kidnapped was the detective's, who was working the case. Does Curtis have any kids in the area?"

"No." Vail quickened her pace, running toward, and then up, the stairs.

Underwood followed. "Where are you going?"

"I know where she's headed. She's going after my son."

"How would she know how to find him?"

Because I told her.

Vail ran out the front door and down the steps, not even thinking about slipping on the ice. Not thinking about *anything* other than getting to Jonathan. She sprinted to her car, suddenly realizing Underwood was right behind her as she fumbled for the remote, attempting to unlock the door.

He took it and hit the correct button. She grabbed the key

fob back and got in. Underwood jumped into the Honda's passenger seat as she turned the engine over.

"I'll kill her, Thomas," she said as she accelerated hard away from the curb. "I'll kill her."

"Your son's gonna be fine."

Vail was comforted—slightly—by his words. But she knew they were just that. Words. Without any power behind them. Well, perhaps faith. *Is that enough?*

Vail pulled out her cell and handed it to Underwood. "Call Jonathan. Look in the call log."

Underwood made the call, then swiveled it away from his mouth. "Voice mail." He pulled it back to his lips. "Jonathan, call your mother immediately. Very important."

Vail clenched her jaw and shook her head. "She hurts him, I'll hunt her down, anywhere in the world, if it's the last thing I do." Thoughts of Uzi and DeSantos and their OPSIG black ops buddies flashed through her mind. *Would they do that for me?*

"Karen," Underwood said firmly. "He's going to be okay."

"He'll be okay if I make it okay. He's a young man, in college. He doesn't know the darkness of evil. He's not prepared for that kind of malevolence."

"He grew up with a mother who's a cop. Who's a profiler. Give him more credit than that."

"I've done my best to shield him from that stuff."

"He watches TV. He plays video games. He's got an idea."

And he had an abusive father. Thomas is right. He's been exposed to more than I'd like to admit.

As Vail screeched around a corner, she thought about that. Again, she asked herself, was that enough? *Against a prolific, unfeeling serial killer? An attractive, intelligent, manipulative female serial killer who had no problems getting close to her male and female victims?*

"Call Robby. My fiancé. He's DEA, he's in town."

He handed the Samsung back to her. As she read off the number, Underwood began tapping the digits into his iPhone—then nearly dropped the handset as she swerved around a curve. He pushed his right hand against the dashboard to steady himself. "If we get killed in a car accident, we're not going to be able to help Jonathan."

"Let me worry about that."

"Is this Robby? . . . This is a colleague of Karen's, Thomas Underwood."

"Put it on speaker," Vail said.

Underwood pressed the button and held up the cell.

"Robby. I think Jasmine's taken Jonathan."

"Taken—why would she do that?"

"Because I fucked up. And because Jasmine's the Blood Lines killer."

There was silence.

"I need you to head toward GW. I don't know where Jonathan's class is. Can you look it up? He's not answering his phone."

"I'm on it. I'll text it to you and head over there. I'm on my way but I'm out by Silver Hill. Just hold it together, Karen. We'll find him."

More hollow assurances.

Vail's phone vibrated. "Gotta go. Let me know what you find out." She looked at her Samsung and tried to read the text.

"How 'bout I drive?" Underwood said, his gaze fixed on the streets ahead of them.

"Under the seat, I've got an auxiliary light."

He scooted forward against the shoulder restraint, reached for—and found—the device. He rolled down the window and a blast of cold air wrapped around Vail's exposed neck.

She heard the magnetic clunk as it attached to the roof.

"Done. Now please, drive carefully."

"Curtis has the app and he's got a location," she said, dropping the cell onto the seat between her thighs. "Whole task force is en route." *No. Too easy.* She grabbed up the Samsung again, called Uzi.

"Karen, got your text, sent the link to Curt—"

"I need you to help me find Jonathan. He's not answering his phone and I think he's in danger."

"What kind of phone does he use?"

Vail accelerated around a Hyundai waiting to make a turn. "iPhone."

"You can track him using the Find my iPhone app, but you'll need his Apple ID. And it's not pinpoint accurate."

"Don't have his ID. What about Stingray? The Bureau's got that equipment, right?"

"Even better," Uzi said. "You're working with the Marshals Service. They've got *mobile* Stingrays, vans outfitted with the devices that can—"

"Got it. Call you back if I hit a roadblock." She hit "end" and struggled to bring up Hurdle's number on her handset. He answered on the third ring.

"Kinda busy," he said. "I'm on my—"

"You got a mobile Stingray deployed in the area? Anywhere near Foggy Bottom?"

"We do. Why, you think Jasmine Marcks is using her phone?"

"My son. I think Jasmine's taken him—or she's gonna take him."

"Give me his number, I'll try to get a location."

After Vail read it off to Hurdle, she swerved around a slow-moving pickup and nearly sideswiped a parked car.

"What's Stingray?" Underwood asked, gripping the door handle with white-knuckled intensity.

"A mobile device that mimics a cell phone tower. It sends out a stronger signal than nearby towers to force a specific phone to connect to *it* instead of the real tower. It then triangulates the signal strength of that cell signal and uses software to give you a location. It can do a lot more than that, but if it can find Jonathan—"

"That's all we need," Underwood said.

"No, that's *not* all we need. We'll be blocks from the White House in a matter of minutes. Law enforcement all over the place. Let's call in the troops."

"And say what? I think a prolific serial killer's on the loose somewhere in Foggy Bottom, but I'm running on pure speculation without an ounce of proof? Once they hear she may have your son they're gonna write you off as a hysterical mother trying desperately to save her boy."

Vail looked at him.

"Keep your eyes on the road. And tell me I'm wrong."

"Fine, right now I'm a hysterical mother trying desperately to save her son. But I don't know what else to do. And I *do* know Jasmine, and I'm pretty damn sure she's going after Jonathan."

"I think you're right. But we need some proof before we pull that fire alarm."

"Because if I'm wrong, they'll never give me any credibility? Right now I couldn't give a shit about tomorrow. Or the day after. All I care about is *tonight*—making sure my son's safe."

"No, Karen. Problem is that they won't deploy. And if we *do* get some proof, they'll have already said no. It'll be harder to convince them. You'd be the woman who cried wolf."

"Fine. We'll give it five minutes. At most. Meantime, call campus police, alert them to a potential problem."

As Underwood looked up the number, Vail tightened her grip on the wheel.

Potential problem may be an understatement.

60

Jasmine stood inside the large, packed campus Starbucks café, a hot cappuccino in her left hand and her face seemingly fixated on her phone. But in reality she was watching the Phillips Hall exit for Jonathan Vail.

With the information Vail had given her, combined with some internet sleuthing, a phone call, and a couple of assumptions, she was able to ascertain that Jonathan was likely in one of five classes. Upon further narrowing the parameters following a conversation with a helpful junior, she figured he would be coming out of his criminology class at 6:03 PM.

At 6:02, with snow flurries falling and the temperature dropping into the twenties, Jasmine left the warmth of Starbucks and started walking slowly toward the building. It was possible she had miscalculated—her crack detective work notwithstanding, she had to admit she did not have a lot of time to think it through.

But she would deal with a failed attempt by withdrawing and living to fight another day. There were other ways to take care of business. And as long as she was smart about it, she would have enough time to get to both her father and Vail, even if it meant a direct assault rather than taking out Jonathan, someone who meant more to Vail than anything else.

There were, of course, advantages to offing Jonathan: Vail would be forced to live with the pain of having her son murdered by a killer she failed to recognize, despite years of interaction. It would be an ongoing nightmare.

As she approached the recessed glass doors—now only about fifty feet away—Jonathan emerged, phone pressed against his ear.

She quickened her pace, closing the distance, ready to begin her spiel.

"Yeah," Jonathan said into the handset. "Just got out of class. Taking Uber. Be there in ten." He started to cross H Street, where a white Toyota Camry had stopped in front of a line of cars.

Jasmine slowed. Change of plans.

Jonathan said something to the driver through the partially cracked window, then pulled open the rear door and got in. As he started to swing it closed, Jasmine grabbed it and stuck her head in. "Mind if I share?"

"This is Uber," Jonathan said. "I've already paid—"

"Not a problem." Jasmine dug into her purse and pulled out a twenty. "On me. I've gotta meet my girlfriend and it's so cold." She gave him an award-winning shiver and sad face.

"I'm going into Georgetown, friends are wait—"

"So am I. Please . . ." she said, drawing it out, again holding up the twenty.

A horn honked behind them. The driver, a slight middle-aged black man, swiveled in his seat and looked at Jonathan. "We need to get going."

Jonathan took the money and slid over.

Jasmine pulled the door closed as the driver accelerated. "Where in Georgetown are you going?" She could feel Jonathan's eyes on her as she sorted herself out, reaching into her purse and glancing up at him, then stopping to make eye contact. She could tell he was just now noticing her beauty.

"Uh—Booeymonger's on Prospect."

"So what are you studying at GW?" She giggled. "I saw you come out of Phillips."

Jonathan glanced at the building out the rear window as it receded into the distance. "You know GW?"

"Alum. Criminal justice major."

"Me, too. Really? Did you have Weitzer?"

"For criminology, of course."

The driver turned left onto 20th Street, which was clear. He sped up and hung a left onto Pennsylvania.

She adjusted her left hand inside her purse and held out her right. "I'm Jessica."

He took it and shook. "I'm Jona—"

But he did not get the word out because she yanked him close and slapped a soaked rag up against his mouth and nose. He tried to pull back, but she had done this too many times. She knew the way a person resisted, and she was ready. His fight lessened as he drifted into an unconscious state.

"Hey," the driver shouted. "The fuck's going on back there?"

"He passed out," Jasmine said. "I've got him, it's okay." She removed the garrote from her purse and whipped it over the driver's head and pulled it tight. Both hands left the steering wheel as he tried—as they all do—to pry the wire off his neck.

It never worked. Jasmine leaned forward, using leverage

and her 135 pounds of weight to cut off the blood supply from the man's brain.

The Toyota drifted right, sideswiped a car, and wedged itself behind another vehicle. The driver's body went limp and she quickly gathered up the garrote and shoved it back into her purse. Jasmine grabbed his jacket and yanked him to the right, toward the passenger's seat.

She had never done this before, and although he was thin and relatively short, he probably weighed 150 pounds. While she was accustomed to lifting weights in the gym, the confined space made this a much more difficult task: she could not use her powerful leg muscles very efficiently. It was harder to move him than she thought.

Jasmine did not have much time. Mere seconds had passed but the Camry was partially blocking the right lane and people had undoubtedly seen the accident, though it was unlikely anyone saw what transpired inside the dark interior.

She gave a quick glance around: it was a three-lane road in each direction and they were next to a small community park on the right side, so there were not many people in the area on a cold and snowy night. And cars were flowing around the Toyota, rushing to wherever they were going. Sometimes the apathy of time-stressed Americans was useful.

Jasmine got his torso draped over the center armrest—leaving enough room for her to fit behind the wheel. She turned off the dome light and opened the back door, careful to avoid the passing vehicles in the adjacent lane.

Jasmine forced her bottom onto the front seat, then grabbed the man's jeans and pushed and lifted and groaned, then reached over and pulled his shirt forward, directing his head toward the floor. That helped, and she was able to get his ass onto the console. She bent his knees and wedged them up near his chest.

Seconds later, her upper body drenched in perspiration from the Herculean effort, she directed the Camry down Pennsylvania Avenue. She would use Washington Circle, only a few blocks down, to turn around and head back to Arlington.

She had not made it very far when she heard a noise. A cell phone vibrating? Stopped at a light, she leaned closer to the driver's body—but it was coming from the backseat.

Jonathan.

As soon as she got the green, she made her way over to the right and parked in front of a bus stop. She got into the rear of the vehicle and dosed Jonathan once again to buy more time, then patted him down and found his phone. There was a text from someone named Patrick:

in the back. got a table.

And a missed call. From Vail.

Jasmine craned her neck toward the windshield but did not see anyone taking an interest in the car. She returned to the task at hand and listened to Vail's message.

She knew that voice.

Impossible.

I killed him.

No longer concerned about passersby, Jasmine pulled out her own phone and opened the SecureHome app for her surveillance cameras. She squeezed the handset while waiting for it to make the connection. Seconds later, she saw the basement of her house.

And Thomas Underwood's body, which she had left on the floor in the middle of the hidden room, was not there.

I can't go back there. They know.

Jasmine picked up Jonathan's phone, returned to the driver's seat, and pulled away. No need to use Washington Circle now. She had to find another place for her kill.

As she mulled that thought, she tore Jonathan's iPhone from its case and tossed the device out the window. It struck the snowy asphalt and bounced a split second before a car tire crushed it.

And that's when she figured out where she should go.

61

Vail's phone buzzed—and Underwood answered. He listened a moment, then put it on speaker. "It's Erik Curtis. That tracking device of yours is working."

Thank god. "Curtis? What've you got?"

"Jasmine's in motion, but so far we've got a clean signal."

"Am I right? GW?"

"GW's huge, but yeah, looks like the outskirts. On our way, not that far."

"Can you text the location to us? I'm driving and Thomas has never used Uzi's app."

"Will do. And I'll let you know soon as we get there."

The second Underwood hung up, her phone vibrated.

"That was fast."

Underwood shook his head. "It's not Curtis. It's a message from your boss, Lewis Hurdle. They're locked onto Jonathan's phone. Stingray."

Vail straightened up in her seat. "Now we're in business."

Her Samsung dinged again. "Curtis's text?"

"Yeah," Underwood said. "He sent us the location."

"Tell me where I'm going."

"Uh . . ." His head jerked up from the screen. "They're different."

"What do you mean?"

"That tracker is not in the same place as Jonathan."

"Call him, call Jonathan. If he's moving, he's no longer in class. He should hear his phone. Assuming he turned the volume up after class ended." *And assuming Jasmine doesn't have him.*

"I still need to call campus PD. Gonna do that first, get them on board. We could use their eyes and ears on the ground. They know their streets and buildings better than us. Then we can figure out what's going on. Hurdle's headed toward the Stingray location and Curtis is going after that tracking device you've got on Jasmine. We're covered. Hang tight."

Hang tight? Is he serious? Hang tight?

Underwood went through some verbal sparring with campus police but ultimately convinced them they could have a serial killer on-site and that a target could be a student, Jonathan Vail, who was leaving one of his classes. "Which one? Which building?" Underwood asked Vail.

"No idea. I asked him for his schedule but I don't think he gave it to me. I just know he's done with classes today at six."

Underwood related that information and told them he had two potential locations. "Yes, this is a federal agent's son. Vail, Karen Vail. FBI." He listened a moment, thanked them, then hung up.

"So?"

"So I was right. They don't know what to make of it. You have a photo of Jonathan? And Jasmine?"

"Nothing of Jasmine. But I took a good one of Jonathan a couple weeks ago with my fiancé." She gestured at the phone. "In 'gallery.'"

Underwood navigated the screen, tapping and swiping. "Got it. Sending it through to them now."

"There's probably one of Jasmine on her website. Have them google it. No idea what it is."

"They're getting a couple of cars out to circulate in the area and alerting foot patrols. But other than looking for Jonathan— which is why I wanted the picture—they didn't seem to have a plan of action. Can't say I blame them."

"Open up that app. Let's see if I can talk you through how to use it."

Underwood had the program up and running as Vail turned right onto 23rd Street NW, now blocks from GW. As she began her explanation, Hurdle called through.

Vail reached over and put it on the Bluetooth speaker.

"We got a problem," Hurdle said.

"I don't want to hear about problems."

Hurdle ignored the comment and continued: "Stingray had a fix on Jonathan's phone along Pennsylvania Avenue and then it winked out."

"Winked out? What the hell does that mean?"

"It means the signal disappeared. They said it can be caused by the phone powering down. But Stingray can do all kinds of shit, including tracking the phone even if it's off."

"And?"

"And they're not getting anything. Which means the phone's probably broken."

Vail felt a knot in her intestines. "As in smashed."

"Yeah, something violent, like hitting it with a hammer. Or throwing it from a moving vehicle."

Vail took a deep breath, trying to keep herself calm. "Where on Pennsylvania Avenue was the last known position?"

"Near 22nd. But we're here right now and there's nothing. No sign of Jonathan. Or the phone. But there's all kinds of shit in the road, snow and slush and salt. Not sure we'd find it unless we plowed it and went through the crap by hand."

Dammit. Jonathan would not do this. She has him. "Can we all agree that Jasmine's got him?"

Hurdle hesitated a second, then: "Yeah. That'd be my assumption."

"That tracking device I planted on her, it started working again. Curtis has it up and running."

"I'll get the location from them. Keep me posted. I'll do the same."

Vail continued driving, unsure of where she was going or even what they would do when they got there.

"Where would she take him?" Underwood asked.

"Depends on why she wants him. Could be to lure me to her."

"If she wanted you, she'd *call* you."

"Then why else?"

"To kill him. I'm sorry, Karen. But now's the time for independent, rational thought. You have to somehow divorce your emotions, think logically. Clearly. Can you do that?"

I'm his mother. How can I do that?

"I asked you a question," Underwood said firmly. "Can I count on you to think clearly?"

"Yes. Yes." Vail took a deep breath and slowed the vehicle. She had unknowingly brought it up to forty in a twenty-five zone, with college students milling about on the sidewalks. "If she wants to kill this victim, she'd take him back to her house in Arlington, where she killed her other victims."

"Except that we have to assume that by now she's looked in on Rusty."

Vail nodded. "And she'll see that he's no longer there."

"And in his place there's a bunch of crime scene personnel."

Vail pulled to a spot by the curb. "So she'd think we probably found her Arlington house, too. And you. Right?"

Underwood blew some air through his lips. "I don't know. It's possible she also had a camera there. It's likely. Why not? That's probably how she knew I wasn't trying to escape. She must've looked in on me from time to time."

"Wait. There were two victims the Blood Lines killer— Jasmine—murdered on-site. Deviations from her other kills."

"Yeah." Underwood nodded slowly, staring straight out the windshield. "Carla Rackonelli and Nancy Ermine."

"Ermine was killed in Fredericksburg, Prince William Forest. The national park."

"Yeah, that's how we got federal jurisdiction to prosecute Marcks."

Fredericksburg is too far away. "She offed Rackonelli somewhere in Georgetown, right?"

"Yes."

Vail thought about that. "None of what's going down right now was planned. Maybe Jonathan wasn't part of what she wanted to do. She feels cornered. She now knows that *we* know she's the Blood Lines killer. She's desperate, thinking on the fly. Not much to lose. And now she wants to get back at the person who ruined her life, who figured out she was the killer. Me. And that's why she took Jonathan." She swung her gaze over to Underwood. "And if that's the case, she needs a place to—" Her voice caught. "A place to kill her victim." *Focus, Karen. Get past this. Be objective.*

"I agree."

"She'll go back to where she killed Rackonelli, a place she knows will give her decent cover. A place *nearby*. Do you remember exactly where her body was found?"

"Kind of—the general area. Head toward Georgetown, we'll figure it out."

Vail pulled away from the curb and accelerated.

62

The auxiliary light was still flashing, so Vail leaned on the horn and cars cleared a way for them.

"We need to get the exact location," she said. "Don't have time to guess wrong. Call Gifford. I've got his cell."

A moment later it was ringing through the Bluetooth. Voice mail came on and Vail left a message.

"Try my unit chief. Look in 'contacts.' Stacey DiCarlo."

"I've got it." Underwood manipulated the phone and it again began ringing. "You think she's still at the office this late?"

"No idea. Don't know much about her. Except that I don't like her."

"DiCarlo."

Vail shot a look at Underwood. *Maybe I need to reevaluate her.* "This is Karen Vail. I need some help. Can you look something up in my files?"

"Your files? For what?"

"I don't have time to explain. But it's got to do with the Blood Lines case. Thomas Underwood's in the car with me. The killer's not who we thought it was. And she's got my son."

"Whoa, back up a second, Vail. What the hell are you going on about?"

"Look, I don't mean any disrespect, but I don't have time for this. Just pull up my files. If you can't do that, I'll find someone else to help—"

"We'll deal with your insubordination later. Tell me what you need."

I need a new unit chief.

"Exact location where the Rackonelli body was found. Carla Rackonelli."

"Where am I looking?"

"I organized the file by victim," Underwood said. "Everything's cross-referenced, but fastest way to get what we need is to go to the Rackonelli tab." He turned to Vail. "Did you change the file?"

"Just added to it. All your original reports and notes are just as you left them."

"I'm calling it up on the server," DiCarlo said. "Give me a few minutes to sort through everything."

If it was your son you wouldn't need a few minutes.

"Text me the location as soon as you've got it. I need to make another call."

Underwood hit the red "end call" icon and looked to Vail for instructions.

"Call Curtis."

He was on the line seconds later. "Good timing, Karen. We're closing in on the tracking signal's twenty."

63

Curtis pulled to a stop in front of The Gibson at 23rd and L, a ten-story brick apartment building. Tarkoff got out, his Glock in hand, moving forward cautiously.

Curtis followed, consulting the iPhone's display as he walked up to a large chain-link fence.

"Well?"

He could barely hear Vail's voice emanating from the speaker but did not want to take his eyes off the screen until they got a fix on Jasmine.

"Used to be a Metro PD building here but it's now a huge construction site," he said, keeping his voice low. "Give us a minute." They stood shoulder to shoulder, Tarkoff looking out at the street while Curtis peered through the narrow openings between the privacy slats at the steel girders that represented the structure's skeleton. "Ben, you see anything?"

Tarkoff looked down the block, turned in a 360-degree arc, and faced Curtis. "No."

He again checked the map on the iPhone. "She should be right there, thirty feet away. Maybe around the corner? I can't see because of all that heavy equipment behind the fence."

They walked about fifteen paces when Curtis stopped and elbowed Tarkoff. "That woman in the parka, crossing L."

"She's got a hood up, can't see her face. But there's no one else nearby."

"Let's check it out."

Tarkoff dodged an approaching taxi and jogged across 23rd, approaching from the left as Curtis came up behind her.

"Police," Curtis yelled. "Don't move. Get down on the ground!"

64

Vail turned to Underwood, her eyes wide, her pulse racing. She kept driving, leaning forward in her seat, listening for any clues as to what was happening.

"Is it her?"

Tarkoff's voice.

"No," Curtis said. "Goddammit. Sonofabitch." Into the handset: "Not her, Karen. She's got the tracking device in her jacket pocket but it's not Jasmine."

She beat me at my own game.

"Karen, you hear me?"

"Yeah, I got it. Thomas and I are on our way to a place that may have meaning to her. Where she killed before. Rackonelli."

"Rackonelli. That was somewhere on the outskirts of Georgetown. A park?"

"We're trying to get an address. Soon as we have it, I'll send it to you."

Underwood disconnected the call—but Vail's phone rang almost immediately. He held up the Samsung. "Someone named Oliver Aldrich."

Vail whipped her head toward him so hard it popped. "What?"

He showed her the screen. "Oliver Aldrich."

"Aldrich was killed by—" She stopped. "Answer it."

A familiar voice came through the speakers. Smooth, cold, unemotional. "Hello, Karen."

65

Marcks."

He chuckled. "You don't sound happy to hear from me."

"I've got more important matters to deal with. And unless you can give me your daughter's whereabouts, you're wasting my time."

"My daughter?" His voice got deeper. "I'm going to kill her. Then I'm going to kill you."

"Good luck trying to find her. I'm looking for her, too."

He snorted. "I know exactly where she is."

Vail turned slowly to face Underwood. "You do?"

"She's in the car right in front of me. And I completely understand why you've got 'more important matters to deal with.' Looks like she's got your son."

"Where are you?" She leaned closer to the speaker. "Marcks! Where are you?"

"He hung up," Underwood said. "I'm sorry."

Vail cursed under her breath then told him to call Hurdle.

"Got something for me?" Hurdle asked.

"Yeah," she said, "a new number. Get Stingray on it."

Underwood read it off to him.

"Belongs to a phone Marcks is using—but do not engage him. He's following Jasmine. If we play this right, we'll get them both."

"Hope you're right. Hurdle out."

Makes two of us. Vail pointed at the Samsung. "Get back to DiCarlo, see if she's got that twenty."

Underwood made the call but kept it off Bluetooth. "No, this is Tom Underwood. Agent Vail's driving. You have the location?" He listened a moment. "Yeah, that's the one." He waited, exchanged a glance with Vail, then slapped his thigh. "That's it," he said into the phone. "Got it." Another beat, then, "We're on our way, we're pretty close."

As he hung up, Vail said, "Text it to Curtis, Robby, and Hurdle."

She sat up in her seat and accelerated.

"Keep it under control," Underwood said calmly as he tried to tap out the message. His finger kept flying off the keyboard with each bump and jerk of the car. "We need to get there in one piece."

"I'm going to kill that bitch, Thomas."

"I understand," he said as he hit "send." "And I'd feel the same way. But—"

"Unless someone gets there before me." *Someone named Roscoe Lee Marcks.*

"You're not listening, Karen," he said with the even firmness of a father imparting wisdom to his daughter. "Let justice take its course. Jasmine needs to stand trial and be properly convicted of the murders we'd wrongly pinned on Marcks."

"With what evidence? Do you have her admission on tape? 'Cause I sure don't. And unless I'm missing something, I don't see much of a case. You want justice, it's gonna have to come some other way."

"Can't say I like the sound of this."

"You'll like it even less when she walks out of the courtroom with a 'case dismissed' smile plastered all over her face."

"Promise me you'll show restraint. Let the system do its job. I have faith."

She gave him a quick glance. "This isn't one of your TV shows, Thomas. Not every case ends happily ever after. Did you forget what it's like out there?"

"No. Did you?"

Touché. Vail took a breath. *Shit, I've been spending too much time with black operators, where there are no rules other than accomplishing the mission. But this isn't that.*

"You're right. I'm sorry. I'm just—very upset."

Underwood seemed to accept that because he did not reply.

"But Thomas. I'm telling you now. If she . . . if she hurts my son, everything goes out the window."

"Including your career?"

Vail did not hesitate. "Including my career."

66

The vibration of her phone made her heart skip a beat. "Who is it?"

"Lewis Hurdle."

"On speaker."

Underwood pressed a button and the wind noise of an SUV filled the Honda's passenger compartment.

"Please tell me you've got a location on Marcks."

"We do," Hurdle said. "He's on the move, so I'm gonna patch us through to the Stingray team. Hang on while I make the connection."

Seconds later, Vail heard more voices on the line.

"I think we've got Deputy Henderson. Correct?"

"Ten-four," Henderson said. "Agent Vail, I've got that phone number and I'm sending the location beacon directly to your handset."

"You can do that?"

"Yes, ma'am. And here's another thing we can do: I tapped into Marcks's cell and I'm using it as a microphone. But doesn't sound like there's anyone else in the car with him because no one's talking."

Underwood held up Vail's Samsung. "Got it. I see the beacon on the map."

Vail glanced over at the screen but could not keep her eyes off the road long enough to make anything out. "Is it near the location where she killed Carla Rackonelli?" Vail asked.

"Looks like it," Underwood said. "He's headed right for it."

"We're minutes out," Hurdle said. "Curtis and Tarkoff are meeting the rest of us en route, so sounds like you'll get there first."

"Understood." Vail tightened her grip on the wheel. "Problem is, Marcks is gonna get there before *me*."

67

Jasmine was concentrating on the dark streets, looking for one particular location. Every minute or so, she glanced back at Jonathan—who, she figured, would be waking up very shortly.

She had been thinking of how she needed to approach the coming hours. If Vail had discovered Underwood's body in the basement, they would have left him there until the medical examiner arrived. And that meant her first impression—bolstered by the message she heard on Jonathan's phone—was correct: Underwood had somehow survived. And that altered the dynamic of all that would need to come.

It was a fatal error, one of the few she had ever made. Perhaps the only one. Everything had been so well calculated, so well planned. Her execution was almost always near flawless—and even when it was not, it still worked. Her father landed in prison but she was free to continue killing.

True, she had to modify her methods, using crime concealment fires to hide her handiwork. But even that had gone well. She enjoyed the fires more than she thought when she came across the idea in Underwood's book.

And then her father had called, letting her know he had escaped and was coming for her. He thought it would scare her. Intimidate her. But it was exactly what she had been planning all along.

While she had not yet disposed of him, she figured she had plenty of time to do so—because he would forever be looking for her. He was like that, to a fault. Fixated, unable to let go of a grudge. And this was more than a mere grudge. This was more than personal. She knew that. She constructed it that way. She would either kill him or a cop would kill him. She doubted he would allow himself to go back to prison.

Now, however, the entire equation had changed.

Time was no longer hers to manipulate. She might not be able to get to him before the cops did—because with all the publicity surrounding her father's escape and now the revelation that she was the Blood Lines killer, she had to believe that law enforcement would spare little to track her down.

Sticking around increased the likelihood she would be captured.

She had to take what she could, what was in reach. And right now, that meant Jonathan. It would destroy Vail. She was sure of that. Like Superman's kryptonite, killing her son would zap her of her essence, emasculate her like nothing else could. The more she thought about it, this was the better call, far better than killing Vail herself.

As Jasmine approached the wooded neighborhood, Jonathan stirred. She wanted to dose him again because he would undoubtedly attempt to fight back, and it would be easier to get rid of him without all the drama.

Jasmine now realized that this kill would not be as enjoyable as the others had been. It couldn't be. With Vail and Curtis and the task force now likely looking for her, she would have less time with the body.

This pissed her off—but she knew the smarter thing would be to get it over with and get away. Another city, another state. Maybe Canada or Mexico. She did not know how big the net would be, but she was sure they would make it difficult.

She had a contingency plan in place with a neat little diversion—a pipe bomb along with a phony tweet and Facebook post replete with a bombastic radical Islamic claim of responsibility. If she timed her escape right, in the minutes and hours after the explosion, she might be able to make it work. A serial killer did not warrant the attention and resources a terror group did.

She pulled down the tree-lined street and slowed opposite some densely wooded parkland. Flurries were still fluttering this way and that, making the icy ground even more slick.

Jasmine found the spot she was looking for and brought the Toyota to a stop.

Jonathan moaned as she shoved the gearshift into "park." She dug into her purse to ready the ether and reached for the door handle—

But the driver's side window shattered, showering her face with glass.

"What the f—"

She felt two hands on her neck

Looked up and saw

Her father

She grabbed his forearms, knowing instinctively not to try to pry his fingers away from her skin.

She heard him yelling something—"I'm gonna fuckin' kill you!"—and for the first time in her life, she believed him.

Dug her nails into his muscle-taut flesh, had to be drawing blood.

But he did not yield.

She slid her arms down to his wrists. With all her body weight, she yanked suddenly and forcefully to the right.

Marcks was not expecting it and lost his balance, striking his head on the door frame. She leaned left and again pulled hard right and again slammed his face into the metal, the jagged remains of glass slicing his nose and eyes.

One more blow to the head and his grip loosened and his hands left her neck and he dropped out of sight.

Unconscious.

But for how long?

Jasmine turned around toward Jonathan—but the rear passenger door was swinging closed.

And the seat was empty.

68

Jasmine hoisted herself into the back of the Camry. With the Uber driver blocking the passenger seat and her father likely, hopefully, unconscious outside her front door, it was the fastest way out.

She stepped into the freezing night air. Fifteen yards away Jonathan was stumbling forward, slipping and sliding like a drunken sailor chasing a pretty woman down the street.

Jasmine jogged after him, using a broad-based gait to maintain her balance. She knew that ahead of him was a tall fence that enclosed a children's play area. As he would soon see, he had nowhere to run, even if he was fully lucid—which, by now, he might be. Her prior victims were older individuals. A young man's metabolism could be different, so she had to assume the drug had cleared, or was close to clearing, his system.

She caught up to him and tackled him from behind, took him facedown onto the icy ground.

But he twisted onto his back and kicked her in the nose, stunning her and driving her head back.

She literally saw black—and pinpricks of stars twinkling all around her. Her vision cleared and she got slowly to her feet, careful to keep her footing—but Jonathan was in full escape mode and he was scrabbling forward on the slick, frozen snow, moving his legs fast but not getting very far.

He suddenly stopped and straightened up. He had undoubtedly seen the obstacle in his path because he turned to face her.

Nowhere to run.

Nowhere to hide.

Jasmine pulled out an exceptionally lethal knife and smiled. Maybe this would be more enjoyable than she had thought.

69

W e're half a mile away," Underwood said.

"Is Marcks there yet?"

"His signal just stopped moving. Maybe."

Vail accelerated and swerved on a patch of black ice, side-swiping a car. *C'mon, Karen. Stay in control.*

"You need to slow down," Underwood said, his voice steady even though his right hand was clutching the dashboard while his left maintained a white-knuckled grip on the Samsung.

"If Marcks is there—" She did not finish the sentence—because she did not want to consider the implications. *Two killers with my son.* No matter how she parsed it, this was not a good situation.

Vail's brights illuminated the landscape in front of her. "This is that park. Where she killed Rackonelli."

"Right up ahead," Underwood said, pointing into the snowy darkness. "A block away."

Her lights hit what looked like a man lying still in the street beside a white sedan.

"Big body," Underwood said. "Could be Marcks."

Vail was going too fast for a residential street in this weather. She tapped her brakes and skidded a bit. "Wait in the car, Thomas."

"What?"

"You're not a cop anymore, you don't even have a gun."

"And you don't have any backup."

As they approached, Vail saw *two* cars, not just the white sedan.

"You're retired."

"Fifteen years from now, you think you'd be waiting in the car while someone else goes after the killer?"

Off to the right were two figures. "That's Jonathan!"

"And Jasmine."

Oh my god.

70

Jasmine advanced on Jonathan, a karambit knife fisted in her right hand, its anodized black blade all but hidden from his sight.

"I'm not gonna hurt you," she said. "I'm trying to help you."

Jonathan's breathing was rapid and shallow, spewing vapor into the dark, moist air. "Who are you?"

"Your mom's friend."

"Bullshit. You—you drugged me or something."

"That was Jessica, the woman who got into the car before me."

Jonathan's eyes were darting back and forth. She knew that look, had seen it in her prior victims. He was trying to fight through the cobwebs to reason it out.

"Come with me, I'll take you to Robby. He asked me to pick you up. That guy who escaped, Roscoe Lee Marcks, is trying to kill you."

"What are you talking about? Why would he—"

"To get back at your mother. She helped put him in prison."

"I don't—"

"Didn't you see Marcks back there by the car? He was trying to get to you. I fought him off." She yanked down on her collar and showed him what surely looked like red marks encircling her neck. "He almost killed me. Now, c'mon! We don't have time to debate this. He's gonna wake up, he's very dangerous."

Jasmine sensed weakness. He was buying her story and letting his guard down. She held out her left hand and wiggled her fingers. "C'mon," she said with a reassuring smile. "Let's go. It's freezing."

Jonathan took a step toward her and then stopped. "No."

Headlights splashed across them as she lunged forward, arcing the karambit in a sweeping motion. Jonathan blocked it with his left forearm then threw a quick right jab, catching Jasmine in the chin and driving her back.

The knife dropped from her hand and Jonathan went for it—but so did Jasmine.

Jonathan snatched the karambit off the ice a second before she could get there and buried the blade in her abdomen.

Jasmine gasped and froze in place, hunched over.

She stumbled a couple of steps, then fell to her knees.

71

Vail lurched, slipped, and slid toward her son, Glock in hand. She glanced at Jasmine on the ground and ran into Jonathan, embracing him so hard he had to pry her away to breathe.

"Thank God. Thank God."

"Is she dead?"

Vail let go of Jonathan and knelt beside Jasmine. She holstered her Glock and felt for a pulse, then rolled Jasmine onto her back.

A knife was buried deep in her stomach, only the handle protruding.

Jasmine brought a hand up and made a weak attempt to pull it out. Vail placed her palm atop the karambit and kept it in place.

Blood pulsed from the wound.

"You're pathetic," Jasmine whispered, struggling to keep her eyes open. "Seven years . . . you were . . . clueless . . ."

Vail tightened her grip on the knife's handle. "Took me a while. But in the end we got it right." She looked into Jasmine's eyes. "Time to meet your maker, to pay for what you did."

Jasmine stared at her and seconds later, her hand dropped from the knife.

Vail stood up and handed Jonathan her cell. "Call an ambulance." She hustled over to the Camry and bent over Marcks to feel for a pulse.

But two meaty hands grabbed her wrist, tight and unyielding.

He got to his feet and swung Vail around as if she were a sack of apples and pulled her against his body. He put her in a headlock, both arms forced skyward.

She could not move. Could not reach her gun. Or the tanto.

Vail squirmed and tried swinging her left forearm back, but he had a good hold on her, so good that she had only a limited range of motion with that limb. The right was completely immobilized.

He pushed forward slightly, forcing her head farther down toward her chest.

"Trying to snap my neck?"

"If I was trying, it'd be broken already. But make one wrong move and I'll do just that."

"Yeah," she said, struggling to breathe over the intense pain. "I got that."

He removed her Glock and tossed it to the ground behind him. He felt around and located the tanto, then slid it out of its sheath and brought it around the front of her neck. Pressed it against her carotid.

"Mom!" Jonathan had Jasmine's bloody knife in his hands, forearm taut, his body infused with anger. "Let go of her," he said between clenched teeth. "Now."

Marcks snorted. "You know who I am?"

"Let go of her."

"I've got a better idea," Marcks said. "Put that knife down or I'll kill her."

"No way do you put that knife down," Vail said. "If he's going to kill me, he's going to kill me. He's not going to spare me because you drop your weapon. He's a killer, Jonathan."

Jonathan eyes were wavering, looking at Marcks, the knife, back to Marcks—everywhere but his mother.

"There's no way out of this for you," Vail said. "You're going back to prison for all the people you killed. William Reynolds, Nathan Anderson, Oliver—"

Marcks squeezed harder, pushing her arm forward another inch.

He's gonna break my neck.

"I've had enough of you, Vail. You're gonna do what I tell you to do. First you're going to admit you got it wrong. In front of your son, tell him you fucked up, that you made my life a living hell, helped put me in prison for murders I didn't commit."

"That was my doing, asshole." Underwood's voice.

Vail did not know what was happening—she was forced to stare at the snow-covered ground—but she had a pretty good idea: Underwood had taken the Glock Marcks had thrown aside and was holding it against the man's ear. Or temple. Or back.

"You got a beef?" Underwood said. "It's with me. *I'm* the one who drew up that profile. Anyone's responsible, it's me. Now drop the knife or I'll pull this trigger and feel damn good about it."

"Jonathan," Vail said, "go wait in the car."

"I'm not going anywhere," he said. "Make him drop that knife!"

"First I want an apology," Marcks said.

"An apology?" Underwood grunted. "You know, you're right. I'm really sorry you killed your wife and a bunch of other innocent people. Because you're gonna get the death penalty.

Now drop the fucking knife or I'll drive a 9-millimeter round through your goddamn skull and save the taxpayers a few million dollars. You have till three. Three."

Marcks loosened his grip on both Vail and the tanto, which fell to the ground. Vail knocked his hands away and grabbed his wrists, pulled out her handcuffs and ratcheted them down hard.

The headlights of two approaching SUVs bounced a few dozen yards away. The vehicles drove over the curb and into the park, stopping just in front of them.

Hurdle got out of the lead vehicle, followed by Curtis and Walters, Morrison and Tarkoff.

"Damn," Hurdle said, surveying the scene. "Looks like we missed all the fun."

"Well, well, well," Curtis said, taking hold of Marcks's cuffed forearm. "Look who caught the fugitive, Hurdle. The FBI."

Hurdle holstered his sidearm. "Give me a break."

"No, no, no," Vail said. "It was a team effort. In fact, why don't you guys *both* do the honors."

Curtis and Hurdle led Marcks away toward the SUV as another car pulled up.

Robby jumped out, leaving his door open. He said something to Curtis before seeing Vail and Jonathan—then ran over to them.

"Got here as soon as I could." As he gathered them in an embrace, he squinted into the darkness.

"Is that Jasmine?"

"Yeah."

Robby stepped back and looked at Vail. "How?"

Vail told Robby what happened, letting Jonathan fill in the details.

Robby held out his fist and Jonathan bumped it.

"When I saw Jasmine go at him," Vail said, "my heart stopped."

"C'mon, Mom. I had it under control."

Vail lifted her brow.

Jonathan shrugged. "She lunged at me. I saw the blade at the last second and parried it, then counterattacked with a riposte."

Vail looked at Robby. "What did he just say?"

"I think he's talking fencing."

"Yeah," Jonathan said. "Fencing. When you parry, or block, an attack you've got a split second to launch a counterstrike—a riposte. Instead of pulling back, you attack quickly, before your opponent can recover and defend."

"But you didn't have a sword," Robby said.

"Concept is tactical, whether you have a weapon or not. It's reactions, balance, muscle memory. I reacted without thinking."

I do that all the time without such good results. Maybe I should take up fencing.

"Strategic analysis aside," Robby said, "I'm real proud of you." He grabbed Jonathan's shoulders and looked into his eyes. "You okay?"

Jonathan thought a moment. "I'm not sure. I—no, I don't know what I think. I mean, I killed someone." He stared off for a second, as if it had just sunk in.

"Sweetie, you killed someone who'd murdered about two dozen people. You didn't have a choice. She was coming at you. And believe me, she was trying to kill you. This is a lot to grasp. I know, I've been there. We'll have you talk to someone. It'll help."

"Like a shrink?"

Vail drew a hand down his left cheek. "Exactly like a shrink.

And I don't want any pushback. I'm still your mother, even if you're technically an adult."

He shivered. "Fine. I'll talk with someone."

"Tomorrow. You'll talk with someone tomorrow."

"C'mon, it's friggin' cold out here." Robby clamped a hand around Jonathan's shoulders and led him toward the car. "I mean it, bud. I'm very proud of you."

Jonathan was silent for a few steps and then stopped. "I—I think I feel good about what I did. Is that wrong?"

"Wrong?" Vail asked. *Well there's a loaded question. From my son, no less.* "No. You defended yourself. You did what needed to be done."

Jonathan absorbed that for a second. "Is this what it's like to be a cop?"

"Sometimes," Robby said with a shrug. "Yeah. Getting the bad guy. You feel good you made things safer for people. That's what it's all about. Keeping order, upholding the law, saving lives."

Jonathan gazed off into the distance as he considered that. "Maybe I should think more seriously about a career in law enforcement."

Vail and Robby shared a concerned look.

"How about *not*?" Vail said.

"This isn't something you should decide after what just happened," Robby said. "You've got plenty of time to think it through. You're a criminal justice major. That's the right path if you want to carry a badge. That's all you need to think about now."

Jonathan nodded slowly. "Okay."

But Vail could tell by the look on his face that he had just decided what he wanted to do with the rest of his life. She knew that look.

She knew it because she had seen it once before.

In the mirror.

ACKNOWLEDGMENTS

Each novel presents unique challenges in telling the story. One constant, however, is my desire to "get it right"—or as close to accurate as is possible—and feasible, which is of course an important point: there are a million facts in each of my books, so it's inevitable something is going to be wrong because no one can know everything about everything. Even with all the experts I consult during the course of my research, it's impossible to fact-check every sentence, statement, or assertion. (That doesn't stop me from trying.) There are also those rare times when I take some literary license for a variety of reasons— which, my editor reminds me, is perfectly acceptable because, after all, I do write fiction!

With that in mind, I'd like to acknowledge and offer my sincere thanks to these individuals, who greatly enhanced the reality I dream up in my head:

Mark Safarik, FBI Supervisory Special Agent and senior FBI profiler (ret.) and principal of Forensic Behavioral Services International, spent hours with me discussing maximum-security prison procedures, FBI case management, crime concealment fires, and arson basics. In addition, he assisted me with the profiling and behavioral analysis nuances, including those involving homosexual offenders, sexual mutilators, and all the other goodies that go along with those pillars of society, serial killers. Brainstorming with Mark, whose law enforcement expertise extends well beyond profiling, was invaluable. As Mark knows, no detail is too small, and his fine-tooth review of the manuscript was extremely helpful in bringing to the pages the verisimilitude I always strive to achieve.

Micheal Weinhaus, Special Agent, ICE (Immigration and Customs Enforcement), Department of Homeland Security, Homeland Security Investigations, wore several hats. Mike is a former Fairfax County police officer and served on the US Marshals Service's Capital Area Regional Fugitive Task Force (CARFTF), so his stories, background, and fugitive hunting tips were invaluable. In addition, his intimate knowledge of the area helped me find proper locations for my action and characters, and his experience working with the Bureau of Prisons and its correctional facilities oriented me as to how an escape could occur and what would happen in its wake. Mike also schooled me on warrant procedures, helped me get the police procedure ballpark accurate, and he refreshed my memory of the Mason District station. As if that were not enough, his review of the manuscript and attention to detail helped me get it right.

David Diliberti, Deputy US Marshal and inspector on the Pacific Southwest Regional Fugitive Task Force, was a wealth of information, recounting stories of the wild cases he has handled in his long career, instructing me on US Marshal fugitive task force procedures and the art of fugitive tracking, providing Bureau of Prison and correctional facility background, and sharing insider terminology and stories of what's it's like in the trenches of the job. He also related the nuances that exist in the relationship between members of the Marshals Service and the FBI. Last but just as important, he reviewed the manuscript to ensure I didn't make any egregious procedural flubs.

Carl Caulk, Assistant Director, Office of Professional Responsibility, US Marshals Service, for his many hours of counsel and instruction on procedure. I first met with Carl back in 2003 when he was a Supervisory Deputy Marshal in charge of the fugitive squad in Phoenix. He gave me my first in depth look into the tough work this crucial arm of the Department of Justice does—and does very successfully—in apprehending dangerous offenders. Carl also gave me my first look into maximum-security prisons and how escapes are often perpetrated. I've carried that knowledge with me since then, and it served me well in *Darkness of Evil*.

Mary Ellen O'Toole, FBI Supervisory Special Agent and senior FBI profiler (ret.) and Program Director for the Forensic Science Program at George Mason University's College of Science, reviewed the manuscript and provided key input on psychopathic personalities, which helped me fine-tune both Marcks characters. And all I had to do was promise that I'd one day feature GW rival GMU in a future book—yes, that's a joke.

The accelerant/anesthetic issue required specialized information from a number of experts to make sure I was not writing fiction (which is, of course, what I am doing). **Rachel Jacobson**, Pharm.D., pharmacist, helped with my initial search, and research, into flammable anesthetics. **David Sheinbein**, MD, anesthesiologist, picked up the ball and counseled me on inhaled anesthetics in general and sevoflurane in particular, and brought in diethyl ether expert and anesthetics historian **R. Dennis Bastron**, MD, anesthesiologist, University of Arizona College of Medicine, who gave me historical perspective on ether's prior use in anesthesia and stories of accidental misuse (including the explosions mentioned in the novel); his discussions regarding ether and cyclopropane and the properties, usage, and effects of both were invaluable.

I then consulted with **Jane Willoughby**, PhD, biochemist, for her background and experiences working with ether; its chemical nature and properties; types of storage vessels; and how the killer would deploy it. She then reviewed, researched, and corrected the pertinent excerpts of the novel that deal with ether. It all ended up being a much bigger deal than I had initially thought, but because it was an important piece of the story I wanted to make sure I didn't muck it up.

John Cooney, Special Agent, ATF (Bureau of Alcohol, Tobacco, and Firearms), supplied arson and bombing information, and reviewed those parts of the novel to make sure I was true to life, and fact, with my fire-related references, procedures, and terminology.

Joseph Ramos, Captain, San Diego Police Department and former SWAT Lieutenant reviewed—and corrected—the SWAT chapters. Joe's attention to detail is extraordinary and he knows exactly what I'm looking to accomplish in a scene. **Christopher Schneider**, assistant SWAT Team Leader, Anaheim Police Department (ret.) and Executive Director, agency relations, 5.11 Tactical, provided background on SWAT's approach to Gaines's trailer, including the Bearcat deployment and breaching procedure.

Mark Waldo, Crime Scene Investigator, Santa Ana Police

Department, Forensic Services Section, helped me get the forensics right relative to indented writing and latent prints.

Larry Wein, Squad Detective, New York Police Department, explained the scenarios involving the commissioner's good guy letter and Leslie Johnson's dismissal from the police force.

Jeffrey Jacobson, Esq., Associate General Counsel, Federal Law Enforcement Officers Association, and former Assistant US Attorney, gave me a general overview of the CARFTF and how it operates, as well as the Stingray program, the proper legal approach to the Kubiak scene, and other legal issues/procedures

Robert Jordan, automotive industry consultant, gave me the background behind the anti-theft ignition locks and safety device that were not present on the 1964 Buick LeSabre. My parents owned one, similar to the storyline, and it was the car I drove when I got my license. I remember quite well the ability to remove the keys while the engine was running. According to Robert, who researched it for me, the ignitions were, indeed, designed this way until 1969, when General Motors was the first carmaker to comply with the new federal law, which went into effect in 1970. It was technically an anti-theft device, but it was enacted, ultimately, as a safety measure. Stolen vehicles were more frequently involved in accidents, 200 times the normal rate. So preventing people from shutting the engine and leaving the keys in the ignition was a safety device that functioned as one designed to prevent vehicular theft.

Kenneth LaMaster, twenty-seven-year Correctional Officer at the United States Penitentiary, Leavenworth (ret.) and prison historian, educated me relative to prison escape procedure, including lockdowns and emergency bed counts; we also discussed inmate mug shot update intervals and the treatment of homosexual inmates by heterosexual prisoners.

Tómas Palmer, cryptographer, helped me equip Vail with the correct geek stuff. Tómas reviewed the Find/Me app, its explanation and hardware functionality for operational authenticity.

Matthew Jacobson lent his experience with fencing, its physical demands and techniques; he also shared his ideas for, and knowledge of, **George Washington University**, its buildings, and locations. The **George Washington University Columbian College of Arts & Sciences department** staff and the **GW registrar** provided the particulars I needed regarding Phillips Hall, including interior photos of the rooms and lecture halls.

The terrific team at Open Road Integrated Media toiled behind the scenes in the publishing and promotion of my novels. I hesitate to name specific individuals because there are so many who, unbeknownst to me, perform vital tasks to bring my novels to your hands. Of those I've worked with closely, I'd like to thank **Emma Pulitzer**, **Lauren Chomiuk**, **Megan Buckman**, **Colleen Lindsay**, **Nathan Barker**, **Tina Pohlman**, and, without question, **Jane Friedman** and **Paul Slavin**. It would be tough to find a finer group of publishing professionals in the industry.

John Hutchinson and **Virginia Lenneville** of Norwood Press worked tirelessly to make my hardcover editions a reality. Pride goes into every novel they publish, and it shows. They love books—and most importantly, they love Alan Jacobson's books!

My editorial team has gone to battle quite a few times now, and we've always come away victorious. *The Darkness of Evil* is the ninth book of mine that **Kevin Smith** has edited, which is amazing in and of itself. (See the dedication at the beginning of this novel for more on Kevin's contributions.) My copyeditor, **Chrisona Schmidt**, helps me refine the prose and makes sure all the grammatical i's and t's are dotted and crossed (and in their proper order). Style manuals make my eyes blur, but Chrisona can quote chapter and verse. The winning goal is to turn out the best product possible, and my team works hard to make that happen. We've got many more battles to come.

My agents, **Joel Gotler** and **Frank Curtis**, once again lent their agenting and legal expertise/advice, respectively, that has kept me afloat in the brave new world of publishing.

Richard Prati and **Steven and Leslie Johnson** were instrumental in making Norwood Press's hardcover of *The Darkness of Evil* a reality.

My fans and readers are really what it's all about. Without you guys, my novels would go unappreciated. To that end, my Facebook fan group administrators, **Sandra Soreano** and **Terri Landreth**, keep everyone engaged in the "Alan Jacobson universe" and encourage people to post and maintain lively discussions.

I've written about my wife **Jill** in each of my eleven books and her contributions toward keeping me sane throughout the *in*sane process of plotting, outlining, researching, writing, and editing. But in *The Darkness of Evil*, she made an editorial catch that—in the words of my editor—"saved our bacon." I don't eat bacon but I understood the sentiment, and I agree. So the ultimate thanks goes to my soulmate and . . . um, bacon saver.

ABOUT THE AUTHOR

Alan Jacobson is the award-winning, *USA Today* bestselling author of eleven thrillers, including the FBI profiler Karen Vail series and the OPSIG Team Black novels. His books have been translated internationally and several have been optioned by Hollywood.

Jacobson has spent over twenty years working with the FBI's Behavioral Analysis Unit, the DEA, the US Marshals Service, SWAT, the NYPD, Scotland Yard, local law enforcement, and the US military. This research and the breadth of his contacts help bring depth and realism to his characters and stories.

For video interviews and a free personal safety eBook co-authored by Alan Jacobson and FBI Profiler Mark Safarik, please visit Jacobson's website at www.AlanJacobson.com.

You can connect with Jacobson on Twitter (@JacobsonAlan), on Facebook (www.Facebook.com/AlanJacobsonFans), and on Instagram (alan.jacobson).

THE WORKS OF ALAN JACOBSON

Alan Jacobson has established a reputation as one of the most insightful suspense/thriller writers of our time. His exhaustive research, coupled with years of unprecedented access to law enforcement agencies, including the FBI's Behavioral Analysis Unit, bring realism and unique characters to his pages. Following are his current, and forthcoming, releases.

STAND ALONE NOVELS

False Accusations > Dr. Phillip Madison has everything: wealth, power, and an impeccable reputation. But in the predawn hours of a quiet suburb, the revered orthopedic surgeon is charged with double homicide—a cold-blooded hit-and-run that leaves an innocent couple dead. Blood evidence has brought the police to his door. An eyewitness has placed him at the crime scene, and Madison has no alibi. With his family torn apart, his career forever damaged, no way to prove his innocence and facing life in prison, Madison must find the person who has engineered the case against him. Years after reading it, people still talk about his shocking ending. *False Accusations* launched Jacobson's career and became a national bestseller, prompting

CNN to call him, "One of the brightest stars in the publishing industry." Note: Detective Ryan Chandler reprises his role in *Spectrum* (Karen Vail #6).

FBI PROFILER KAREN VAIL SERIES

The 7th Victim (Karen Vail #1)> Literary giants Nelson DeMille and James Patterson describe Karen Vail, the first female FBI profiler, as "tough, smart, funny, very believable," and "compelling." In *The 7th Victim*, Vail—with a dry sense of humor and a closet full of skeletons—heads up a task force to find the Dead Eyes Killer, who is murdering young women in Virginia . . . the backyard of the famed FBI Behavioral Analysis Unit. The twists and turns that Karen Vail endures in this tense psychological suspense thriller build to a powerful ending no reader will see coming. Named one of the Top 5 Best Books of the Year (*Library Journal*).

Crush (Karen Vail #2)> In light of the traumatic events of *The 7th Victim*, FBI Profiler Karen Vail is sent to the Napa Valley for a mandatory vacation—but the Crush Killer has other plans. Vail partners with Inspector Roxxann Dixon to track down the architect of death who crushes his victims' windpipes and leaves their bodies in wine caves. However, the killer is unlike anything the profiling unit has ever encountered, and Vail's miscalculations have dire consequences for those she holds dear. *Publishers Weekly* describes *Crush* as "addicting" and *New York Times* bestselling author Steve Martini calls it a thriller that's "Crisply written and meticulously researched," and "rocks from the opening page to the jarring conclusion." (Note: the *Crush* storyline continues in *Velocity*.)

Velocity (Karen Vail #3) > *A missing detective. A bold serial killer. And evidence that makes FBI profiler Karen Vail question the loyalty of those she has entrusted her life to.* In the shocking conclusion to *Crush*, Karen Vail squares off against foes more dangerous than any she has yet encountered. In the process, shocking personal and professional truths emerge—truths that may be more than Vail can handle. *Velocity* was named to *The Strand Magazine*'s Top 10 Best Books for 2010, *Suspense Magazine*'s Top 4 Best Thrillers of 2010, *Library Journal*'s Top 5 Best Books of the Year, and the *Los Angeles Times*' top picks of the year. Michael Connelly said *Velocity* is "As relentless as a bullet. Karen Vail is my kind of hero and Alan Jacobson is my kind of writer!"

Inmate 1577 (Karen Vail #4) > When an elderly woman is found raped and murdered, Karen Vail heads west to team up with Inspector Lance Burden and Detective Roxxann Dixon. As they follow the killer's trail in and around San Francisco, the offender leaves behind clues that ultimately lead them to the most unlikely of places, a mysterious island ripped from city lore whose long-buried, decades-old secrets hold the key to their case: Alcatraz. The Rock. It's a case that has more twists and turns than the famed Lombard Street. The legendary Clive Cussler calls *Inmate 1577* "a powerful thriller, brilliantly conceived and written." Named one of *The Strand Magazine*'s Top 10 Best Books of the Year.

No Way Out (Karen Vail #5) > Renowned FBI profiler Karen Vail returns in *No Way Out*, a high-stakes thriller set in London. When a high profile art gallery is bombed, Vail is dispatched to England to assist with Scotland Yard's investigation. But what she finds there—a plot to destroy a controversial, recently unearthed 440-year-old manuscript—turns into something much larger, and a whole lot more dangerous, for the UK, the US—and herself. With his trademark spirited dialogue, page-turning scenes, and well drawn characters, National Bestselling author Alan Jacobson ("My kind of writer," per Michael Connelly) has crafted the thriller of the year. Named a top ten "Best thriller of 2013" by both *Suspense Magazine* and *Strand Magazine*.

Spectrum (Karen Vail #6) > It's 1995 and the NYPD has just graduated a promising new patrol officer named Karen Vail. During the rookie's first day on the job, she finds herself at the crime scene of a woman murdered in an unusual manner. As the years pass and more victims are discovered, Vail's career takes unexpected twists and turns—as does the case that's come to be known as "Hades." Now a skilled FBI profiler, will Vail be in a better position to catch the offender? Or will Hades prove to be Karen Vail's hell on earth? # 1 *New York Times* bestseller Richard North Patterson called *Spectrum*, "Compelling and crisp . . . A pleasure to read."

The Darkness of Evil (Karen Vail #7) > Roscoe Lee Marcks, one of history's most notorious serial killers, sits in a maximum-security prison serving a life sentence—until he stages a brutal and well-executed escape. Although the US Marshals Service's fugitive task force enlists the help of FBI profiler Karen Vail to launch a no holds barred manhunt, the bright and law enforcement–wise Marcks has other plans—which include killing his daughter. But a retired profiling legend, who was responsible for Marcks's original capture, may just hold the key to stopping him. Perennial #1 *New York Times* bestselling author John Sandford compared *The Darkness of Evil* to *The Girl with the Dragon Tattoo*, calling it "smoothly written, intricately plotted," and "impressive," while fellow *New York Times* bestseller Phillip Margolin said *The Darkness of Evil* is "slick" and "full of very clever twists. Karen Vail is one tough heroine!"

OPSIG TEAM BLACK SERIES

The Hunted (OPSIG Team Black Novel #1) > How well do you know the one you love? How far would you go to find out? When Lauren Chambers' husband Michael disappears, her search reveals his hidden past involving the FBI, international assassins—and government secrets that some will go to great lengths to keep hidden. As *The Hunted* hurtles toward a conclusion mined with turn-on-a-dime twists, no one is who he appears to be and nothing is as it seems. *The Hunted* introduces the dynamic Department of Defense covert operative Hector DeSantos and FBI Director Douglas Knox, characters who return in future OPSIG Team Black novels, as well as the Karen Vail series (*Velocity, No Way Out,* and *Spectrum*).

Hard Target (OPSIG Team Black Novel #2)> An explosion pulverizes the president-elect's helicopter on Election Night. The group behind the assassination attempt possesses far greater reach than anything the FBI has yet encountered—and a plot so deeply interwoven in the country's fabric that it threatens to upend America's political system. But as covert operative

Hector DeSantos and FBI Agent Aaron "Uzi" Uziel sort out who is behind the bombings, Uzi's personal demons not only jeopardize the investigation but may sit at the heart of a tangle of lies that threaten to trigger an international terrorist attack. Lee Child called *Hard Target*, "Fast, hard, intelligent. A terrific thriller." Note: FBI Profiler Karen Vail plays a key role in the story.

The Lost Codex (OPSIG Team Black Novel #3)> In a novel Jeffery Deaver called "brilliant," two ancient biblical documents stand at the heart of a geopolitical battle between foreign governments and radical extremists, threatening the lives of millions. With the American homeland under siege, the president turns to a team of uniquely trained covert operatives that includes FBI profiler Karen Vail, Special Forces veteran Hector DeSantos, and FBI terrorism expert Aaron Uziel. Their mission: find the stolen documents and capture—or kill—those responsible for unleashing a coordinated and unprecedented attack on US soil. Set in Washington, DC, New York, Paris, England, and Israel, *The Lost Codex* is international historical intrigue at its heart-stopping best.

SHORT STORIES

"Fatal Twist" > The Park Rapist has murdered his first victim—and FBI profiler Karen Vail is on the case. As Vail races through the streets of Washington, DC to chase down a promising lead that may help her catch the killer, a military-trained sniper takes aim at his target, a wealthy businessman's son. But what brings these two unrelated offenders together is something the nation's capital has never before experienced. "Fatal Twist" provides a taste of Karen Vail that will whet your appetite.

"Double Take" > NYPD detective Ben Dyer awakens from cancer surgery to find his life turned upside down. His fiancée has disappeared and Dyer, determined to find her, embarks on a journey mined with potholes and startling revelations—revelations that have the potential to forever change his life. "Double Take" introduces NYPD Lieutenant Carmine Russo and Detective Ben Dyer, who return to play significant roles in *Spectrum* (Karen Vail #6).

More to come > For a peek at recently released Alan Jacobson novels, interviews, reading group guides, and more, visit www. AlanJacobson.com.

THE KAREN VAIL SERIES

FROM OPEN ROAD MEDIA

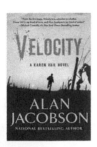

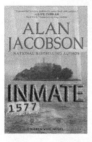
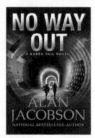

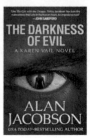
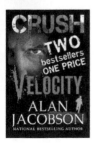

HE OPSIG TEAM BLACK SERIES

FROM OPEN ROAD MEDIA

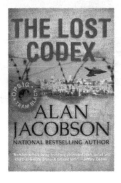

INTEGRATED MEDIA

Find a full list of our authors and
titles at www.openroadmedia.com

FOLLOW US
@OpenRoadMedia

CPSIA information can be obtained
at www.ICGtesting.com
Printed in the USA
BVHW07s1620040818
523257BV00001B/1/P